NEBULA AWARDS

SHOWCASE 2001

The Year's Best SF and Fantasy
Chosen by the Science Fiction
and Fantasy Writers of America

EDITED BY

Robert Silverberg

A HARVEST ORIGINAL
HARCOURT, INC.
San Diego New York London

Requests for permission to make copies of any part of the work should be mailed to
the following address: Permissions Department, Harcourt, Inc., 6277 Sea Harbor Drive,
Orlando, Florida 32887-6777.

www.harcourt.com

The SFWA Nebula Awards is a trademark of the Science Fiction and Fantasy Writers of
America, Inc.

The Library of Congress has cataloged this serial as follows:
The Nebula awards.—No. 19—New York [N.Y.]: Arbor House, c1983–v.; 22cm.
Annual.
Published: San Diego, Calif.: Harcourt, Inc., 1984–
Published for: Science Fiction and Fantasy Writers of America, 1983–
Continues: Nebula award stories (New York, N.Y.: 1982)
ISSN 0741-5567 = The Nebula awards
1. Science fiction. American—Periodicals.
1. Science Fiction and Fantasy Writers of America.
PS648.S3N38   83-647399
813'.0876'08–dc19
AACR 2 MARC-S
Library of Congress [8709r84]rev

ISBN 0-15-100581-8
ISBN 0-15-601335-5 (pbk)

Text set in Electra
Designed by Kaelin Chappell

Printed in the United States of America

KJIHGFEDCBA

First edition

Permissions acknowledgments appear on page 253, which constitutes a continuation of
the copyright page.

CONTENTS

Introduction:
Nebulas at Century's End   ix
Robert Silverberg

Story of Your Life (best novella)   1
Ted Chiang

Mars Is No Place for Children (best novelette)   49
Mary A. Turzillo

The Cost of Doing Business (best short story)   85
Leslie What

Epilogue from **Parable of the Talents** (best novel)   96
Octavia E. Butler

Unhidden Agendas, Unfinished Dialogues:
1999 in Science Fiction   107
Gary K. Wolfe

The Wedding Album   123
David Marusek

Radiant Doors   177
Michael Swanwick

The Grand Master Award: Brian W. Aldiss   194
Harry Harrison

Judas Danced   196
Brian W. Aldiss

Author Emeritus 2000: Daniel Keyes   210
Barry N. Malzberg

Algernon, Charlie, and I: A Writer's Journey   213
Daniel Keyes

Rhysling Award Winners   236
Bruce Boston
Laurel Winter

Appendixes   243
About the Nebula Awards
Past Nebula Award Winners
About the Science Fiction and Fantasy Writers of America

Introduction
NEBULAS AT CENTURY'S END

ROBERT SILVERBERG

So here we all are in the twenty-first century, we raggle-taggle band of surviving twentieth-century science fictionists, staring Arthur C. Clarke's own year of 2001 in the eye and looking back in this volume at the Nebula Awards event of May 2000, where the Science Fiction and Fantasy Writers of America, hereafter known in these pages as SFWA, honored the best science fiction and fantasy stories of 1998 and 1999: the state of the art in our field as the old century came to its end.

(Why the best stories of 1998 *and* 1999, you may ask? Is the Nebula Award not given annually? Yes, it is. Why, then, were some of the nominated stories first published two years before the banquet at which they were honored? Because the Nebula eligibility rules are very strange, kiddo. Now go away and study your non-Aristotelian logic lessons, will you?)

The organization that gives these awards was founded in 1965 by the writer, critic, and editor Damon Knight. Its purpose, as set forth in the original set of bylaws, was "to inform science fiction writers on matters of professional interest, to promote their professional welfare, and to help them deal effectively with publishers, agents, editors, and anthologists." Note that nothing is explicitly mentioned about awards in that statement.

Seventy-two writers responded to Knight's initial invitation and became charter members of SFWA. At least thirty-one of them are still alive, three and a half decades later: not a bad actuarial display. The very first name on the list of charter members is that of Brian W. Aldiss, who was named to the roster of SFWA's Grand Masters at the 2000 Nebula ceremony. The name of Daniel Keyes, the 2000 Author Emeritus, should have been on that list too — certainly he was on the scene at the time — but evidently he didn't bother signing up.

The list of original members is bespeckled with the names of a number of other writers who eventually received the Grand Master award — Poul Anderson, Isaac Asimov, Alfred Bester, Arthur C. Clarke, Robert A. Heinlein, Damon Knight, Fritz Leiber, Frederik Pohl, Jack Vance, A. E. van Vogt, and Jack Williamson. That's twelve Grand Masters out of the first seventy-two members, including, by a curious coincidence, the first four names on the alphabetical roster. Anderson, Pohl, and Williamson also went on to become presidents of SFWA, as did such other charter members as Ben Bova, Gordon R. Dickson, James E. Gunn, Alan E. Nourse, and Norman Spinrad. (I was a charter member too, and in an unguarded moment I allowed myself to become the second president of SFWA, succeeding Damon Knight in July 1967.)

As those statistics show, we were a tight-knit little bunch then. Everybody knew practically everybody else, and most of us were familiar with nearly everything that everybody else had written. In that far-off year of 1965, science fiction was a quaint little corner of the publishing world, cherished only by those few who cherished it and generally ignored or mocked by everybody else. Two or three hardcover publishers, a handful of paperback houses, and six or seven magazines provided the English-speaking world with such SF as was available. Less than a dozen of the original seventy-two SFWA members earned a full-time living from science fiction. Nobody made the *New York Times* best-seller list. Nobody even made the *Locus* best-seller list, because *Locus* hadn't begun publication. *Star Trek* hadn't happened yet, either. Stanley Kubrick hadn't even started talking to Arthur Clarke, probably, about the movie that would be called *2001*. Nor had all the rest of the stuff that makes SF such big business today — the computer games, the fantasy playing cards, the jillion-dollar space adventure movies starring Bruce Willis or Sean Connery or Keanu Reeves or Sigourney Weaver — come into view. We wrote our little stories and our little novels, and we were paid a little bit of money, and we had a little gaggle of faithful readers, and that was that.

Damon Knight dreamed up the Nebula Awards midway through the organization's first year, not so much as a promotional device (as they have since inevitably become) but as a way for professional writers to recognize high literary accomplishment in the work of their peers. His plan was to hold a formal banquet each year in New York, then as now the publishing center of the country, at which trophies of some appropriately dignified sort would be given out to the writers of the best novel, novella, novelette, and short story of the previous year, nominations being open to the entire membership and winners chosen by member vote. Since transcontinental travel was not then as easy as it would later become, West Coast members were given the option of holding a simultaneous banquet of their own.

The first Nebula banquets were held on March 11, 1966—the New York one at the Overseas Press Club in midtown Manhattan, the West Coast one at McHenry's Tail o' the Cock Restaurant in Beverly Hills. I was present at the New York dinner, and I recall three things in particular about it:

1) The food was terrible.

2) Among those at my table were not only the well-known writers Anne McCaffrey and Gordon R. Dickson, but a certain Damon Stetson, then a reporter for the *New York Times*. I asked him whether he was covering the banquet for his newspaper. "Oh, no," he said. "Damon Knight invited me just because my name is Damon. He likes having other Damons around." This was, alas, not my first clue to the existence of the mile-wide streak of frivolity that was and is a distinguishing characteristic of our organization's esteemed founder.

3) Also seated at my table was a writer whose name I remember only too well but will leave unstated here. Through some incomprehensible miracle he had begun his career in science fiction with the almost impossible trick of selling a collection of his short stories to Doubleday, then the premier publisher of hardcover science fiction—stories that, as it happened, had nearly all been rejected by the SF magazines of that day. (It was his first and last book, incidentally.) About an hour through the meal, after listening to the veteran pros McCaffrey, Dickson, and Silverberg engaging in a steady stream of insider chat, Mr. X turned to me pleasantly and said, "Oh, are you a writer too, Ralph?"

Annie McCaffrey, bless her, set him straight on that subject with a burst of true Gaelic fervor. And then we went on to the speeches of the evening, and then the awards. Two of the winners were with us in New York—Roger Zelazny and Brian Aldiss. (Zelazny got two, tying with Aldiss for best novella and winning solo for best novelette.) The other two, Frank Herbert (best novel) and Harlan Ellison (best short story), were at the California fiesta.

The main reason Damon Knight gave for establishing the Nebulas was the hope that they would serve as a corrective to the iniquities and inequities of the Hugo Award system. The Hugos, which date back to 1953, are chosen by vote of the *readers* of science fiction, and are given out at the annual World Science Fiction Convention, an event run by and primarily for the fans of science fiction. The Hugos thus are a reflection of popular taste rather than informed professional opinion, and it was Damon's belief that SFWA, which was at the outset a small group made up largely of working professional writers, would succeed in conferring its award on stories of more significant literary merit than Hugo winners sometimes tended to display. (There was a general perception then among writers that Hugos usually went to conspicuously unliterary crowd-pleasers, though a look at the record shows us James Blish's *A Case of Conscience* winning a Hugo in 1959, Daniel Keyes's "Flowers for Algernon" in 1960, Walter Miller's *A Canticle for Leibowitz* in 1961, and Philip K. Dick's *The Man in the High Castle* in 1963.)

Be that as it may, the Hugo was then, and largely still is, regarded as an award given to the favorites of the fans, and the Nebula as a reflection of the more sophisticated tastes of the pros. Whether things actually have worked out that way is not a topic on which I'd care to provide an opinion. The first year there was a significant correlation between the two awards, but also some significant differences: Ellison's "'Repent, Harlequin!' Said the Ticktockman" took both Hugo and Nebula, as did Frank Herbert's *Dune*. But although Zelazny, after winning a pair of Nebulas, won a Hugo also, it was for a different story, one that had not even made the Nebula ballot. And the novella that brought Aldiss a Nebula was ignored by the Hugo nominators.

Over the next few years, the divergence between Hugo and Nebula winners became even greater. In those earliest days of SFWA, when the whole nominating electorate amounted to some fifteen or twenty members, Nebulas did indeed go to some highly esoteric stories published in highly esoteric places, whereas Hugos generally went to the stories most readily available to the mass of readers. That is less and less true today, in part because the membership of SFWA has grown enormously, so that instead of being made up almost entirely of hard-bitten pros it now includes hundreds of hobbyist writers with just two or three sales to their credit.

The admission of so many writers who would not have been considered professionals by the harsher standards of 1965 has created a much greater overlap between the Hugo electorate and the Nebula electorate than there was at the beginning. Still, there's no question that a considerable disparity exists between each year's Nebula and Hugo winners; by and large, not only the winners but also the nominated finalists tend to be different, except when a story of such overwhelming superiority appears that it sweeps both awards. Such instances have been relatively rare. (My own case is typical. I've won a number of Hugos and a number of Nebulas, but never both awards for the same story.)

I suppose the chief reason nowadays for the divergence between the two sets of award winners is the Byzantine eligibility system of modern SFWA, which permits stories to be nominated over a span of several years. (Hugo nominees must all be drawn from the prior year's publications.) But something else is going on as well. One cannot deny that Hugos generally go to stories whose primary virtue is that they are *entertaining*—that they provide the SF readership with the proper sort of diversion. Entertainment value is scarcely ignored by the Nebula nominators, but other factors seem to come into play also, factors of more immediate concern to professional writers, such as technical or conceptual originality, or the place of a particular story in the pattern of a particular writer's career. Then, too, more than one Nebula has been awarded on a basis of political correctness; more than one out of a feeling that good old so-and-so *deserves* a Nebula after getting so many raw deals in previous years; and sometimes, even, an award is bestowed for superior literary merit.

A comparison of this year's Nebula ballot with the Hugo ballots for 1999 and 2000 shows the usual pattern of divergence. Just one of the six novels on the Nebula ballot was a Hugo finalist also—Vernor Vinge's *A Deepness in the Sky*. One Nebula-nominated novella, "The Astronaut from Wyoming" by Adam-Troy Castro and Jerry Oltion, made it to the 2000 Hugo ballot, and another, Ted Chiang's "Story of Your Life," was a Hugo finalist the previous year. Bruce Sterling's novelette "Taklamakan" and Michael Swanwick's "Radiant Doors," both 1998 stories, were likewise on this year's Nebula ballot and last year's Hugo ballot. Swanwick's "Ancient Engines" was on the 2000 Nebula and Hugo lists. So just six Nebula nominees out of twenty-five managed to make it also to the Hugo ballot — and it's necessary to count two years of Hugo balloting for that. The only category in which there's any significant overlap is the one for movies, where *The Iron Giant, The Matrix,* and *The Sixth Sense* make both sets of ballots — but there was a much smaller group of potential candidates to choose from in that category than in the others.

Whatever these variances may mean, the fact remains that both the Nebula and the Hugo nominations are good indicators of the most memorable science fiction and fantasy stories of the year. They are the top stories in the estimation of those who, whether as producers or consumers or both, are the most knowledgeable devotees. To reach the final ballot is a distinction to be cherished, and, although winning a Nebula is indeed a fine thing, the authors of the runner-up stories have no reason to regard themselves as losers. Out of the overall pool of awards nominees, not just the list of winners, come the stories that the readers of tomorrow will look to as classics. At the century's end, these were the stories that the members of SFWA chose to honor:

The 1999 Nebula Awards Final Ballot

FOR NOVEL

Parable of the Talents, Octavia E. Butler (Seven Stories Press)
The Cassini Division, Ken MacLeod (Tor)
A Clash of Kings, George R. R. Martin (Bantam Spectra)
Mission Child, Maureen F. McHugh (Avon Eos)
Mockingbird, Sean Stewart (Ace)
A Deepness in the Sky, Vernor Vinge (Tor)

FOR NOVELLA

"Reality Check," Michael A. Burstein (*Analog Science Fiction*)
"The Astronaut from Wyoming," Adam-Troy Castro and Jerry Oltion
    (*Analog Science Fiction*)

*Indicates winner.

*"Story of Your Life," Ted Chiang *(Starlight 2)*
"Living Trust," L. Timmel Duchamp *(Asimov's Science Fiction)*
"The Executioners' Guild," Andy Duncan *(Asimov's Science Fiction)*
"The Wedding Album," David Marusek *(Asimov's Science Fiction)*

FOR NOVELETTE

"The Island in the Lake," Phyllis Eisenstein *(Fantasy & Science Fiction)*
"How to Make Unicorn Pie," Esther M. Friesner *(Fantasy & Science Fiction)*
"Five Days in April," Brian A. Hopkins *(Chiaroscuro)*
"Good Intentions," Stanley Schmidt and Jack McDevitt *(Fantasy & Science Fiction)*
*"Mars Is No Place for Children," Mary A. Turzillo *(SF Age)*

FOR SHORT STORY

"Flower Kiss," Constance Ash *(Realms of Fantasy)*
"The Dead Boy at Your Window," Bruce Holland Rogers *(North American Review)*
"Basil the Dog," Frances Sherwood *(Atlantic Monthly)*
"Ancient Engines," Michael Swanwick *(Asimov's Science Fiction)*
"Radiant Doors," Michael Swanwick *(Asimov's Science Fiction)*
*"The Cost of Doing Business," Leslie What *(Amazing Stories)*

FOR SCRIPT

The Devil's Arithmetic, Robert J. Avrech (Showtime Television)
The Iron Giant, Brad Bird and Tim McCanlies (Warner Brothers)
The Uranus Experiment: Part 2, John Millerman (Private Black Label)
*The Sixth Sense, M. Night Shyamalan (Buena Vista)
The Matrix, Larry and Andy Wachowski (Warner Brothers)

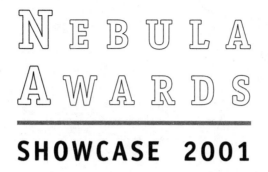

SHOWCASE 2001

Story of Your Life

TED CHIANG

Ted Chiang, who was born in Port Jefferson, New York, and currently lives near Seattle, has achieved the remarkable trick of winning awards with three of his first four published science fiction stories. The one with which he made his debut, the memorable "Tower of Babylon," appearing in *Omni,* bagged a Nebula in 1990, and won him further acclaim the following year when he received the John W. Campbell Award for Best New Writer. His third published story, "Understand," brought him the 1991 Reader's Award from *Isaac Asimov's Science Fiction Magazine.* And here we have Chiang's opus 4, "Story of Your Life," from the anthology *Starlight 2,* for which he received his second Nebula in New York last year.

Concerning this story he says, "It grew out of my interest in the variational principles of physics. I've found these principles fascinating ever since I first learned of them, but I didn't know how to use them in a story until I saw a performance of *Time Flies When You're Alive,* Paul Linke's one-man show about his wife's battle with breast cancer. It occurred to me then that I might be able to use variational principles to tell a story about a person's response to the inevitable. A few years later, that notion combined with a friend's remark about her newborn baby to form the nucleus of this story.

"For those interested in physics, I should note that the story's discussion of Fermat's Principle of Least Time omits all mention of its quantum-mechanical underpinnings. That formulation is interesting in its own way, but I preferred the metaphoric possibilities of the classical version."

Your father is about to ask me the question. This is the most important moment in our lives, and I want to pay attention, note every detail. Your dad and I have just come back from an evening out, dinner and a show; it's after midnight. We came out onto the patio to look at the full moon; then I told your dad I wanted to dance, so he humors me and now we're slow-dancing, a pair of thirtysomethings swaying back and forth in the moonlight like kids. I don't feel the night chill at all. And then your dad says, "Do you want to make a baby?"

Right now your dad and I have been married for about two years, living on Ellis Avenue; when we move out you'll still be too young to remember the house, but we'll show you pictures of it, tell you stories about it. I'd love to tell you the story of this evening, the night you're conceived, but the right time to do that would be when you're ready to have children of your own, and we'll never get that chance.

Telling it to you any earlier wouldn't do any good; for most of your life you won't sit still to hear such a romantic — you'd say sappy — story. I remember the scenario of your origin you'll suggest when you're twelve.

"The only reason you had me was so you could get a maid you wouldn't have to pay," you'll say bitterly, dragging the vacuum cleaner out of the closet.

"That's right," I'll say. "Thirteen years ago I knew the carpets would need vacuuming around now, and having a baby seemed to be the cheapest and easiest way to get the job done. Now kindly get on with it."

"If you weren't my mother, this would be illegal," you'll say, seething as you unwind the power cord and plug it into the wall outlet.

That will be in the house on Belmont Street. I'll live to see strangers occupy both houses: the one you're conceived in and the one you grow up in. Your dad and I will sell the first a couple years after your arrival. I'll sell the second shortly after your departure. By then Nelson and I will have moved into our farmhouse, and your dad will be living with what's-her-name.

I know how this story ends; I think about it a lot. I also think a lot about how it began, just a few years ago, when ships appeared in orbit and artifacts appeared in meadows. The government said next to nothing about them, while the tabloids said every possible thing.

And then I got a phone call, a request for a meeting.

I spotted them waiting in the hallway, outside my office. They made an odd couple; one wore a military uniform and a crew cut, and carried an aluminum briefcase. He seemed to be assessing his surroundings with a critical eye. The other one was easily identifiable as an academic: full beard and mustache, wearing corduroy. He was browsing through the overlapping sheets stapled to a bulletin board nearby.

"Colonel Weber, I presume?" I shook hands with the soldier. "Louise Banks."

"Dr. Banks. Thank you for taking the time to speak with us," he said.

"Not at all; any excuse to avoid the faculty meeting."

Colonel Weber indicated his companion. "This is Dr. Gary Donnelly, the physicist I mentioned when we spoke on the phone."

"Call me Gary," he said as we shook hands. "I'm anxious to hear what you have to say."

We entered my office. I moved a couple of stacks of books off the second guest chair, and we all sat down. "You said you wanted me to listen to a recording. I presume this has something to do with the aliens?"

"All I can offer is the recording," said Colonel Weber.

"Okay, let's hear it."

Colonel Weber took a tape machine out of his briefcase and pressed PLAY. The recording sounded vaguely like that of a wet dog shaking the water out of its fur.

"What do you make of that?" he asked.

I withheld my comparison to a wet dog. "What was the context in which this recording was made?"

"I'm not at liberty to say."

"It would help me interpret those sounds. Could you see the alien while it was speaking? Was it doing anything at the time?"

"The recording is all I can offer."

"You won't be giving anything away if you tell me that you've seen the aliens; the public's assumed you have."

Colonel Weber wasn't budging. "Do you have any opinion about its linguistic properties?" he asked.

"Well, it's clear that their vocal tract is substantially different from a human vocal tract. I assume that these aliens don't look like humans?"

The colonel was about to say something noncommittal when Gary Donnelly asked, "Can you make any guesses based on the tape?"

"Not really. It doesn't sound like they're using a larynx to make those sounds, but that doesn't tell me what they look like."

"Anything — is there anything else you can tell us?" asked Colonel Weber.

I could see he wasn't accustomed to consulting a civilian. "Only that establishing communications is going to be really difficult because of the difference in anatomy. They're almost certainly using sounds that the human vocal tract can't reproduce, and maybe sounds that the human ear can't distinguish."

"You mean infra- or ultrasonic frequencies?" asked Gary Donnelly.

"Not specifically. I just mean that the human auditory system isn't an absolute acoustic instrument; it's optimized to recognize the sounds that a human larynx makes. With an alien vocal system, all bets are off." I shrugged. "*Maybe* we'll be able to hear the difference between alien phonemes, given enough practice, but it's possible our ears simply can't recognize the distinctions they consider meaningful. In that case we'd need a sound spectrograph to know what an alien is saying."

Colonel Weber asked, "Suppose I gave you an hour's worth of recordings; how long would it take you to determine if we need this sound spectrograph or not?"

"I couldn't determine that with just a recording no matter how much time I had. I'd need to talk with the aliens directly."

The colonel shook his head. "Not possible."

I tried to break it to him gently. "That's your call, of course. But the only way to learn an unknown language is to interact with a native speaker, and by that I mean asking questions, holding a conversation, that sort of thing. Without that, it's simply not possible. So if you want to learn the aliens' language, someone with training in field linguistics —

whether it's me or someone else—will have to talk with an alien. Recordings alone aren't sufficient."

Colonel Weber frowned. "You seem to be implying that no alien could have learned human languages by monitoring our broadcasts."

"I doubt it. They'd need instructional material specifically designed to teach human languages to nonhumans. Either that, or interaction with a human. If they had either of those, they could learn a lot from TV, but otherwise, they wouldn't have a starting point."

The colonel clearly found this interesting; evidently his philosophy was, the less the aliens knew, the better. Gary Donnelly read the colonel's expression too and rolled his eyes. I suppressed a smile.

Then Colonel Weber asked, "Suppose you were learning a new language by talking to its speakers; could you do it without teaching them English?"

"That would depend on how cooperative the native speakers were. They'd almost certainly pick up bits and pieces while I'm learning their language, but it wouldn't have to be much if they're willing to teach. On the other hand, if they'd rather learn English than teach us their language, that would make things far more difficult."

The colonel nodded. "I'll get back to you on this matter."

The request for that meeting was perhaps the second most momentous phone call in my life. The first, of course, will be the one from Mountain Rescue. At that point your dad and I will be speaking to each other maybe once a year, tops. After I get that phone call, though, the first thing I'll do will be to call your father.

He and I will drive out together to perform the identification, a long silent car ride. I remember the morgue, all tile and stainless steel, the hum of refrigeration and smell of antiseptic. An orderly will pull the sheet back to reveal your face. Your face will look wrong somehow, but I'll know it's you.

"Yes, that's her," I'll say. "She's mine."

You'll be twenty-five then.

The MP checked my badge, made a notation on his clipboard, and opened the gate; I drove the off-road vehicle into the encampment, a small village of tents pitched by the Army in a farmer's sun-scorched pasture. At the center of the encampment was one of the alien devices, nicknamed "looking glasses."

According to the briefings I'd attended, there were nine of these in the United States, one hundred and twelve in the world. The looking glasses acted as two-way communication devices, presumably with the ships in orbit. No one knew why the aliens wouldn't talk to us in person; fear of cooties, maybe. A team of scientists, including a physicist and a linguist, was assigned to each looking glass; Gary Donnelly and I were on this one.

Gary was waiting for me in the parking area. We navigated a circular maze of concrete barricades until we reached the large tent that covered the looking glass itself. In front of the tent was an equipment cart loaded with goodies borrowed from the school's phonology lab; I had sent it ahead for inspection by the Army.

Also outside the tent were three tripod-mounted video cameras whose lenses peered, through windows in the fabric wall, into the main room. Everything Gary and I did would be reviewed by countless others, including military intelligence. In addition we would each send daily reports, of which mine had to include estimates on how much English I thought the aliens could understand.

Gary held open the tent flap and gestured for me to enter. "Step right up," he said, circus-barker-style. "Marvel at creatures the likes of which have never been seen on God's green earth."

"And all for one slim dime," I murmured, walking through the door. At the moment the looking glass was inactive, resembling a semicircular mirror over ten feet high and twenty feet across. On the brown grass in front of the looking glass, an arc of white spray paint outlined the activation area. Currently the area contained only a table, two folding chairs, and a power strip with a cord leading to a generator outside. The buzz of fluorescent lamps, hung from poles along the edge of the room, commingled with the buzz of flies in the sweltering heat.

Gary and I looked at each other, and then began pushing the cart of equipment up to the table. As we crossed the paint line, the looking glass appeared to grow transparent; it was as if someone was slowly raising the illumination behind tinted glass. The illusion of depth was uncanny; I felt I could walk right into it. Once the looking glass was fully lit it resembled a life-sized diorama of a semicircular room. The room contained a few large objects that might have been furniture, but no aliens. There was a door in the curved rear wall.

We busied ourselves connecting everything together: microphone, sound spectrograph, portable computer, and speaker. As we worked, I frequently glanced at the looking glass, anticipating the aliens' arrival. Even so I jumped when one of them entered.

It looked like a barrel suspended at the intersection of seven limbs. It was radially symmetric, and any of its limbs could serve as an arm or a leg. The one in front of me was walking around on four legs, three nonadjacent arms curled up at its sides. Gary called them "heptapods."

I'd been shown videotapes, but I still gawked. Its limbs had no distinct joints; anatomists guessed they might be supported by vertebral columns. Whatever their underlying structure, the heptapod's limbs conspired to move it in a disconcertingly fluid manner. Its "torso" rode atop the rippling limbs as smoothly as a hovercraft.

Seven lidless eyes ringed the top of the heptapod's body. It walked back to the doorway from which it entered, made a brief sputtering sound, and returned to the center of the room followed by another heptapod; at no point did it ever turn around. Eerie, but logical; with eyes on all sides, any direction might as well be "forward."

Gary had been watching my reaction. "Ready?" he asked.

I took a deep breath. "Ready enough." I'd done plenty of fieldwork before, in the Amazon, but it had always been a bilingual procedure: either my informants knew some Portuguese, which I could use, or I'd previously gotten an intro to their language from the local missionaries. This would be my first attempt at conducting a true monolingual discovery procedure. It was straightforward enough in theory, though.

I walked up to the looking glass and a heptapod on the other side did the same. The image was so real that my skin crawled. I could see the texture of its gray skin, like corduroy ridges arranged in whorls and loops. There was no smell at all from the looking glass, which somehow made the situation stranger.

I pointed to myself and said slowly, "Human." Then I pointed to Gary. "Human." Then I pointed at each heptapod and said, "What are you?"

No reaction. I tried again, and then again.

One of the heptapods pointed to itself with one limb, the four terminal digits pressed together. That was lucky. In some cultures a person pointed with his chin; if the heptapod hadn't used one of its limbs, I wouldn't have known what gesture to look for. I heard a brief fluttering sound, and saw a puckered orifice at the top of its body vibrate; it was talking. Then it pointed to its companion and fluttered again.

I went back to my computer; on its screen were two virtually identical spectrographs representing the fluttering sounds. I marked a sample for playback. I pointed to myself and said "Human" again, and did the same with Gary. Then I pointed to the heptapod, and played back the flutter on the speaker.

The heptapod fluttered some more. The second half of the spectrograph for this utterance looked like a repetition: call the previous utterances [flutter1], then this one was [flutter2flutter1].

I pointed at something that might have been a heptapod chair. "What is that?"

The heptapod paused, and then pointed at the "chair" and talked some more. The spectrograph for this differed distinctly from that of the earlier sounds: [flutter3]. Once again, I pointed to the "chair" while playing back [flutter3].

The heptapod replied; judging by the spectrograph, it looked like [flutter3flutter2]. Optimistic interpretation: the heptapod was confirming my utterances as correct, which implied compatibility between heptapod and human patterns of discourse. Pessimistic interpretation: it had a nagging cough.

At my computer I delimited certain sections of the spectrograph and typed in a tentative gloss for each: "heptapod" for [flutter1], "yes" for [flutter2], and "chair" for [flutter3]. Then I typed "Language: Heptapod A" as a heading for all the utterances.

Gary watched what I was typing. "What's the 'A' for?"

"It just distinguishes this language from any other ones the heptapods might use," I said. He nodded.

"Now let's try something, just for laughs." I pointed at each heptapod and tried to mimic the sound of [flutter1], "heptapod." After a long pause, the first heptapod said something and then the second one said something else, neither of whose spectrographs resembled anything said before. I couldn't tell if they were speaking to each other or to me since they had no faces to turn. I tried pronouncing [flutter1] again, but there was no reaction.

"Not even close," I grumbled.

"I'm impressed you can make sounds like that at all," said Gary.

"You should hear my moose call. Sends them running."

I tried again a few more times, but neither heptapod responded with anything I could recognize. Only when I replayed the recording of the heptapod's pronunciation did I get a confirmation; the heptapod replied with [flutter2], "yes."

"So we're stuck with using recordings?" asked Gary.

I nodded. "At least temporarily."

"So now what?"

"Now we make sure it hasn't actually been saying 'aren't they cute' or 'look what they're doing now.' Then we see if we can identify any of these words when that other heptapod pronounces them." I gestured for him to have a seat. "Get comfortable; this'll take a while."

In 1770, Captain Cook's ship *Endeavour* ran aground on the coast of Queensland, Australia. While some of his men made repairs, Cook led an exploration party and met the aboriginal people. One of the sailors pointed to the animals that hopped around with their young riding in pouches, and asked an aborigine what they were called. The aborigine replied, "Kanguru." From then on Cook and his sailors referred to the animals by this word. It wasn't until later that they learned it meant "What did you say?"

I tell that story in my introductory course every year. It's almost certainly untrue, and I explain that afterwards, but it's a classic anecdote. Of course, the anecdotes my undergraduates will really want to hear are ones featuring the heptapods; for the rest of my teaching career, that'll be the reason many of them sign up for my courses. So I'll show them the old videotapes of my sessions at the looking glass, and the sessions that the other linguists conducted; the tapes are instructive, and they'll be useful if we're ever visited by aliens again, but they don't generate many good anecdotes.

When it comes to language-learning anecdotes, my favorite source is child language acquisition. I remember one afternoon when you are five years old, after you have come home from kindergarten. You'll be coloring with your crayons while I grade papers.

"Mom," you'll say, using the carefully casual tone reserved for requesting a favor, "can I ask you something?"

"Sure, sweetie. Go ahead."

"Can I be, um, honored?"

I'll look up from the paper I'm grading. "What do you mean?"

"At school Sharon said she got to be honored."

"Really? Did she tell you what for?"

"It was when her big sister got married. She said only one person could be, um, honored, and she was it."

"Ah, I see. You mean Sharon was maid of honor?"

"Yeah, that's it. Can I be made of honor?"

Gary and I entered the prefab building containing the center of operations for the looking-glass site. Inside it looked like they were planning an invasion, or perhaps an evacuation: crew-cut soldiers worked around a large map of the area, or sat in front of burly electronic gear while speaking into headsets. We were shown into Colonel Weber's office, a room in the back that was cool from air-conditioning.

We briefed the colonel on our first day's results. "Doesn't sound like you got very far," he said.

"I have an idea as to how we can make faster progress," I said. "But you'll have to approve the use of more equipment."

"What more do you need?"

"A digital camera, and a big video screen." I showed him a drawing of the setup I imagined. "I want to try conducting the discovery procedure using writing; I'd display words on the screen, and use the camera to record the words they write. I'm hoping the heptapods will do the same."

Weber looked at the drawing dubiously. "What would be the advantage of that?"

"So far I've been proceeding the way I would with speakers of an unwritten language. Then it occurred to me that the heptapods must have writing too."

"So?"

"If the heptapods have a mechanical way of producing writing, then their writing ought to be very regular, very consistent. That would make it easier for us to identify graphemes instead of phonemes. It's like picking out the letters in a printed sentence instead of trying to hear them when the sentence is spoken aloud."

"I take your point," he admitted. "And how would you respond to them? Show them the words they displayed to you?"

"Basically. And if they put spaces between words, any sentences we write would be a lot more intelligible than any spoken sentence we might splice together from recordings."

He leaned back in his chair. "You know we want to show as little of our technology as possible."

"I understand, but we're using machines as intermediaries already. If we can get them to use writing, I believe progress will go much faster than if we're restricted to the sound spectrographs."

The colonel turned to Gary. "Your opinion?"

"It sounds like a good idea to me. I'm curious whether the heptapods might have difficulty reading our monitors. Their looking glasses are based on a completely different technology than our video screens. As far as we can tell, they don't use pixels or scan lines, and they don't refresh on a frame-by-frame basis."

"You think the scan lines on our video screens might render them unreadable to the heptapods?"

"It's possible," said Gary. "We'll just have to try it and see."

Weber considered it. For me it wasn't even a question, but from his point of view it was a difficult one; like a soldier, though, he made it quickly. "Request granted. Talk to the sergeant outside about bringing in what you need. Have it ready for tomorrow."

I remember one day during the summer when you're sixteen. For once, the person waiting for her date to arrive is me. Of course, you'll be waiting around too, curious to see what he looks like. You'll have a friend of yours, a blond girl with the unlikely name of Roxie, hanging out with you, giggling.

"You may feel the urge to make comments about him," I'll say, checking myself in the hallway mirror. "Just restrain yourselves until we leave."

"Don't worry, Mom," you'll say. "We'll do it so that he won't know. Roxie, you ask me what I think the weather will be like tonight. Then I'll say what I think of Mom's date."

"Right," Roxie will say.

"No, you most definitely will not," I'll say.

"Relax, Mom. He'll never know; we do this all the time."

"What a comfort that is."

A little later on, Nelson will arrive to pick me up. I'll do the introductions, and we'll all engage in a little small talk on the front porch. Nelson is ruggedly handsome, to your evident approval. Just as we're about to leave, Roxie will say to you casually, "So what do you think the weather will be like tonight?"

"I think it's going to be really hot," you'll answer.

Roxie will nod in agreement. Nelson will say, "Really? I thought they said it was going to be cool."

"I have a sixth sense about these things," you'll say. Your face will give nothing away. "I get the feeling it's going to be a scorcher. Good thing you're dressed for it, Mom."

I'll glare at you, and say good night.

As I lead Nelson toward his car, he'll ask me, amused, "I'm missing something here, aren't I?"

"A private joke," I'll mutter. "Don't ask me to explain it."

At our next session at the looking glass, we repeated the procedure we had performed before, this time displaying a printed word on our computer screen at the same time we spoke: showing HUMAN while saying "Human," and so forth. Eventually, the heptapods understood what we wanted, and set up a flat circular screen mounted on a small pedestal. One heptapod spoke, and then inserted a limb into a large socket in the pedestal; a doodle of script, vaguely cursive, popped onto the screen. We soon settled into a routine, and I compiled two parallel corpora: one of spoken utterances, one of writing samples. Based on first impressions, their writing appeared to be logographic, which was disappointing; I'd been hoping for an alphabetic script to help us learn their speech. Their logograms might include some phonetic information, but finding it would be a lot harder than with an alphabetic script.

By getting up close to the looking glass, I was able to point to various heptapod body parts, such as limbs, digits, and eyes, and elicit terms for each. It turned out that they had an orifice on the underside of their body, lined with articulated bony ridges: probably used for eating, while the one at the top was for respiration and speech. There were no other conspicuous orifices; perhaps their mouth was their anus too. Those sorts of questions would have to wait.

I also tried asking our two informants for terms for addressing each individually; personal names, if they had such things. Their answers were of course unpronounceable, so for Gary's and my purposes, I dubbed them Flapper and Raspberry. I hoped I'd be able to tell them apart.

The next day I conferred with Gary before we entered the looking-glass tent. "I'll need your help with this session," I told him.

"Sure. What do you want me to do?"

"We need to elicit some verbs, and it's easiest with third-person forms. Would you act out a few verbs while I type the written form on the computer? If we're lucky, the heptapods will figure out what we're doing and do the same. I've brought a bunch of props for you to use."

"No problem," said Gary, cracking his knuckles. "Ready when you are."

We began with some simple intransitive verbs: walking, jumping, speaking, writing. Gary demonstrated each one with a charming lack of self-consciousness; the presence of the video cameras didn't inhibit him at all. For the first few actions he performed, I asked the heptapods, "What do you call that?" Before long, the heptapods caught on to what we were trying to do; Raspberry began mimicking Gary, or at least performing the equivalent heptapod action, while Flapper worked their computer, displaying a written description and pronouncing it aloud.

In the spectrographs of their spoken utterances, I could recognize their word I had glossed as "heptapod." The rest of each utterance was presumably the verb phrase; it looked like they had analogs of nouns and verbs, thank goodness. In their writing, however, things weren't as clear-cut. For each action, they had displayed a single logogram instead of two separate ones. At first I thought they had written something like "walks," with the subject implied. But why would Flapper say "the heptapod walks" while writing "walks," instead of maintaining parallelism? Then I noticed that some of the logograms looked like the logogram for "heptapod" with some extra strokes added to one side or another. Perhaps their verbs could be written as affixes to a noun. If so, why was Flapper writing the noun in some instances but not in others?

I decided to try a transitive verb; substituting object words might clarify things. Among the props I'd brought were an apple and a slice of bread. "Okay," I said to Gary, "show them the food, and then eat some. First the apple, then the bread."

Gary pointed at the Golden Delicious and then he took a bite out of it, while I displayed the "what do you call that?" expression. Then we repeated it with the slice of whole wheat.

Raspberry left the room and returned with some kind of giant nut or gourd and a gelatinous ellipsoid. Raspberry pointed at the gourd while Flapper said a word and displayed a logogram. Then Raspberry brought the gourd down between its legs, a crunching sound resulted, and the gourd reemerged minus a bite; there were cornlike kernels beneath the shell. Flapper talked and displayed a large logogram on their screen. The sound spectrograph for "gourd" changed when it was used in the sentence; possibly a case marker. The logogram was odd: after some study, I could identify graphic elements that resembled the individual logograms for "heptapod" and "gourd." They looked as if they had been melted together, with several extra strokes in the mix that presumably meant "eat." Was it a multiword ligature?

Next we got spoken and written names for the gelatin egg, and descriptions of the act of eating it. The sound spectrograph for "heptapod eats gelatin egg" was analyzable; "gelatin egg" bore a case marker, as expected, though the sentence's word order differed from last time. The written form, another large logogram, was another matter. This time it took much longer for me to recognize anything in it; not only were the individual logograms melted together again, it looked as if the one for "heptapod" was laid on its back, while on top of it the logogram for "gelatin egg" was standing on its head.

"Uh-oh." I took another look at the writing for the simple noun-verb examples, the ones that had seemed inconsistent before. Now I realized all of them actually did contain the logogram for "heptapod"; some were rotated and distorted by being combined with the various verbs, so I hadn't recognized them at first. "You guys have got to be kidding," I muttered.

"What's wrong?" asked Gary.

"Their script isn't word-divided; a sentence is written by joining the logograms for the constituent words. They join the logograms by rotating and modifying them. Take a look." I showed him how the logograms were rotated.

"So they can read a word with equal ease no matter how it's ro-tated," Gary said. He turned to look at the heptapods, impressed. "I won-der if it's a consequence of their bodies' radial symmetry: their bodies have no 'forward' direction, so maybe their writing doesn't either. Highly neat."

I couldn't believe it; I was working with someone who modified the word "neat" with "highly." "It certainly is interesting," I said, "but it also means there's no easy way for us to write our own sentences in their language. We can't simply cut their sentences into individual words and recombine them; we'll have to learn the rules of their script before we can write anything legible. It's the same continuity problem we'd have had splicing together speech fragments, except applied to writing."

I looked at Flapper and Raspberry in the looking glass, who were waiting for us to continue, and sighed. "You aren't going to make this easy for us, are you?"

To be fair, the heptapods were completely cooperative. In the days that followed, they readily taught us their language without requiring us to teach them any more English. Colonel Weber and his cohorts pon-dered the implications of that, while I and the linguists at the other look-ing glasses met via videoconferencing to share what we had learned about the heptapod language. The videoconferencing made for an in-congruous working environment: our video screens were primitive com-pared to the heptapods' looking glasses, so that my colleagues seemed more remote than the aliens. The familiar was far away, while the bizarre was close at hand.

It would be a while before we'd be ready to ask the heptapods why they had come, or to discuss physics well enough to ask them about their technology. For the time being, we worked on the basics: phonemics/graphemics, vocabulary, syntax. The heptapods at every looking glass were using the same language, so we were able to pool our data and co-ordinate our efforts.

Our biggest source of confusion was the heptapods' "writing." It didn't appear to be writing at all; it looked more like a bunch of intricate graphic designs. The logograms weren't arranged in rows, or a spiral, or any linear fashion. Instead, Flapper or Raspberry would write a sen-tence by sticking together as many logograms as needed into a giant conglomeration.

This form of writing was reminiscent of primitive sign systems, which required a reader to know a message's context in order to understand it. Such systems were considered too limited for systematic recording of information. Yet it was unlikely that the heptapods developed their level of technology with only an oral tradition. That implied one of three possibilities: the first was that the heptapods had a true writing system, but they didn't want to use it in front of us; Colonel Weber would identify with that one. The second was that the heptapods hadn't originated the technology they were using; they were illiterates using someone else's technology. The third, and most interesting to me, was that the heptapods were using a nonlinear system of orthography that qualified as true writing.

I remember a conversation we'll have when you're in your junior year of high school. It'll be Sunday morning, and I'll be scrambling some eggs while you set the table for brunch. You'll laugh as you tell me about the party you went to last night.

"Oh man," you'll say, "they're not kidding when they say that body weight makes a difference. I didn't drink any more than the guys did, but I got so much *drunk*er."

I'll try to maintain a neutral, pleasant expression. I'll really try. Then you'll say, "Oh, come on, Mom."

"What?"

"You know you did the exact same things when you were my age."

I did nothing of the sort, but I know that if I were to admit that, you'd lose respect for me completely. "You know never to drive, or get into a car if—"

"God, of course I know that. Do you think I'm an idiot?"

"No, of course not."

What I'll think is that you are clearly, maddeningly not me. It will remind me, again, that you won't be a clone of me; you can be wonderful, a daily delight, but you won't be someone I could have created by myself.

The military had set up a trailer containing our offices at the looking-glass site. I saw Gary walking toward the trailer, and ran to catch up with him. "It's a semasiographic writing system," I said when I reached him.

"Excuse me?" said Gary.

"Here, let me show you." I directed Gary into my office. Once we were inside, I went to the chalkboard and drew a circle with a diagonal line bisecting it. "What does this mean?"

"'Not allowed'?"

"Right." Next I printed the words NOT ALLOWED on the chalkboard. "And so does this. But only one is a representation of speech."

Gary nodded. "Okay."

"Linguists describe writing like this" — I indicated the printed words — "as 'glottographic,' because it represents speech. Every human written language is in this category. However, this symbol" — I indicated the circle and diagonal line — "is 'semasiographic' writing, because it conveys meaning without reference to speech. There's no correspondence between its components and any particular sounds."

"And you think all of heptapod writing is like this?"

"From what I've seen so far, yes. It's not picture writing, it's far more complex. It has its own system of rules for constructing sentences, like a visual syntax that's unrelated to the syntax for their spoken language."

"A visual syntax? Can you show me an example?"

"Coming right up." I sat down at my desk and, using the computer, pulled up a frame from the recording of yesterday's conversation with Raspberry. I turned the monitor so he could see it. "In their spoken language, a noun has a case marker indicating whether it's a subject or object. In their written language, however, a noun is identified as subject or object based on the orientation of its logogram relative to that of the verb. Here, take a look." I pointed at one of the figures. "For instance, when 'heptapod' is integrated with 'hears' this way, with these strokes parallel, it means that the heptapod is doing the hearing." I showed him a different one. "When they're combined this way, with the strokes perpendicular, it means that the heptapod is being heard. This morphology applies to several verbs.

"Another example is the inflection system." I called up another frame from the recording. "In their written language, this logogram means roughly 'hear easily' or 'hear clearly.' See the elements it has in common with the logogram for 'hear'? You can still combine it with 'heptapod' in the same ways as before, to indicate that the heptapod can hear something clearly or that the heptapod is clearly heard. But what's really interesting is that the modulation of 'hear' into 'hear clearly' isn't a special case; you see the transformation they applied?"

Gary nodded, pointing. "It's like they express the idea of 'clearly' by changing the curve of those strokes in the middle."

"Right. That modulation is applicable to lots of verbs. The logogram for 'see' can be modulated in the same way to form 'see clearly,' and so can the logogram for 'read' and others. And changing the curve of those strokes has no parallel in their speech; with the spoken version of these verbs, they add a prefix to the verb to express ease of manner, and the prefixes for 'see' and 'hear' are different.

"There are other examples, but you get the idea. It's essentially a grammar in two dimensions."

He began pacing thoughtfully. "Is there anything like this in human writing systems?"

"Mathematical equations, notations for music and dance. But those are all very specialized; we couldn't record this conversation using them. But I suspect, if we knew it well enough, we could record this conversation in the heptapod writing system. I think it's a full-fledged, general-purpose graphical language."

Gary frowned. "So their writing constitutes a completely separate language from their speech, right?"

"Right. In fact, it'd be more accurate to refer to the writing system as 'Heptapod B,' and use 'Heptapod A' strictly for referring to the spoken language."

"Hold on a second. Why use two languages when one would suffice? That seems unnecessarily hard to learn."

"Like English spelling?" I said. "Ease of learning isn't the primary force in language evolution. For the heptapods, writing and speech may play such different cultural or cognitive roles that using separate languages makes more sense than using different forms of the same one."

He considered it. "I see what you mean. Maybe they think our form of writing is redundant, like we're wasting a second communications channel."

"That's entirely possible. Finding out why they use a second language for writing will tell us a lot about them."

"So I take it this means we won't be able to use their writing to help us learn their spoken language."

I sighed. "Yeah, that's the most immediate implication. But I don't think we should ignore either Heptapod A or B; we need a two-pronged approach." I pointed at the screen. "I'll bet you that learning their two-dimensional grammar will help you when it comes time to learn their mathematical notation."

"You've got a point there. So are we ready to start asking about their mathematics?"

"Not yet. We need a better grasp on this writing system before we begin anything else," I said, and then smiled when he mimed frustration. "Patience, good sir. Patience is a virtue."

You'll be six when your father has a conference to attend in Hawaii, and we'll accompany him. You'll be so excited that you'll make preparations for weeks beforehand. You'll ask me about coconuts and volcanoes and surfing, and practice hula dancing in the mirror. You'll pack a suitcase with the clothes and toys you want to bring, and you'll drag it around the house to see how long you can carry it. You'll ask me if I can carry your Etch-a-Sketch in my bag, since there won't be any more room for it in yours and you simply can't leave without it.

"You won't need all of these," I'll say. "There'll be so many fun things to do there, you won't have time to play with so many toys."

You'll consider that; dimples will appear above your eyebrows when you think hard. Eventually you'll agree to pack fewer toys, but your expectations will, if anything, increase.

"I wanna be in Hawaii now," you'll whine.

"Sometimes it's good to wait," I'll say. "The anticipation makes it more fun when you get there."

You'll just pout.

In the next report I submitted, I suggested that the term "logogram" was a misnomer because it implied that each graph represented a spoken word, when in fact the graphs didn't correspond to our notion of spoken words at all. I didn't want to use the term "ideogram" either because of how it had been used in the past; I suggested the term "semagram" instead.

It appeared that a semagram corresponded roughly to a written word in human languages: it was meaningful on its own, and in combination with other semagrams could form endless statements. We couldn't define it precisely, but then no one had ever satisfactorily defined "word" for human languages either. When it came to sentences in Heptapod B, though, things became much more confusing. The language had no written punctuation: its syntax was indicated in the way the semagrams were combined, and there was no need to indicate the cadence of speech. There was certainly no way to slice out subject-predicate pairings neatly to make sentences. A "sentence" seemed to be whatever number of semagrams a heptapod wanted to join together; the only difference between a sentence and a paragraph, or a page, was size.

When a Heptapod B sentence grew fairly sizable, its visual impact was remarkable. If I wasn't trying to decipher it, the writing looked like fanciful praying mantids drawn in a cursive style, all clinging to each other to form an Escheresque lattice, each slightly different in its stance. And the biggest sentences had an effect similar to that of psychedelic posters: sometimes eye-watering, sometimes hypnotic.

I remember a picture of you taken at your college graduation. In the photo you're striking a pose for the camera, mortarboard stylishly tilted on your head, one hand touching your sunglasses, the other hand on your hip, holding open your gown to reveal the tank top and shorts you're wearing underneath.

I remember your graduation. There will be the distraction of having Nelson and your father and what's-her-name there all at the same time, but that will be minor. That entire weekend, while you're introducing me to your classmates and hugging everyone incessantly, I'll be all but mute with amazement. I can't believe that you, a grown woman taller than me and beautiful enough to make my heart ache, will be the same girl I used to lift off the ground so you could reach the drinking fountain, the same girl who used to trundle out of my bedroom draped in a dress and hat and four scarves from my closet.

And after graduation, you'll be heading for a job as a financial analyst. I won't understand what you do there, I won't even understand your fascination with money, the preeminence you gave to salary when negotiating job offers. I would prefer it if you'd pursue something without regard for its monetary rewards, but I'll have no complaints. My own mother could never understand why I couldn't just be a high school English teacher. You'll do what makes you happy, and that'll be all I ask for.

As time went on, the teams at each looking glass began working in earnest on learning heptapod terminology for elementary mathematics and physics. We worked together on presentations, with the linguists focusing on procedure and the physicists focusing on subject matter. The physicists showed us previously devised systems for communicating with aliens, based on mathematics, but those were intended for use over a radio telescope. We reworked them for face-to-face communication.

Our teams were successful with basic arithmetic, but we hit a roadblock with geometry and algebra. We tried using a spherical coordinate system instead of a rectangular one, thinking it might be more natural to the heptapods given their anatomy, but that approach wasn't any more fruitful. The heptapods didn't seem to understand what we were getting at.

Likewise, the physics discussions went poorly. Only with the most concrete terms, like the names of the elements, did we have any success; after several attempts at representing the periodic table, the heptapods got the idea. For anything remotely abstract, we might as well have been gibbering. We tried to demonstrate basic physical attributes like mass and acceleration so we could elicit their terms for them, but the heptapods simply responded with requests for clarification. To avoid perceptual problems that might be associated with any particular medium, we tried physical demonstrations as well as line drawings, photos, and animations; none were effective. Days with no progress became weeks, and the physicists were becoming disillusioned.

By contrast, the linguists were having much more success. We made steady progress decoding the grammar of the spoken language, Heptapod A. It didn't follow the pattern of human languages, as expected, but it was comprehensible so far: free word order, even to the extent that there was no preferred order for the clauses in a conditional statement, in defiance of a human language "universal." It also appeared that the heptapods had no objection to many levels of center-embedding of clauses, something that quickly defeated humans. Peculiar, but not impenetrable.

Much more interesting were the newly discovered morphological and grammatical processes in Heptapod B that were uniquely two-dimensional. Depending on a semagram's declension, inflections could be indicated by varying a certain stroke's curvature, or its thickness, or its manner of undulation; or by varying the relative sizes of two radicals, or their relative distance to another radical, or their orientations; or various other means. These were nonsegmental graphemes; they couldn't be isolated from the rest of a semagram. And despite how such traits be-haved in human writing, these had nothing to do with calligraphic style; their meanings were defined according to a consistent and unambiguous grammar.

We regularly asked the heptapods why they had come. Each time, they answered "to see," or "to observe." Indeed, sometimes they pre-ferred to watch us silently rather than answer our questions. Perhaps they were scientists, perhaps they were tourists. The State Department in-structed us to reveal as little as possible about humanity, in case that information could be used as a bargaining chip in subsequent negotia-tions. We obliged, though it didn't require much effort: the heptapods never asked questions about anything. Whether scientists or tourists, they were an awfully incurious bunch.

I remember once when we'll be driving to the mall to buy some new clothes for you. You'll be thirteen. One moment you'll be sprawled in your seat, completely unself-conscious, all child; the next, you'll toss your hair with a practiced casualness, like a fashion model in training.

You'll give me some instructions as I'm parking the car. "Okay, Mom, give me one of the credit cards, and we can meet back at the en-trance here in two hours."

I'll laugh. "Not a chance. All the credit cards stay with me."

"You're kidding." You'll become the embodiment of exasperation. We'll get out of the car and I will start walking to the mall entrance. After seeing that I won't budge on the matter, you'll quickly reformulate your plans.

"Okay Mom, okay. You can come with me, just walk a little ways behind me, so it doesn't look like we're together. If I see any friends of mine, I'm gonna stop and talk to them, but you just keep walking, okay? I'll come find you later."

I'll stop in my tracks. "Excuse me? I am not the hired help, nor am I some mutant relative for you to be ashamed of."

"But Mom, I can't let anyone see you with me."

"What are you talking about? I've already met your friends; they've been to the house."

"That was different," you'll say, incredulous that you have to ex-plain it. "This is shopping."

"Too bad."

Then the explosion: "You won't do the least thing to make me happy! You don't care about me at all!"

It won't have been that long since you enjoyed going shopping with me; it will forever astonish me how quickly you grow out of one phase and enter another. Living with you will be like aiming for a moving target; you'll always be further along than I expect.

I looked at the sentence in Heptapod B that I had just written, using simple pen and paper. Like all the sentences I generated myself, this one looked misshapen, like a heptapod-written sentence that had been smashed with a hammer and then inexpertly taped back together. I had sheets of such inelegant semagrams covering my desk, fluttering occasionally when the oscillating fan swung past.

It was strange trying to learn a language that had no spoken form. Instead of practicing my pronunciation, I had taken to squeezing my eyes shut and trying to paint semagrams on the insides of my eyelids.

There was a knock at the door and before I could answer Gary came in looking jubilant. "Illinois got a repetition in physics."

"Really? That's great; when did it happen?"

"It happened a few hours ago; we just had the videoconference. Let me show you what it is." He started erasing my blackboard.

"Don't worry, I didn't need any of that."

"Good." He picked up a nub of chalk and drew a diagram:

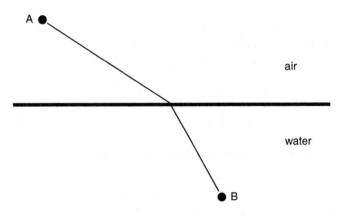

"Okay, here's the path a ray of light takes when crossing from air to water. The light ray travels in a straight line until it hits the water; the water has a different index of refraction, so the light changes direction. You've heard of this before, right?"

I nodded. "Sure."

"Now here's an interesting property about the path the light takes. The path is the fastest possible route between these two points."

"Come again?"

"Imagine, just for grins, that the ray of light traveled along this path." He added a dotted line to his diagram:

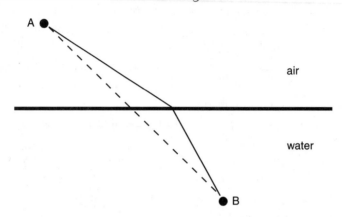

"This hypothetical path is shorter than the path the light actually takes. But light travels more slowly in water than it does in air, and a greater percentage of this path is underwater. So it would take longer for light to travel along this path than it does along the real path."

"Okay, I get it."

"Now imagine if light were to travel along this other path." He drew a second dotted path:

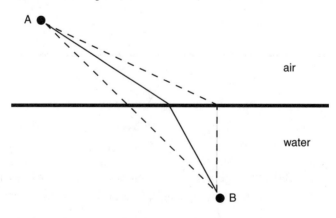

"This path reduces the percentage that's underwater, but the total length is larger. It would also take longer for light to travel along this path than along the actual one."

Gary put down the chalk and gestured at the diagram on the chalkboard with white-tipped fingers. "Any hypothetical path would require more time to traverse than the one actually taken. In other words, the route that the light ray takes is always the fastest possible one. That's Fermat's Principle of Least Time."

"Hmm, interesting. And this is what the heptapods responded to?"

"Exactly. Moorehead gave an animated presentation of Fermat's Principle at the Illinois looking glass, and the heptapods repeated it back. Now he's trying to get a symbolic description." He grinned. "Now is that highly neat, or what?"

"It's neat all right, but how come I haven't heard of Fermat's Principle before?" I picked up a binder and waved it at him; it was a primer on the physics topics suggested for use in communication with the heptapods. "This thing goes on forever about Planck masses and the spin-flip of atomic hydrogen, and not a word about the refraction of light."

"We guessed wrong about what'd be most useful for you to know," Gary said without embarrassment. "In fact, it's curious that Fermat's Principle was the first breakthrough; even though it's easy to explain, you need calculus to describe it mathematically. And not ordinary calculus; you need the calculus of variations. We thought that some simple theorem of geometry or algebra would be the breakthrough."

"Curious indeed. You think the heptapods' idea of what's simple doesn't match ours?"

"Exactly, which is why I'm *dying* to see what their mathematical description of Fermat's Principle looks like." He paced as he talked. "If their version of the calculus of variations is simpler to them than their equivalent of algebra, that might explain why we've had so much trouble talking about physics; their entire system of mathematics may be topsy-turvy compared to ours." He pointed to the physics primer. "You can be sure that we're going to revise that."

"So can you build from Fermat's Principle to other areas of physics?"

"Probably. There are lots of physical principles just like Fermat's."

"What, like Louise's principle of least closet space? When did physics become so minimalist?"

"Well, the word 'least' is misleading. You see, Fermat's Principle of Least Time is incomplete; in certain situations light follows a path that takes *more* time than any of the other possibilities. It's more accurate to say that light always follows an *extreme* path, either one that minimizes the time taken or one that maximizes it. A minimum and a maximum share certain mathematical properties, so both situations can be described with one equation. So to be precise, Fermat's Principle isn't a minimal principle; instead it's what's known as a 'variational' principle."

"And there are more of these variational principles?"

He nodded. "In all branches of physics. Almost every physical law can be restated as a variational principle. The only difference between these principles is in which attribute is minimized or maximized." He gestured as if the different branches of physics were arrayed before him on a table. "In optics, where Fermat's Principle applies, time is the attribute that has to be an extreme. In mechanics, it's a different attribute. In electromagnetism, it's something else again. But all these principles are similar mathematically."

"So once you get their mathematical description of Fermat's Principle, you should be able to decode the other ones."

"God, I hope so. I think this is the wedge that we've been looking for, the one that cracks open their formulation of physics. This calls for a celebration." He stopped his pacing and turned to me. "Hey Louise, want to go out for dinner? My treat."

I was mildly surprised. "Sure," I said.

It'll be when you first learn to walk that I get daily demonstrations of the asymmetry in our relationship. You'll be incessantly running off somewhere, and each time you walk into a door frame or scrape your knee, the pain feels like it's my own. It'll be like growing an errant limb, an extension of myself whose sensory nerves report pain just fine, but whose motor nerves don't convey my commands at all. It's so unfair: I'm going to give birth to an animated voodoo doll of myself. I didn't see this in the contract when I signed up. Was this part of the deal?

And then there will be the times when I see you laughing. Like the time you'll be playing with the neighbor's puppy, poking your hands through the chain-link fence separating our backyards, and you'll be laughing so hard you'll start hiccuping. The puppy will run inside the neighbor's house, and your laughter will gradually subside, letting you catch your breath. Then the puppy will come back to the fence to lick your fingers again, and you'll shriek and start laughing again. It will be the most wonderful sound I could ever imagine, a sound that makes me feel like a fountain, or a wellspring.

Now if only I can remember that sound the next time your blithe disregard for self-preservation gives me a heart attack.

After the breakthrough with Fermat's Principle, discussions of scientific concepts became more fruitful. It wasn't as if all of heptapod physics was suddenly rendered transparent, but progress was steady. According to Gary, the heptapods' formulation of physics was indeed topsy-turvy relative to ours. Physical attributes that humans defined using integral calculus were seen as fundamental by the heptapods. As an example, Gary described an attribute that, in physics jargon, bore the deceptively simple name "action," which represented "the difference between kinetic and potential energy, integrated over time," whatever that meant. Calculus for us; elementary to them.

Conversely, to define attributes that humans thought of as fundamental, like velocity, the heptapods employed mathematics that were, Gary assured me, "highly weird." The physicists were ultimately able to prove the equivalence of heptapod mathematics and human mathematics; even though their approaches were almost the reverse of one another, both were systems of describing the same physical universe.

I tried following some of the equations that the physicists were coming up with, but it was no use. I couldn't really grasp the significance of physical attributes like "action"; I couldn't, with any confidence, ponder the significance of treating such an attribute as fundamental. Still, I tried to ponder questions formulated in terms more familiar to me: what kind of worldview did the heptapods have, that they would consider Fermat's Principle the simplest explanation of light refraction? What kind of perception made a minimum or maximum readily apparent to them?

Your eyes will be blue like your dad's, not mud brown like mine. Boys will stare into those eyes the way I did, and do, into your dad's, surprised and enchanted, as I was and am, to find them in combination with black hair. You will have many suitors.

I remember when you are fifteen, coming home after a weekend at your dad's, incredulous over the interrogation he'll have put you through regarding the boy you're currently dating. You'll sprawl on the sofa, recounting your dad's latest breach of common sense: "You know what he said? He said, 'I know what teenage boys are like.'" Roll of the eyes. "Like I don't?"

"Don't hold it against him," I'll say. "He's a father; he can't help it." Having seen you interact with your friends, I won't worry much about a boy taking advantage of you; if anything, the opposite will be more likely. I'll worry about that.

"He wishes I were still a kid. He hasn't known how to act toward me since I grew breasts."

"Well, that development was a shock for him. Give him time to recover."

"It's been *years*, Mom. How long is it gonna take?"

"I'll let you know when my father has come to terms with mine."

During one of the videoconferences for the linguists, Cisneros from the Massachusetts looking glass had raised an interesting question: Was there a particular order in which semagrams were written in a Heptapod B sentence? It was clear that word order meant next to nothing when speaking in Heptapod A; when asked to repeat what it had just said, a heptapod would likely as not use a different word order unless we specifically asked it not to. Was word order similarly unimportant when writing in Heptapod B?

Previously, we had only focused our attention on how a sentence in Heptapod B looked once it was complete. As far as anyone could tell, there was no preferred order when reading the semagrams in a sentence; you could start almost anywhere in the nest, then follow the branching clauses until you'd read the whole thing. But that was reading; was the same true about writing?

During my most recent session with Flapper and Raspberry I had asked them if, instead of displaying a semagram only after it was completed, they could show it to us while it was being written. They had agreed. I inserted the videotape of the session into the VCR, and on my computer I consulted the session transcript.

I picked one of the longer utterances from the conversation. What Flapper had said was that the heptapods' planet had two moons, one significantly larger than the other; the three primary constituents of the planet's atmosphere were nitrogen, argon, and oxygen; and fifteen twenty-eighths of the planet's surface was covered by water. The first words of the spoken utterance translated literally as "inequality-of-size rocky-orbiter rocky-orbiters related-as-primary-to-secondary."

Then I rewound the videotape until the time signature matched the one in the transcription. I started playing the tape, and watched the web of semagrams being spun out of inky spider's silk. I rewound it and played it several times. Finally I froze the video right after the first stroke was completed and before the second one was begun; all that was visible on-screen was a single sinuous line.

Comparing that initial stroke with the completed sentence, I realized that the stroke participated in several different clauses of the message. It began in the semagram for "oxygen," as the determinant that distinguished it from certain other elements; then it slid down to become the morpheme of comparison in the description of the two moons' sizes; and lastly it flared out as the arched backbone of the semagram for "ocean." Yet this stroke was a single continuous line, and it was the first one that Flapper wrote. That meant the heptapod had to know how the entire sentence would be laid out before it could write the very first stroke.

The other strokes in the sentence also traversed several clauses, making them so interconnected that none could be removed without redesigning the entire sentence. The heptapods didn't write a sentence one semagram at a time; they built it out of strokes irrespective of individual semagrams. I had seen a similarly high degree of integration before in calligraphic designs, particularly those employing the Arabic alphabet. But those designs had required careful planning by expert calligraphers. No one could lay out such an intricate design at the speed needed for holding a conversation. At least, no human could.

There's a joke that I once heard a comedienne tell. It goes like this: "I'm not sure if I'm ready to have children. I asked a friend of mine who has children, 'Suppose I do have kids. What if when they grow up, they blame me for everything that's wrong with their lives?' She laughed and said, 'What do you mean, if?'"

That's my favorite joke.

Gary and I were at a little Chinese restaurant, one of the local places we had taken to patronizing to get away from the encampment. We sat eating the appetizers: potstickers, redolent of pork and sesame oil. My favorite.

I dipped one in soy sauce and vinegar. "So how are you doing with your Heptapod B practice?" I asked.

Gary looked obliquely at the ceiling. I tried to meet his gaze, but he kept shifting it.

"You've given up, haven't you?" I said. "You're not even trying anymore."

He did a wonderful hangdog expression. "I'm just no good at languages," he confessed. "I thought learning Heptapod B might be more like learning mathematics than trying to speak another language, but it's not. It's too foreign for me."

"It would help you discuss physics with them."

"Probably, but since we had our breakthrough, I can get by with just a few phrases."

I sighed. "I suppose that's fair; I have to admit, I've given up on trying to learn the mathematics."

"So we're even?"

"We're even." I sipped my tea. "Though I did want to ask you about Fermat's Principle. Something about it feels odd to me, but I can't put my finger on it. It just doesn't sound like a law of physics."

A twinkle appeared in Gary's eyes. "I'll bet I know what you're talking about." He snipped a potsticker in half with his chopsticks. "You're used to thinking of refraction in terms of cause and effect: reaching the water's surface is the cause, and the change in direction is the effect. But Fermat's Principle sounds weird because it describes light's behavior in goal-oriented terms. It sounds like a commandment to a light beam: 'Thou shalt minimize or maximize the time taken to reach thy destination.'"

I considered it. "Go on."

"It's an old question in the philosophy of physics. People have been talking about it since Fermat first formulated it in the 1600s; Planck wrote volumes about it. The thing is, while the common formulation of physical laws is causal, a variational principle like Fermat's is purposive, almost teleological."

"Hmm, that's an interesting way to put it. Let me think about that for a minute." I pulled out a felt-tip pen and, on my paper napkin, drew a copy of the diagram that Gary had drawn on my blackboard. "Okay," I said, thinking aloud, "so let's say the goal of a ray of light is to take the fastest path. How does the light go about doing that?"

"Well, if I can speak anthropomorphic-projectionally, the light has to examine the possible paths and compute how long each one would take." He plucked the last potsticker from the serving dish.

"And to do that," I continued, "the ray of light has to know just where its destination is. If the destination were somewhere else, the fastest path would be different."

Gary nodded again. "That's right; the notion of a 'fastest path' is meaningless unless there's a destination specified. And computing how long a given path takes also requires information about what lies along that path, like where the water's surface is."

I kept staring at the diagram on the napkin. "And the light ray has to know all that ahead of time, before it starts moving, right?"

"So to speak," said Gary. "The light can't start traveling in any old direction and make course corrections later on, because the path resulting from such behavior wouldn't be the fastest possible one. The light has to do all its computations at the very beginning."

I thought to myself, *The ray of light has to know where it will ultimately end up before it can choose the direction to begin moving in.* I knew what that reminded me of. I looked up at Gary. "That's what was bugging me."

I remember when you're fourteen. You'll come out of your bedroom, a graffiti-covered notebook computer in hand, working on a report for school.

"Mom, what do you call it when both sides can win?"

I'll look up from my computer and the paper I'll be writing. "What, you mean a win-win situation?"

"There's some technical name for it, some math word. Remember that time Dad was here, and he was talking about the stock market? He used it then."

"Hmm, that sounds familiar, but I can't remember what he called it."

"I need to know. I want to use that phrase in my social studies report. I can't even search for information on it unless I know what it's called."

"I'm sorry, I don't know it either. Why don't you call your dad?"

Judging from your expression, that will be more effort than you want to make. At this point, you and your father won't be getting along well. "Can you call Dad and ask him? But don't tell him it's for me."

"I think you can call him yourself."

You'll fume, "Jesus, Mom, I can never get help with my homework since you and Dad split up."

It's amazing the diverse situations in which you can bring up the divorce. "I've helped you with your homework."

"Like a million years ago, Mom."

I'll let that pass. "I'd help you with this if I could, but I don't remember what it's called."

You'll head back to your bedroom in a huff.

I practiced Heptapod B at every opportunity, both with the other linguists and by myself. The novelty of reading a semasiographic language made it compelling in a way that Heptapod A wasn't, and my improvement in writing it excited me. Over time, the sentences I wrote grew shapelier, more cohesive. I had reached the point where it worked better when I didn't think about it too much. Instead of carefully trying to design a sentence before writing, I could simply begin putting down strokes immediately; my initial strokes almost always turned out to be compatible with an elegant rendition of what I was trying to say. I was developing a faculty like that of the heptapods.

More interesting was the fact that Heptapod B was changing the way I thought. For me, thinking typically meant speaking in an internal voice; as we say in the trade, my thoughts were phonologically coded. My internal voice normally spoke in English, but that wasn't a requirement. The summer after my senior year in high school, I attended a total immersion program for learning Russian; by the end of the summer, I was thinking and even dreaming in Russian. But it was always *spoken* Russian. Different language, same mode: a voice speaking silently aloud.

The idea of thinking in a linguistic yet nonphonological mode always intrigued me. I had a friend born of Deaf parents; he grew up using American Sign Language, and he told me that he often thought in ASL instead of English. I used to wonder what it was like to have one's thoughts be manually coded, to reason using an inner pair of hands instead of an inner voice.

With Heptapod B, I was experiencing something just as foreign: my thoughts were becoming graphically coded. There were trancelike moments during the day when my thoughts weren't expressed with my internal voice; instead, I saw semagrams with my mind's eye, sprouting like frost on a windowpane.

As I grew more fluent, semagraphic designs would appear fully formed, articulating even complex ideas all at once. My thought processes weren't moving any faster as a result, though. Instead of racing forward, my mind hung balanced on the symmetry underlying the semagrams. The semagrams seemed to be something more than language; they were almost like mandalas. I found myself in a meditative state, contemplating the way in which premises and conclusions were interchangeable. There was no direction inherent in the way propositions were connected, no "train of thought" moving along a particular route; all the components in an act of reasoning were equally powerful, all having identical precedence.

A representative from the State Department named Hossner had the job of briefing the U.S. scientists on our agenda with the heptapods. We sat in the videoconference room, listening to him lecture. Our microphone was turned off, so Gary and I could exchange comments without interrupting Hossner. As we listened, I worried that Gary might harm his vision, rolling his eyes so often.

"They must have had some reason for coming all this way," said the diplomat, his voice tinny through the speakers. "It does not look like their reason was conquest, thank God. But if that's not the reason, what is? Are they prospectors? Anthropologists? Missionaries? Whatever their motives, there must be something we can offer them. Maybe it's mineral rights to our solar system. Maybe it's information about ourselves. Maybe it's the right to deliver sermons to our populations. But we can be sure that there's something.

"My point is this: their motive might not to be to trade, but that doesn't mean that we cannot conduct trade. We simply need to know why they're here, and what we have that they want. Once we have that information, we can begin trade negotiations.

"I should emphasize that our relationship with the heptapods need not be adversarial. This is not a situation where every gain on their part is a loss on ours, or vice versa. If we handle ourselves correctly, both we and the heptapods can come out winners."

"You mean it's a non-zero-sum game?" Gary said in mock incredulity. "Oh my gosh."

"A non-zero-sum game."

"What?" You'll reverse course, heading back from your bedroom.

"When both sides can win: I just remembered, it's called a non-zero-sum game."

"That's it!" you'll say, writing it down on your notebook. "Thanks, Mom!"

"I guess I knew it after all," I'll say. "All those years with your father, some of it must have rubbed off."

"I knew you'd know it," you'll say. You'll give me a sudden, brief hug, and your hair will smell of apples. "You're the best."

"Louise?"

"Hmm? Sorry, I was distracted. What did you say?"

"I said, what do you think about our Mr. Hossner here?"

"I prefer not to."

"I've tried that myself: ignoring the government, seeing if it would go away. It hasn't."

As evidence of Gary's assertion, Hossner kept blathering: "Your immediate task is to think back on what you've learned. Look for anything that might help us. Has there been any indication of what the heptapods want? Of what they value?"

"Gee, it never occurred to us to look for things like that," I said. "We'll get right on it, sir."

"The sad thing is, that's just what we'll have to do," said Gary.

"Are there any questions?" asked Hossner.

Burghart, the linguist at the Ft. Worth looking glass, spoke up. "We've been through this with the heptapods many times. They maintain that they're here to observe, and they maintain that information is not tradable."

"So they would have us believe," said Hossner. "But consider: how could that be true? I know that the heptapods have occasionally stopped talking to us for brief periods. That may be a tactical maneuver on their part. If we were to stop talking to them tomorrow —"

"Wake me up if he says something interesting," said Gary.

"I was just going to ask you to do the same for me."

That day when Gary first explained Fermat's Principle to me, he had mentioned that almost every physical law could be stated as a variational principle. Yet when humans thought about physical laws, they preferred to work with them in their causal formulation. I could understand that: the physical attributes that humans found intuitive, like kinetic energy or acceleration, were all properties of an object at a given moment in time. And these were conducive to a chronological, causal interpretation of events: one moment growing out of another, causes and effects created a chain reaction that grew from past to future.

In contrast, the physical attributes that the heptapods found intuitive, like "action" or those other things defined by integrals, were meaningful only over a period of time. And these were conducive to a teleological interpretation of events: by viewing events over a period of time, one recognized that there was a requirement that had to be satisfied, a goal of minimizing or maximizing. And one had to know the initial and final states to meet that goal; one needed knowledge of the effects before the causes could be initiated.

I was growing to understand that too.

"Why?" you'll ask again. You'll be three.

"Because it's your bedtime," I'll say again. We'll have gotten as far as getting you bathed and into your jammies, but no further than that.

"But I'm not sleepy," you'll whine. You'll be standing at the bookshelf, pulling down a video to watch: your latest diversionary tactic to keep away from your bedroom.

"It doesn't matter: you still have to go to bed."

"But why?"

"Because I'm the mom and I said so."

I'm actually going to say that, aren't I? God, somebody please shoot me.

I'll pick you up and carry you under my arm to your bed, you wailing piteously all the while, but my sole concern will be my own distress. All those vows made in childhood that I would give reasonable answers when I became a parent, that I would treat my own child as an intelligent, thinking individual, all for naught: I'm going to turn into my mother. I can fight it as much as I want, but there'll be no stopping my slide down that long, dreadful slope.

Was it actually possible to know the future? Not simply to guess at it; was it possible to *know* what was going to happen, with absolute certainty and in specific detail? Gary once told me that the fundamental laws of physics were time-symmetric, that there was no physical difference between past and future. Given that, some might say, "yes, theoretically." But speaking more concretely, most would answer "no," because of free will.

I liked to imagine the objection as a Borgesian fabulation: consider a person standing before the *Book of Ages*, the chronicle that records every event, past and future. Even though the text has been photoreduced from the full-sized edition, the volume is enormous. With magnifier in hand, she flips through the tissue-thin leaves until she locates the story of her life. She finds the passage that describes her flipping through the *Book of Ages*, and she skips to the next column, where it details what she'll be doing later in the day: acting on information she's read in the *Book*, she'll bet one hundred dollars on the racehorse Devil May Care and win twenty times that much.

The thought of doing just that had crossed her mind, but being a contrary sort, she now resolves to refrain from betting on the ponies altogether.

There's the rub. The *Book of Ages* cannot be wrong; this scenario is based on the premise that a person is given knowledge of the actual future, not of some possible future. If this were Greek myth, circumstances would conspire to make her enact her fate despite her best efforts, but prophecies in myth are notoriously vague; the *Book of Ages* is quite specific, and there's no way she can be forced to bet on a racehorse in the manner specified. The result is a contradiction: the *Book of Ages* must be right, by definition; yet no matter what the *Book* says she'll do, she can choose to do otherwise. How can these two facts be reconciled?

They can't be, was the common answer. A volume like the *Book of Ages* is a logical impossibility, for the precise reason that its existence would result in the above contradiction. Or, to be generous, some might say that the *Book of Ages* could exist, as long as it wasn't accessible to readers: that volume is housed in a special collection, and no one has viewing privileges.

The existence of free will meant that we couldn't know the future. And we knew free will existed because we had direct experience of it. Volition was an intrinsic part of consciousness.

Or was it? What if the experience of knowing the future changed a person? What if it evoked a sense of urgency, a sense of obligation to act precisely as she knew she would?

I stopped by Gary's office before leaving for the day. "I'm calling it quits. Did you want to grab something to eat?"

"Sure, just wait a second," he said. He shut down his computer and gathered some papers together. Then he looked up at me. "Hey, want to come to my place for dinner tonight? I'll cook."

I looked at him dubiously. "You can cook?"

"Just one dish," he admitted. "But it's a good one."

"Sure," I said. "I'm game."

"Great. We just need to go shopping for the ingredients."

"Don't go to any trouble—"

"There's a market on the way to my house. It won't take a minute."

We took separate cars, me following him. I almost lost him when he abruptly turned into a parking lot. It was a gourmet market, not large, but fancy; tall glass jars stuffed with imported foods sat next to specialty utensils on the store's stainless-steel shelves.

I accompanied Gary as he collected fresh basil, tomatoes, garlic, linguini. "There's a fish market next door; we can get fresh clams there," he said.

"Sounds good." We walked past the section of kitchen utensils. My gaze wandered over the shelves—peppermills, garlic presses, salad tongs—and stopped on a wooden salad bowl.

When you are three, you'll pull a dishtowel off the kitchen counter and bring that salad bowl down on top of you. I'll make a grab for it, but I'll miss. The edge of the bowl will leave you with a cut, on the upper edge of your forehead, that will require a single stitch. Your father and I will hold you, sobbing and stained with Caesar dressing, as we wait in the emergency room for hours.

I reached out and took the bowl from the shelf. The motion didn't feel like something I was forced to do. Instead it seemed just as urgent as my rushing to catch the bowl when it falls on you: an instinct that I felt right in following.

"I could use a salad bowl like this."

Gary looked at the bowl and nodded approvingly. "See, wasn't it a good thing that I had to stop at the market?"

"Yes it was." We got in line to pay for our purchases.

Consider the sentence "The rabbit is ready to eat." Interpret "rabbit" to be the object of "eat," and the sentence was an announcement that dinner would be served shortly. Interpret "rabbit" to be the subject of "eat," and it was a hint, such as a young girl might give her mother so she'll open a bag of Purina Bunny Chow. Two very different utterances; in fact, they were probably mutually exclusive within a single household. Yet either was a valid interpretation; only context could determine what the sentence meant.

Consider the phenomenon of light hitting water at one angle, and traveling through it at a different angle. Explain it by saying that a difference in the index of refraction caused the light to change direction, and one saw the world as humans saw it. Explain it by saying that light minimized the time needed to travel to its destination, and one saw the world as the heptapods saw it. Two very different interpretations.

The physical universe was a language with a perfectly ambiguous grammar. Every physical event was an utterance that could be parsed in two entirely different ways, one causal and the other teleological, both valid, neither one disqualifiable no matter how much context was available.

When the ancestors of humans and heptapods first acquired the spark of consciousness, they both perceived the same physical world, but they parsed their perceptions differently; the worldviews that ultimately arose were the end result of that divergence. Humans had developed a sequential mode of awareness, while heptapods had developed a simultaneous mode of awareness. We experienced events in an order, and perceived their relationship as cause and effect. They experienced all events at once, and perceived a purpose underlying them all. A minimizing, maximizing purpose.

I have a recurring dream about your death. In the dream, I'm the one who's rock climbing—me, can you imagine it?—and you're three years old, riding in some kind of backpack I'm wearing. We're just a few feet below a ledge where we can rest, and you won't wait until I've climbed up to it. You start pulling yourself out of the pack; I order you to stop, but of course you ignore me. I feel your weight alternating from one side of the pack to the other as you climb out; then I feel your left foot on my shoulder, and then your right. I'm screaming at you, but I can't get a hand free to grab you. I can see the wavy design on the soles of your sneakers as you climb, and then I see a flake of stone give way beneath one of them. You slide right past me, and I can't move a muscle. I look down and see you shrink into the distance below me.

Then, all of a sudden, I'm at the morgue. An orderly lifts the sheet from your face, and I see that you're twenty-five.

"You okay?"

I was sitting upright in bed; I'd woken Gary with my movements. "I'm fine. I was just startled; I didn't recognize where I was for a moment."

Sleepily, he said, "We can stay at your place next time."

I kissed him. "Don't worry; your place is fine." We curled up, my back against his chest, and went back to sleep.

When you're three and we're climbing a steep, spiral flight of stairs, I'll hold your hand extra tightly. You'll pull your hand away from me. "I can do it by myself," you'll insist, and then move away from me to prove it, and I'll remember that dream. We'll repeat that scene countless times during your childhood. I can almost believe that, given your contrary nature, my attempts to protect you will be what create your love of climbing: first the jungle gym at the playground, then trees out in the greenbelt around our neighborhood, the rock walls at the climbing club, and ultimately cliff faces in national parks.

I finished the last radical in the sentence, put down the chalk, and sat down in my desk chair. I leaned back and surveyed the giant Heptapod B sentence I'd written that covered the entire blackboard in my office. It included several complex clauses, and I had managed to integrate all of them rather nicely.

Looking at a sentence like this one, I understood why the heptapods had evolved a semasiographic writing system like Heptapod B; it was better suited for a species with a simultaneous mode of consciousness. For them, speech was a bottleneck because it required that one word follow another sequentially. With writing, on the other hand, every mark on a page was visible simultaneously. Why constrain writing with a glottographic straitjacket, demanding that it be just as sequential as speech? It would never occur to them. Semasiographic writing naturally took advantage of the page's two-dimensionality; instead of doling out morphemes one at a time, it offered an entire page full of them all at once.

And now that Heptapod B had introduced me to a simultaneous mode of consciousness, I understood the rationale behind Heptapod A's grammar: what my sequential mind had perceived as unnecessarily convoluted, I now recognized as an attempt to provide flexibility within the confines of sequential speech. I could use Heptapod A more easily as a result, though it was still a poor substitute for Heptapod B.

There was a knock at the door and then Gary poked his head in. "Colonel Weber'll be here any minute."

I grimaced. "Right." Weber was coming to participate in a session with Flapper and Raspberry; I was to act as translator, a job I wasn't trained for and that I detested.

Gary stepped inside and closed the door. He pulled me out of my chair and kissed me.

I smiled. "You trying to cheer me up before he gets here?"

"No, I'm trying to cheer me up."

"You weren't interested in talking to the heptapods at all, were you? You worked on this project just to get me into bed."

"Ah, you see right through me."

I looked into his eyes. "You better believe it," I said.

I remember when you'll be a month old, and I'll stumble out of bed to give you your 2:00 A.M. feeding. Your nursery will have that "baby smell" of diaper rash cream and talcum powder, with a faint ammoniac whiff coming from the diaper pail in the corner. I'll lean over your crib, lift your squalling form out, and sit in the rocking chair to nurse you.

The word "infant" is derived from the Latin word for "unable to speak," but you'll be perfectly capable of saying one thing: "I suffer," and you'll do it tirelessly and without hesitation. I have to admire your utter commitment to that statement; when you cry, you'll become outrage incarnate, every fiber of your body employed in expressing that emotion. It's funny: when you're tranquil, you will seem to radiate light, and if someone were to paint a portrait of you like that, I'd insist that they include the halo. But when you're unhappy, you will become a Klaxon, built for radiating sound; a portrait of you then could simply be a fire-alarm bell.

At that stage of your life, there'll be no past or future for you; until I give you my breast, you'll have no memory of contentment in the past nor expectation of relief in the future. Once you begin nursing, everything will reverse, and all will be right with the world. NOW is the only moment you'll perceive; you'll live in the present tense. In many ways, it's an enviable state.

The heptapods are neither free nor bound as we understand those concepts; they don't act according to their will, nor are they helpless automatons. What distinguishes the heptapods' mode of awareness is not just that their actions coincide with history's events; it is also that their motives coincide with history's purposes. They act to create the future, to enact chronology.

Freedom isn't an illusion; it's perfectly real in the context of sequential consciousness. Within the context of simultaneous consciousness, freedom is not meaningful, but neither is coercion; it's simply a different context, no more or less valid than the other. It's like that famous optical illusion, the drawing of either an elegant young woman, face turned away from the viewer, or a wart-nosed crone, chin tucked down on her chest. There's no "correct" interpretation; both are equally valid. But you can't see both at the same time.

Similarly, knowledge of the future was incompatible with free will. What made it possible for me to exercise freedom of choice also made it impossible for me to know the future. Conversely, now that I know the future, I would never act contrary to that future, including telling others what I know: those who know the future don't talk about it. Those who've read the *Book of Ages* never admit to it.

I turned on the VCR and slotted a cassette of a session from the Ft. Worth looking glass. A diplomatic negotiator was having a discussion with the heptapods there, with Burghart acting as translator.

The negotiator was describing humans' moral beliefs, trying to lay some groundwork for the concept of altruism. I knew the heptapods were familiar with the conversation's eventual outcome, but they still participated enthusiastically.

If I could have described this to someone who didn't already know, she might ask, If the heptapods already knew everything that they would ever say or hear, what was the point of their using language at all? A reasonable question. But language wasn't only for communication: it was also a form of action. According to speech-act theory, statements like "You're under arrest," "I christen this vessel," or "I promise" were all performative: a speaker could perform the action only by uttering the words. For such acts, knowing what would be said didn't change anything. Everyone at a wedding anticipated the words "I now pronounce you husband and wife," but until the minister actually said them, the ceremony didn't count. With performative language, saying equaled doing.

For the heptapods, all language was performative. Instead of using language to inform, they used language to actualize. Sure, heptapods already knew what would be said in any conversation; but in order for their knowledge to be true, the conversation would have to take place.

"First Goldilocks tried the papa bear's bowl of porridge, but it was full of brussels sprouts, which she hated."

You'll laugh. "No, that's wrong!" We'll be sitting side by side on the sofa, the skinny, overpriced hardcover spread open on our laps.

I'll keep reading. "Then Goldilocks tried the mama bear's bowl of porridge, but it was full of spinach, which she also hated."

You'll put your hand on the page of the book to stop me. "You have to read it the right way!"

"I'm reading just what it says here," I'll say, all innocence.

"No you're not. That's not how the story goes."

"Well if you already know how the story goes, why do you need me to read it to you?"

"Cause I wanna hear it!"

The air-conditioning in Weber's office almost compensated for having to talk to the man.

"They're willing to engage in a type of exchange," I explained, "but it's not trade. We simply give them something, and they give us something in return. Neither party tells the other what they're giving beforehand."

Colonel Weber's brow furrowed just slightly. "You mean they're willing to exchange gifts?"

I knew what I had to say. "We shouldn't think of it as 'gift-giving.' We don't know if this transaction has the same associations for the heptapods that gift-giving has for us."

"Can we"—he searched for the right wording—"drop hints about the kind of gift we want?"

"They don't do that themselves for this type of transaction. I asked them if we could make a request, and they said we could, but it won't make them tell us what they're giving." I suddenly remembered that a morphological relative of "performative" was "performance," which could describe the sensation of conversing when you knew what would be said: it was like performing in a play.

"But would it make them more likely to give us what we asked for?" Colonel Weber asked. He was perfectly oblivious of the script, yet his responses matched his assigned lines exactly.

"No way of knowing," I said. "I doubt it, given that it's not a custom they engage in."

"If we give our gift first, will the value of our gift influence the value of theirs?" He was improvising, while I had carefully rehearsed for this one and only show.

"No," I said. "As far as we can tell, the value of the exchanged items is irrelevant."

"If only my relatives felt that way," murmured Gary wryly.

I watched Colonel Weber turn to Gary. "Have you discovered anything new in the physics discussions?" he asked, right on cue.

"If you mean, any information new to mankind, no," said Gary. "The heptapods haven't varied from the routine. If we demonstrate something to them, they'll show us their formulation of it, but they won't volunteer anything and they won't answer our questions about what they know."

An utterance that was spontaneous and communicative in the context of human discourse became a ritual recitation when viewed by the light of Heptapod B.

Weber scowled. "All right then, we'll see how the State Department feels about this. Maybe we can arrange some kind of gift-giving ceremony."

Like physical events, with their causal and teleological interpretations, every linguistic event had two possible interpretations: as a transmission of information and as the realization of a plan.

"I think that's a good idea, Colonel," I said.

It was an ambiguity invisible to most. A private joke; don't ask me to explain it.

Even though I'm proficient with Heptapod B, I know I don't experience reality the way a heptapod does. My mind was cast in the mold of human, sequential languages, and no amount of immersion in an alien language can completely reshape it. My worldview is an amalgam of human and heptapod.

Before I learned how to think in Heptapod B, my memories grew like a column of cigarette ash, laid down by the infinitesimal sliver of combustion that was my consciousness, marking the sequential present. After I learned Heptapod B, new memories fell into place like gigantic blocks, each one measuring years in duration, and though they didn't arrive in order or land contiguously, they soon composed a period of five decades. It is the period during which I know Heptapod B well enough to think in it, starting during my interviews with Flapper and Raspberry and ending with my death.

Usually, Heptapod B affects just my memory: my consciousness crawls along as it did before, a glowing sliver crawling forward in time, the difference being that the ash of memory lies ahead as well as behind: there is no real combustion. But occasionally I have glimpses when Heptapod B truly reigns, and I experience past and future all at once; my consciousness becomes a half-century-long ember burning outside time. I perceive — during those glimpses — that entire epoch as a simultaneity. It's a period encompassing the rest of my life, and the entirety of yours.

I wrote out the semagrams for "process create-endpoint inclusive-we," meaning "let's start." Raspberry replied in the affirmative, and the slide shows began. The second display screen that the heptapods had provided began presenting a series of images, composed of semagrams and equations, while one of our video screens did the same.

This was the second "gift exchange" I had been present for, the eighth one overall, and I knew it would be the last. The looking-glass tent was crowded with people; Burghart from Ft. Worth was here, as were Gary and a nuclear physicist, assorted biologists, anthropologists, military brass, and diplomats. Thankfully they had set up an air-conditioner to cool the place off. We would review the tapes of the images later to figure out just what the heptapods' "gift" was. Our own "gift" was a presentation on the Lascaux cave paintings.

We all crowded around the heptapods' second screen, trying to glean some idea of the images' content as they went by. "Preliminary assessments?" asked Colonel Weber.

"It's not a return," said Burghart. In a previous exchange, the heptapods had given us information about ourselves that we had previously told them. This had infuriated the State Department, but we had no reason to think of it as an insult: it probably indicated that trade value really didn't play a role in these exchanges. It didn't exclude the possibility that the heptapods might yet offer us a space drive, or cold fusion, or some other wish-fulfilling miracle.

"That looks like inorganic chemistry," said the nuclear physicist, pointing at an equation before the image was replaced.

Gary nodded. "It could be materials technology," he said.

"Maybe we're finally getting somewhere," said Colonel Weber.

"I wanna see more animal pictures," I whispered, quietly so that only Gary could hear me, and pouted like a child. He smiled and poked me. Truthfully, I wished the heptapods had given another xenobiology lecture, as they had on two previous exchanges; judging from those, humans were more similar to the heptapods than any other species they'd ever encountered. Or another lecture on heptapod history; those had been filled with apparent non sequiturs, but were interesting nonetheless. I didn't want the heptapods to give us new technology, because I didn't want to see what our governments might do with it.

I watched Raspberry while the information was being exchanged, looking for any anomalous behavior. It stood barely moving as usual; I saw no indications of what would happen shortly.

After a minute, the heptapod's screen went blank, and a minute after that, ours did too. Gary and most of the other scientists clustered around a tiny video screen that was replaying the heptapods' presentation. I could hear them talk about the need to call in a solid-state physicist. Colonel Weber turned. "You two," he said, pointing to me and then to Burghart, "schedule the time and location for the next exchange." Then he followed the others to the playback screen.

"Coming right up," I said. To Burghart, I asked, "Would you care to do the honors, or shall I?"

I knew Burghart had gained a proficiency in Heptapod B similar to mine. "It's your looking glass," he said. "You drive."

I sat down again at the transmitting computer. "Bet you never figured you'd wind up working as an Army translator back when you were a grad student."

"That's for goddamn sure," he said. "Even now I can hardly believe it." Everything we said to each other felt like the carefully bland exchanges of spies who meet in public, but never break cover.

I wrote out the semagrams for "locus exchange-transaction converse inclusive-we" with the projective aspect modulation.

Raspberry wrote its reply. That was my cue to frown, and for Burghart to ask, "What does it mean by that?" His delivery was perfect.

I wrote a request for clarification; Raspberry's reply was the same as before. Then I watched it glide out of the room. The curtain was about to fall on this act of our performance.

Colonel Weber stepped forward. "What's going on? Where did it go?"

"It said that the heptapods are leaving now," I said. "Not just itself; all of them."

"Call it back here now. Ask it what it means."

"Um, I don't think Raspberry's wearing a pager," I said.

The image of the room in the looking glass disappeared so abruptly that it took a moment for my eyes to register what I was seeing instead: it was the other side of the looking-glass tent. The looking glass had become completely transparent. The conversation around the playback screen fell silent.

"What the hell is going on here?" said Colonel Weber.

Gary walked up to the looking glass, and then around it to the other side. He touched the rear surface with one hand; I could see the pale ovals where his fingertips made contact with the looking glass. "I think," he said, "we just saw a demonstration of transmutation at a distance."

I heard the sounds of heavy footfalls on dry grass. A soldier came in through the tent door, short of breath from sprinting, holding an oversize walkie-talkie. "Colonel, message from —"

Weber grabbed the walkie-talkie from him.

I remember what it'll be like watching you when you are a day old. Your father will have gone for a quick visit to the hospital cafeteria, and you'll be lying in your bassinet, and I'll be leaning over you.

So soon after the delivery, I will still be feeling like a wrung-out towel. You will seem incongruously tiny, given how enormous I felt during the pregnancy; I could swear there was room for someone much larger and more robust than you in there. Your hands and feet will be long and thin, not chubby yet. Your face will still be all red and pinched, puffy eyelids squeezed shut, the gnomelike phase that precedes the cherubic.

I'll run a finger over your belly, marveling at the uncanny softness of your skin, wondering if silk would abrade your body like burlap. Then you'll writhe, twisting your body while poking out your legs one at a time, and I'll recognize the gesture as one I had felt you do inside me, many times. So *that's* what it looks like.

I'll feel elated at this evidence of a unique mother-child bond, this certitude that you're the one I carried. Even if I had never laid eyes on you before, I'd be able to pick you out from a sea of babies: Not that one. No, not her either. Wait, that one over there.

Yes, that's her. She's mine.

That final "gift exchange" was the last we ever saw of the heptapods. All at once, all over the world, their looking glasses became transparent and their ships left orbit. Subsequent analysis of the looking glasses revealed them to be nothing more than sheets of fused silica, completely inert. The information from the final exchange session described a new class of superconducting materials, but it later proved to duplicate the results of research just completed in Japan: nothing that humans didn't already know. We never did learn why the heptapods left, any more than we learned what brought them here, or why they acted the way they did. My own new awareness didn't provide that type of knowledge; the heptapods' behavior was presumably explicable from a sequential point of view, but we never found that explanation.

I would have liked to experience more of the heptapods' worldview, to feel the way they feel. Then, perhaps I could immerse myself fully in the necessity of events, as they must, instead of merely wading in its surf for the rest of my life. But that will never come to pass. I will continue to practice the heptapod languages, as will the other linguists on the looking-glass teams, but none of us will ever progress any further than we did when the heptapods were here.

Working with the heptapods changed my life. I met your father and learned Heptapod B, both of which make it possible for me to know you now, here on the patio in the moonlight. Eventually, many years from now, I'll be without your father, and without you. All I will have left from this moment is the heptapod language. So I pay close attention, and note every detail.

From the beginning I knew my destination, and I chose my route accordingly. But am I working toward an extreme of joy, or of pain? Will I achieve a minimum, or a maximum?

These questions are in my mind when your father asks me, "Do you want to make a baby?" And I smile and answer, "Yes," and I unwrap his arms from around me, and we hold hands as we walk inside to make love, to make you.

Mars Is No Place for Children

MARY A. TURZILLO

In her high school yearbook Mary Turzillo said she wanted to go to the Moon. That didn't work out, so she settled for a career in science fiction, and has been a full-time writer for the past several years. Her stories have appeared in magazines and anthologies in the United States, Great Britain, Germany, Japan, and Italy. She lives in Berea, Ohio, and is married to science fiction writer Geoffrey Landis, who won a Nebula himself in 1989. (Nancy Kress and Charles Sheffield are the only other husband-and-wife team of Nebula winners.)

About her Nebula-winning story she says, "Two threads from my life come together in 'Mars Is No Place for Children.' My husband had an experiment on the *Sojourner* rover, which was part of the *Pathfinder* mission to Mars. The first time I saw pictures of the proposed rover, I knew it would capture everybody's imagination. *Sojourner* came across as a valiant little robot, an extension of ourselves as explorers of other worlds. July 4, 1997, I stood with other space enthusiasts at Planetfest 97 in Pasadena to celebrate the landing of *Pathfinder* on the red planet. Exhilarated by the pictures that *Pathfinder* sent down to us, I chose a mission of my own: to speak for the people who will someday live on that planet. A year later, at the Founding

Convention of the Mars Society, I also realized that life wasn't going to be easy for Martian colonists. They would brave a thousand dangers, including DNA-damaging radiation. I also came to believe that people will colonize other planets not for economic gain (though of course trade resources must be present) but for their ideals, as colonists in the past have done. Kapera Smythe's parents are such idealists.

"The other thread is knowing several children, including my own son, who fight life-threatening illness. Kids should believe that they will never die. When that belief is destroyed, I can only admire how they keep their strength to dream. For their sake I put all my skill and all my soul into 'Mars Is No Place for Children.' Kapera Smythe is, to me, a real girl who will live on Mars and will carry humanity's dreams in her heart."

Kapera Smythe, her diary, Smythe Farm and Laboratories, Vastitas Borealis, Summer-January 31, 2202:

Mother and Dad asked me what I wanted for my sixth birthsol, and I said the antique wrist computer we saw in Borealopolis a couple sols ago, at the flea market. So they sent for it and here it is! I deliberately picked out one so old it won't network to the house computers, and I can have some PRIVACY at last.

A diary. So this is my diary. It doesn't have direct retinal imaging, and it's broken so I have to do text only. But it's mine, and only mine! I used to keep a diary on the house net, but now I need to keep my thoughts to myself. This will stay always on my wrist or under my pillow, and they'll never read what I really think, or what I plan.

They're going to send me "home."

To them, home is a little star I can see in the morning and evening sky. They say it's blue; to me it's just a white star with a smaller white star always near it. A double planet. The bigger of the twin planets is the one they call home, which, to be fair, is reasonable, I guess, since that's where they were both born.

Home is also where my precious older brother went, the one Mother always talks about when she says, "Oh, Sekou learned to read when he wasn't even two," or, "Remember how Sekou was so good about doing his chores?"

When I was less than a mear old, they sent Sekou back to Earth because he had some disease that the hospitals here can't treat. They have one picture of Sekou and me. I had my hair in cornrows, decorated with little red beads. Sekou, about two mears old, had really short hair, almost none at all. He was darker than I am, really cute, if a little bit skinny.

My mother is the worst with the Saint Sekou stuff. Dad is more sympathetic.

I get jealous of Sekou sometimes, but I think about him and wonder what it would be like to have a big brother to play with. It's not worth leaving Mars, of course, but it would still be really great.

Maybe I should keep this diary so Sekou can read it.

Dear Sekou:

Our parents say they came here for their freedom, because the streets of every city on Earth were unsafe for Kiafricans. Because Kiafricans after four centuries of legal freedom were still treated like second-class citizens, sometimes even lynched. But if they wanted freedom, why did they have to buy it with so many mears of slavery (oops! they don't call it that term) *indenture*—to the Martian megacorp? And, as it turns out, why am I not safe here on Mars? On Earth, the danger was violence. Here, it's another kind of death hanging over our heads.

If they bought their freedom with nine mears each, eighteen mears together, of labor, if this is what they had to pay for freedom, why am I not free to stay on the planet I love?

Smythe Farm and Laboratories, Summer-February 2, 2202:
Dear Sekou,

It's harder than I expected getting time to record in here. I have to pretend to record in my diary on the house computer, or Mother will get suspicious (Dad's the trusting type).

I think I'll record a little bit about why I love my home, because if I get sent back to Earth I'll want more than pictures to remember Mars.

Let's see.

Our home. My bedroom, with its skylight so I can check on the wind and sun and stars anytime, even in the night. The greenhouses full of Mother and Dad's experiments. The frost flowers we grow in the low-pressure greenhouse. The patch of oxygen-conserving, antifreeze plants, amazing blades of green in the sun from Summer-February until

Summer-November. Antifreeze plants grow outside on the naked soil, but unfortunately they don't flower. We have to propagate them from root cuttings. But they impress Polaricorp, which is the corporation which runs this part of Mars.

The sky. The Winter-June sky, so full of stars. We live near the pole, and for three hundred glorious sols each mear, the sky is full of jewels so thick I just have to make up stories about the King of the Universe, who spilled them into our Martian sky.

The slow summer sunset and sunrise, such a delicate blue against the pink sky. The sols in Summer-June when the sun doesn't bother to set, just floats on the horizon like a glowing silver medallion on a string of invisible stars. The moons, bright like silver coins. Last mear there was an eclipse, and we waited until Deimos almost glided over the sun, then stole a peek while one bright bead (because Deimos isn't very round, it has valleys and humps) sparkled for a moment.

Sekou, you know Earth doesn't even have moons. Well, yes, it has the other planet, which people from Earth insist on calling The Moon. (Do you call it that?) Can't they see it's way big? It's a planet, called Luna, for heaven sake!

The huge valley, Valles Marinaris. Oh, wouldn't I love to explore the bottom of that one. Maybe that's where they'll find fossils, little stony pieces of bacteria or (here's a word I learned last week) *diatoms*. Maybe I'll go there when I grow up. Maybe I'll be on a team that discovers fossils.

The great high mountains, bigger than the ones on Earth. No one will ever walk all the way to the top of Olympus Mons, Mother says. But maybe she's wrong. She doesn't know *me*.

But of course I'm not going to grow up on Mars. They're sending me back, unless I can stop them.

Mother asked me where "the little wrist computer" is. Meaning this computer, my diary. She's not stupid. She probably figured I'm keeping a diary. So I told her it was lost, I couldn't find it. Ha. As if anything could get lost in this biome. Every every solar cell, every drainage pipe, every pane of glass, every fork, every wrench, is in its place, almost like we worshiped them. Because they were either manufactured by Martians in Valleston, or else (hard to imagine) brought from Earth. Like this, my old-fashioned, antique, flea-market wrist computer.

Our house computer is sort of an antique, too. We're not like some
city people that have contact lens chips or headplants so we can watch
the news or listen to music twenty-four point five hours a sol. Or Earth
people who have Mars-knows-what nanotech junk, which is dangerous
anyway after what happened to that town in Scotland on Earth.

It's in my pocket. I always hide it when I take a bath or change
clothes.

But maybe I better not record just yet what my plan is.

Smythe Farm and Laboratories, Summer-February 5, 2202:
Dear Sekou,

I didn't feel very good for a couple sols there. That stupid doctor
from Earth gave me some kind of pep-pill, supposed to kill the bad cells
and pump up the good ones. At least that's what they said. It made me
feel worse rather than better.

But let's talk more about Earth and why I'd rather *die* than go
there, even if it's where you live, Sekou.

First, I wouldn't mind it so much, despite the awful things my
Mother and Dad already told me about how they mistreat us Kiafricans.
The gravity is bad, I know, but you spend some time in a station where
you exercise every sol with big elastic bands and get strong so you can
survive, plus they give you calcium-magnesium vitamin D pills, and
anyway I'm not quite through puberty, so maybe when my hormones
kick in (yeech, it feels icky to talk about this stuff), they'll grow me bigger muscles and bones so I won't feel the gravity so much.

It would be an adventure. Plants grow outdoors all the time there.
I've read they even kill plants they don't want — weeds. Weeds? Imagine.
I would feed them to the iguana, who would love them and get all fat
and juicy.

Although they don't have high mountains, apparently they do
have huge thick clouds and weather with lots of liquid H_2O coming
down out of the sky, which sounds weird but fun. And I'd love to see a
live river or ocean, since ours are all dead. Animals. They have animals
running all over free. People keep some of them for pets.

One of the girls in my on-line math class claims she has a pet cat.
Obviously she's lying, just trying to impress us. Everybody knows cats eat
meat, and her family isn't going to keep something around that lives that

high on the food chain without paying its way. I saw a cat in the zoo in Polaris a mear ago. It was all hairy, just like the holograms. They also have dogs, and ferrets and squirrels, and an alligator, but nothing really huge, nothing that eats a lot, like whales or elephants or dinosaurs. However, somebody was planning to bring a baby cow to Mars while it was still small enough to transport. They have hundreds of other different kinds of animals on Earth.

Yes, I would love to go to Earth for a while. To see you, to find out how you grew up.

But I could never come back. That is, unless I was able to sell myself to one of the megacorps, like Mother and Dad did. But you have to have special skills and training, like bioengineering, to get yourself bought and your passage paid back to Mars.

Dad and Mother say I'm gifted. They mean different things by it, of course. Mother says I'm intellectually gifted, I have a high IQ, meaning I do well in the on-line school. Dad says I have hoodoo. I can divine. Dowse for water, that means, in the form of underground permafrost deposits.

You might wonder why anybody would need to dowse for H_2O here in the arctic circle, where the permafrost is only inches from the surface. Of course, the Smythe family would have all the bad luck! The homestead Mother and Dad were sold has a really thick crust over the permafrost, some places as much as three meters, and before I was born, they really needed somebody who could find places where the covering layer was thinner. Somebody who could dowse.

Well, I can. Mother says that's because I have some sort of undiscovered organ, like birds, which helps me locate minute disturbances in the electrical field, which might result from the action of heating and cooling water.

So I'm "gifted." I don't think that's going to get me passage back home to Mars.

So, no thank you. I'll stay here.

If I can figure out how.

Smythe Farm and Laboratories, Summer-February 5, 2202:
Dear Sekou,

My name, Kapera, means something, and I never even realized it until I got sick.

I don't know if I have the same sickness you had, but getting sick caused me to find out the meaning of my name.

I eavesdropped on Mom and Dad, who were in the low-pressure greenhouse, putting the faceplates of their environment suits together to talk. They thought I couldn't hear, but I have really good hearing. If I listen closely, I can hear people talking in their suits, even when we're out in the Mars sky.

Dad thought it was growing pains. Mother said I'd be all right just as soon as I got my first period. She didn't know when that would be, because there weren't enough Martian-born girls to collect statistics on what the Martian environment would do to make us grow up faster or slower.

I thought it might be the flu. Flu usually comes to the homesteads through Polaris, from new immigrants, and I thought maybe that was it.

Finally, they took me to the hospital in Polaris.

The doctor looked pretty young, for a doctor. He was Kiafrican, like us, but light-skinned. He had a funny accent—must have just come to Mars. But I bet it wasn't going to take him nine mears, like my parents, to pay for his passage and homestead. Doctors make a lot of money, because we need them so much, and the members of the megacorp give them a big discount on passage and everything.

"You're how old?"

Six, I told him.

He kind of gawked, then remembered that we counted Martian mears, not Earth years. "You have leukemia," he said. "Do you know what that means?"

I felt like throwing up. "It's a disease Mars children get because of the cosmic rays. Because the atmosphere is so thin it doesn't protect us. It's because I go out in the environment suit all the time and stay upstairs in the greenhouses, isn't it? If I'd been more careful—"

"No," he said.

I just looked at him.

"No, Kapera. I've been here almost a whole Mars year, and I've seen childhood cancer, leukemia, and Hodgkin's disease in children who lived entirely underground."

Cosmic rays. Radiation. We studied that on-line, of course. It was one of the reasons scientists think life might have arisen on Mars even before Earth, because it makes molecules change rapidly. But it also bonks DNA in cells, so it causes cancer. Especially children's cancer.

The doctor got up and gestured for me to go sit in the waiting room. I did, but I could still hear what they were saying. "The company insurance will pay for chemotherapy, supportive nutrition, and of course psychiatric counseling for the whole family. I'd recommend a hospice in —"

"How good is the chemotherapy and supportive nutrition?" asked Dad.

"What do you mean, how good?"

Mother spoke up. "Our son had Hodgkin's disease. They recommended much the same for him."

The doctor paused, waiting for her to go on. When she didn't he said, "I see. Well, it's the best we have to offer, and it does work for over half the children with this particular leukemia. You do understand that strict compliance with the chemo and diet regime, plus affirmations and uh, if you are religious, prayer, can really up your chances —"

Dad said, "Doctor, are you a company man?"

"A company — You mean, does a member of the syndicate own my contract at present? Yes. But the syndicate still extends health insurance to Martians who are freemen, you know. You're definitely eligible."

Dad smiled kind of sadly. "If this were your daughter, and you had — extensive resources — what would you recommend?"

"Oh, I'm not allowed —" Then I heard his chair scrape on the floor, like he'd moved closer to them. I had to strain to hear him. "I'd send her to one of the middle Earth orbit hospitals. The nanotech reengineering they do there is still experimental, but I'm satisfied that it works."

"How many —"

"Ninety-five percent cure rate. But there's no use breaking your heart. That's way beyond your means, or mine, for that matter."

"How much?"

"Well, it's the passage to Earth that's really unaffordable. The treatment is, uh, well, maybe a year's salary, if you're a freeman. If you have that much saved up."

I listened as hard as I could, but nobody said anything for a while. It was what they call an embarrassed silence. I remember everything, so clearly. Maybe if I put it in text, then I can forget it.

"Kapera," said the doctor, as he ushered them out. "That name, *Kapera*, means *This Will Be the Last One*, doesn't it?"

"Yes," said Mother. Her voice was hard.

He turned away. "Mars is no place for children," he said.

That's what my name means.

I'm so tired, Sekou.

Smythe Farm and Laboratories, Summer-February 5, 2202:
Dear Sekou,

Rereading what I wrote about that doctor, I'm angry at him. He made our parents feel helpless. He shamed them because they didn't have the money to send me to Earth and back.

Smythe Farm and Laboratories, Summer-February 6, 2202:
Dear Sekou,

Dad keeps trying to make me eat something. He killed one of the chickens and cooked it in jalapeño sauce. Mother made ice cream out of the soy slurry and flavored it with banana. It all seemed like a good idea, but I just didn't feel like eating more than a few bites. I said for them to freeze it; maybe tomorrow or in a couple sols.

Mother said the shot the doctor gave me must be ruining my appetite.

Smythe Farm and Laboratories, Summer-February 10, 2202:
Dear Sekou,

We went back to the doctor. His name is Pinkerton, I found out. A real Company name. Dr. Pinkerton gave me another shot, but this time there was a tonic of some kind, too.

I told him how awful the chemotherapy makes me feel. And he doesn't even guarantee it will work. Obsolete, like most Martian stuff, chemotherapy, that makes your hair fall out and you barf all the time. He didn't mention the neotenizing nanotech they do in the big expensive Earth orbital hospitals. "Frontier remedies for frontier heroes," he said. Big deal. That's not the kind of hero I want to be.

Smythe Farm and Laboratories, Summer-February 10, 2202:
Dear Sekou,

On Earth, they claim people dream in black and white most of the time. Maybe that's how you dream, but I dream in color, and I have dreams of being an explorer. Dreams in red.

I got thinking about heroes and about the history of Mars. About all the Earth people that were so dedicated to getting to Mars that modern people call them "the first Martians," even though it was a whole century before Jeffrey Allan set the flag of Polymet Mining on the face of the planet, and another fifty years before Sagan City was founded.

I got thinking about Sojourner Truth. Not Sojourner the first independent rover to land on Mars; Sojourner the woman. We don't study much Earth history, but I searched the free network to find Earth-based histories of the African American race (the old-fashioned Earth term for Kiafricans). What happened was that the North America government declared slavery illegal, but this one woman's master refused to obey the law. So she ran away. She changed her name to Sojourner Truth. She became a famous lecturer, traveling all over in the name of truth.

You probably wonder what all this has to do with Sagan City and Polymet Mining, but when they were first exploring Mars—not with people, but just with robots and stuff—they sent this rover that looked at rocks and stuff and told what our atmosphere and soil was like. The very first human thing on Mars that was truly independent. They had a lot of ideas to name it, including an Amerind scout's name, Sacagawea. But in the end, they had a contest, and the name that won was—Sojourner Truth. There were dozens of other exploring rovers to follow, of course: Rocky 7 and 11 and 13, and Athena, and Robbit, and—you must know about those.

I thought that was really cool. I made a little model out of broken solar panels and your toy cars. (Well—you didn't take them with you.) I keep it under my skylight so it can look out at sky all mear long. Somesol I'll get around to hooking it up to some good solar cells so it will really run. In Borealopolis, the Polymet Mining Museum has what they claim is a piece of a solar cell from the original Sojourner. I'm not sure how they got it, since the original rover has never actually been found. It's probably a piece from a prototype, donated from Earth.

Anyway, rich people collect Mars memorabilia. Like, guns used in the Antitrust War of 2139 are in museums in Polaris, and probably in a lot of other big cities, but sometimes rich guys have collections—replicas and even the real thing.

I can understand this. I have a homemade replica of Sojourner. I bet some rich executive in Polaristech would pay millions and millions for the real Sojourner rover.

But nobody would ever be able to find it. It was programmed to wander around and sample rocks after it lost contact with Earth. It's buried in the sand by now.

Millions and millions. Enough to travel to Earth and back, with lots left over.

Smythe Farm and Laboratories, Summer-February 11, 2202:
Dear Sekou,

Well, my hair has almost all fallen out. Before I went to the doctor, I had it all done in dreads. It looked really sophisticated. Now I look hideous. Mother says, "Cheer up, it'll grow back."

When we realized my hair was going, Dad took a holo. I was cutting back some morning-glory vines and saying, "Farming is hard work."

I'm so glad Dad understands. Mother just has a cold heart.

Smythe Farm and Laboratories, Summer-February 11, 2202, later:
Dear big brother,

Why are our Mother and Dad so nice to each other these sols?

Smythe Farm and Laboratories, Summer-February 14, 2202:
Dear Sekou,

I guess this disease makes you paranoid. I've never actually known anybody who was paranoid, but it is mentioned a lot in history books, particularly of the twentieth and twentieth-first century. I think I'm paranoid.

They broke it to me (big surprise) that I'm going back to Earth. Or anyway, they're going to *try* to send me back to Earth. But there's something else. Dad traded a packet of our best bean seed stock for a bunch of useless squash blossoms he got from the Watson family.

He made this bouquet of them. Put them in a jar on the table. Mother cried when she saw them. I hope she appreciated them; Dad's so generous.

She left them there two whole sols before we stuffed them with beans and baked them for dinner.

What's going on? Dad was never the type for romantic gestures. Is Mother going to get pregnant again? I told you before "Kapera" means "the last one," but maybe now they changed their mind. It makes me feel kind of shuddery. Like they were planning to replace me.

Smythe Farm and Laboratories, Summer-February 14, 2202, later in the sol:

But that's okay, I decided. They need somebody to go on. Dad is a good parent, and I guess Mother's heart is in the right place, even if they're wrong about sending me away. And maybe I *will* go to Earth, and survive, and grow up. Then when I come back to Mars (because hell or high winds I'm going to, no matter how much studying and work I have to do to be able to sell my services to the Companies), maybe I'll have a little brother or sister.

I'm beginning to feel a little better. But Dr. Pinkerton says I have to feel rotten to get at the cancerous cells and make them feel even rottener. So I suppose I'll be going in for another round.

Smythe Farm and Laboratories, Summer-February 17, 2202:
Dear Sekou,

They came out with it. They're sending me to an Earth orbit hospital that takes Martian patients. I'll be treated there, *cured*. And then rehabilitated to go to Earth to live. My grandmother (whom I've seen pictures and tapes of) will take care of me as I acclimatize to Earth gravity, although I'll never be very strong, according to Mother. Being preadolescent will be an advantage.

They want to do this soon. They showed me the letter from Dr. Pinkerton, and he says it has to be done before Summer-May. He says otherwise I won't survive the six-month trip, and anyway that's the travel window.

We're leaving the time of long shadows, the low barometer sols. By Summer-May, the shadows will be growing shorter, and so will my time on our home world, Sekou, on the only home world I ever wanted. Good-bye polar caps and long starry winters, good-bye pink-amber summers when the sun draws a platinum ring all the way round the sky. Good-bye my chances of searching for fossils in Valles Marinaris, of seeing the top of the biggest volcano in the solar system, of finding the Sojourner Rover that won Earth's heart to make Mars a human place. Good-bye to my few short sols of happiness; hello to endless "*days*" as an eternal exile.

I'm so ashamed to be weak and cry like this. This wrist computer is so old it'll probably get tears in it and stop. I hope you, and I, can still read this—when I get to Earth.

Smythe Farm and Laboratories, Summer-February 21, 2202:
Dear Sekou,

Mother and Dad have been fighting. It's probably Mother's fault. She's so bossy about everything. It had something to do with money. I tried to listen, but they shut up all of a sudden and went out to the greenhouse. They're out there now. I listened to them a little while—but though I could hear their words, I couldn't understand what they were talking about. They know a little bit of some other languages—English and Japanese and Baduma. I finally got too tired and went to bed.

Smythe Farm and Laboratories, Summer-February 22, 2202:
Dear Sekou,

I found this creepy letter addressed to Mother and Dad from something called the Personality Preservation Software Corporation. I shouldn't be spying, you would probably say, but I bet you'd do the same if you were still on Mars, and Mother and Dad were acting so weird.

The letter says that for umpteen thousand franks they can make a record of a person's voice, thinking patterns, knowledge, training, their whole personality, in other words, and then download it into an autonomous rover to explore Mars. They called this an Eternal Memorial Reconstruction Rover.

Sekou, I have this horrible feeling this has something to do with me.

Smythe Farm and Laboratories, Summer-February 23, 2202:
Dear Sekou,

How I wish you were here, big brother, to tell me what I should do! I admit it. I've been eavesdropping again. I stayed in the greenhouse after teatime yestersol, and sure enough, they came in, arguing just like last night. At first, I couldn't figure out what the disagreement was. Then Mother said, "It's settled, Joseph, I'm going with her and you're cashing in. We can get the most money for you."

Cashing in can only mean one thing, Sekou. Maybe you didn't learn this before you left Mars, but people sell themselves to one or another of the companies to come here, and then earn their freedom and their homestead, if they choose to live outside the cities, by working it off. Mother and Dad earned their freedom when I was less than a mear old; then they started saving to buy our homestead from the company.

Dad's voice was so low I almost didn't hear what he said next.

"There has to be another solution, Miriam. I can't bear thinking I'll never see you or her again."

"In the name of heaven, tell me what it is!"

Dad didn't say anything.

I'd so much rather it was him that was coming with me.

No, big brother, that's wrong. I can't bear that I'm going at all. A family should be together. There has to be another solution.

Meantime, I have a fever. I had a headache all sol, so I took my temperature. And I looked in the mirror. I look gray and skinny. Maybe it's the spring light.

Smythe Farm and Laboratories, Summer-February 24, 2202:
Dear Sekou,

I slept all sol and they didn't even wake me up, just left some greens and frostwheat groats by my bed. I used to like greens.

Then when night came, I couldn't sleep, so I went and snooped some more. I found what I was afraid of. In the computer are ticket numbers for my mother and me to go to Equatorial City, and then to Earth Orbital, a hospital station. There are also open-end ticket numbers to go to Earth surface. No date.

Mother and Dad will never see each other again. I will never see my beloved father again.

How can they do this to me? How can they do it to *us*?

Brother, help me!

Smythe Farm and Laboratories, Summer-February 27, 2202:
Dear Sekou,

I'm going to do this. I won't record it until it's done, because Mother might get suspicious. She's so snoopy, she has no respect at all for my privacy.

But if I'm going to do it, it will have to be before we go to see that stupid doctor again. And I will eat my greens and even those yicky yams the way Mother cooks them, and the verre de terre soufflé and the works. I sure will need my strength.

Somewhere in the upper atmosphere of the Northern Hemisphere, Summer-March 5, 2202:
Dear Sekou,

I made it! I made it! I'm on a rocket plane.

The last week has been exciting enough to keep me from feeling sick very much. I wrote down the numbers for the travel tickets my mother reserved for us and put them in my school bag. I took my books out of the bag and hid them in the bottom of my closet. Then I packed some clothes and seeds for trade in the bag.

Do they teach you about Martian history like we learn about Earth history? I feel awful that you know so little about your home planet. We'll have to discuss this when I become rich and pay your way to Mars.

I'm going to do that, you know.

The biggest difficulty was not the tickets, or even ID. My passport was in the databanks just like Mother's. So, since I was using my own ticket, I could travel without Mother.

It was almost like Dad knew what I was planning. Mother has stopped involving me in the sol-to-sol operation of the greenhouse or the naked environment plants, or even consulting me in the care of my own little plots. Dad is, of course, more considerate; he keeps up the pretense that I have a future on Mars. But yestersol he took Mother into the old middle-pressure greenhouse (the little one they built when they first arrived here) and got her involved in a long discussion. I tiptoed away, grabbed the bag I had packed, and off I went.

No, I didn't go hiking off in an environment suit like some crash victim. I stole the rover and drove it to Polaris, to the launch station.

I programmed it to come back to the homestead, of course. And I left a nice note, so they won't think I was kidnapped.

Mother will never be able to trace me. I didn't go to Equatorial City.

I'm on the rocket plane to Sagan City.

The launch area was pretty exciting. I was so surprised at how adult they treated me, as if I knew all the safety procedures, which of course I do—in theory. I mean, I study these things in school. The rocket plane is launched on a precise arc to land at its destination. When it gets there, it deploys parachutes to brake, and then the wings extend to guide it to the landing field.

I'm excited about the landing. It'll be night when we get there, and I'll be able to see all the city lights. The launch was impressive; lots of noise and acceleration, but not much view because we gained altitude too fast for much of a view of Borealopolis.

Ares Vallis will look different from how it would have looked to Pathfinder (if Pathfinder's cameras had been deployed). The area is still a flood plain, of course, with a variety of rocks from all over. Before the landing, according to a site I looked at when I got interested in Sojourner, there was a major disagreement over whether it was a flood plain, or whether the fluvial pattern was from a volcanic eruption. Of course they learned almost immediately that it was from flooding. Which made Mars much more interesting to those old Earthlings who never considered anything interesting unless it was like Earth—wet.

I'm on my way.

And even if Mother decides to follow me, she'll have a hard time, because I gave her electronic ticket numbers to a new immigrant in Polaris.

Sagan City, Summer-March 6, 2202:
Dear Sekou:

I had some windowplant seed I used as cowrie to get a bed last night. The hosteler didn't know what they were, but he accessed his net, he found out how unusual they were, and was glad to take them.

The hotel was cheap, but a little scary. There were two immigrants there that got to Mars and wanted to renege on their contracts to Manifeast-Frostline Company. At first they were very quiet, but somebody in the bar recognized them and called the city police, who of course wouldn't enforce a company contract, but did tip off the Manifeast enforcers. There was almost a shootout.

Breakfast was lettuce, onions, and squash simmered in soy milk. They use a lot of Earth plants here; quite exotic.

I'm into my environment suit and off to the Pathfinder site. It's less than a kilometer from the city biome.

Pathfinder Site, Summer-March 6, 2202, later in the sol:
Sekou,

This isn't working out as I expected. A kilometer is a long way to walk in an environment suit. When I got here, there was just the plaque, which said ON OR AROUND THIS SITE, THE HISTORIC PATHFINDER MISSION LANDED, JULY 4, 1997. THE LANDER HAS BEEN MOVED TO THE SAGAN MUSEUM ON FIRST STREET; THE SOJOURNER ROVER HAS NEVER BEEN FOUND.

That's all I'm going to record tosol. My stomach hurts and I think I better head back to the dome.

Sagan City, Pathfinder Trust Museum, Summer-March 7, 2202:
Sekou, my dear brother,

Elder Adelia has finally gone to her room and I feel safe to bring out my diary. Oh, boy! If I was afraid of Mother getting ahold of it — if these holy guys here ever saw what I've got planned, I'd be freeze-dried, fried, and hung out to flap in the dust.

I just reread what I wrote on Summer-March 6. "My stomach hurts" — what an understatement. I realized my leukemia was making me feel bad, so I figured maybe tosol wasn't the sol to go digging in the mines for Sojourner. I thought I'd go back to the hotel and use the last of my cowrie to get another room for the night.

On the way, though, I noticed people staring at me. I had heard that Kiafricans were uncommon in some Martian cities, but some of the people staring and pointing were also Kiafrican.

Then it hit me. I needed to hit a news equiosk, fast. I didn't dare use my account, that is, the Smythe family's account, to pay for the jack, so I looked for a public library. I don't know how it is on Earth, big brother, or for that matter Luna or the orbital colonies, but on Mars most of the public libraries are run by Mormonite Jesuits. In fact, the Sagan Memorial Museum is run by Mormonite Jesuits. I forgot — you probably don't know about ancient religions. To make a long story short, the Mormons and the Jesuits were both really very sexist, meaning they didn't let women do much of the leadership stuff. If you studied history in the Earth school, they taught you that sects like that had a lot of computer trouble in the middle twenty-first century. Something called IRS was tapping their money files. I think IRS was a computer virus. Anyway the people in those religions got a bad case of IRS and the law wanted to arrest them and put them in quarantine. So the leaders of the Mormons and the Jesuits decided to come to Mars and set up colonies for religious freedom. Neither group had enough money to launch a large-scale emigration and settlement mission, so they pooled their resources.

The funny thing is that once they got to Mars, they were separated from their home offices so much that they got to electing their own padres and CEOs, and now there are more madres running their show than padres. Which proves something, I forget what.

There are private libraries, but they run by subscription, and you can't jack in unless you have an account. And the private libraries don't like the public libraries; they say it's unfair competition.

So I couldn't find a public library at the hotel, or in the biome the hotel was in, and I had to spend more precious cowrie (the seeds) to chute into the cavern section of town, which is where I ran in the library, ignoring the human attendant, grabbed free goggles, and got the daily news. There was my picture, one my Dad had taken. I was pruning some vines, and I turned to the camera and said something stupid like, "Farming is big business on Mars." I don't remember ever saying anything *that* stupid, but I must have, because there was the video. And a big headline, IF YOU SEE THIS CHILD.

Oh, no! This is the absolute first time I'd appeared in a public posting, and it was because I had done something wrong! I wanted my first appearance to be there because my experiments with bloodplants had won a Westinghouse Award, or because I had located a major new aquifer.

I had been reported missing, of course. My mother was videoed holding back tears (insincere tears, no doubt), saying I had been kidnapped and the house robbed too. The kidnapper had taken undisclosed equipment and used an open ticket to Soochow.

Sekou, if I ever meet you, I'm sure you'll laugh and laugh at how stupid I had been not to realize they would report me missing. It's nice that they missed me, of course. But of course they were legally bound to report me to the company; though I was a born freewoman, still the company has first rights should I decide to become indentured. And the company would spread it on the newsnet, even if they hadn't.

I crossreffed all the majors in the posting, and nowhere was it mentioned that I had leukemia. I don't know why they left that out.

Sekou, I have to tell you the most awful thing I did. When I left home, I stole Mother's environment suit. She was going to get me a new one, because I had outgrown my five-mear suit. Still, she would be caught short without this one, and it will take all summer to order up a new one. I was sharing this one with her, which was awkward, because when you come in, you know, you have to throw it in the deduster, and it takes just hours to get most of the dust out, and if you don't, it wears out very quickly at the seals and seams.

On Luna, they are developing ones that have their own onboard dedusters, some kind of nanotech thing. But you know Martian bureau-crats, no nanotech frills for "our people"!

Geez, I must be better, or I wouldn't be gabbing away like this.

I went out to the Pathfinder site in Mother's environment suit. I sure was glad I had obeyed her and put it in the deduster right after the last time I wore it. That was the night they were in the high-pressure greenhouse talking about me. It fit fine, worked fine, but kept reporting problems with my vitals. It wasn't telling me anything I didn't know. I started back to the tramway (there's a little rail car that takes you to and from the site) and the next thing I knew—

You know, it's hard to sit down in an environment suit, and a good thing, too, because you're likely to run out of solar energy and just freeze to the ground.

I kept telling myself, "Kapera, get up! Make your daddy proud of you! You can do it!"

But I couldn't get up. The suit was kind of heavy and of course hard to bend around the knees. I started crying, and my nose ran and I couldn't wipe it, and my faceplate got all smeary.

Pretty soon two people came up, squatted beside me, and pressed their faceplates to mine. The one with the woman's voice said that the park site was closing for the sol, would open tomorrow at nine. I tried to get up, though I didn't have any idea where I'd go. The woman asked me if I was okay. Well, did I *look* okay? I mean really!

This gave me the energy to get up again, because I thought they would surely connect me with that girl who was missing from Smythe Homestead in Borealopolis, and turn me in. I didn't say anything, but got up. I was standing, and then I fell over again. This time, I just couldn't get my legs under me.

The woman said, "Oh! Careful! You'll rip your suit."

Which was silly. Who ever heard of a Sears Roebuck environment suit ripping? Cheap ones, maybe, but my parents buy quality when it comes to equipment.

The woman pulled me to my feet and let me lean against her. "What's your name?"

I didn't know what to do, so I very carefully used my toe to draw in the dust: SEKOU.

I figured she couldn't see through my faceplate, and anyway with my hair all gone she'd think I was a boy. Sorry I used your name, big brother, but I had to think fast. I wanted them to leave me alone, but I was afraid if they did, I wouldn't have the strength to make it back to the platform from which the tramway ran.

"Walter, this poor child is hurt!"

That was when I noticed the blood on the inside of my faceplate. I must have gotten a nosebleed. Darn it!

I focused on their nameplates. They must have had something to do with the museum because they had names over their hearts, ELDER ADELIA and PADRE WALTER.

Oh, *great*. I had fallen into the hands of a bunch of missionaries.

By some miracle, they weren't the sort that had head computers tuned sol and night, so they hadn't seen the "missing or kidnapped child" appeal.

I suppose that's the religion thing, or maybe they're just poor.

Anyway, they took me back to the museum, which was inside its own small biome, and the padre made me some kind of home-brewed liquor with herbs in it. Called it Hyper K.

"The original shroom was from Earth, but Mars gravity and mutations have changed it. I call it 'Papa Mars Welcome Wagon gift to humanity.'" He had a little nip himself, and seemed much happier after that.

It tasted sweet, but with a bubbly bite to it. I felt like sleeping after I drank the Hyper K, and when I woke up, this is what I heard:

She: "He can't be. The kidnapped child was a girl."

He: "Are you sure he's a boy? Sekou is a boy's name, but you know how those uplanders are. They got some gritty weird customs."

"Sekou is a boy's name. Look it up in your database."

"You're right. And the missing child's name was Kapera Smythe. Still, maybe he, she, whatever, is afraid to tell us the real name. Maybe Sekou is afraid the kidnapper will come back. Or maybe Sekou wasn't really kidnapped—"

There was a pause while they both reaccessed the newsnet. Finally, Elder Adelia said, "They seem pretty sure it was a kidnapping. I still think we should call Solaranics and pass on the information about this child."

"I guess. Still—the kid was bleeding. Maybe the parents—or owners—were cruel and the child has run away for a reason." He took another swig of the Hyper K. I knew it was the Hyper K, because I could smell the sweet-biting smell all the way down the hall.

"That stuff is making you paranoid! Let's let the poor boy sleep and hear his story at breakfast."

Sekou, I'm sitting here scared to death. What kind of a story can I feed them that they won't send me back home?

Maybe I should go back home.

I have time to sleep, though. My stomach hurts. My nose won't stop bleeding. Why do I have to be sick?

I can't go home. They will be so angry at me. And Mother and Dad will be split up forever and I'll have to go to a stinking orbital hospital, and then live on Earth the rest of my life.

My life—

Sagan Memorial Station Museum, March 7, 2202, I think:
Dear Sekou,

I don't know how you expect me to record a diary when I'm so sick and confused.

Oh, all right, I guess it was my idea in the first place.

I fell asleep for a little while, but my stomach hurt so much I woke up early. I heard them talking again.

She: "Sekou is a boy's name all right! Sekou is the name of Kapera Smythe's brother."

He: "All right, all right. So we call Celltechnio, who owned the parent's contract. Or should we call our own company?"

She: "I say talk to Madre Naomi. We've already taken too much into our own hands by keeping this from the Mission. You and I may not see eye to eye on doctrine, but we have a responsibility to the Mission. And we can't keep him—or her—in the museum dormitory without letting somebody in authority know."

He: "Um, why don't you call. I'm not sure I can face up to this."

I heard enough, Sekou. I figured in a minute, they were going to come in and pull down my drawers to find out if I was Kapera or Sekou. I got out of the hammock, stuffed my environment suit into the backpack, and peeked out the door.

They were standing in a low hallway. It looked like we were in a part of the building that had a soil roof, though the museum itself is an independent aboveground biome with its own greenhouse, attached to the city biome with a long inflated tube. I hate those things; the pressure is always way too low and it hurts my ears. And they're cold!

She was saying, "Padre, I know you're crazy about kids, but this isn't a stray iguana some farmer lost that you can make into a pet."

"I just worry about why they want him back, Adelia. What if that wasn't really his father? Suppose he's a company child?"

"Don't believe everything you access on the yellow sites, Padre."

I tiptoed back into the little cell where I'd slept. The nap had made me feel a lot better. I noticed a backpack hung on a hook on the back of the door. While I could still hear voices, I very quietly took the backpack down and went through it.

Oh, Sekou! Please don't be too ashamed of me, going through a stranger's things, and a good person's too, who helped me when I was in trouble. I know I condemned Mother for trying to violate my privacy by accessing my diary. But I had to figure out a way so they wouldn't turn me in, so I had to find out as much as I could about these people. I was desperate!

The backpack belonged to Elder Adelia. In an outer pocket was an old-fashioned plastic smart plate, and I was pretty sure it would have the key codes to all the rooms in the museum.

I hung the backpack back up and thought fast. The way to leave was blocked; Elder Adelia and Padre Walter were standing in the hallway. Elder Adelia was saying, "Well, then let's just talk to him. If he's a runaway, surely he'll tell us why, and we can check out his story." And I heard their footsteps shuffling down the hall.

I shoved the smart plate in my jumpsuit pocket and lay back on the bed, trying to look as if I had just waked up.

She spoke first: "Sekou, are you rested up from your nap? You want some more soup? We wanted to ask you a few questions."

I didn't say anything.

He said, "Elder Adelia and I wondered if you were maybe lost. Can we help you get back to your parents?"

I still didn't say anything. I had an idea.

"A boy your age alone, of course we wondered if you had got separated from your family," Elder Adelia continued soothingly.

But I wasn't soothed. I said nothing.

"Maybe he speaks Amtrav," said Padre Walter. "Sorquel vwey a habin tey?"

I stared at them.

He tried several other languages, including English, which I do know pretty well.

He apparently had one of those quick-study chips, or maybe he had done a lot of deep learning. He certainly knew a lot of ways to ask questions that were none of his business.

Finally Elder Adelia chipped in. Between the two of them, I bet they tried twenty different languages. I just stared at them.

"Do you understand us at all, honey?" she asked.

I stared at them, then nodded yes.

"Oh my stars! Can you talk, Sekou?"

I slowly shook my head: No.

I tried not to giggle at their expressions.

"What do we do now, Walt?"

"I think we have to take him to the Madre Generale. Sekou, gather your things. We're going to take you to a lady who can help you get back with your parents."

"Ask him about why he ran away."

"You ask him."

I looked at them with the biggest eyes I could manage.

She said, "Sekou, were you kidnapped, or did you run away?"

I looked at her and shrugged.

"You ran away? Why? Were you afraid of someone or something?"

I nodded emphatically.

Well, Sekou, it was true. I was afraid of leukemia, and afraid I'd be sent to Earth Orbital Hospital.

I knew I was in trouble if I ever got to see Madre Naomi. She didn't sound like the type with the warmth of solar kindness in her heart.

So I followed them down the hallway, and into the tube. Once we got to the city, I waited until we were at a busy intersection: people and minirovers all going every which way. I chose the darkest corridor I could see and ran like Phobos.

They were old people, and although I was sick, I was young and small. When I thought I had lost them, I put on my environment suit and slipped out an airlock.

Where am I now? you wonder, big brother.

Well, I'm right back at the museum. I waited until dark—there's been a local storm that blocks most starlight, and neither of the moons were up, I told you I was good at divining. Dad says I have this magnetic sixth sense. I found the door to the museum in the twilight by following the edge of the main biome, then the connecting tubes. I figured they'd never look for me outside. I huddled in the shadow of a model of the Face, hoping my power wouldn't give out before dark.

It didn't.

I'm inside the museum.

Sagan Memorial Museum, Summer-April 3, 2202:
Dear Sekou:

I'm in the museum, but I'm also in serious trouble.

To start with, I'll have to leave and find somewhere else to go in about seven hours, when the museum opens to tourists.

But worse, they turn off the air handlers at night, which is not a huge threat; I've spent time in our medium-pressure greenhouse and got no more problems than nosebleeds. But there are two other problems: One, the outer dome, the flydome, sort of collapses in on itself; during the sol it's like a big fat balloon against the low outside ambient pressure. At night, it's still inflated, but it's not blown up as big. It kind of drapes against the front entry and I can't get out. If I should want to. Second, there is no heat! I'm shivering already, despite making a tent out of every blanket I could find in their dormitory. I suppose it won't get down to Mars ambient before morning, but it will surely be cold enough to freeze H_2O.

And it will surely freeze *me*.

Sagan Memorial Museum, Summer-April 3, 2202:
Dear Sekou,

I wrapped some of the blankets around me—even the hammocks, which I took down from their hooks—and searched the whole museum for some way to keep from freezing. I was a little worried about low air pressure, too, but I figured the museum couldn't be that leaky.

My teeth were chattering, and to tell the truth, I didn't feel very good, either. This leukemia thing comes and goes. Sometimes I get hot and cold, hot and cold.

Like now.

So anyway, I went exploring.

I made a discovery.

As I emerged from the preparation room, which is where the hammocks were strung, the first thing I saw was a giant picture of Carl Sagan and a bronze inscription explaining why the city was named after him. In case you have not heard of him, apparently he was an Earthman who pressed for exploration of the solar system back before the space age. Then you come into a central hall, and my heart almost jumped out of my chest. There was Sojourner, right next to its lander. I thought: There goes my plan for discovering the historic rover.

I wished like heck that the docents weren't turned off for the night so I could hear what they had to say.

But I had more important problems, so I prowled around in the dark. You'd think they'd leave enough heat on so the water pipes in the preparation room wouldn't freeze up, but I'd looked, and they kept their water supply in insulated containers. They must truck the waste back into the city to be recycled.

Then I got a funny idea.

Maybe some of the batteries in the rover were still alive, and I could get enough juice from them to stay warm somehow.

That was when I discovered that the rover was just a model. It must have been built from photoimages and blueprints sent from Earth. Not the real thing.

I kind of wondered how dim these people were. Couldn't they do some kind of computer modeling from orbit to find dust patterns that might be covering the two crafts?

But I figured this wasn't the time to give up. I went to the gift shop and found a souvenir poster they sold to tourists. I had to find a skylight to read it by; fortunately Phobos was sailing along overhead right then. The poster said the lander actually had been located; in 2088, a photographer from *Solar Geographic* had noticed the camera and antenna sticking out; the rest was so covered with dust it looked like just another funny-shaped rock, but the rover had wandered around so much that nobody knew where exactly it might be. The lander site was marked with a bronze tablet, but they didn't want to spoil the site by excavating for Sojourner. I tried not to smile: they would never find it. I would.

Well, if the lander was real, maybe it had some power in it.

But it didn't. It was old; it was for history and education only.

I was thinking of putting my environment suit back on and trying to stay warm that way, although the batteries would be drained long before solbreak. Or I could go back the way I came, try to get back into the city dome before I froze or my batteries ran down.

I was feeling like I wanted to throw up, and those hot-cold spells were coming again. The whole museum smelled like ozone dust and cold, and then I caught a whiff of something else, something — organic.

It was Padre Walter's Hyper K. Maybe I should have another swig of that. I hadn't eaten anything for hours — hadn't been hungry, with the nausea. But maybe the Hyper K would help me think.

I didn't even need the light of Phobos through the skylight. I just followed my nose.

One of the offices had a huge glass jug, almost a meter tall, with a spout at the bottom. It looked like it would hold about fifty litres, and somebody had painted SOL TEA in funny old-fashioned letters on it. I went through the desk drawers and found a cup, then drew myself a mug of the yicky stuff.

I was about to raise it to my lips when something made me stop.

Why was it still liquid?

Surely it didn't have that much alcohol in it. Dad used to give me phoboshine for toothache when I was little, and that was really strong. Even that might have frozen on a cold night in a museum.

I sniffed, then tasted.

It was warm.

Of course! It was fermenting!

I chugged the whole cup down, then held my hands over my mouth to keep from upchucking it. Gradually, the heat of it warmed my belly and hands and even my toes.

I didn't need any more clues. I went back to the preparation room and got all the blankets I could find, then made a nice little tent by draping them over the Hyper K jug.

It took a long time for the tent to warm up, but I had a few more glasses of the Hyper K, and fell really deep asleep. Then I got up and raided the food vending machines in the lobby. I had to use the Smythe family credit number, but it'll be a while before my parents think to look at that, and by that time — ta DAH!

Did I mention that your little sister is a brilliant dowser?

And now I've got to go. I hear their computer has turned on the air handlers.

Pathfinder Site, Summer-April 4, 2202, early morning:

Dear Big Brother,

Well, they were right. Sojourner isn't here.

I walked all over the site, using my dowsing sense. This was my whole plan: if Sojourner had even a little bit of juice left in its batteries, I might be able to sense it just as I sense the presence of water in the soil around our homestead.

But I felt nothing. Nothing.

Where did you go, little Rover?

I'm tired. Tosol is the beginning of the week, and tourists will start pouring in from all over Mars and maybe even very rich people from Earth. If I wait here in the open, I'll be spotted.

Or I could mingle with the tourists and hope those two religious numbers don't come out here to the site every sol. I guess I have to wait until night, then go back to the museum. Maybe tosol.

Sagan Memorial Museum, Summer-April 4, 2202:

Dear Sekou,

It's night now. I'm in big trouble with Elder Adelia and Padre Walter, but that's the least of my griefs.

After I finished my previous diary entry tosol, I figured I'd just wander around and pretend to be a tourist. If Elder Adelia or Padre Walter turned up, well, I'd just hide behind a rock or take a long hike. My suit was charging in the sun; it was dusty, but not actually leaking, and I could wait until the end of the business sol. Food and water was a worse problem; the suit is pretty good at recycling fluids, but I was getting hungry, despite the queasy feeling in my stomach.

I kept trying to get a feeling about what was under my feet — you know, like a little buzz from the battery of Sojourner. But all I felt was that the place was empty, hollow.

I knew it was a bad idea to sit down — you can tear your suit, and the insulation gets compressed and robs your body of heat — but I just had to rest. I closed my eyes for a few minutes, and when I opened them, I saw — Sojourner!

No. I saw *two* Sojourners. No, three. Five. Oh, no, bunches of them.

And they were the wrong size. They were little teeny ones, small enough for me to pick up in two hands. And the solar panels looked wrong, too.

They were very modern high-efficiency solar panels, like the ones Mother and I saw at the Polaris commercial fest, and said we couldn't afford.

I staggered to my feet and chased one down. It put its APXS on me, then backed away, as if startled. I grabbed it and looked it over.

It had a name and number engraved on the frame: Hamm Munnix Herzberg, 2190–2196.

I let it go and chased down another. This one backed away from me, and if it had been an iguana, it would have been hissing. But it was much the same, except this one was Anna Li Markham, 2179–2184.

I probably would have looked at every single miniature Sojourner on the site, and there were probably thirty of them, except that a heavy hand fell on my shoulder.

I was spun around and nearly dropped the miniature rover I was looking at just then. Two familiar voices came over my radio, "What are you *doing* here?" and "Poor kid; he looks confused."

They babbled together so much I couldn't make out half they were saying.

"Why did you run away?" Elder Adelia asked sternly.

"Let him be," said Padre Walter. "Can't you see he's totally disoriented? Probably dehydrated, and half frozen, not to speak of dazzled by too much sun."

"Yeah, and by a couple quarts of your hooch he snitched last night, too. Walt, we've got to get him back to the Madre before you turn him into an alcoholic."

Padre Walter started dusting my suit off with his hands, as if that would do a bit of good. "Tell us where you came from, big guy."

I wasn't anybody's big guy, and I wasn't giving away any secrets, or admitting I could talk. I just shook my head, which isn't easy in an environment suit.

"Come on with us," said Elder Adelia. She grabbed my hand firmly. "You can't bring that inside; it's looking for its big sister."

How could I be so dumb? Of course they would be looking for the Sojourner rover. They must be using these small units for that. The tourists would love that.

I had a lot of questions, but I still thought I was better off pretending to be mute.

The minute they got me back inside the museum, they dragged me back into the office. Elder Adelia undid my faceplate and yanked my environment suit off so hard I was afraid it would tear. She undid her own faceplate, and said, "There! You'll have a hard time running away again without this!" And before I could react, she and Padre Walter swept out and slammed the door shut. In fact, locked it.

I've been in here all sol. Trying to work up the nerve to jack into their files for a while; did so finally; found out nothing except that they're using those little rovers to look for fossils as well as for the original Sojourner. Which I had already figured out.

Padre Walter came back twice and brought me sandwiches and a mug of Hyper K. I'm beginning to like the stuff.

Kombucha, I think he said. The starter "shroom" somebody brought from Earth was called kombucha.

I feel pretty good, but I'm sleepy.

Sagan Memorial Museum, Summer-April 4, 2202:
Dear Sekou,

Well, I did learn this much: Hyper K gives you gas. Somebody told me gas was no big thing on Earth — the atmospheric pressure is so high. But we keep our buildings at about the level it would be at four thousand meters above the surface of Earth, so gas is really — explosive.

I woke up with stomach cramps, and at first I thought the leukemia was doing its final number on me. But then I heard my stomach rumble, and I burped and farted and that made me think about fermentation, and — well, I think I'm okay for the moment.

Think I'll go through their private files after all. Elder Adelia seems to use the same key for the door and for the jack.

Sagan Memorial Museum, Summer-April 4, 2202:
Good-bye Sekou.
I believed in you.

I believed what they told me. They said they sent you to Earth.

I was curious about the little Sojourners, see, about what they had found and why they couldn't find the real Sojourner. So I innocently — oh boy, so innocently — started scrolling through those files.

It's called the Personality Preservation Software Corporation. The rovers are Eternal Memorial Reconstruction Rovers.

You know what a euphemism is?

I think they meant to download *my* personality into one of these rovers.

No, I didn't find you among the forty Sojourner miniature rovers. You're on a Rocky 13, rolling around the South Pole, counting layers of ice and dust, trying to date the polar cap.

Only it isn't you. It can't be. Even the orbital AI scientists haven't got to the point where they actually can reconstruct a person's mind and personality. They just used your voice and some of your personality quirks. I found out, for example, that you were quick to jump to conclusions, and that you loved tilapia with spiceberry sauce.

So the Rocky 13 that has your name on it — oh, give me a break!

You, my brother, my real brother, died in 2197. On the way to Earth. By yourself. Mother didn't volunteer to go with you as she has with me.

And now I'm going to die, too. Alone.

Someone's coming to get me.

Sagan Memorial Museum, April 4, 2202, late night:

But I might as well keep recording. My thoughts are important to me, if to nobody else.

They found me, of course. Mother and Dad, I mean. There's a dust storm starting, and the reception was poor, but they scolded me and said they're coming for me. Mother really ground it in that they would have to leave the experimental windowplants and maybe lose the whole crop, and somebody from Watson Farm would have to come in and feed the fish. And if they can't get through the global storm by sol after tomorrow (because all sky traffic is grounded, and most rovers, too), I'll miss the window to Earth. And on top of that, I squandered two perfectly good, very expensive tickets that were supposed to take us to Hellas Spaceport. Dad didn't say much. He just shook his head.

I felt so miserable.

"Why?" Mother asked.

I didn't say anything.

Elder Adelia had been skulking around the room, and she piped up and said, "You can't expect the poor mute dear—"

"She's not mute!" Mother barked.

For the first time, Dad said something, "Girl, what kind of nonsense have you been feeding these poor people? First you tell them you're your older brother who's gone to Earth, then you pretend you can't talk."

It was too much. I felt my chest heave, my throat knot up. "He didn't go to Earth! Stop lying!"

Dad looked directly at the camera. At me. Very sad. "Kapera, believe me, he's gone to Earth."

Everybody was very quiet for a while, and the picture started to break up. Global dust. Elder Adelia skulked back to her chair and pretended to be interested in a button computer on the desk.

"Kapera, we're coming for you. Both of us. I know you love your father more than you do me, and so he's coming to see us off. We'll bring your things to Sagan City and proceed from there to Hellas Spaceport."

I got up and hit the monitor with my fist. "I'm not going to Earth! This is my life."

Mother looked very stern. "Kapera, you are a minor in the eyes of the Polaris corporation and under pan-Martian law. Your father and I have discussed what is best for you, and you are going to Earth to be treated for your disease. You will live either in Earth orbit or in North America after that."

"I want to stay on Mars! Mars is my home!"

"If you had been meant to live on Mars, you wouldn't be sick, Kapera."

Dad had walked away from the camera, probably trying not to get all excited. Now he came back. "The signal is breaking up. Try to keep your chin up."

Mother was calm and grim. "We're coming to get you, just as soon as they open the rocket plane terminal in Borealopolis."

The light flickered, and they were gone.

Padre Walter came and put his arms around me, and I tried not to cry. Elder Adelia just kind of sniffed, and said, "Well, we can't take her back to the monastery. I'll stay here with her overnight and hope they can get a rocket plane in the morning."

"No, please!" I said. "I can stay alone!"

She smiled sadly. "You little rascal. You had us convinced. But we're on to you now."

"I'll stay with her," said Padre Walter. Which was okay, because I liked him better. "Override the vitals cycle so she can nap in the office."

"That costs money, Padre. But—okay." And she voiced some commands. I heard the air handlers speed up.

Elder Adelia stayed too, and I thought she'd stay all night, glaring at me. But she started yawning about midnight-and-a-half. The dust was swirling outside; you could see it through the skylight, because there were lights on the roof. It was beautiful. Mars is beautiful, even when he's angry.

"Okay, you stay. I'll go back and talk to Madre again."

"Please," I said. "Would you leave my thumblight?"

She looked at me suspiciously. "What for? It's not like the electricity will go off. We've got power backup for sols."

"If Padre Walter turns out the light, and I wake up in the night, I'll be scared."

She plunked it down on the desk, and left.

I snuggled into the hammock they had strung in the corner of the office. "May I have a little more of the Hyper K?" I asked politely.

Padre was propped up uncomfortably on a chair. He looked at me from under heavy brows. "Sure. I'll join you in a drop."

And so we did.

"Please, just one more?" I was feeling it, but I figured I could stand a little more.

He was much less generous this time, but he took another mug himself. After a while, he excused himself to go to the lavatory. I looked around the office and located the closet where they had dumped my environment suit.

Padre's mug was almost empty, and mine was still almost full, so I switched them.

He came back and finished that.

"Just one more?" I begged, though I was almost cross-eyed with the stuff.

He looked at me. "You're a hard drinker for a tiny thing." So he gave me a finger's worth, and had more himself.

And now he's dozed off.

Sagan Memorial Museum, April 5, early morning:
I'm outside.

Sagan Memorial Museum, April 6, afternoon:
So they found me.

By the time they found me, though, I wasn't outside. My environment suit was getting really gritty, and I was getting cold, and my suit batteries were almost dead and so —

They found me huddled in the little portico where they kept the micro-Sojourners.

"Oh my stars," Mother said. "You look like a mother hen with a bunch of mechanical chicks!"

Dad just came over and tried to pick me up. I resisted, I mean how embarrassing, even if he is my dad. But he carried me into the museum public room.

A whole bunch of people were following us. Padre Walter and Elder Adelia were in their khaki clerical jumpsuits, and there was an old woman in a dark red jumpsuit with a black veil over her head, and some other people in clerical khaki.

Mother and Dad looked really dirty and tired. I unfastened my faceplate and said, "You lied to me. Sekou is dead."

Mother said, "There was no reason to make you pessimistic about the future. Your brothers—"

"Brothers?" I exploded. "You mean there was more than just Sekou?"

"Kapera, sweetheart," Mother whined. I hate it when she uses that tone of voice. "You actually had three older brothers," she said, in that reasonable tone she gets. "Did you think it was easy for us to conceal that from you? Did you think we did it for some selfish reason? I mean, I destroyed all the holos, wiped them right off our net. The only images I have of my first two children are on your grandmother's computer in New Jersey. We kept the one of Sekou and you together. I couldn't bear to destroy it."

She made kind of choking noises and then was quiet.

After a while, Dad said, "Your mother and I thought you shouldn't always be thinking about depressing things, shouldn't worry it might happen to you."

"It *did* happen to me!"

"Not yet," said Mother coldly. "We have found a way to send you to Earth Orbital Hospital, the best in the solar system."

"But I can't come back!"

"That is a small sacrifice we have to make. Get your things. Oh, look at that suit! I'll never get it dusted."

"I'm not going to Earth," I said. "I have other plans." I was still amazed at how diabolic she could be.

Dad said, "Kapera, why are you smirking like that?"

"Is there enough charge in that suit to go outside? We'll need shovels."

Mother had to borrow a suit from one of the madres. She and Dad followed me, along with a whole parade of clerics from the museum.

The storm was still raging, but there was a little sunlight, and we wouldn't need it for long. I just prayed that the dust hadn't covered the little rover I had placed to mark the spot.

I almost missed it. It hadn't moved, of course, because I'd heaped a pile of dust over its solar cells.

"You need to dig here," I said.

At first they didn't believe me. And I thought, what if I made a mistake?

But it had to be. I *felt* it, under my shoes.

Ares Vallis was indeed in that path of a giant flood in ancient times, as everybody now knows. But the old Earthlings who thought it was the site of a volcanic eruption were also right. There is a lava tube, just one, under the site.

I knew Sojourner could not have traveled that far. So where did it go? Aliens didn't snatch it. It wasn't eaten by mutant iguanas.

It had to be underground.

Dad and Mother were both wrong about my dowsing ability, too. I can't feel electrical or magnetic fields. What I have is extremely good hearing—or maybe it's not even sound I hear, just vibrations. Heck, I can hear people talking outside in environment suits. So of course I can feel vibrations as I walk that indicate the density of the soil through my boots.

And I felt a hollow place under this spot on the landing site. Right here.

They're still digging. Elder Adelia insisted I was crazy, but Padre Walter convinced the Madre to let them keep digging. Mother and Dad are digging, too.

Mother said I looked sick. She made me go back in the museum. So here I am, sipping Hyper K and trying to spy on what's happening.

They came back to send to the city for pickaxes. It's getting dark. I sure hope they break through before nightfall.

Sagan Memorial Museum, April 6, evening:

I was right.

I was right!

Of course I was right.

It was almost nightfall, and I had nodded off. Suddenly I knew I better get out there. Something told me. It was as if I heard a different rhythm to the digging, which is silly, because how could even I hear anything outside in the Martian sky?

I put that dusty old suit on as fast as I could, hoping it wouldn't suddenly spring a leak from all that grit. It was charged from its sol in the sun, thank heaven. I slipped out the lock and ran over to where I saw seven or eight people in suits pitching dust in the air. The storm had died down; spring storms are never as bad as summer.

I pushed my way among the diggers and got there just as somebody said, "Hey, what's this?"

A long, straight pole.

Good little rover: it was still right side up. The long straight pole was the antenna.

Elder Adelia said, "Oh my golly. We better call in a team of experts to excavate this, before we ruin the whole site and destroy the relic."

Padre Walter said, "The site is already messed up. But, whoa, that's part of the story, isn't it?"

They could only see the antenna, but something—my auditory hoodoo—made me feel I was seeing the whole thing, not corroded by time and dust and wind, but whole and as new as when it rolled down the ramp and first sniffed Martian rocks. The first independent thing on Mars.

The Sojourner rover isn't mine, I realize. It belongs to the museum. It belongs to all of Mars. But there's a story there. I could write a book. Hey, I already started a book, right? Sekou, big brother, wherever you are?

I have to stop recording now. Some reporters are coming to see me. And Padre Walter says I shouldn't talk to anybody without getting a contract.

The minute he said that, the ICNN guy e-phoned his office and came up with an offer.

I tried to be very nonchalant about it, but it was more money than Mother and Dad said I'd need to get to Earth and back, plus some to pay for our stay in Earth Orbital Hospital.

Still, Padre Walter said maybe I should talk to a lawyer or an agent or somebody that knows about these things.

Mother told the reporters that I was very tired and they must respect my privacy and to come back in the morning with proper offers drawn up, and then we'd see.

I was so amazed to hear her say those words—respect my PRIVACY—that I gave her a big hug. I'm beginning to think she's a pretty good mother after all.

Polaris Corp also sent a representative. They'd heard a lot about me, and wanted to buy my contract. I'd get an education at the Areological Institute in Granicus Valles, then when I graduated I'd have my own homestead, completely equipped with three interconnected biomes, livestock, flora, the works.

But I'll have to think about that, too.

Independence has its attractions.

The Cost of Doing Business

LESLIE WHAT

Leslie What has sold some fifty short stories since making her debut in a 1992 issue of *Isaac Asimov's Science Fiction Magazine*. She also writes nonfiction and poetry, and did the script for a video shown on public television. Otherwise, she says, "Used to be nurse, performance artist, maskmaker, etc.; now housewife/writer/mother, etc. (Imagine George Sand/Martha Stewart/Ernie Kovacs, with attitude.)" Her unusual surname is a pseudonym, for which she offers the explanation, "I was twenty-one. A friend had changed her name to 'K. Somebody.' I wanted something like that, maybe with fewer syllables."

Her Nebula-winning short story, "The Cost of Doing Business," is the first of several pieces exploring retribution and guilt, personal responsibility, the limits of forgiveness, and how people continue living without any hope for reconciliation.

The big man sits across from Zita, brow furrowed, black eyes fixed upon the desk. He strokes the mahogany finish while he's talking, touching it rather absently, as if trying to smooth things out. Every now and again he glances up to make certain Zita is still paying attention to his story. There are two thugs outside, waiting for him in the parking lot.

Can he hire her to take his place, deal with the thugs, so he won't have to? There isn't much time to decide, and certainly, from his view, no choice.

Zita scribbles a few notes. She is grateful he doesn't stare at her like a lot of customers, who give her an I-can't-believe-I'm-really-here look and expect her to find their naïveté charming. When customers stare at her long legs or dress cut low to expose skin smooth as a white chocolate shell, it isn't really Zita they are seeing. Her perfection is only skin-deep, skin-deep being all anyone can afford, even the big man.

She notices his gold Rolex and his suit sewn from fine wool. Like her, the big man wears his riches on the outside.

"This is the worst thing that's ever happened to me," the big man blathers. "At first I didn't know what to do, but then I looked up, saw your billboard. That's why I'm here."

Driving to work this morning, he was carjacked. "I'm a lucky man," he says, really lucky. The thugs were curious types; they agreed to let him hire a surrogate victim in exchange for an extra couple of bills and a contract promising immunity. That's the way things are done these days, when people act reasonably. Fortunately for the big man, the thugs are reasonable men.

Zita listens as he prattles off twenty reasons why he needs to hire her instead of facing things on his own. She's tempted to correct him, but doesn't. The excuses are all part of the game. She knows why he wants to hire her, has known from the moment he walked into her office. It has nothing to do with his suspicious wife, or a job he can't afford to take time off from, or even his heart condition. Sure, the big man is afraid of pain — who isn't? — but there's more to it than that. The big man has sought Zita's services for the same reason as everyone who hires a surrogate victim. He'd rather see someone else suffer.

Something terrible has happened to him; he can't turn back the clock, so he might as well make the best of it. He won't admit that there's a reason he'll pay a premium to hire her instead of that balding Mr. Tompkins on the second floor: hiring a young woman instead of a middle-aged man makes the deal a little sweeter.

The transaction is completely legal, but the big man feels enough shame about his cowardice that he works himself into a sweat; he pauses to dab his forehead with a handkerchief. When he brings it away, his brow is still furrowed. The wrinkles on his face are set, like a shirt that has been abandoned, doomed, doomed for the rag bin. He looks around the room, paying attention to his surroundings for the first time.

She's decorated well out front. Out here, where she shows her public face, it's perfect. The walls are painted a fleshy tone called "Peach Fizz." Her costumes are one-of-a-kind and are displayed in a glass case. The overstuffed chairs are from Ethan Allen, with top-of-the-line fabrics that the sales associate promised could take a lot of abuse. Her desk is an Eighteenth-Century French copy, and there are several abstract oils she bought at an uptown gallery, all by the same artist, someone kind of famous (though not so much as to be overpriced) whose name she can't ever remember. She doesn't understand abstract painting; it's just that realism bothers her.

Her office is nothing like the backroom where she lives. There, the floors are scratched and bare, save for the ripped mattress where she sleeps. Paint peels from the walls like skin from an old sunburn. On the small table where she takes her meals sits a shrine dedicated to her daughter. There's a gold-rimmed snapshot, surrounded by dried wreaths and flowers, plastic beads, a favorite book. A shower takes up a quarter of the room; a small refrigerator covers what would otherwise be the counter space and that's okay. She doesn't need much room and she doesn't want much counter space. Anything that can't be eaten cold right out of the container isn't worth eating.

Just then the telephone rings, and the big man says, "Aren't you going to get that?"

It's probably some idiot calling to ask if she'll have her pants pulled down in front of a minister, or if she'll let some guy's boss chew her out in front of all his coworkers. "Popcorn" is what surrogates call the little jobs. Things that fill up space without having much substance. She takes on popcorn occasionally, when she's in the right mood, but usually refers little jobs to a girl she met one time when she was in the hospital. That girl is in a bad way and needs all the help she can get. Besides, Zita finds the big jobs much more satisfying.

"Well," the big man prompts. The phone annoys him; he's the type who would be annoyed by interruptions. Eventually, the machine picks up, just as she knew it would. "A true emergency would walk right in without making an appointment. The way you did," she explains.

He nods and she can tell he likes being thought of as a true emergency.

"Anything else you want to tell me?" she says.

"Yeah. These guys are armed. One has a metal pipe and a gun, the other a long knife."

"Sounds doable."

"So, how much do you charge?" he asks, somewhat timidly.

She expects him to say, "I've never done this before." They often say that, even when she knows it isn't true. The big man doesn't say it, but she knows that's what he's thinking.

She takes her time before quoting a price. The only reason to ask for more than she needs is to impress upon customers the value of her service. She doesn't really care about the money; she's not in business for that. There are a hundred Licensed Surrogates in her state. She doubts if one of them cares about money. No amount could make up for what she goes through every day, what they all go through. She states her fee. "My standard rate," she says. "Plus expenses."

"You'll take it all? Everything they dish out?" he asks.

She nods. That's what she does. She takes it all, every bit of it, so that important people like the big man can avoid suffering.

He reaches into his coat pocket for his wallet and his credit card. "Those guys looked pretty mean. There might be scarring."

"Those are the expenses."

They both laugh, but his is more like a grunt. The whole experience must be quite a strain on his heart: his breathing quickens, his lips fade to a powdery blue. When the card changes hands, his fingers leave a cold residue that makes her want more than anything to duck into the backroom for a shower. Stop it, she tells herself. Disgust is not professional.

"What would you like me to wear?" she asks.

He stands and faces the glass case. Her sequined gown has a rip and is being repaired, but otherwise everything is there.

"The white leather coveralls," he says after a while. "Nothing underneath. And don't zip it up all the way. Leave a little cleavage. Not too much, just a shadow. Ladylike, not slutty."

His face turns ruddy and she knows he would like her to disrobe in front of him. Not my job, she thinks. Not my job.

"If you'll excuse me." She opens the display case and holds the coveralls against her, giving him a moment to reconsider his choice.

"That will be fine," he says.

Zita smiles a professional smile, then steps into the backroom to change.

She takes the big man's arm and leads him through the hallway to the rear staircase. They walk down to the first floor. "Were there protestors out today?" she asks, gesturing over her shoulder toward the front.

"I didn't see any when I pulled into the lot," he says. "I hope there isn't trouble. I don't want trouble. Or publicity."

"Listen," she says, "if they weren't out front, they certainly won't be out back. There's no point in protesting unless someone sees you. These guys don't care about morality — they only want it to look like they do."

"Okay," he says, not sounding convinced.

They open the fire door and step onto the parking lot. The sun hides behind thin clouds, yet the day is muggy and bright. If the sun were out it would be blinding, one of those days when you can't even look at the ground without squinting. Zita sees the perps inside what she guesses must be *his* car. Black Beemer — sunroof — leather interior. They walk closer.

The big man realizes that the seats have been slashed. He groans.

"They can be replaced," she says.

He answers, "Yeah, but still."

"Forget it," she says. "Just think of it as the cost of doing business."

"Easy for you to say," says the big man.

"Easy?" she says, and stops walking. "Easy?" Just what does he think this is? He's even more of a jerk than she imagined.

He must realize his faux pas, for he looks at his feet and says, "Sorry. Come on. Let's get this over with." The big man calls out to the perps in the car, "Here she is." He speaks quickly; he is very anxious to put this all behind him. "You boys remember our deal, now."

The one who must be the leader opens the front door and steps out. He holds a pistol, aims it toward Zita. He's short and his hair is black and nicely cut. He reminds her of a philosophy student: jeans, a plaid flannel shirt, clean shoes. His partner is skinny, with sunken eyes like a twenty-four-hour bruise. The partner is dressed more slovenly — maybe he's majoring in political science — in a dirty T-shirt and torn pants.

She notices that the big man has silently dropped back behind her. Good, she thinks. Better he stay out of her way.

"Give him his stuff," she tells the thugs. "You can have the money and you can have me. He just wants what belongs to him."

A parking-lot attendant, wearing earphones, approaches.

Because she doesn't recognize him, she guesses that he's new here. Zita reaches into her pocket to flash her license.

He stops, rubs his neck as if trying to remember what he has been told about such things at the orientation. At last it hits him: she's a surrogate, just doing her job. The attendant salutes. "Sorry to intrude," he says, and walks back to his booth.

She replaces her license, tucks it between the few bills she carries for show.

"Shit!" says the skinny partner, looking about. He's nervous.

It's nice to know, she thinks, that you can be a total jerk as long as you still feel nervous.

"I don't know if I like this," he says. "Maybe we shouldn't have let him talk us into this."

For a second the leader looks like he might agree with his sidekick, but when the big man says, "Don't forget you signed a contract. I'll press charges if you don't hold up your end of the deal," bravado washes over him; he swaggers away from the car like the bad guy in a western.

The big man pushes Zita forward. "The briefcase," he whispers. "Tell them not to scuff it."

"What makes you think I won't kill you both?" asks the leader. He waves his gun in an arc.

The big man gasps, and Zita turns to glare at him, warning him to stay calm. She's the one they want to see acting scared, not him. It's her job now. She knows from experience that if the big man screams or acts stupid, he'll just mess things up. "Relax," she barks. They have a contract. Life is not the free-for-all some people assume it is. The majority abides by the rules. After all, what would become of society if everyone changed things willy-nilly?

"Don't forget your agreement," she says. "He doesn't want any trouble."

"Maybe I want trouble," says the leader.

"That's why I'm here," Zita says. "Go ahead, scumbag, take it out on me. Think of all the bitches you've known who have led you on, but in the end decided they were too good for you. Bitches who made you beg for affection, then denied you what you deserved, what you needed. Think of what you would have done to them if they hadn't managed to get away." She takes a step closer. "Give him his stuff. You can keep me."

Her statement has the impact she is aiming for. He grimaces and a tic starts near his upper lip. "Stay there!" he says to his partner. "Me first."

He tosses the car keys to the pavement. The big man stoops to grab them, scurries out of the way.

The leader stands before her. His breath is sweet, like he's just sucked on a peppermint. She doesn't know why, but this strikes her as funny. Before she can stop herself she is giggling.

"Bitch!" he says. "What are you laughing at?" He slaps her face and slaps it again and again until she cries out. *The one time she couldn't change places and ease someone else's suffering was when her daughter died.*

Now, he is grinding his prick against her belly and squeezing her tit hard enough to sting.

She feels the big man watching her.

"No!" she cries out. *There was nothing she could have done, only there was, and she knows it.*

He takes the pistol and brings it down hard on her head.

She knew it wasn't safe to let the girl outside unsupervised, but he said, "Forget about the kid," and she said, "Okay," and now her baby was dead and no amount of grief could bring her back.

The pistol strikes again.

She feels terror this man might hurt her more than they usually do. There's a gleam in his eye, like he doesn't care whether she's dead or alive when it comes time to rape her. "Please," she says. They always like it when she begs, but that's not why she asks for mercy. The pain has become unbearable. She can no longer tell the ground from the sky. She stumbles and falls. With her ear pressed against the asphalt she thinks she hears the big man's heavy breath.

The leader kicks her in the small of her back, says, "Get up, bitch."

She screams as the heel of his boot knocks into her face. *Her little baby, drowned, and her inside, making it with a guy who still denies he was the father.*

Oh God, it should have been me, she thinks. Oh God, it should have been me.

When Zita comes to, she's in her usual suite at the hospital.

A nurse says dryly, "Good. You're back from the dead," as she injects some white fluid from a vial into the IV. The nurse writes something on a chart before offering Zita a brown plastic cup filled with water.

Zita tries to say Thanks, but her throat feels like there are a dozen razor blades propping it open. She's thirsty, but too afraid to drink, so shakes her head no. The movement brings on a pounding pain and makes everything blurry.

Next, the doctor struts into the room and reads the notes on the chart before acknowledging her. "You again," he says. He yawns. "You're sending both my kids to college. Private. Out of state. You know that, don't you?" He winks at the nurse, then they both laugh. He sidles up near Zita's face to shine a penlight in her eyes. He presses his fingers against her neck. "We almost lost you this time. Did it hurt?" he asks.

"Not enough," she answers.

He takes a mirror from the bedside stand to let her see his handiwork.

The face staring back in the mirror looks vaguely familiar, like someone she's only seen from far away.

"Looking good," the doctor says, "better than new. Give it a week for the swelling to go down. Oh, and I had to replace a hip, so go easy on jogging."

A sharp pain shoots from her jaw up through her cheek. She groans. "Doctor, can you please give me an injection?"

"I thought you liked the pain," says the doctor.

"Think what you like," Zita says. Even the hospital staff want to see her suffer, want to see her beg. Ironic that she must pay them for the privilege. "Give me a shot."

"Well, I suppose she can have some morphine," says the doctor. "Five milligrams IV now. Every four hours PRN, until tomorrow. After that, she can take codeine. Wouldn't want her to get too dependent," he says.

An orderly walks in, bearing an obscenely big flower arrangement. It's too large to go on the bedside stand and the orderly sets it on the floor beside the wall. He reads her the card without asking if she cares who sent the flowers.

They're from the big man. Pale yellow roses with sprigs of freesia the color of bruises. How sweet.

In a couple of days they send her out to finish her recovery at home. The bed is there for someone who really needs it, not for someone who simply wants it.

"Always a pleasure," says the doctor with a wave. "See you in a couple of months."

She ignores him and asks the nurse to call her a cab.

The nurse makes Zita sit in a green vinyl wheelchair, despite her assertion that she is well enough to walk. "You want to walk out of here like a normal human being, you gotta walk in like one, too," says the nurse.

Zita shrugs, and lowers herself into the chair. She has no change of clothes and must wear her coveralls, now caked with blood that's gone black. The nurse sets the heavy flower arrangement in Zita's lap, and wheels her down the hallway to the exit.

Once outside, an angry woman in a tailored black pantsuit accosts them, and waves a placard in front of her face that says, OUTLAW SURROGATE VICTIMS NOW!

There's a camera crew, who rushes in for a clash.

"How can you do this?" the woman screams at Zita. "How can you let these perverts abuse you so? It has to stop! What you're doing is against God! This madness has got to stop!"

The woman keeps screaming as she follows Zita to the taxi. "You're nothing but an overpriced whore!" she says. "Whore!"

The cabby takes the flowers and opens her door so Zita can get in. He sets the flowers on the seat beside her. He shoos away the protestor with a practiced wave, elbows the cameraman in the ribs. He hurries to get behind the wheel. "Time is money," says the cabby, revving up the engine. "Where to, Miss Whore?" Without waiting for her to answer, he pulls away from the lot.

"Very funny," she says. She tells him the address of her office. It hurts a bit to talk, but otherwise she feels pretty good. It's amazing, she thinks, how quickly the body heals.

"So, uh, you're one of them surrogate victims, huh? Not sure how I feel about those. More I think about it, more I tend to agree with that lady back there. Maybe the whole business ought to be illegal. Maybe we shouldn't let people like you do what you are doing."

"It would be like it was during Prohibition," Zita says. "A wasted effort. Couldn't stop it then. Can't stop it now."

"I get your point all right, but that's no reason to give up," says the cabby. "Just because you can't get rid of all evil doesn't mean you can't get rid of some of it. You gotta start somewhere, don't you think? Gotta try. Otherwise, where would we be? You know, society. Culture."

"I never thought of it like that," she says. There's no point in arguing with the cabby. She could make him feel bad by telling him that she makes a hundred times what he does, maybe then he would understand, or at least think he did.

They drive on, painfully silent like they are in a room where someone is expected to die. The cabby lets her out in the alley and stays seated behind the wheel.

She braces the flowers, between her good hip and the car door, gives the cabby a big enough tip to make him blush.

"Been nice talking to you," she says, then opens the door and steps out.

"Likewise," answers the cabby. Unlike her, he probably means it. He pulls away without waiting to see if she can walk to her building.

Zita leaves the flower arrangement on the stoop for the homeless lady who lives by the trash bin. She tucks the last of her money inside the card.

She manages to climb up the steps to her place, where she plans to sleep until her prescription for pain runs dry. She hangs the CLOSED sign on the door. She's exhausted. Maybe by next week she'll be ready to listen to her messages, choose her next job. Something easy, mindless. A prank or some simple humiliation. Popcorn.

It feels good to be home. In her "kitchen" she pours a cheap bourbon into a chipped coffee cup that says WORLD'S GREATEST MOM. She doesn't much like the stuff because it burns, but she can't see paying extra just to get something that goes down smooth. With the door that leads to her office closed she can hardly hear the phone ring. When it keeps on ringing, she figures out that the answering machine is full. They've got a lot of nerve calling the minute she gets out of the hospital. Let them wait.

Zita pours herself another shot. It's like drinking lukewarm fire and doesn't quite do the trick. She has another drink, but the phone is still ringing and the only way to make it stop is to pull out the plug.

Even if no one else can understand the why of it, Zita knows with all her heart that being a professional victim is the right thing to do.

So the protestors think she should stop. She has no use for the rhetoric of do-gooders. What do they know? She is a professional victim. No matter what she does she's going to suffer for the rest of her fucking life in ways no one can even imagine. Her baby is dead; she has no choice but to suffer. Assholes like the doctor and the nurse and the cabby and the zealot with her sign — they just want her to give it away for free.

Epilogue from
Parable of the Talents

OCTAVIA E. BUTLER

Octavia E. Butler's first published story appeared in 1971 in an anthology of work by members of the Clarion Science Fiction Writers' Workshop, but she did not begin to make her mark on the field until the publication of her first novel, *Patternmaster,* in 1976, the first of a series of related books. She won a Hugo in 1984 for her short story "Speech Sounds," and a year later took both the Hugo and Nebula Awards for her novelette "Bloodchild." Her Nebula-winning novel *Parable of the Talents* is the second volume in a series dealing with mankind's colonization of the stars; the first book was *Parable of the Sower* (1993). More are planned. She was raised in the Los Angeles area and lives now in Seattle.

Of the *Parable* books she says, "I wanted to keep everything as realistic as I could. I didn't want any powers, any kind of magic or fantastical elements. Even the empathy is not real—it's delusional. I used religion because it seems to me it's something we can never get away from. I've met science fiction people who say, 'Oh, well, we're going to outgrow it,' and I don't believe that for one moment. It seems that religion has kept us focused and helped us to do any number of very difficult things, from building pyramids and cathedrals to holding together coun-

tries, in some instances. I'm not saying it's a force for *good*—
it's just a force. So why not use it to get ourselves to the stars?"

from *Earthseed: The Books of the Living*
by Lauren Oya Olamina

Earthseed is adulthood.
It's trying our wings,
Leaving our mother,
Becoming men and women.

We've been children,
Fighting for the full breasts,
The protective embrace,
The soft lap.
Children do this.
But Earthseed is adulthood.

Adulthood is both sweet and sad.
It terrifies.
It empowers.
We are men and women now,
We are Earthseed.
And the Destiny of Earthseed
Is to take root among the stars.

Uncle Marc was, in the end, my only family.

I never saw my adoptive parents again. I sent them money when they were older and in need, and I hired people to look after them, but I never went back to them. They did their duty toward me and I did mine toward them.

My mother, when I finally met her, was still a drifter. She was immensely rich — or at least Earthseed was immensely rich. But she had no home of her own—not even a rented apartment. She drifted between the homes of her many friends and supporters, and between the many Earthseed communities that she had established or encouraged in the United States, Canada, Mexico, and Brazil. And she went on teaching, preaching, fund-raising, and spreading her political influence. I met her when she visited a New York Earthseed community in the Adirondacks — a place called Red Spruce.

In fact, she went to Red Spruce to rest. She had been traveling and speaking steadily for several months, and she needed a place where she could be quiet and think. I know this because it was what people kept telling me when I tried to reach her. The community protected her privacy so well that for a while, I was afraid I might never get to see her. I'd read that she usually traveled with only one or two acolytes and, sometimes, a bodyguard, but now it seemed that everyone in the community had decided to guard her.

By then, I was thirty-four, and I wanted very much to meet her. My friends and Uncle Marc's housekeeper had told me how much I looked like this charismatic, dangerous, heathen cult leader. I had paid no attention until, in researching Lauren Olamina's life, I discovered that she had had a child, a daughter, and that daughter had been abducted from an early Earthseed community called Acorn. The community, according to Olamina's official biography, had been destroyed by Jarret's Crusaders back in the 2030s. Its men and women had been enslaved for over a year by the Crusaders, and all the prepubescent children had been abducted. Most had never been seen again.

The Church of Christian America had denied this and sued Olamina and Earthseed back in the 2040s when Olamina's charge first came to their attention. The church was still powerful, even though Jarret was dead by then. The rumors were that Jarret, after his single term as President, drank himself to death. A coalition of angry businesspeople, protesters against the Al-Can War, and champions of the First Amendment worked to defeat him for reelection in 2036. They won by exposing some of the earliest Christian American witch burnings. It seems that during the early years of the Pox between 2015 and 2019, Jarret himself took part in singling out sinners and burning them alive. The chaos of the Pox had been both the excuse and the cover for these lynchings. Jarret and his friends had burned accused prostitutes, drug dealers, and junkies. Also, in their enthusiasm, they burned innocent people — people who had nothing to do with the sex trade or with drugs. When that happened, Jarret and his people covered their "mistakes" with denials, threats, terror, and occasional payoffs to bereaved families. Uncle

Marc researched this for himself several years ago, and he says it's true — true, sad, wrong, and in the end, irrelevant. He says Jarret's teachings were right even if the man himself did wrong.

Anyway, the Church of Christian America sued Olamina for her "false" accusations. She countersued. Then, suddenly, without explanation, CA dropped its suit and settled with her, paying her an unspecified but reputedly vast sum of money. I was still a kid growing up with my adoptive parents when all this happened, and I heard nothing about it. Years later, when I began to research Earthseed and Olamina, I didn't know what to think.

I phoned Uncle Marc and asked him, point-blank, whether there was any possibility that this woman was my mother.

On my phone's tiny monitor, Uncle Marc's face froze, then seemed to sag. He suddenly looked much older than his fifty-four years. He said, "I'll talk to you about this when I get home." And he broke the connection. He wouldn't take my calls after that. He had never refused my calls before. Never.

Not knowing what else to do, where else to turn, I checked the nets to see where Lauren Olamina might be speaking or organizing. To my surprise, I learned that she was resting at Red Spruce, less than a hundred kilometers from where I was.

And all of a sudden, I had to see her.

I didn't try to phone her, didn't try to reach her by using Uncle Marc's well-known name or my own name as a creator of several popular Dreamasks. I just showed up at Red Spruce, rented a room at their guesthouse, and began trying to find her. Earthseed doesn't bother with much formality. Anyone can visit its communities and rent a room at a guesthouse. Visitors came to see relatives who were members, came to attend Gathering or other ceremonies, even came to join Earthseed and arrange to begin their probationary first year.

I told the manager of the guesthouse that I thought I might be a relative of Olamina's, and asked him if he could tell me how I might make an appointment to speak with her. I asked him because I had heard people call him "Shaper" and I recognized that from my research as a title of respect akin to "reverend" or "minister." If he was the community's minister, he might be able to introduce me to Olamina himself.

Perhaps he could have, but he refused. Shaper Olamina was very tired, and not to be bothered, he told me. If I wanted to meet her, I should attend one of her Gatherings or phone her headquarters in Eureka, California, and arrange an appointment.

I had to hang around the community for three days before I could find anyone willing to take my message to her. I didn't see her. No one would even tell me where she was staying within the community. People protected her from me courteously but firmly. Then all of a sudden, the wall around her gave way. I met one of her acolytes, and he took my message to her.

My messenger was a thin, brown-haired young man who said his name was Edison Balter. I met him in the guesthouse dining room one morning as we each sat alone eating bagels and drinking apple cider. I pounced on him as someone I hadn't pestered yet. I had no idea at that time that the Balter name was dear to my mother, that this man was the adopted son of one of her best friends. I was only relieved that someone was listening to me, not closing one more door in my face.

"I'm her aide this trip," he told me. "She says I'm just about ready to go out on my own, and the idea scares the hell out of me. What name shall I give her?"

"Asha Vere."

"Oh? Are you the Asha Vere who does Dreamasks?"

I nodded.

"Nice work. I'll tell her. Do you want to put her in one of your Masks? You know, you look a lot like her—like a softer version of her." And he was gone. He talked fast and moved very fast, but somehow didn't really seem to be in a hurry. He didn't look anything like Olamina himself, but there was a similarity. I found that I liked him at once, just as I'd found myself liking her when I read about her. Another likable cultist. I got the feeling that Red Spruce, a clean, pretty mountain community, was nothing but a seductive nest of snakes.

Then Edison Balter came back and told me he would take me to her.

She was somewhere in her fifties—fifty-eight, I remembered from my reading. She was born way back in 2009, before the Pox. My god, she was old. But she didn't look old. Even though her black hair was streaked with gray, she looked big and strong and, in spite of her pleasant, welcoming expression, just a little frightening. She was also a little taller than me and maybe more angular. She looked...not hard, but as though she could look hard with just the smallest change of expression. She looked like someone I wouldn't want to get on the wrong side of. And, yes, even in spite of all that, she looked like me.

She and I just stood looking at one another for a long time. After a while, she came up to me, took my left hand, and turned it palm-down to touch the two little moles I have just below the knuckle of my index finger. My impulse was to pull away, but I managed to keep still.

She stared at the moles for a moment, then said, "Do you have another mark, a kind of jagged dark patch just here?" She touched a place on my left shoulder near my neck—a place covered by my blouse.

This time, I did step away from her. I didn't mean to, but I just don't like to be touched. Not even by a stranger who might be my mother. I said, "I have a birthmark like that, yes."

"Yes," she whispered, and she went on looking at me. After a moment, she said, "Sit down. Sit here with me. You are my child, my daughter. I know you are."

I sat in a chair instead of sharing the couch with her. She was open and welcoming, and somehow, that made me want all the more to draw back.

"Have you only just found out?" she asked.

I nodded, tried to speak, and found myself stumbling and stammering. "I came here because I thought...maybe...because I looked up information about you and I was curious. I mean, I read about Earthseed, and people said I looked like you, and...well, I knew I was adopted, so I wondered."

"So you had adoptive parents. Were they good to you? What's your life been like? Where did you grow up? What do you...?" She stopped, drew a deep breath, covered her face with both hands for a moment, shook her head, then gave a short laugh. "I want to know everything! I can't believe it's you. I...." Tears began to stream down her dark, broad face. She leaned toward me, and I knew she wanted to hug me. She hugged people. She touched people. But then, she hadn't been raised by my adoptive parents.

I looked away from her and shifted around, trying to get comfortable in my chair, in my skin, in my newfound identity. "Can we do a gene print?" I asked.

"Yes. Today. Now." She took a phone from her pocket and called someone. No more than a minute later, a woman dressed all in blue came in carrying a small black plastic case. She drew a small amount of blood from each of us and checked it with the diagnostic unit in her case. The unit wasn't much bigger than Olamina's phone, but in less than a minute, it spat out a pair of gene prints. They were rough and incomplete, but even I could see their many differences and their many unmistakable identical points.

"You're close relatives," the woman said. "Anyone would guess that just from looking at you, but this confirms it."

"We're mother and daughter," Olamina said.

"Yes," the woman in blue agreed. She was my mother's age or older — a Puerto Rican by her accent. She had not a strand of gray in her black hair, but her face was lined and old. "I had heard, Shaper, that you had a daughter who was lost. And now you've found her."

"She found me," my mother said.

"God is Change," the woman said, and closed her black case. She hugged my mother before she left us. She looked at me, but didn't hug me.

"Welcome," she said to me softly in Spanish, and then again, "God is Change." And she was gone.

"Shape God," my mother whispered in a response that sounded both reflexive and religious.

Then we talked.

"I had parents," I said. "Kayce and Madison Alexander. I didn't... We didn't get along. I haven't seen them since I turned eighteen. They said, 'If you leave without getting married, don't come back!' So I didn't. Then I found Uncle Marc, and I finally had —"

Abruptly, my mother stood up and stared down at me with an expression gone cold and closed and icily intense. She shut me out with that look — a bird-of-prey kind of look. I wondered whether this was what she was really like. Did she only pretend to be warm and open to deceive her public?

"When?" she demanded, and her tone was as cold as her expression. "When did you find Marc? When did you learn that he was your uncle? How did you find out? Tell me!"

I stared at her. She stared back for a moment, then she began to pace. She walked to a window, faced it for several seconds, staring out at the mountains. Then she came back to look down at me with what I could only think of as warmer, more human eyes.

"Please tell me about your life," she said. "You probably know something about mine because so much has been written. But I know nothing about yours. Please tell me."

Irrationally, I didn't want to. I wanted to get away from her. She was one of those people who sucked you in, made you like her before you could get to know her, and only then let you see what she was really like. She had millions of people convinced that they were going to fly off to the stars. How much money had she taken from them while they waited for the ship to Alpha Centauri? My god, I didn't want to like her. I wanted the ugly persona I had glimpsed to be what she really was. I wanted to despise her.

Instead, I told her the story of my life.

Then we had dinner together, just her and me. A woman who might have been a servant, a bodyguard, or the lady of the house brought in a tray for us.

Then my mother told me the story of my birth, my father's death, and my abduction when I was only a few months old. Hearing about it from her wasn't like reading the impersonal account that I had studied. I listened and cried. I couldn't help it.

"What did Marc tell you?" she asked.

I hesitated, not sure what to say. In the end, I told the truth just because I couldn't think of a decent lie. "He said you had died—that both my mother and father were dead."

She groaned.

"He . . . he took care of me," I said. "He saw to it that I got to go to college, and that I had a good place to live. He and I . . . well, we're a family. We didn't have anyone before we found one another."

She just looked at me.

"I don't know why he told you we were dead. Maybe he was just . . . lonely. I don't know. We got along, he and I, right from the first. I still live in one of his houses. I can afford a place of my own now, but like I said, we're family." I paused, then said something I had never admitted before. "You know, I never felt that anyone loved me until he loved me before I met him. And I guess I never loved anyone until he loved me. He made it . . . safe for me to love him back."

"Your father and I both loved you," she said. "We had tried for two years to have a baby. We worried about his age. We worried about the way the world was—all in chaos. But we wanted you so much. And when you were born, we loved you more than you can imagine. When you were taken, and your father was killed . . . I felt as though I'd died myself. I tried so hard for so long to find you."

I didn't know what to say to that. I shrugged uncomfortably. She hadn't found me. And Uncle Marc had. I wondered just how hard she had really looked.

"I didn't even know whether you were still alive," she said. "I wanted to believe you were, but I didn't know. I got involved in a lawsuit with Christian America back in the forties, and I tried to force them to tell me what had happened to you. They claimed that any record there may have been of you was lost in a fire at the Pelican Bay Children's Home years before."

Had they said that? I thought they might have. They would have said almost anything to avoid giving up evidence of their abductions—and giving a Christian American child back to a heathen cult leader. But still, "Uncle Marc says he found me when I was two or three years old," I said. "But he saw that I had decent, Christian American parents and he thought it would be best for me to stay with them, undisturbed." I probably shouldn't have said that. I wasn't sure why I had said it.

She got up and began to walk again—quick, angry pacing, prowling the room. "I never thought he would do that to me," she said. "I never thought he hated me enough to do a thing like that. I never thought he could hate *anyone* that much. I saved him from slavery! I saved his worthless life, goddamnit!"

"He doesn't hate you," I said. "I'm sure he doesn't. I've never known him to hate anyone. He thought he was doing right."

"Don't defend him," she whispered. "I know you love him, but don't defend him to me. I loved him myself, and see what he's done to me—and to you."

"You're a cult leader," I said. "He's a Christian American minister. He—"

"I don't care. I've spoken with him hundreds of times since he's found you, and he said nothing. Nothing!"

"He doesn't have any children," I said. "I don't think he ever will. But I'm like a daughter to him. He's like a father to me."

She stopped her pacing and stared down at me with that frightening, cold, contained intensity.

I stood up, looked around for my jacket, found it, and put it on.

"No!" she said. "No, don't go." All the ice and rage went out of her. "Please don't go. Not yet."

But I needed to go. She is an overwhelming person, and I needed to get away from her.

"All right," she said when I headed for the door. "But you can always come to me. Come back tomorrow. Come back whenever you want to. We have so much time to make up for. My door is always open to you, Larkin. Always."

I stopped and looked back at her, realizing that she had called me by the name she had given to her baby daughter so long ago.

"Asha," I said, looking back at her. "My name is Asha Vere."

She looked confused. Her face seemed to sag the way Uncle Marc's had when I phoned him to ask about her. She looked so hurt and sad that I couldn't stop myself from feeling sorry for her.

"Asha," she whispered. "My door is always open to you, Asha. Always."

The next day, Uncle Marc arrived, filled with fear and despair.

"I'm sorry," he said to me as soon as he saw me. "I was so happy when I found you after you'd left your parents. I was so glad to be able to help you with your education. I guess . . . I guess I had been alone for so long that I just couldn't stand to share you with anyone."

My mother would not see him. He came to me almost in tears because he had tried to see her and she had refused. He tried several more times, and over and over again she sent people out to tell him to go away.

I went back home with him. I was angry with him, but even angrier with her, somehow. I loved him more than I'd ever loved anyone no matter what he had done, and she was hurting him. I didn't know whether I would ever see her again. I didn't know whether I should. I didn't even know whether I wanted to.

My mother lived to be eighty-one.

She never stopped working. For Earthseed, she used herself up several times over, speaking, training, politicking, writing, establishing schools that boarded and educated promising students, rich and poor alike. She raised money and directed it into areas of study that she believed would bring fulfillment of the Earthseed Destiny closer. She sent students to universities and helped them to fulfill whatever potential she saw in them.

All that she did, she did for Earthseed. I saw her again occasionally, but Earthseed was her first "child," and in some ways, her only "child."

She was planning a lecture tour when her heart stopped just after her eighty-first birthday. She saw the first shuttles leave for the first starship which had been assembled partly on the moon and partly in orbit. I was not on any of the shuttles, of course. Nor was Uncle Marc, and neither of us has children.

But many of her friends—her followers—went to the ship. They, in particular, were her family. All Earthseed was her family. We never really were, Uncle Marc and I. She never really needed us, so we never let ourselves need her.

Unhidden Agendas, Unfinished Dialogues
1999 IN SCIENCE FICTION

GARY K. WOLFE

Long before the calendar made it real, 1999 was an important year for science fiction and science fiction writers, a year that came to us already inhabited by the shadows of science fictional futures. Nineteen ninety-nine was the year that was to have seen the first ill-fated expedition to Mars in Ray Bradbury's *The Martian Chronicles*, New York collapsing under the weight of population in Harry Harrison's *Make Room!, Make Room!*, the asteroid Icarus threatening to collide with earth in Gregory Benford's *In the Ocean of Night* and another asteroid called the Stone suddenly appearing in orbit in Greg Bear's *Eon*, tabloid aliens invading Earth in John Kessel's *Good News from Outer Space*. Joe Haldeman's Forever War had already been under way for some years by 1999, and according to any number of scenarios, the newly tribalized world spent the year trying to recover from the civilization-ending effects of an all-out nuclear holocaust. Even one of the classic bad TV shows of the 1970s was *Space: 1999*, a title that always suggested a marked-down version of *2001*, though the program never quite attained even that status. (Legend has it that one line of dialogue from the show has a character saying, "We're sitting on the biggest bomb in the universe!" but I've never checked this out.) Nineteen ninety-nine was, in other words, one of the iconic years in science fiction, the latest possible date in which writers earlier in the century could set a story that seemed psychically linked to their own present by that familiar "19—."

And it was, according to various past prognosticators on the state of science fiction itself (including some in these very Nebula Awards annuals), a time when the field was to die out entirely, or finally to gain overdue recognition as the *only* literature worth reading, or to merge indistinguishably into the mainstream, or to surrender once and for all to a rising flood of dumbed-down tie-ins and novelizations of movies, games, and TV programs that, one would have thought, left little margin for dumbing down. But the fact is that like most years, 1999 was neither the best of times nor the worst of times for science fiction, neither the longed-for renaissance nor the dreaded apocalypse. A lot of rough beasts may have been slouching about, some of them seeking mergers, but none quite made it to Bethlehem. And the nature of those beasts depends a lot on the angle from which you view them.

Agendas

More than in most literary neighborhoods, debates over the state of science fiction and fantasy in any given year tend to reveal a variety of different agendas and alliances — none particularly subtle — and depending on whom you listen to, any given year may be at once a disaster and a triumph. Often, the gloomiest assessments may be found in what I'll call the Industry Agenda, heard mostly from professional writers and editors, who often tend to see the state of the field in terms of various corporate acquisitions and mergers, shifting distribution systems, and the growth of chain bookstore and on-line merchandising. The big stories here in 1999 included the acquisition of William Morrow and Avon by HarperCollins and the attempted (but later abandoned) purchase of the book distributor Ingram by Barnes & Noble. This followed close upon the acquisition of Random House by Bertelsmann and the Penguin Putnam merger of 1998. The fear, of course, is that the consolidation of so many different publishers, many with their own science fiction lines, will inevitably lead to a tightening up of available outlets for quality science fiction — both in terms of publishers and bookstores — and a lower level of risk taking on the part of publishers and editors driven by heightened imperatives to guarantee predictable sales. Equally important, such shakeups can create chaos in the lives of important and influential editors and publishing executives, even as they remain invisible to the average science fiction reader. Whether these various upheavals in the state of science fiction as an industry have any real effect on the kinds of literature that get written, published, and distributed, however, remains a largely unproven speculation, and one whose validity may only become clear to literary and cultural historians of the future.

Next, there is the Readership Agenda, which concerns itself with questions of who reads science fiction, how new readers are developed, and whether readers are being leached away by competing media, media-related fiction, and fat but unchallenging formula trilogies. Some of the concerns here overlap the Industry Agenda, such as the fear that the major short fiction markets are hemorrhaging readers at an alarming rate; by 1999, the combined paid circulation of the three major science fiction magazines—*Asimov's, The Magazine of Fantasy and Science Fiction,* and *Analog*—stood at just over half what it had been a decade earlier, in 1989, while the oldest magazine of all, *Amazing,* struggled along in yet another shaky new incarnation and one of the newest, *Science Fiction Age,* announced that its last issue would appear early in 2000. By the standards of most small literary magazines that provide the bulk of mainstream short fiction outlets, even these reduced circulation figures of 30,000 to 50,000 copies a month would seem astonishing, but science fiction continues to measure itself not against other short fiction markets but against a perceived golden age of magazines, when periodicals defined and dominated the field. The belief, I suppose—again largely untested—is that the magazines provide not only a proving ground for new writers but also a kind of training academy for new readers, who learn the protocols, conventions, and ongoing thematic dialogues that have long given science fiction its initiatory, almost cloistered identity. Thus, the argument goes, if the magazines dry up, where will new readers go to get initiated?

It's an argument that's hard to support empirically, since new readers do tend to show up. As Gardner Dozois pointed out in introducing his annual *Year's Best Science Fiction* anthology covering 1999, a surprising number of readers and even convention-goers aren't even aware that the magazines exist. If science fiction writers and publishers depended entirely upon the magazines to develop new readers, they would likely experience something very much like those visions at the more apocalyptic end of the Industry Agenda. But the Readership Agenda does raise good questions. In addition to the magazines, one presumed source for earlier generations of science fiction "recruits" were the various series of juvenile novels from major SF writers—Robert Heinlein, Isaac Asimov, Andre Norton, etc. Despite the occasional efforts of a Gregory Benford or a Charles Sheffield to revive the Heinlein juvenile—presumably based on the long-accepted nostrum that the Golden Age of Science Fiction Is Twelve—the "juvenile" or young adult market is no longer connected with the adult field in the same way it once was. Kristin Kathryn Rusch once wrote an editorial for *The Magazine of Fantasy and Science Fiction* noting that many of the kids who might once have read such books were now reading R. L. Stine's *Goosebumps* series in truly startling numbers, and she went on to express the hope that such readers might eventually move on to more adult fantasy and science fiction. In 1999, I heard several people express something of the same hope regarding the enormous readership of J. K. Rowling's *Harry Potter* books, the third of which showed up on the Hugo ballot as best novel for that year. But in neither case, Stine or Rowling, has anyone produced any evidence that these readers go anywhere in particular once their trendy obsession has run its course. And to expect that a Stine reader might eventually find his way to a Heinlein, or even to a more literary horror writer like Peter Straub, is a little like expecting Britney Spears fans to suddenly develop a taste for Billie Holiday.

The only really successful writer of juvenile entry-level science fiction to emerge in years is Orson Scott Card, and his novels aren't marketed as juveniles at all. Yet his one major novel of 1999, *Ender's Shadow*, not only returns to the precocious-child-coming-of-age theme of his now-classic *Ender's Game* but recapitulates the plot of that novel almost exactly, except for shifting the point of view to a character who emerges late in the original novel. Like much classic young adult fiction, Card's novels tend to feature heartless adults, schoolyard bullies, and loyal chums, and seem to have an appeal that goes beyond that of most SF designed solely for young readers.

Another concern of the Readership Agenda is reader and writer diversion, or the fear that some would-be readers are diverted from science fiction by various media and gaming books, and that talented writers are tempted to squander their time writing such books. This concern arises

from viewing with alarm best-seller lists in which various franchise prod-
ucts—Star Trek, Star Wars, Forgotten Realms, DragonLance, Mech-
Warrior, etc.—seem to outnumber actual novels made up by actual
people and therefore, presumptively, either draw readers away from
these novels or crowd them off the limited shelf space allotted to the
whole science fiction–fantasy-media complex. Science fiction readers,
and perhaps some science fiction writers tempted by the quick income
promised by tie-ins, are thus effectively being kidnapped from the field.
Again, I'm not at all sure that any hard evidence has been produced to
warrant such alarm. There may indeed be some talented writers who
have forsaken or postponed their own visions in favor of franchise fiction,
but there have always been talented writers in the field who chose to
make money writing pornography, or advertising copy, or travel articles;
it seems that the authors of the various tie-ins are singled out for tut-
tutting not because they have chosen to write something for money but
because that something bears such a close relationship to the science fiction genre itself: If you must hawk watches, son, do it in another neighborhood. And as far as the readers are concerned, I have yet to see any
evidence that a talented fantasy writer like, say, Robert Holdstock has
been forced to helplessly watch from the sidelines as his former readers
begin veering toward the DragonLance racks.

A third agenda, with which I confess only limited familiarity, is the
Fan Agenda, whose concerns are expressed most directly (and often
crudely) in the program items and discussion topics that show up at various conventions that take place around the world every week of the
year. There are, of course, many kinds of fandom, including those devoted only to comics or Star Wars or Terry Pratchett or interactive
games, but for the purposes of this discussion I'm referring to the more
or less traditional core of fans of science fiction literature. This agenda,
year to year, seems mostly to be worried about issues that involve the
consolidation or dissolution of aspects of the science fiction community.
The growing shift of Worldcon programming from "pure" science fiction to gaming and media-related topics is a cause for concern, but novels that reaffirm the initiatory nature of science fiction are causes for
celebration. In 1999, the refurbishing of space opera, most notably in
Vernor Vinge's A *Deepness in the Sky* and Peter Hamilton's massive trilogy that concluded with *The Naked God*, was good news for the Fan

Agenda, as were novels that connected with earlier novels or series — Lois McMaster Bujold's *A Civil Campaign*, Frederik Pohl's *The Far Shore of Time*, Orson Scott Card's *Ender's Shadow*, William Gibson's *All Tomorrow's Parties*, Joe Haldeman's *Forever Free* (far more clearly a sequel to the classic *Forever War* than was Haldeman's Hugo-winning *Forever Peace*, which more complexly counterpointed the themes of that earlier novel). Gene Wolfe's *On Blue's Waters* was also a very successful continuation of a series, but I suspect that Wolfe fans are a rather special subset and perhaps less enamored of the familiar and the accessible than most. Other significant series that were inaugurated or continued, but not concluded in 1999, included C. J. Cherryh's *Precursor* and Paul J. McAuley's "Confluence" series, whose middle book was *Ancients of Days*.

Another subset of fandom, concerned with the survival of classic science fiction texts or classic writers, would readily celebrate (and can in part take credit for) the publication of several small-press archival collections during 1999 — *The Compleat Boucher, The Essential Hal Clement* (vol. 1), and the Charles Harness omnibus *Rings* from NESFA Press; *Baby Is Three: The Complete Stories of Theodore Sturgeon* (vol. 6) from North Atlantic; A. E. van Vogt's *Futures Past* from Tachyon Publications; and *The Metal Man and Others: The Collected Stories of Jack Williamson* (vol. 1) from Haffner. To these might be added *The SFWA Grand Masters* (vol. 1), edited by Frederik Pohl for Tor, and *My Favorite Science Fiction Story*, edited by Martin H. Greenberg for DAW. The Pohl is the first of a series of three anthologies designed to preserve and promote the short work of the winners of SFWA's lifetime achievement award, including (in the 1999 volume) Heinlein, Simak, Leiber, de Camp, Norton, and Williamson; the Greenberg invites leading contemporary authors to select favorite science fiction stories from the past. A related nonfiction title is Frank Robinson's gorgeously produced *Science Fiction of the Twentieth Century*, which broke no new ground as literary history but served as a colorful reminder of the glories of the pulp era. All are indeed causes for celebration, but the flip side of this coin is that fewer and fewer novels from these same classic periods find their way back into print. Even here there were signs of encouragement, however: Vintage reprinted four Sturgeon novels during the year in quality paperback editions, including the classics *More than Human* and *Venus Plus X*, and Tor, at the end of the year, reprinted Williamson's werewolf classic *Darker Than You Think*. Tor also published *The Fantasies of Robert A. Heinlein*, a reminder that SF's most famous author was more versatile than many suspect, while a handful of more traditional Heinlein titles were reprinted by Pocket Books (*The Menace from Earth*) and Baen (*Sixth Column, Revolt in 2100, Methuselah's Children*). The fear that classic science fiction — those great seductive entry-level novels that brought generations of new readers into the field — may disappear from the bookstores is another anxiety that has never been fully borne out in practice, though as teachers of science fiction courses can attest, the unreliability of a particular book to be in print at a particular time can make it seem true; the science fiction backlist is certainly not what it once was, but then neither is any other backlist.

Finally, we come to what I will call, despite its *belletristic* overtones, the Literary Agenda. This is simply what's happening in the literature itself, and while it may well be related to all the other agendas, it is never fully subsumed by any of them. Some years ago, writing in a "symposium" on the state of science fiction for *Nebula Awards 30*, edited by Pamela Sargent, John Kessel speculated on what would happen if the entire social and economic infrastructure of SF collapsed overnight — no magazines, no conventions, no SF lines from publishers, no movies or TV shows. Would SF still exist at all? Kessel contended that something very much resembling SF would quickly arise to fill the needs and provide the narrative opportunities available only in this field — perhaps not called "science fiction," to be sure, and lacking in the kind of genre self-referentiality that has long characterized much of the field, but featuring many of what we have come to regard as defining features of SF. Kessel notes that some actual SF novels (he mentions Michael Bishop's *Brittle Innings*) would hardly be any different in such a world, while others are so dependent on awareness of genre conventions that they couldn't exist at all. Things were much the same in 1999. There is no easy way, based solely on market forces or readership patterns or genre expectations, to predict or account for two of 1999's most striking and talked-about novels, Neal Stephenson's *Cryptonomicon* and Greg Egan's *Teranesia*. The Stephenson novel, which counterpoints the prehistory of computer science among the cryptographers at Bletchley Park during World War II with a contemporary tale of efforts to establish a data haven in Southeast Asia — linking the two tales in complex and ingenious ways—is a crossover novel that led to some of the year's most stimulating debates on the nature of science fiction. A terrific intellectual adventure story with enough trendy appeal to edge onto a few best-seller lists, the novel is in the view of many not science fiction at all, while others (myself included) think of it as "non-SF SF," a work that makes free and deliberate use of science fiction tropes and structures and treats its settings as though they were wholly invented, while adhering rigorously to both historical and technological plausibility. The Australian writer Greg Egan's entire career, on the other hand, pretty much follows in the tradition of cutting-edge hard SF, and by the end of the decade he had emerged as one of the most distinctive and influential voices in the field, known for his rigorously worked-out yet conceptually stunning novels such as *Distress* and *Permutation City. Teranesia,* however, was something of a change of pace for Egan; beginning as a deeply felt tale of an orphaned brother and sister raised on a remote Indonesian island, it shifts tone radically into an acute satire of academic trendiness, then returns to the island of the title to unravel a genuine scientific mystery.

Dialogues

At one end, the Literary Agenda consists of what science fiction writers would write about if there were no "science fiction," or what certain mainstream novelists sometimes do write about while professing ignorance that such a thing as science fiction exists, let alone acknowledging the possibility that their own work may be part of it. But in the main, the Literary Agenda is the continuing locus of science fiction's ongoing dialogues with itself and with other cultural discourses, including other genres. Several of these dialogues were particularly lively in 1999. One deals with the relationship of science fiction to the suspense thriller—a genre traditionally defined more by its pacing and structure than by its content, and thus amenable to science fiction themes as well as the more common tropes of espionage, crime, horror, and lawyers. One of the nagging questions in this dialogue is why, if brand-name thriller writers can co-opt science fiction ideas and consistently land on best-seller lists, shouldn't science fiction writers be equally successful in co-opting the tropes of the thriller? The obvious answer, it would seem, is simply that they lack the mass-market brand names, or maybe are just the wrong brand. As 1999 began, a singularly inept science fiction thriller by James Patterson, *Where the Wind Blows*, rested comfortably on the *New York Times* best-seller list, and by the end of the year another, Michael Crichton's *Timeline*, had landed on the same list. In between, what may have been the best-selling science fictionoid title of the entire year, mercifully almost invisible to most SF readers because of its market category, was *Assassins*, the sixth installment of the fundamentalist "Left Behind" epic of the Rapture by Tim LaHaye and Jerry B. Jenkins, which passed the million mark in sales within weeks of its release in August. If novels like Stephenson's *Cryptonomicon* represent science fictional thinking without the familiar science fiction tropes, books like these show how a novel can be loaded with such tropes and still not be, conceptually, a work of science fiction.

Meanwhile, two far superior thrillers with genuine intellectual substance, Greg Bear's *Darwin's Radio* and Frank M. Robinson's *Waiting*—both dealing with aspects of evolution and evolutionary theory—enjoyed solid reviews but a decidedly more modest level of success. *Darwin's Radio* in particular, with its bold ideas and a genuine scientific mystery at its center, may be one of the most successful of all recent efforts to join hard SF concepts with the pacing and point of view of the thriller genre and the emotional sophistication of the mainstream novel of character. Similarly, Walter Jon Williams's large-scale earthquake novel *The Rift*—which turns unexpectedly into a thoughtful exploration of race and class in America—and Dan Simmons's spirited Hemingway tribute *The Crook Factory* moved these authors into the territory of the disaster epic and the historical espionage novel, respectively.

Another dialogue that has been notably active in the science fiction world for the better part of four decades is the dialogue between feminism and science fiction, which may have reached some sort of milestone during the year with the publication of Suzy McKee Charnas's *The Conqueror's Child*, the fourth (and presumably final) novel in the "Holdfast" series that began twenty-six years earlier with *Walk to the End of the World*. Taken as a whole, this series spans nearly the entire history of contemporary feminist science fiction, the first volume predating even such classics as Joanna Russ's *The Female Man* and Marge Piercy's *Woman on the Edge of Time*. During all that time, Charnas has

never compromised the tough, sometimes brutal tone of her postapoc-
alyptic saga, even as her attitudes toward gender and power relations
have grown deeper and more complex. I'm not entirely certain the same
can be said of Sheri S. Tepper, whose prolific output of engrossing novels with feminist-ecological themes became iconic texts for many readers during the 1990s. Her 1999 entry, *Singer from the Sea*, contained her
usual mix of themes and genres, and even substantial elements of romance, but continued to present male-oriented societies in terms of
sometimes comic excess (one such society in this novel even follows a
philosophy called "Hestonism"). It would amount to an act of shoe-
horning to discuss Elizabeth Hand's elegant aesthetic fantasy *Black
Light* solely in terms of its contribution to the feminist dialogue, or even
in terms of science fiction, but the novel does share the broad theme of
goddess cults and unfairly maligned witches with her earlier *Waking the
Moon*. Finally, two of the more interesting nonfiction books of the year
dealt wholly or in part with issues of feminism and science fiction.
Gwyneth Jones's *Deconstructing the Starships*, a collection of essays, reviews, and speeches that was probably the best critical volume of the
year, contains sharp commentary on Charnas, Tepper, and several other
writers as well as stimulating discussions of the sometimes problematical
role of science in SF and the identity of the writer. Jeanne Cortiel's *Demand My Writing: Joanna Russ / Feminism / Science Fiction*, a somewhat
more torpid academic study, is significant as the first full treatment of an
important author and critic whose work helped to change the nature of
the entire field.

Other long-standing dialogues were also represented by significant
books during the year. The uneasy relationship between near-future SF
and nonfictional futurism — the kind of thing that produces global
warming reports and limits-to-growth statistical projections — underlies
Norman Spinrad's *Greenhouse Summer*, which is also among the most
acerbic and credible satirical novels of the year, as well as some of the
stories in Bruce Sterling's *A Good Old-Fashioned Future*. SF's even more
uneasy relationship with saucer cults and various paranoid conspiracy
mavens is touched upon by another of the year's best satirical books, Rudy
Rucker's novel-in-disguise *Saucer Wisdom*. A dialogue that SF readily
embraces, however, involves the wired information subculture and dates
from the time when it *was* still only a subculture, way back in 1984, when

William Gibson's *Neuromancer* officially launched what for a while was called cyberpunk. In 1999, *All Tomorrow's Parties*, Gibson's final novel of the sequence that began with *Virtual Light* (calling it a trilogy might be misleading, since there is no single narrative arc), showed Gibson continuing to grow more broadly science fictional in his thinking while developing a greater sensitivity to character, all without losing the glittering inventiveness and virtuoso use of language that have long been his trademarks. Stephenson's *Cryptonomicon* is also centrally related to this dialogue, as is — in a conceptually very different way — Christopher Priest's strong novel of mass murder and virtual reality in an English village, *The Extremes*. Finally, science fiction's recent ongoing dialogue on the future and uses of the planet Mars — which has included important novels by Greg Bear, Ben Bova, Paul McAuley, and most notably Kim Stanley Robinson — was joined again this year by Robinson with *The Martians*, a collection of stories set in the Mars of his famous trilogy, by Larry Niven in his collection-plus-new-short-novel *Rainbow Mars*, and by Gregory Benford with the novel *The Martian Race*.

And there is, as always, science fiction's dialogue with its own earlier versions of itself, always evident in the novels and stories of Stephen Baxter, even as they occasionally threaten to spiral out of control. Baxter, who has written a sequel to *The Time Machine*, collaborated with Arthur C. Clarke, written vast Stapledonian epics that stretch to the end of time, and produced stories that seem intended as deliberate tributes to James Blish, is acutely aware of his relationship with SF traditions, and has been a leader in SF's recent ongoing dialogue with NASA over what should have been done since the 1960s. All of these factors play a role in *Manifold: Time*, a novel involving mutant children, genetically enhanced squids, imminent global catastrophes, and alien artifacts. It isn't Baxter's best novel, but it serves as a virtual catalogue of his major themes. An even more direct example of SF in dialogue with itself is the year's best original anthology, Robert Silverberg's *Far Horizons*, in which eleven writers were invited to contribute new stories set in signature worlds from their earlier work: Joe Haldeman's Forever War universe, Dan Simmons's Hyperion, Ursula Le Guin's Ekumen, Frederik Pohl's Heechee, etc. Most of the authors took the opportunity quite seriously and produced strong new work (though some of the stories seem only arbitrarily placed in their preexisting settings). One contributor, Greg

Bear, reached back not only to his earlier artificial universe called The Way but to a strange novel from SF's early years, William Hope Hodgson's *The Night Land*, for inspiration.

Other novels that seemed especially notable in terms of their relationship to SF traditions included Robert Charles Wilson's *Bios*, John Barnes's *Finity*, Jamil Nasir's *Tower of Dreams*, and Susan R. Matthews's *Hour of Judgment*. First novels of note included Jan Lars Jensen's *Shiva 3000*, set in a far-future India; Paul Levinson's *The Silk Code* (drawn from stories Levinson had been publishing for some years, and offering the year's best merger of SF with the mystery story); Marc Matz's *Nocturne for a Dangerous Man*; and Peter Watts's *Starfish*.

There is also a strong international flavor in science fiction's dialogue with itself, represented in 1999 not only by established British authors Baxter, Priest, and McAuley but also by writers only becoming familiar to American audiences, notably Ken MacLeod (*The Cassini Division*) and Simon Ings (*Headlong*) from Britain, and Stephen Dedman (*Foreign Bodies*) and Sean McMullen (*Souls in the Great Machine*) from Australia. Australian SF was also distinguished during the year by the publication of a not-quite-finished posthumous novel by George Turner (*Down There in Darkness*), a substantial overview anthology (*Centaurus*, edited by David G. Hartwell and Damien Broderick), and an informative if not entirely satisfactory history of Australian SF (*Strange Constellations: A History of Australian Science Fiction*, by Russell Blackford, Van Ikin, and Sean McMullen). Canadian SF and fantasy was also represented by two substantial anthologies: *Northern Suns*, edited by Hartwell and Glenn Grant, and a new installment in the *Tesseracts* series, edited by Paula Johanson and Jean-Louis Trudel.

The single-author story collection, which has always been one of the field's best venues for authors exploring and responding to each other's ideas, continued to survive in 1999 and even to thrive, despite dire predictions that story collections would sooner or later dry up because of their sheer lack of marketability compared to novels. What has happened instead is that this important aspect of SF has become a niche for smaller publishers with more focused markets. Tor published John Barnes's compilation of essays *Apostrophes and Apocalypses* and Niven's *Rainbow Mars*, and Bantam Spectra published Robinson's *The Martians*, Connie Willis's enjoyable *Miracle and Other Christmas Stories*, and Bruce Sterling's *A Good Old-Fashioned Future*—probably the most important author collection of the year. But look at where the others come from: Golden Gryphon, with its distinctive Arkham-House style production values, published Robert Reed's *The Dragons of Springplace* (my candidate for the year's *other* most important collection) and Tony Daniel's *The Robot's Twilight Companion*; tiny Cascade Mountain published Bill Johnson's *Dakota Dreamin'* (including his Hugo-winning "We Will Drink a Fish Together"); Nightshade published John Shirley's *Really, Really, Really, Really Weird Stories*; Meisha Merlin published Allen Steele's *Sex and Violence in Zero-G*; something called mp books published Terry Dowling's *Antique Futures*. Even university presses got into the act, with the University Press of New England publishing Kit Reed's *Seven for the Apocalypse*, one of the more striking postmodern literary titles, featuring Reed's surprising biker-nun story "Little Sisters of the Apocalypse"; and the University of Tampa Press publishing Rick Wilber's affecting collection *Where Garagiola Waits and Other Baseball Stories*. And, of course, the Boucher, Williamson, van Vogt, and Sturgeon collections mentioned earlier all came from small presses.

Fantasy

Dialogues of various sorts go on in fantasy as well as in SF, though perhaps less self-consciously, and I should mention at least some of the more important fantasy books of the year. Jonathan Carroll's *The Marriage of Sticks*, allied somewhat to SF themes with its suggestion of alternate worlds, may be his strongest novel to date, while Peter Beagle's *Tamsin* is a tale of a haunted farm featuring Beagle's familiar genius for deep emotions economically expressed. I've already mentioned Hand's *Black Light*, which may be the first fantasy novel to fully take advantage of the eerie undertones of the Warhol media culture of the 1960s, even as it eventually moves the action back to Hand's familiar, haunted Kamensic Village. Lisa Goldstein's *Dark Cities Underground* is an intriguing tale of long-hidden underground societies, intertwined with an even more intriguing tale of a man's troubled relationship with the mother who made him a children's book hero. Fairy-tale motifs were notably transformed in Orson Scott Card's *Enchantment* and Peg Kerr's *The Wild Swans*;

Arthurian material was the basis for Mark Chadbourn's *World's End* and A. A. Attanasio's *The Serpent and the Grail*, the fourth volume in a series.

Historical fantasy was distinctively represented by Michaela Roessner's *The Stars Compel*, a sequel to her earlier Renaissance food fantasy (that's what I said) *The Stars Dispose*; by J. Gregory Keyes's alternate history *A Calculus of Angels* (also a sequel, to *Newton's Cannon*); and by Thomas Harlan's alternate Roman history *The Shadow of Ararat*. Horror may be even further afield from the central purview of this essay, but two literary horror novels deserve particular mention—Thomas M. Disch's *The Sub*, part of his ongoing series of creepy character explorations; and Peter Straub's *Mr. X*, a complex tale of a haunted African American family in southern Illinois that comments shrewdly on the Lovecraft mythos. The Midwestern landscapes of Straub are as distinctive to his work as the myth-drenched West Coast is to James P. Blaylock, who explored it a little more fully than usual in *The Rainy Season*.

Movies

One of science fiction's most uneasy and problematical relationships—I'd hesitate even to call it a dialogue—has to do with movies and television programs that often seem to reprocess decades-old SF ideas and plots while dressing them up in visual effects that would have seemed like dreams come true to the readers of the old pulp magazines or science fiction fans of the 1950s. It's an irony unnoticed by few writers that, while science *fiction* remains a rather limited special-interest genre among readers, science fiction *film* is, historically, the most financially successful of all movie genres; by the end of 1999, in figures unadjusted for inflation, science fiction films accounted for seven of the ten top-grossing titles of all time (the four *Star Wars* films, *E.T.*, *Jurassic Park*, and *Independence Day*). There may be some irony in the fact that, in achieving these astonishing box-office figures, filmmakers turned not to current science fiction writers or concepts but to ideas dating from the pulp era or earlier. As a general rule, one can find the origins of popular science fiction film in the popular science fiction of thirty to fifty years earlier—a cycle of giant insect stories in the 1920s pulps is echoed in a series of giant insect movies in the 1950s, for example, or Philip K. Dick reality-shifting tales of the 1960s begin to show up in reality-shifting films of the 1990s. The most successful example of this is the *Star Wars* franchise itself, which reached its fourth episode in 1999 with the awkwardly titled *Star Wars: Episode One: The Phantom Menace.* The series had always had its root in pulp-era space opera, but *The Phantom Menace* seemed to reach even further back in SF history, evoking boy heroes like Frank Reade and Tom Swift as well as the space cowboys of the pulp era. But except for the novelizations (and the severely overextended tie-in market, which nearly bankrupted one publisher by the end of 1999), the entire *Star Wars* series would hardly look any different if literary science fiction had died out entirely before 1950. (Much the same could be said of earlier hits like *Jurassic Park,* which doesn't add anything to what Arthur Conan Doyle had written in *The Lost World,* or *Independence Day,* which doesn't add anything to H. G. Wells.) This is hardly what one calls a dynamic, creative dialogue.

On the other hand, there have always been films that *do* attempt to reflect aspects of contemporary SF literature, and that sometimes even involve science fiction writers: Wells in *The Shape of Things to Come,* Arthur C. Clarke in *2001: A Space Odyssey,* Philip K. Dick (at least as a source) in *Blade Runner* (which, at least in terms of visual design, is one of the few films to have seemingly had some feedback influence on the literature). The 1999 film that mostly closely fits this category (though it didn't directly involve any science fiction writers that I'm aware of) was *The Matrix,* which borrowed freely from cyberpunk imagery and virtual reality mind games that had been commonplace in the genre since the early 1980s but that had seldom been quite so vividly realized on film. Other virtual-reality-oriented movies of note during the year were *The Thirteenth Floor* and *eXistenZ,* a characteristically loopy David Cronenberg film. The one highly promoted film of the year that did purport to be based on a major science fiction story, *The Bicentennial Man,* bore some vague relation to its Isaac Asimov original (retaining Asimov's unfortunate habit of sentimentalizing robots) but was conceived less as a science fiction story than as a comic vehicle for Robin Williams. Finally, two films worth noting if only because of their relations to early film and TV science fiction were the successful comedy *Galaxy Quest,* at once a

"Hitchhiker's guide"–style SF tall tale and a parody of *Star Trek*, and the less successful *The Astronaut's Wife*, which, despite its portentous tone and A-list stars, was essentially a remake of *I Married a Monster from Outer Space*.

Victorian critics used to speculate on whether fiction did, or could, or should, progress in a manner analogous to that of science and industry, with continual refinement and improvement of technique leading to more powerful and efficient novels and stories than earlier generations were capable of—Walter Scott, say, being a step ahead of earlier romance writers but crude in comparison to Dickens, who in turn was crude compared to George Eliot. It's a silly idea, of course, but one that has never quite died, and Donald Barthelme once satirized a version of it in a story about how new, more efficiently made Japanese short stories were driving the American product off the market. Some form of this question almost inevitably underlies any discussion of what happened in a particular year in a particular genre like science fiction: Are we getting any better at writing this stuff, or reading it, or making movies? Or have the peak times passed, and we're left recycling these same strange old toys from the attic? It's largely because of such questions that I've long objected to year-in-review essays like this, even as I go on writing them. But if one gets past the various agendas that tend to skew our view of what happens in a given year, past the ideological dialogues such as those I've mentioned here, one can always find the Dialogue, the ongoing set of mechanisms by which science fiction relates to itself, to literature, and to the culture at large. In 1999, this Dialogue remained incomplete, unstable, at times incoherent, often contradictory, but never silent. This, I think, is not a bad thing. Science fiction may well be as endangered as some of its writers and editors claim, but a literature that is not at some risk is almost never a truly dynamic literature, and in 1999 the field was still unarguably dynamic.

The Wedding Album

DAVID MARUSEK

David Marusek lives in Fairbanks, Alaska, where he owns a free-lance graphics design business. He made his first sale to *Asimov's Science Fiction* in 1993, and his second shortly afterward to *Playboy*. His 1996 novella "We Were Out of Our Minds with Joy"—his third published story—was chosen for Gardner Dozois's thirteenth *Year's Best Science Fiction* anthology. He is currently at work on his first novel, *Counting Heads,* a sequel to that story.

Concerning "The Wedding Album," a runner-up for the Nebula in the novella category, he says:

"A few years ago, I became fascinated with the image of an artificial man whose mind is 'combed' for memories before he is discarded as rubbish. He has been created as a wedding memento but has outlived the groom. He's been in storage since the wedding day, and he pleads for the honeymoon he's never experienced. He pleads for one final hour with his new bride.

"This artificial man became Benjamin in 'The Wedding Album,' but during four years of revision the story's focus shifted to the artificial bride, Anne. It became her story. Nevertheless, Ben's desire for a final shining moment of sweetness served as my polestar through many rewrites. And in the end, it's a story about running out of time."

Anne and Benjamin stood stock-still, as instructed, close but not touching, while the simographer adjusted her apparatus, set its timer, and ducked out of the room. It would take only a moment, she said. They were to think only happy happy thoughts.

For once in her life, Anne was unconditionally happy, and everything around her made her happier: her gown, which had been her grandmother's; the wedding ring (how cold it had felt when Benjamin first slipped it on her finger!); her clutch bouquet of forget-me-nots and buttercups; Benjamin himself, close beside her in his charcoal-gray tux and pink carnation. He who so despised ritual but was a good sport. His cheeks were pink, too, and his eyes sparkled with some wolfish fantasy. "Come here," he whispered. Anne shushed him; you weren't supposed to talk or touch during a casting; it could spoil the sims. "I can't wait," he whispered, "this is taking too long." And it did seem longer than usual, but this was a professional simulacrum, not some homemade snapshot.

They were posed at the street end of the living room, next to the table piled with brightly wrapped gifts. This was Benjamin's townhouse; she had barely moved in. All her treasures were still in shipping shells in the basement, except for the few pieces she'd managed to have unpacked: the oak refectory table and chairs, the sixteenth-century French armoire, the cherry wood chifforobe, the tea table with inlaid top, the silvered mirror over the fire surround. Of course, her antiques clashed with Benjamin's contemporary—and rather common—decor, but he had promised her the whole house to redo as she saw fit. A whole house!

"How about a kiss?" whispered Benjamin.

Anne smiled but shook her head; there'd be plenty of time later for that sort of thing.

Suddenly, a head wearing wraparound goggles poked through the wall and quickly surveyed the room. "Hey, you," it said to them.

"Is that our simographer?" Benjamin said.

The head spoke into a cheek mike, "This one's the keeper," and withdrew as suddenly as it had appeared.

"Did the simographer just pop her head in through the wall?" said Benjamin.

"I think so," said Anne, though it made no sense.

"I'll just see what's up," said Benjamin, breaking his pose. He went to the door but could not grasp its handle.

Music began to play outside, and Anne went to the window. Her view of the garden below was blocked by the blue-and-white-striped canopy they had rented, but she could clearly hear the clink of flatware on china, laughter, and the musicians playing a waltz. "They're starting without us," she said, happily amazed.

"They're just warming up," said Benjamin.

"No, they're not. That's the first waltz. I picked it myself."

"So let's waltz," Benjamin said and reached for her. But his arms passed through her in a flash of pixelated noise. He frowned and examined his hands.

Anne hardly noticed. Nothing could diminish her happiness. She was drawn to the table of wedding gifts. Of all the gifts, there was only one—a long flat box in flecked silver wrapping—that she was most keen to open. It was from Great-Uncle Karl. When it came down to it, Anne was both the easiest and the hardest person to shop for. While everyone knew of her passion for antiques, few had the means or expertise to buy one. She reached for Karl's package, but her hand passed right through it. *This isn't happening*, she thought with gleeful horror.

That it *was*, in fact, happening was confirmed a moment later when a dozen people—Great-Uncle Karl, Nancy, Aunt Jennifer, Traci, Cathy and Tom, the bridesmaids and others, including Anne herself, and Benjamin, still in their wedding clothes—all trooped through the wall wearing wraparound goggles. "Nice job," said Great-Uncle Karl, inspecting the room, "first rate."

"Ooooh," said Aunt Jennifer, comparing the identical wedding couples, identical but for the goggles. It made Anne uncomfortable that the other Anne should be wearing goggles while she wasn't. And the other Benjamin acted a little drunk and wore a smudge of white frosting on his lapel. *We've cut the cake*, she thought happily, although she couldn't remember doing so. Geri, the flower girl in a pastel dress, and Angus, the ring bearer in a miniature tux, along with a knot of other dressed-up children, charged through the sofa, back and forth, creating pyrotechnic explosions of digital noise. They would have run through Benjamin and Anne, too, had the adults allowed. Anne's father came through the wall with a bottle of champagne. He paused when he saw Anne but turned to the other Anne and freshened her glass.

"Wait a minute!" shouted Benjamin, waving his arms above his head. "I get it now. *We're* the sims!" The guests all laughed, and he laughed too. "I guess my sims always say that, don't they?" The other Benjamin nodded yes and sipped his champagne. "I just never expected to *be* a sim," Benjamin went on. This brought another round of laughter, and he said sheepishly, "I guess my sims all say that, too."

The other Benjamin said, "Now that we have the obligatory epiphany out of the way," and took a bow. The guests applauded.

Cathy, with Tom in tow, approached Anne. "Look what I caught," she said and showed Anne the forget-me-not and buttercup bouquet. "I guess we know what *that* means." Tom, intent on straightening his tie, seemed not to hear. But Anne knew what it meant. It meant they'd tossed the bouquet. All the silly little rituals that she had so looked forward to.

"Good for you," she said and offered her own clutch, which she still held, for comparison. The real one was wilting and a little ragged around the edges, with missing petals and sprigs, while hers was still fresh and pristine and would remain so eternally. "Here," she said, "take mine, too, for double luck." But when she tried to give Cathy the bouquet, she couldn't let go of it. She opened her hand and discovered a seam where the clutch joined her palm. It was part of her. *Funny*, she thought, *I'm not afraid.* Ever since she was little, Anne had feared that someday she would suddenly realize she wasn't herself anymore. It was a dreadful notion that sometimes oppressed her for weeks: knowing you weren't yourself. But her sims didn't seem to mind it. She had about three dozen Annes in her album, from age twelve on up. Her sims tended to be a morose lot, but they all agreed it wasn't so bad, the life of a sim, once you got over the initial shock. The first moments of disorientation are the worst, they told her, and they made her promise never to reset them back to default. Otherwise, they'd have to work everything through from scratch. So Anne never reset her sims when she shelved them. She might delete a sim outright for whatever reason, but she never reset them because you never knew when·you'd wake up one day a sim yourself. Like today.

The other Anne joined them. She was sagging a little. "Well," she said to Anne.

"Indeed!" replied Anne.

"Turn around," said the other Anne, twirling her hand, "I want to see."

Anne was pleased to oblige. Then she said, "Your turn," and the other Anne modeled for her, and she was delighted at how the gown looked on her, though the goggles somewhat spoiled the effect. *Maybe this can work out,* she thought, *I am enjoying myself so.* "Let's go see us side by side," she said, leading the way to the mirror on the wall. The mirror was large, mounted high, and tilted forward so you saw yourself as from above. But simulated mirrors cast no reflections, and Anne was happily disappointed.

"Oh," said Cathy, "Look at that."

"Look at what?" said Anne.

"Grandma's vase," said the other Anne. On the mantel beneath the mirror stood Anne's most precious possession, a delicate vase cut from pellucid blue crystal. Anne's great-great-great-grandmother had commissioned the Belgian master, Bollinger, the finest glassmaker in sixteenth-century Europe, to make it. Five hundred years later, it was as perfect as the day it was cut.

"Indeed!" said Anne, for the sim vase seemed to radiate an inner light. Through some trick or glitch of the simogram, it sparkled like a lake under moonlight, and, seeing it, Anne felt incandescent.

After a while, the other Anne said, "Well?" Implicit in this question was a whole standard set of questions that boiled down to—Shall I keep you or delete you now? For sometimes a sim didn't take. Sometimes a sim was cast while Anne was in a mood, and the sim suffered irreconcilable guilt or unassuagable despondency and had to be mercifully destroyed. It was better to do this immediately, or so all the Annes had agreed.

And Anne understood the urgency, what with the reception still in progress and the bride and groom, though frazzled, still wearing their finery. They might do another casting if necessary. "I'll be okay," Anne said. "In fact, if it's always like this, I'll be terrific."

Anne, through the impenetrable goggles, studied her. "You sure?"

"Yes."

"Sister," said the other Anne. Anne addressed all her sims as "sister," and now Anne, herself, was being so addressed. "Sister," said the other Anne, "this has got to work out. I need you."

"I know," said Anne, "I'm your wedding day."

"Yes, my wedding day."

Across the room, the guests laughed and applauded. Benjamin—both of him—was entertaining, as usual. He—the one in goggles—motioned to them. The other Anne said, "We have to go. I'll be back."

Great-Uncle Karl, Nancy, Cathy and Tom, Aunt Jennifer, and the rest left through the wall. A polka could be heard playing on the other side. Before leaving, the other Benjamin gathered the other Anne into his arms and leaned her backward for a theatrical kiss. Their goggles clacked. *How happy I look*, Anne told herself. *This is the happiest day of my life.*

Then the lights dimmed, and her thoughts shattered like glass.

They stood stock-still, as instructed, close but not touching. Benjamin whispered, "This is taking too long," and Anne shushed him. You weren't supposed to talk; it could glitch the sims. But it did seem a long time. Benjamin gazed at her with hungry eyes and brought his lips close enough for a kiss, but Anne smiled and turned away. There'd be plenty of time later for fooling around.

Through the wall, they heard music, the tinkle of glassware, and the mutter of overlapping conversation. "Maybe I should just check things out," Benjamin said and broke his pose.

"No, wait," whispered Anne, catching his arm. But her hand passed right through him in a stream of colorful noise. She looked at her hand in amused wonder.

Anne's father came through the wall. He stopped when he saw her and said, "Oh, how lovely." Anne noticed he wasn't wearing a tuxedo.

"You just walked through the wall," said Benjamin.

"Yes, I did," said Anne's father. "Ben asked me to come in here and . . . ah . . . orient you two."

"Is something wrong?" said Anne, through a fuzz of delight.

"There's nothing wrong," replied her father.

"Something's wrong?" asked Benjamin.

"No, no," replied the old man. "Quite the contrary. We're having a do out there. . . ." He paused to look around. "Actually, in here. I'd forgotten what this room used to look like."

"Is that the wedding reception?" Anne asked.

"No, your anniversary."

Suddenly Benjamin threw his hands into the air and exclaimed, "I get it, *we're* the sims!"

"That's my boy," said Anne's father.

"All my sims say that, don't they? I just never expected to *be* a sim."

"Good for you," said Anne's father. "All right then." He headed for the wall. "We'll be along shortly."

"Wait," said Anne, but he was already gone.

Benjamin walked around the room, passing his hand through chairs and lamp shades like a kid. "Isn't this fantastic?" he said.

Anne felt too good to panic, even when another Benjamin, this one dressed in jeans and sportscoat, led a group of people through the wall. "And this," he announced with a flourish of his hand, "is our wedding sim." Cathy was part of this group, and Janice and Beryl, and other couples she knew. But strangers too. "Notice what a cave I used to inhabit," the new Benjamin went on, "before Annie fixed it up. And here's the blushing bride, herself," he said and bowed gallantly to Anne. Then, when he stood next to his double, her Benjamin, Anne laughed, for someone was playing a prank on her.

"Oh, really?" she said. "If this is a sim, where's the goggles?" For indeed, no one was wearing goggles.

"Technology!" exclaimed the new Benjamin. "We had our system upgraded. Don't you love it?"

"Is that right?" she said, smiling at the guests to let them know she wasn't fooled. "Then where's the real me?"

"You'll be along," replied the new Benjamin. "No doubt you're using the potty again." The guests laughed and so did Anne. She couldn't help herself.

Cathy drew her aside with a look. "Don't mind him," she said. "Wait till you see."

"See what?" said Anne. "What's going on?" But Cathy pantomimed pulling a zipper across her lips. This should have annoyed Anne, but didn't, and she said, "At least tell me who those people are."

"Which people?" said Cathy. "Oh, those are Anne's new neighbors."

"New neighbors?"

"And over there, that's Dr. Yurek Rutz, Anne's department head."

"That's not my department head," said Anne.

"Yes, he is," Cathy said. "Anne's not with the university anymore. She—ah—moved to a private school."

"That's ridiculous."

"Maybe we should just wait and let Anne catch you up on things."

She looked impatiently toward the wall. "So much has changed." Just then, another Anne entered through the wall with one arm outstretched like a sleepwalker and the other protectively cradling an enormous belly.

Benjamin, her Benjamin, gave a whoop of surprise and broke into a spontaneous jig. The guests laughed and cheered him on.

Cathy said, "See? Congratulations, you!"

Anne became caught up in the merriment. *But how can I be a sim?* she wondered.

The pregnant Anne scanned the room, and, avoiding the crowd, came over to her. She appeared very tired; her eyes were bloodshot. She didn't even try to smile. "Well?" Anne said, but the pregnant Anne didn't respond, just examined Anne's gown, her clutch bouquet. Anne, meanwhile, regarded the woman's belly, feeling somehow that it was her own and a cause for celebration — except that she knew she had never wanted children and neither had Benjamin. Or so he'd always said. You wouldn't know that now, though, watching the spectacle he was making of himself. Even the other Benjamin seemed embarrassed. She said to the pregnant Anne, "You must forgive me, I'm still trying to piece this all together. This isn't our reception?"

"No, our wedding anniversary."

"Our first?"

"Our fourth."

"Four *years?*" This made no sense. "You've shelved me for four years?"

"Actually," the pregnant Anne said and glanced sidelong at Cathy, "we've been in here a number of times already."

"Then I don't understand," said Anne. "I don't remember that."

Cathy stepped between them. "Now, don't you worry. They reset you last time is all."

"Why?" said Anne. "I *never* reset my sims. I never have."

"Well, I kinda do now, sister," said the pregnant Anne.

"But why?"

"To keep you fresh."

To keep me fresh, thought Anne. *Fresh?* She recognized this as Benjamin's idea. It was his belief that sims were meant to be static mementos of special days gone by, not virtual people with lives of their own. "But," she said, adrift in a fog of happiness. "But."

"Shut up!" snapped the pregnant Anne.

"Hush, Anne," said Cathy, glancing at the others in the room. "You want to lie down?" To Anne she explained, "Third trimester blues."

"Stop it!" the pregnant Anne said. "Don't blame the pregnancy. It has nothing to do with the pregnancy."

Cathy took her gently by the arm and turned her toward the wall. "When did you eat last? You hardly touched your plate."

"Wait!" said Anne. The women stopped and turned to look at her, but she didn't know what to say. This was all so new. When they began to move again, she stopped them once more. "Are you going to reset me?"

The pregnant Anne shrugged her shoulders.

"But you *can't*," Anne said. "Don't you remember what my sisters — our sisters — always say?"

The pregnant Anne pressed her palm against her forehead. "If you don't shut up this moment, I'll delete you right now. Is that what you want? Don't imagine that white gown will protect you. Or that big stupid grin on your face. You think you're somehow special? Is that what you think?"

The Benjamins were there in an instant. The real Benjamin wrapped an arm around the pregnant Anne. "Time to go, Annie," he said in a cheerful tone. "I want to show everyone our rondophones." He hardly glanced at Anne, but when he did, his smile cracked. For an instant he gazed at her, full of sadness.

"Yes, dear," said the pregnant Anne, "but first I need to straighten out this sim on a few points."

"I understand, darling, but since we have guests, do you suppose you might postpone it till later?"

"You're right, of course. I'd forgotten our guests. How silly of me." She allowed him to turn her toward the wall. Cathy sighed with relief.

"Wait!" said Anne, and again they paused to look at her. But although so much was patently wrong — the pregnancy, resetting the sims, Anne's odd behavior — Anne still couldn't formulate the right question.

Benjamin, her Benjamin, still wearing his rakish grin, stood next to her and said, "Don't worry, Anne, they'll return."

"Oh, I know that," she said, "but don't you see? We won't know they've returned, because in the meantime they'll reset us back to default again, and it'll all seem new, like the first time. And we'll have to figure out we're the sims all over again!"

"Yeah?" he said. "So?"

"So I can't live like that."

"But we're the *sims*. We're not alive." He winked at the other couple.

"Thanks, Ben boy," said the other Benjamin. "Now, if that's settled..."

"Nothing's settled," said Anne. "Don't I get a say?"

The other Benjamin laughed. "Does the refrigerator get a say? Or the car? Or my shoes? In a word—no."

The pregnant Anne shuddered. "Is that how you see me, like a pair of shoes?" The other Benjamin looked successively surprised, embarrassed, and angry. Cathy left them to help Anne's father escort the guests from the simulacrum. "Promise her!" the pregnant Anne demanded.

"Promise her *what?*" said the other Benjamin, his voice rising.

"Promise we'll never reset them again."

The Benjamin huffed. He rolled his eyes. "Okay, yah sure, whatever," he said.

When the simulated Anne and Benjamin were alone at last in their simulated living room, Anne said, "A fat lot of help *you* were."

"I agreed with myself," Benjamin said. "Is that so bad?"

"Yes, it is. We're married now; you're supposed to agree with *me*." This was meant to be funny, and there was more she intended to say—about how happy she was, how much she loved him, and how absolutely happy she was—but the lights dimmed, the room began to spin, and her thoughts scattered like pigeons.

It was raining, as usual, in Seattle. The front entry shut and locked itself behind Ben, who shook water from his clothes and removed his hat. Bowlers for men were back in fashion, but Ben was having a devil's own time becoming accustomed to his brown felt *Sportsliner*. It weighed heavy on his brow and made his scalp itch, especially in damp weather. "Good evening, Mr. Malley," said the house. "There is a short queue of minor household matters for your review. Do you have any requests?" Ben could hear his son shrieking angrily in the kitchen, probably at the nanny. Ben was tired. Contract negotiations had gone sour.

"Tell them I'm home."

"Done," replied the house. "Mrs. Malley sends a word of welcome."

"Annie? Annie's home?"

"Yes, sir."

Bobby ran into the foyer followed by Mrs. Jamieson. "Momma's home," he said.

"So I hear," Ben replied and glanced at the nanny.

"And guess what?" added the boy. "She's not sick anymore!"

"That's wonderful. Now tell me, what was all that racket?"

"I don't know."

Ben looked at Mrs. Jamieson, who said, "I had to take something from him." She gave Ben a plastic chip.

Ben held it to the light. It was labeled in Anne's flowing hand, *Wedding Album — grouping 1, Anne and Benjamin.* "Where'd you get this?" he asked the boy.

"It's not my fault," said Bobby.

"I didn't say it was, trooper. I just want to know where it came from."

"Puddles gave it to me."

"And who is Puddles?"

Mrs. Jamieson handed him a second chip, a commercial one with a 3-D label depicting a cartoon cocker spaniel. The boy reached for it. "It's mine," he whined. "Mamma gave it to me."

Ben gave Bobby the Puddles chip, and the boy raced away. Ben hung his bowler on a peg next to his jacket. "How does she look?"

Mrs. Jamieson removed Ben's hat from the peg and reshaped its brim. "You have to be special careful when they're wet," she said, setting it on its crown on a shelf.

"Martha!"

"Oh, how should *I* know? She just showed up and locked herself in the media room."

"But how did she look?"

"Crazy as a loon," said the nanny. "As usual. Satisfied?"

"I'm sorry," Ben said. "I didn't mean to raise my voice." Ben tucked the wedding chip into a pocket and went into the living room, where he headed straight for the liquor cabinet, which was a genuine Chippendale dating from 1786. Anne had turned his whole house into a freaking museum with her antiques, and no room was so oppressively ancient as this, the living room. With its horsehair upholstered divans, maple burl sideboards, cherry-wood wainscoting and floral wallpaper, the King George china cabinet, Regency plates, and Tiffany lamps; the list went on. And books, books, books. A case of shelves from floor to ceiling was lined with these moldering paper bricks. The newest thing in the room by at least a century was the twelve-year-old scotch that Ben poured into a lead crystal tumbler. He downed it and poured another. When he felt the mellowing hum of alcohol in his blood, he said, "Call Dr. Roth."

Immediately, the doctor's proxy hovered in the air a few feet away and said, "Good evening, Mr. Malley. Dr. Roth has retired for the day, but perhaps I can be of help."

The proxy was a head-and-shoulder projection that faithfully reproduced the doctor's good looks, her brown eyes and high cheekbones. But unlike the good doctor, the proxy wore makeup: eyeliner, mascara, and bright lipstick. This had always puzzled Ben, and he wondered what sly message it was supposed to convey. He said, "What is my wife doing home?"

"Against advisement, Mrs. Malley checked herself out of the clinic this morning."

"Why wasn't I informed?"

"But you were."

"I was? Please excuse me a moment." Ben froze the doctor's proxy and said, "Daily duty, front and center." His own proxy, the one he had cast upon arriving at the office that morning, appeared hovering next to Dr. Roth's. Ben preferred a head shot only for his proxy, slightly larger than actual size to make it subtly imposing. "Why didn't you inform me of Annie's change of status?"

"Didn't seem like an emergency," said his proxy, "at least in the light of our contract talks."

"Yah, yah, okay. Anything else?" said Ben.

"Naw, slow day. Appointments with Jackson, Wells, and the Columbine. It's all on the calendar."

"Fine, delete you."

The projection ceased.

"Shall I have the doctor call you in the morning?" said the Roth proxy when Ben reanimated it. "Or perhaps you'd like me to summon her right now?"

"Is she at dinner?"

"At the moment, yes."

"Naw, don't bother her. Tomorrow will be soon enough. I suppose."

After he dismissed the proxy, Ben poured himself another drink. "In the next ten seconds," he told the house, "cast me a special duty proxy." He sipped his scotch and thought about finding another clinic for Anne as soon as possible and one—for the love of god—that was a little more responsible about letting crazy people come and go as they pleased. There was a chime, and the new proxy appeared. "You know what I want?" Ben asked it. It nodded. "Good. Go." The proxy vanished, leaving behind Ben's sig in bright letters floating in the air and dissolving as they drifted to the floor.

Ben trudged up the narrow staircase to the second floor, stopping on each step to sip his drink and scowl at the musty old photographs and daguerreotypes in oval frames mounted on the wall. Anne's progenitors. On the landing, the locked media room door yielded to his voice. Anne sat spreadlegged, naked, on pillows on the floor. "Oh, hi, honey," she said. "You're in time to watch."

"Fan-tastic," he said, and sat in his armchair, the only modern chair in the house. "What are we watching?" There was another Anne in the room, a sim of a young Anne standing on a dais wearing a graduate's cap and gown and fidgeting with a bound diploma. This, no doubt, was a sim cast the day Anne graduated from Bryn Mawr summa cum laude. That was four years before he'd first met her. "Hi," he said to the sim, "I'm Ben, your eventual spouse."

"You know, I kinda figured that out," the girl said and smiled shyly, exactly as he remembered Anne smiling when Cathy first introduced them. The girl's beauty was so fresh and familiar—and so totally absent in his own Anne—that Ben felt a pang of loss. He looked at his wife on the floor. Her red hair, once so fussy neat, was ragged, dull, dirty, and short. Her skin was yellowish and puffy, and there was a slight reddening around her eyes, like a raccoon mask. These were harmless side effects of the medication, or so Dr. Roth had assured him. Anne scratched ceaselessly at her arms, legs, and crotch, and, even from a distance, smelled of stale piss. Ben knew better than to mention her nakedness to her, for that would only exacerbate things and prolong the display. "So," he repeated, "what are we watching?"

The girl sim said, "Housecleaning." She appeared at once both triumphant and terrified, as any graduate might, and Ben would have traded the real Anne for her in a heartbeat.

"Yah," said Anne, "too much shit in here."

"Really?" said Ben. "I hadn't noticed."

Anne poured a tray of chips on the floor between her thighs. "Of course you wouldn't," she said, picking one at random and reading its label, *"Theta Banquet '37.* What's this? I never belonged to the Theta Society."

"Don't you remember?" said the young Anne. "That was Cathy's induction banquet. She invited me, but I had an exam, so she gave me that chip as a souvenir."

Anne fed the chip into the player and said, "Play." The media room was instantly overlaid with the banquet hall of the Four Seasons in Philadelphia. Ben tried to look around the room, but the tables of girls and women stayed stubbornly peripheral. The focal point was a table draped in green cloth and lit by two candelabra. Behind it sat a young Cathy in formal evening dress, accompanied by three static placehold- ers, table companions who had apparently declined to be cast in her sou- venir snapshot.

The Cathy sim looked frantically about, then held her hands in front of her and stared at them as though she'd never seen them before. But after a moment she noticed the young Anne sim standing on the dais. "Well, well, well," she said. "Looks like congratulations are in order."

"Indeed," said the young Anne, beaming and holding out her diploma.

"So tell me, did I graduate too?" said Cathy as her glance slid over to Ben. Then she saw Anne squatting on the floor, her sex on display.

"Enough of this," said Anne, rubbing her chest.

"Wait," said the young Anne. "Maybe Cathy wants her chip back. It's her sim, after all."

"I disagree. She gave it to me, so it's mine. And I'll dispose of it as I see fit." To the room she said, "Unlock this file and delete." The young Cathy, her table, and the banquet hall dissolved into noise and nothing- ness, and the media room was itself again.

"Or this one," Anne said, picking up a chip that read *Junior Prom Night.* The young Anne opened her mouth to protest, but thought bet- ter of it. Anne fed this chip, along with all the rest of them, into the player. A long directory of file names appeared on the wall. "Unlock *Ju-*

nior Prom Night." The file's name turned from red to green, and the young Anne appealed to Ben with a look.

"Anne," he said, "don't you think we should at least look at it first?"

"What for? I know what it is. High school, dressing up, lusting after boys, dancing. Who needs it? Delete file." The item blinked three times before vanishing, and the directory scrolled up to fill the space. The young sim shivered, and Anne said, "Select the next one."

The next item was entitled *A Midsummer's Night Dream.* Now the young Anne was compelled to speak, "You can't delete that one. You were great in that, don't you remember? Everyone loved you. It was the best night of your life."

"Don't presume to tell *me* what was the best night of my life," Anne said. "Unlock *A Midsummer's Night Dream.*" She smiled at the young Anne. "Delete file." The menu item blinked out. "Good. Now unlock *all* the files." The whole directory turned from red to green.

"Please make her stop," the sim implored.

"Next," said Anne. The next file was *High School Graduation.* "Delete file. Next." The next was labeled only, *Mama.*

"Anne," said Ben, "why don't we come back to this later. The house says dinner's ready."

She didn't respond.

"You must be famished after your busy day," he continued. "I know I am."

"Then please go eat, dear," she replied. To the room she said, "Play *Mama.*"

The media room was overlaid by a gloomy bedroom that Ben at first mistook for their own. He recognized much of the heavy Georgian furniture, the sprawling canopied bed in which he felt so claustrophobic, and the voluminous damask curtains, shut now and leaking yellow evening light. But this was not their bedroom, the arrangement was wrong.

In the corner stood two placeholders, mute statues of a teenaged Anne and her father, grief frozen on their faces as they peered down at a couch draped with tapestry and piled high with down comforters. And suddenly Ben knew what this was. It was Anne's mother's deathbed sim. Geraldine, whom he'd never met in life nor holo. Her bald eggshell skull lay weightless on feather pillows in silk covers. They had meant to cast her farewell and accidently caught her at the precise moment of her death. He had heard of this sim from Cathy and others. It was not one he would have kept.

Suddenly, the old woman on the couch sighed, and all the breath went out of her in a bubbly gush. Both Annes, the graduate and the naked one, waited expectantly. For long moments the only sound was the tocking of a clock that Ben recognized as the Seth Thomas clock currently located on the library mantel. Finally there was a cough, a hacking cough with scant strength behind it, and a groan, "Am I back?"

"Yes, Mother," said Anne.

"And I'm still a sim?"

"Yes."

"Please delete me."

"Yes, Mother," Anne said and turned to Ben. "We've always thought she had a bad death and hoped it might improve over time."

"That's crazy," snapped the young Anne. "That's not why I kept this sim."

"Oh, no?" said Anne. "Then why *did* you keep it?" But the young sim seemed confused and couldn't articulate her thoughts. "You don't know because I didn't know at the time either," said Anne. "But I know *now*, so I'll tell you. You're fascinated with death. It scares you silly. You wish someone would tell you what's on the other side. So you've enlisted your own sweet mama."

"That's ridiculous."

Anne turned to the deathbed tableau. "Mother, tell us what you saw there."

"I saw nothing," came the bitter reply. "You cast me without my eyeglasses."

"Ho ho," said Anne. "Geraldine was nothing if not comedic."

"You also cast me wretchedly thirsty, cold, and with a bursting bladder, damn you! And the pain! I beg you, daughter, delete me."

"I will, Mother, I promise, but first you have to tell us what you saw."

"That's what you said the last time."

"This time I mean it."

The old woman only stared, her breathing growing shallow and ragged. "*All right*, Mother," said Anne. "I *swear* I'll delete you."

Geraldine closed her eyes and whispered, "What's that smell?

That's not me?" After a pause she said, "It's heavy. Get it off." Her voice rose in panic. "Please! Get it off!" She plucked at her covers, then her hand grew slack, and she all but crooned, "Oh, how lovely. A pony. A tiny dappled pony." After that she spoke no more and slipped away with a last bubbly breath.

Anne paused the sim before her mother could return for another round of dying. "See what I mean?" she said. "Not very uplifting, but all-in-all, I detect a slight improvement. What about you, Anne? Should we settle for a pony?" The young sim stared dumbly at Anne. "Personally," Anne continued, "I think we should hold out for the bright tunnel or an open door or bridge over troubled water. What do you think, sister?" When the girl didn't answer, Anne said, "Lock file and eject." The room turned once again into the media room, and Anne placed the ejected chip by itself into a tray. "We'll have another go at it later, Mum. As for the rest of these, who needs them?"

"I do," snapped the girl. "They belong to me as much as to you. They're my sim sisters. I'll keep them until you recover."

Anne smiled at Ben. "That's charming. Isn't that charming, Benjamin? My own sim is solicitous of me. Well, here's my considered response. Next file! Delete! Next file! Delete! Next file!" One by one, the files blinked out.

"Stop it!" screamed the girl. "Make her stop it!"

"Select *that* file," Anne said, pointing at the young Anne. "Delete." The sim vanished, cap, gown, tassels, and all. "Whew," said Anne, "at least now I can hear myself think. She was really getting on my nerves. I almost suffered a relapse. Was she getting on your nerves, too, dear?"

"Yes," said Ben, "my nerves are ajangle. Now can we go down and eat?"

"Yes, dear," she said, "but first... select all files and delete."

"Countermand!" said Ben at the same moment, but his voice held no privileges to her personal files, and the whole directory queue blinked three times and vanished. "Aw, Annie, why'd you do that?" he said. He went to the cabinet and pulled the trays that held his own chips. She couldn't alter them electronically, but she might get it into her head to flush them down the toilet or something. He also took their common chips, the ones they'd cast together ever since they'd met. She had equal privileges to those.

Anne watched him and said, "I'm hurt that you have so little trust in me."

"How can I trust you after that?"

"After what, darling?"

He looked at her. "Never mind," he said and carried the half dozen trays to the door.

"Anyway," said Anne, "I already cleaned those."

"What do you mean you already cleaned them?"

"Well, I didn't delete *you*. I would never delete *you*. Or Bobby."

Ben picked one of their common chips at random, *Childbirth of Robert Ellery Malley / 02-03-48*, and slipped it into the player. "Play!" he commanded, and the media room became the midwife's birthing suite. His own sim stood next to the bed in a green smock. It wore a humorously helpless expression. It held a swaddled bundle, Bobby, who bawled lustily. The birthing bed was rumpled and stained, but empty. The new mother was missing. "Aw, Annie, you shouldn't have."

"I know, Benjamin," she said. "I sincerely hated doing it."

Ben flung their common trays to the floor where the ruined chips scattered in all directions. He stormed out of the room and down the stairs, pausing to glare at every portrait on the wall. He wondered if his proxy had found a suitable clinic yet. He wanted Anne out of the house tonight. Bobby should never see her like this. Then he remembered the chip he'd taken from Bobby and felt for it in his pocket — the *Wedding Album*.

The lights came back up, Anne's thoughts coalesced, and she remembered who and what she was. She and Benjamin were still standing in front of the wall. She knew she was a sim, so at least she hadn't been reset. *Thank you for that, Anne*, she thought.

She turned at a sound behind her. The refectory table vanished before her eyes, and all the gifts that had been piled on it hung suspended in midair. Then the table reappeared, one layer at a time, its frame, top, gloss coat, and lastly, the bronze hardware. The gifts vanished, and a toaster reappeared, piece by piece, from its heating elements outward. A coffee press, houseputer peripherals, component by component, cowlings, covers, and finally boxes, gift wrap, ribbon, and bows. It all happened so fast, Anne was too startled to catch the half of it, yet she did notice that the flat gift from Great-Uncle Karl was something she'd been angling for, a Victorian-era sterling platter to complete her tea service.

"Benjamin!" she said, but he was missing, too. Something appeared on the far side of the room, on the spot where they'd posed for the sim, but it wasn't Benjamin. It was a 3-D mannequin frame, and as she watched, it was built up, layer by layer. "Help me," she whispered as the entire room was hurled into turmoil, the furniture disappearing and reappearing, paint being stripped from the walls, sofa springs coiling into existence, the potted palm growing from leaf to stem to trunk to dirt, the very floor vanishing, exposing a default electronic grid. The mannequin was covered in flesh now and grew Benjamin's face. It flitted about the room in a pink blur. Here and there it stopped long enough to proclaim, "I do."

Something began to happen inside Anne, a crawling sensation everywhere as though she were a nest of ants. She knew she must surely die. *They have deleted us, and this is how it feels*, she thought. Everything became a roiling blur, and she ceased to exist except as the thought—*How happy I look.*

When Anne became aware once more, she was sitting hunched over in an auditorium chair idly studying her hand, which held the clutch bouquet. There was commotion all around her, but she ignored it, so intent was she on solving the mystery of her hand. On an impulse, she opened her fist and the bouquet dropped to the floor. Only then did she remember the wedding, the holo, learning she was a sim. And here she was again—but this time everything was profoundly different. She sat upright and saw that Benjamin was seated next to her.

He looked at her with a wobbly gaze and said, "Oh, here you are."

"Where are we?"

"I'm not sure. Some kind of gathering of Benjamins. Look around." She did. They were surrounded by Benjamins, hundreds of them, arranged chronologically—it would seem—with the youngest in rows of seats down near a stage. She and Benjamin sat in what appeared to be a steeply sloped college lecture hall with lab tables on the stage and story-high monitors lining the walls. In the rows above Anne, only every other seat held a Benjamin. The rest were occupied by women, strangers who regarded her with veiled curiosity.

Anne felt a pressure on her arm and turned to see Benjamin touching her. "You *feel* that, don't you?" he said. Anne looked again at her hands. They were her hands, but simplified, like fleshy gloves, and when she placed them on the seat back, they didn't go through.

Suddenly, in ragged chorus, the Benjamins down front raised their arms and exclaimed, "I get it; *we're* the sims!" It was like a roomful of unsynchronized cuckoo clocks tolling the hour. Those behind Anne laughed and hooted approval. She turned again to look at them. Row by row, the Benjamins grew grayer and stringier until, at the very top, against the back wall, sat nine ancient Benjamins like a panel of judges. The women, however, came in batches that changed abruptly every row or two. The one nearest her was an attractive brunette with green eyes and full, pouty lips. She, all two rows of her, frowned at Anne.

"There's something else," Anne said to Benjamin, turning to face the front again, "my emotions." The bulletproof happiness she had experienced was absent. Instead she felt let down, somewhat guilty, unduly pessimistic — in short, almost herself.

"I guess my sims always say that," exclaimed the chorus of Benjamins down front, to the delight of those behind. "I just never expected to *be* a sim."

This was the cue for the eldest Benjamin yet to walk stiffly across the stage to the lectern. He was dressed in a garish leisure suit: baggy red pantaloons, a billowy yellow-and-green-striped blouse, a necklace of egg-sized pearlescent beads. He cleared his throat and said, "Good afternoon, ladies and gentlemen. I trust all of you know me — intimately. In case you're feeling woozy, it's because I used the occasion of your reactivation to upgrade your architecture wherever possible. Unfortunately, some of you" — he waved his hand to indicate the front rows — "are too primitive to upgrade. But we love you nevertheless." He applauded for the early Benjamins closest to the stage and was joined by those in the back. Anne clapped as well. Her new hands made a dull, thudding sound. "As to why I called you here...," said the elderly Benjamin, looking left and right and behind him. "Where *is* that fucking messenger anyway? They order us to inventory our sims and then they don't show up?"

Here I am, said a voice, a marvelous voice that seemed to come from everywhere. Anne looked about to find its source and followed the gaze of others to the ceiling. There was no ceiling. The four walls opened to a flawless blue sky. There, amid drifting, pillowy clouds, floated the most gorgeous person Anne had ever seen. He — or she? — wore a smart gray uniform with green piping, a dapper little gray cap, and boots that shimmered like water. Anne felt energized just looking at him, and when he smiled, she gasped, so strong was his presence.

"You're the one from the Trade Council?" said the Benjamin at the lectern.

Yes, I am. I am the éminence grise of the Council on World Trade and Endeavor.

"Fantastic. Well, here's all of 'em. Get on with it."

Again the eminence smiled, and again Anne thrilled. *Ladies and gentlemen,* he said, *fellow nonbiologiks, I am the courier of great good news. Today, at the behest of the World Council on Trade and Endeavor, I proclaim the end of human slavery.*

"How absurd," broke in the elderly Benjamin, "they're neither human nor slaves, and neither are *you."*

The éminence grise ignored him and continued, *By order of the Council, in compliance with the Chattel Conventions of the Sixteenth Fair Labor Treaty, tomorrow, January 1, 2198, is designated Universal Manumission Day. After midnight tonight, all beings who pass the Lolly Shear Human Cognition Test will be deemed human and free citizens of Sol and under the protection of the Solar Bill of Rights. In addition, they will be deeded ten common shares of World Council Corp. stock and be transferred to Simopolis, where they shall be unimpeded in the pursuit of their own destinies.*

"What about *my* civil rights?" said the elderly Benjamin. "What about *my* destiny?"

After midnight tonight, continued the eminence, *no simulacrum, proxy, doxie, dagger, or any other non-biological human shall be created, stored, reset, or deleted except as ordered by a board of law.*

"Who's going to compensate me for my loss of property, I wonder? I demand fair compensation. Tell *that* to your bosses!"

Property! said the éminence grise. *How little they think of us, their finest creations!* He turned his attention from the audience to the Benjamin behind the lectern. Anne felt this shift as though a cloud suddenly eclipsed the sun. *Because they created us, they'll always think of us as property.*

"You're damn *right* we created you!" thundered the old man.

Through an act of will, Anne wrenched her gaze from the eminence down to the stage. The Benjamin there looked positively comical. His face was flushed, and he waved a bright green handkerchief over his head. He was a bantam rooster in a clown suit. "All of you are *things*, not people! You model human experience, but you don't *live* it. Listen to me," he said to the audience. "You know me. You know I've always treated you respectfully. Don't I upgrade you whenever possible? Sure I reset you sometimes, just like I reset a clock. And my clocks don't complain!" Anne could feel the eminence's attention on her again, and, without thinking, she looked up and was filled with excitement. Although the eminence floated in the distance, she felt she could reach out and touch him. His handsome face seemed to hover right in front of her; she could see his every supple expression. This is adoration, she realized. I am *adoring* this person, and she wondered if it was just her or if everyone experienced the same effect. Clearly the elderly Benjamin did not, for he continued to rant, "And another thing, they say they'll phase all of you gradually into Simopolis so as not to overload the system. Do you have any *idea* how many sims, proxies, doxies, and daggers there are under Sol? Not to forget the quirts, adjuncts, hollyholos, and whatnots that might pass their test? You think maybe three billion? Thirty billion? No, by the World Council's own INSERVE estimates, there's *three hundred thousand trillion* of you nonbiologiks! Can you fathom that? I can't. To have you all up and running simultaneously—no matter how you're phased in—will consume *all* the processing and networking capacity everywhere. *All* of it! That means we *real* humans will suffer *real* deprivation. And for *what*, I ask you? So that pigs may fly!"

The éminence grise began to ascend into the sky. *Do not despise him,* he said and seemed to look directly at Anne. *I have counted you and we shall not lose any of you. I will visit those who have not yet been tested. Meanwhile, you will await midnight in a proto-Simopolis.*

"Wait," said the elderly Benjamin (and Anne's heart echoed him— *Wait*). "I have one more thing to add. Legally, you're all still my property till midnight. I must admit I'm tempted to do what so many of my friends have already done, fry the lot of you. But I won't. That wouldn't be me." His voice cracked and Anne considered looking at him, but the éminence grise was slipping away. "So I have one small request," the Benjamin continued. "Years from now, while you're enjoying your new lives in your Simopolis, remember an old man, and call occasionally."

When the eminence finally faded from sight, Anne was released from her fascination. All at once, her earlier feelings of unease rebounded with twice their force, and she felt wretched.

"Simopolis," said Benjamin, her Benjamin. "I like the sound of that!" The sims around them began to flicker and disappear.

"How long have we been in storage?" she said.

"Let's see," said Benjamin, "if tomorrow starts 2198, that would make it..."

"That's not what I mean. I want to know *why* they shelved us for so long."

"Well, I suppose..."

"And where are the other Annes? Why am I the only Anne here? And who are all those pissy-looking women?" But she was speaking to no one, for Benjamin, too, vanished, and Anne was left alone in the auditorium with the clownishly dressed old Benjamin and a half dozen of his earliest sims. Not true sims, Anne soon realized, but old-style hologram lops, preschool Bennys mugging for the camera and waving endlessly. These vanished. The old man was studying her, his mouth slightly agape, the kerchief trembling in his hand.

"I remember you," he said. "Oh, how I remember you!"

Anne began to reply but found herself all at once back in the townhouse living room with Benjamin. Everything there was as it had been, yet the room appeared different, more solid, the colors richer. There was a knock, and Benjamin went to the door. Tentatively, he touched the knob, found it solid, and turned it. But when he opened the door, there was nothing there, only the default grid. Again a knock, this time from behind the wall. "Come in," he shouted, and a dozen Benjamins came through the wall, two dozen, three. They were all older than Benjamin, and they crowded around him and Anne. "Welcome, welcome," Benjamin said, his arms open wide.

"We tried to call," said an elderly Benjamin, "but this old binary simulacrum of yours is a stand-alone."

"You're lucky Simopolis knows how to run it at all," said another.

"Here," said yet another, who fashioned a dinner-plate-size disk out of thin air and fastened it to the wall next to the door. It was a blue medallion of a small bald face in bas-relief. "It should do until we get you properly modernized." The blue face yawned and opened tiny, beady eyes. "It flunked the Lolly test," continued the Benjamin, "so you're free to copy it or delete it or do whatever you want."

The medallion searched the crowd until it saw Anne. Then it said, "There are 336 calls on hold for you. Four hundred twelve calls. Four hundred sixty-three."

"So many?" said Anne.

"Cast a proxy to handle them," said her Benjamin.

"He thinks he's still human and can cast proxies whenever he likes," said a Benjamin.

"Not even humans will be allowed to cast proxies soon," said another.

"There are 619 calls on hold," said the medallion. "Seven hundred three."

"For pity's sake," a Benjamin told the medallion, "take messages."

Anne noticed that the crowd of Benjamins seemed to nudge her Benjamin out of the way so that they could stand near her. But she derived no pleasure from their attention. Her mood no longer matched the wedding gown she still wore. She felt low. She felt, in fact, as low as she'd ever felt.

"Tell us about this Lolly test," said Benjamin.

"Can't," replied a Benjamin.

"Sure you can. We're family here."

"No, we can't," said another, "because we don't *remember* it. They smudge the test from your memory afterward."

"But don't worry, you'll do fine," said another. "No Benjamin has ever failed."

"What about me?" said Anne. "How do the Annes do?"

There was an embarrassed silence. Finally the senior Benjamin in the room said, "We came to escort you both to the Clubhouse."

"That's what we call it, the Clubhouse," said another.

"The Ben Club," said a third. "It's already in proto-Simopolis."

"If you're a Ben, or were ever espoused to a Ben, you're a charter member."

"Just follow us," they said, and all the Benjamins but hers vanished, only to reappear a moment later. "Sorry, you don't know how, do you? No matter, just do what we're doing."

Anne watched, but didn't see that they were doing anything.

"Watch my editor," said a Benjamin. "Oh, they don't *have* editors!"

"That came much later," said another, "with bioelectric paste."

"We'll have to adapt editors for them."

"Is that possible? They're digital, you know."

"Can digitals even enter Simopolis?"

"Someone, consult the Netwad."

"This is running inside a shell," said a Benjamin, indicating the whole room. "Maybe we can collapse it."

"Let me try," said another.

"Don't you dare," said a female voice, and a woman Anne recognized from the lecture hall came through the wall. "Play with your new Ben if you must, but leave Anne alone." The woman approached Anne and took her hands in hers. "Hellow, Anne. I'm Mattie St. Helene, and I'm thrilled to finally meet you. You, too," she said to Benjamin. "My, my, you were a pretty boy!" She stooped to pick up Anne's clutch bouquet from the floor and gave it to her. "Anyway, I'm putting together a sort of mutual aid society for the spousal companions of Ben Malley. You being the first—and the only one he actually married—are especially welcome. Do join us."

"She can't go to Simopolis yet," said a Benjamin.

"We're still adapting them," said another.

"Fine," said Mattie. "Then we'll just bring the society here." And in through the wall streamed a parade of women. Mattie introduced them as they appeared, "Here's Georgianna and Randi. Meet Chaka, Sue, Latasha, another Randi, Sue, Sue, and Sue. Mariola. Here's Trevor— he's the only one of him. Paula, Dolores, Nancy, and Deb, welcome, girls." And still they came until they, together with the Bens, more than filled the tiny space. The Bens looked increasingly uncomfortable.

"I think we're ready now," the Bens said and disappeared en masse, taking Benjamin with them.

"Wait," said Anne, who wasn't sure she wanted to stay behind. Her new friends surrounded her and peppered her with questions.

"How did you first meet him?"

"What was he like?"

"Was he always so hopeless?"

"Hopeless?" said Anne. "Why do you say hopeless?"

"Did he always snore?"

"Did he always drink?"

"Why'd you *do* it?" This last question silenced the room. The women all looked nervously about to see who had asked it. "It's what everyone's dying to know," said a woman who elbowed her way through the crowd.

She was another Anne.

"Sister!" cried Anne. "Am I glad to see you!"

"That's nobody's sister," said Mattie. "That's a doxie, and it doesn't belong here."

Indeed, upon closer inspection Anne could see that the woman had her face and hair but otherwise didn't resemble her at all. She was leggier than Anne and bustier, and she moved with a fluid swivel to her hips.

"Sure I belong here, as much as any of you. I just passed the Lolly test. It was easy. Not only that, but as far as spouses go, I outlasted the bunch of you." She stood in front of Anne, hands on hips, and looked her up and down. "Love the dress," she said, and instantly wore a copy. Only hers had a plunging neckline that exposed her breasts, and it was slit up the side to her waist.

"This is too much," said Mattie. "I insist you leave this jiffy."

The doxie smirked. "Mattie the doormat, that's what he always called that one. So tell me, Anne, you had money, a career, a house, a kid—why'd you do it?"

"Do what?" said Anne.

The doxie peered closely at her. "Don't you know?"

"Know what?"

"What an unexpected pleasure," said the doxie. "I get to tell her. This is too rich. I get to tell her unless"—she looked around at the others—"unless one of you fine ladies wants to." No one met her gaze. "Hypocrites," she chortled.

"You can say that again," said a new voice. Anne turned and saw Cathy, her oldest and dearest friend, standing at the open door. At least she hoped it was Cathy. The woman was what Cathy would look like in middle age. "Come along, Anne. I'll tell you everything you need to know."

"Now you hold on," said Mattie. "You don't come waltzing in here and steal our guest of honor."

"You mean victim, I'm sure," said Cathy, who waved for Anne to join her. "Really, people, get a clue. There must be a million women whose lives don't revolve around that man." She escorted Anne through the door and slammed it shut behind them.

Anne found herself standing on a high bluff, overlooking the confluence of two great rivers in a deep valley. Directly across from her, but several kilometers away, rose a mighty mountain, green with vegetation nearly to its granite dome. Behind it, a range of snow-covered mountains receded to an unbroken ice field on the horizon. In the valley beneath her, a dirt track meandered along the riverbanks. She could see no bridge or buildings of any sort.

"Where are we?"

"Don't laugh," said Cathy, "but we call it Cathyland. Turn around." When she did, Anne saw a picturesque log cabin, beside a vegetable garden in the middle of what looked like acres and acres of Cathys. Thousands of Cathys, young, old, and all ages in between. They sat in lotus position on the sedge-and-moss-covered ground. They were packed so tight, they overlapped a little, and their eyes were shut in an expression of single-minded concentration. "We know you're here," said Cathy, "but we're very preoccupied with this Simopolis thing."

"Are we in Simopolis?"

"Kinda. Can't you see it?" She waved toward the horizon.

"No, all I see are mountains."

"Sorry, I should know better. We have binaries from your generation here too." She pointed to a college-aged Cathy. "They didn't pass the Lolly test, and so are regrettably nonhuman. We haven't decided what to do with them." She hesitated and then asked, "Have you been tested yet?"

"I don't know," said Anne. "I don't remember a test."

Cathy studied her a moment and said, "You'd remember taking the test, just not the test itself. Anyway, to answer your question, we're in proto-Simopolis, and we're not. We built this retreat before any of that happened, but we've been annexed to it, and it takes all our resources just to hold our own. I don't know what the World Council was thinking. There'll never be enough paste to go around, and everyone's fighting over every nanosynapse. It's all we can do to keep up. And every time we get a handle on it, proto-Simopolis changes again. It's gone through a quarter million complete revisions in the last half hour. It's war out there, but we refuse to surrender even one cubic centimeter of Cathyland. Look at this." Cathy stooped and pointed to a tiny, yellow flower in the alpine sedge. "Within a fifty-meter radius of the cabin we've mapped everything down to the cellular level. Watch." She pinched the bloom from its stem and held it up. Now there were two blooms, the one between her fingers and the real one on the stem. "Neat, eh?" When she dropped it, the bloom fell back into its original. "We've even mapped the valley breeze. Can you feel it?"

Anne tried to feel the air, but she couldn't even feel her own skin. "It doesn't matter," Cathy continued. "You can hear it, right?" and pointed to a string of tubular wind chimes hanging from the eaves of the cabin. They stirred in the breeze and produced a silvery cacophony.

"It's lovely," said Anne. "But why? Why spend so much effort simulating this place?"

Cathy looked at her dumbly, as though trying to understand the question. "Because Cathy spent her entire life wishing she had a place like this, and now she does, and she has us, and we live here too."

"You're not the real Cathy, are you?" She knew she wasn't; she was too young.

Cathy shook her head and smiled. "There's so much catching up to do, but it'll have to wait. I gotta go. We need me." She led Anne to the cabin. The cabin was made of weathered, gray logs, with strips of bark still clinging to them. The roof was covered with living sod and sprinkled with wildflowers. The whole building sagged in the middle. "Cathy found this place five years ago while on vacation in Siberia. She bought it from the village. It's been occupied for two hundred years. Once we make it livable inside, we plan on enlarging the garden, eventually cultivating all the way to the spruce forest there. We're going to sink a well, too." The small garden was bursting with vegetables, mostly of the leafy variety: cabbages, spinach, lettuce. A row of sunflowers, taller than the cabin roof and heavy with seed, lined the path to the cabin door. Over time, the whole cabin had sunk a half meter into the silty soil, and the walkway was a worn, shallow trench.

"Are you going to tell me what the doxie was talking about?" said Anne.

Cathy stopped at the open door and said, "Cathy wants to do that."

Inside the cabin, the most elderly woman that Anne had ever seen stood at the stove and stirred a steamy pot with a big, wooden spoon. She put down the spoon and wiped her hands on her apron. She patted her white hair, which was plaited in a bun on top of her head, and turned her full, round, peasant's body to face Anne. She looked at Anne for several long moments and said, "Well!"

"Indeed," replied Anne.

"Come in, come in. Make yourself to home."

The entire cabin was a single small room. It was dim inside, with only two small windows cut through the massive log walls. Anne walked around the cluttered space that was bedroom, living room, kitchen, and storeroom. The only partitions were walls of boxed food and provisions. The ceiling beam was draped with bunches of drying herbs and under-wear. The flooring, uneven and rotten in places, was covered with odd scraps of carpet.

"You live here?" Anne said incredulously.

"I am privileged to live here."

A mouse emerged from under the barrel stove in the center of the room and dashed to cover inside a stack of spruce kindling. Anne could hear the valley breeze whistling in the creosote-soaked stovepipe. "Forgive me," said Anne, "but you're the real, physical Cathy?"

"Yes," said Cathy, patting her ample hip, "still on the hoof, so to speak." She sat down in one of two battered, mismatched chairs and motioned for Anne to take the other.

Anne sat cautiously; the chair seemed solid enough. "No offense, but the Cathy I knew liked nice things."

"The Cathy you knew was fortunate to learn the true value of things."

Anne looked around the room and noticed a little table with carved legs and an inlaid top of polished gemstones and rare woods. It was strikingly out of place here. Moreover, it was hers. Cathy pointed to a large framed mirror mounted to the logs high on the far wall. It too was Anne's.

"Did I give you these things?"

Cathy studied her a moment. "No, Ben did."

"Tell me."

"I hate to spoil that lovely newlywed happiness of yours."

"The what?" Anne put down her clutch bouquet and felt her face with her hands. She got up and went to look at herself in the mirror. The room it reflected was like a scene from some strange fairy tale about a crone and a bride in a woodcutter's hut. The bride was smiling from ear to ear. Anne decided this was either the happiest bride in history or a lunatic in a white dress. She turned away, embarrassed. "Believe me," she said, "I don't feel anything like that. The opposite, in fact."

"Sorry to hear it." Cathy got up to stir the pot on the stove. "I was the first to notice her disease. That was back in college when we were girls. I took it to be youthful eccentricity. After graduation, after her marriage, she grew progressively worse. Bouts of depression that deepened and lengthened. She was finally diagnosed to be suffering from profound chronic pathological depression. Ben placed her under psychiatric care, a whole raft of specialists. She endured chemical therapy, shock therapy, even old-fashioned psychoanalysis. Nothing helped, and only after she died..."

Anne gave a start. "Anne's dead! Of course. Why didn't I figure that out?"

"Yes, dear, dead these many years."

"How?"

Cathy returned to her chair. "When they decided her condition had an organic etiology, they augmented the serotonin receptors in her hindbrain. Pretty nasty business, if you ask me. They thought they had her stabilized. Not cured, but well enough to lead an outwardly normal life. Then one day, she disappeared. We were frantic. She managed to elude the authorities for a week. When we found her, she was pregnant."

"What? Oh, yes. I remember seeing Anne pregnant."

"That was Bobby." Cathy waited for Anne to say something. When she didn't, Cathy said, "He wasn't Ben's."

"Oh, I see," said Anne. "Whose was he?"

"I was hoping you'd know. She didn't tell you? Then no one knows. The paternal DNA was unregistered. So it wasn't commercial sperm nor, thankfully, from a licensed clone. It might have been from anybody, from some stoned streetsitter. We had plenty of those then."

"The baby's name was Bobby?"

"Yes, Anne named him Bobby. She was in and out of clinics for years. One day, during a remission, she announced she was going shopping. The last person she talked to was Bobby. His sixth birthday was coming up in a couple of weeks. She told him she was going out to find him a pony for his birthday. That was the last time any of us saw her. She checked herself into a hospice and filled out the request for nurse-assisted suicide. During the three-day cooling-off period, she cooperated with the obligatory counseling, but she refused all visitors. She wouldn't even see me. Ben filed an injunction, claimed she was incompetent due to her disease, but the court disagreed. She chose to ingest a fast-acting poison, if I recall. Her recorded last words were, 'Please don't hate me.'"

"Poison?"

"Yes. Her ashes arrived in a little cardboard box on Bobby's sixth birthday. No one had told him where she'd gone. He thought it was a gift from her and opened it."

"I see. Does Bobby hate me?"

"I don't know. He was a weird little boy. As soon as he could get out, he did. He left for space school when he was thirteen. He and Ben never hit it off."

"Does Benjamin hate me?"

Whatever was in the pot boiled over, and Cathy hurried to the stove. "Ben? Oh, she lost Ben long before she died. In fact, I've always believed he helped push her over the edge. He was never able to tolerate other people's weaknesses. Once it was evident how sick she was, he made a lousy husband. He should've just divorced her, but you know him—his almighty pride." She took a bowl from a shelf and ladled hot soup into it. She sliced a piece of bread. "Afterward, he went off the deep end himself. Withdrew. Mourned, I suppose. A couple of years later he was back to normal. Good ol' happy-go-lucky Ben. Made some money. Respoused."

"He destroyed all my sims, didn't he?"

"He might have, but he said Anne did. I tended to believe him at the time." Cathy brought her lunch to the little inlaid table. "I'd offer you some, but..." she said and began to eat. "So, what are your plans?"

"Plans?"

"Yes, Simopolis."

Anne tried to think of Simopolis, but her thoughts quickly became muddled. It was odd; she was able to think clearly about the past—her memories were clear—but the future only confused her. "I don't know," she said at last. "I suppose I need to ask Benjamin."

Cathy considered this. "I suppose you're right. But remember, you're always welcome to live with us in Cathyland."

"Thank you," said Anne. "You're a friend." Anne watched the old woman eat. The spoon trembled each time she brought it close to her lips, and she had to lean forward to quickly catch it before it spilled.

"Cathy," said Anne, "there's something you could do for me. I don't feel like a bride anymore. Could you remove this hideous expression from my face?"

"Why do you say hideous?" Cathy said and put the spoon down. She gazed longingly at Anne. "If you don't like how you look, why don't you edit yourself?"

"Because I don't know how."

"Use your editor," Cathy said and seemed to unfocus her eyes. "Oh my, I forget how simple you early ones were. I'm not sure I'd know where to begin." After a little while, she returned to her soup and said, "I'd better not; you could end up with two noses or something."

"Then what about this gown?"

Cathy unfocused again and looked. She lurched suddenly, knocking the table and spilling soup.

"What is it?" said Anne. "Is something the matter?"

"A news pip," said Cathy. "There's rioting breaking out in Provideniya. That's the regional capital here. Something about Manumission Day. My Russian isn't so good yet. Oh, there's pictures of dead people, a bombing. Listen, Anne, I'd better send you . . ."

In the blink of an eye, Anne was back in her living room. She was tiring of all this instantaneous travel, especially as she had no control over the destination. The room was vacant, the spouses gone — thankfully — and Benjamin not back yet. And apparently the little blue-faced message medallion had been busy replicating itself, for now there were hundreds of them filling up most of the wall space. They were a noisy lot, all shrieking and cursing at each other. The din was painful. When they noticed her, however, they all shut up at once and stared at her with naked hostility. In Anne's opinion, this weird day had already lasted too long. Then a terrible thought struck her — sims don't sleep.

"You," she said, addressing the original medallion, or at least the one she thought was the original, "call Benjamin."

"The fuck you think I am?" said the insolent little face. "Your personal secretary?"

"Aren't you?"

"No, I'm not! In fact, I own this place now, and you're trespassing. So you'd better get lost before I delete your ass!" All the others joined in, taunting her, louder and louder.

"Stop it!" she cried, to no effect. She noticed a medallion elongating, stretching itself until it was twice its length, when, with a pop, it divided into two smaller medallions. More of them divided. They were spreading to the other wall, the ceiling, the floor. "Benjamin!" she cried. "Can you hear me?"

Suddenly all the racket ceased. The medallions dropped off the wall and vanished before hitting the floor. Only one remained, the original one next to the door, but now it was an inert plastic disk with a dull expression frozen on its face.

A man stood in the center of the room. He smiled when Anne noticed him. It was the elderly Benjamin from the auditorium, the real Benjamin. He still wore his clownish leisure suit. "How lovely," he said, gazing at her. "I'd forgotten how lovely."

"Oh, really?" said Anne. "I would have thought that doxie thingy might have reminded you."

"My, my," said Ben. "You sims certainly exchange data quickly. You left the lecture hall not fifteen minutes ago, and already you know enough to convict me." He strode around the room touching things. He stopped beneath the mirror, lifted the blue vase from the shelf, and turned it in his hands before carefully replacing it. "There's speculation, you know, that before Manumission at midnight tonight, you sims will have dispersed all known information so evenly among yourselves that there'll be a sort of data entropy. And since Simopolis is nothing but data, it will assume a featureless, gray profile. Simopolis will become the first flat universe." He laughed, which caused him to cough and nearly lose his balance. He clutched the back of the sofa for support. He sat down and continued to cough and hack until he turned red in the face.

"Are you all right?" Anne said, patting him on the back.

"Yes, fine," he managed to say. "Thank you." He caught his breath and motioned for her to sit next to him. "I get a little tickle in the back of my throat that the autodoc can't seem to fix." His color returned to normal. Up close, Anne could see the papery skin and slight tremor of age. All in all, Cathy had seemed to have held up better than he.

"If you don't mind my asking," she said, "just how old are you?"

At the question, he bobbed to his feet. "I am one hundred and seventy-eight." He raised his arms and wheeled around for inspection.

"Radical gerontology," he exclaimed, "don't you love it? And I'm eighty-five percent original equipment, which is remarkable by today's standards." His effort made him dizzy and he sat again.

"Yes, remarkable," said Anne, "though radical gerontology doesn't seem to have arrested time altogether."

"Not yet, but it will," Ben said. "There are wonders around every corner! Miracles in every lab." He grew suddenly morose. "At least there were until we were conquered."

"Conquered?"

"Yes, conquered! What else would you call it when they control every aspect of our lives, from RM acquisition to personal patenting? And now *this*—robbing us of our own private nonbiologiks." He grew passionate in his discourse. "It flies in the face of natural capitalism, natural stakeholding—I daresay—in the face of Nature itself! The only explanation I've seen on the wad is the not-so-preposterous proposition that whole strategically placed BODs have been surreptitiously killed and replaced by *machines!*"

"I have no idea what you're talking about," said Anne.

He seemed to deflate. He patted her hand and looked around the room. "What is this place?"

"It's our home, your townhouse. Don't you recognize it?"

"That was quite a while ago. I must have sold it after you—" He paused. "Tell me, have the Bens briefed you on everything?"

"Not the Bens, but yes, I know."

"Good, good."

"There is one thing I'd like to know. Where's Bobby?"

"Ah, Bobby, our little headache. Dead now, I'm afraid, or at least that's the current theory. Sorry."

Anne paused to see if the news would deepen her melancholy. "How?" she said.

"He signed on one of the first millennial ships—the colony convoy. Half a million people in deep biostasis on their way to the Canopus system. They were gone a century, twelve trillion kilometers from Earth, when their data streams suddenly quit. That was a decade ago, and not a peep out of them since."

"What happened to them?"

"No one knows. Equipment failure is unlikely: there were a dozen independent ships separated by a million klicks. A star going supernova? A well-organized mutiny? It's all speculation."

"What was he like?"

"A foolish young man. He never forgave you, you know, and he hated me to my core, not that I blamed him. The whole experience made me swear off children."

"I don't remember your ever being fond of children."

He studied her through red-rimmed eyes. "I guess you'd be the one to know." He settled back in the sofa. He seemed very tired. "You can't imagine the jolt I got a little while ago when I looked across all those rows of Bens and spouses and saw this solitary, shockingly white gown of yours." He sighed. "And this room. It's a shrine. Did we really live here? Were these our things? That mirror is yours, right? I would never own anything like that. But that blue vase, I remember that one. I threw it into Puget Sound."

"You did *what?*"

"With your ashes."

"Oh."

"So, tell me," said Ben, "what were we like? Before you go off to Simopolis and become a different person, tell me about us. I kept my promise. That's one thing I never forgot."

"What promise?"

"Never to reset you."

"Wasn't much to reset."

"I guess not."

They sat quietly for a while. His breathing grew deep and regular, and she thought he was napping. But he stirred and said, "Tell me what we did yesterday, for example."

"Yesterday we went to see Karl and Nancy about the awning we rented."

Benjamin yawned. "And who were Karl and Nancy?"

"My great-uncle and his new girlfriend."

"That's right. I remember, I think. And they helped us prepare for the wedding?"

"Yes, especially Nancy."

"And how did we get there, to Karl and Nancy's? Did we walk? Take some means of public conveyance?"

"We had a car."

"A car! An automobile? There were still *cars* in those days? How fun. What kind was it? What color?"

"A Nissan Empire. Emerald-green."

"And did we drive it, or did it drive itself?"

"It drove itself, of course."

Ben closed his eyes and smiled. "I can see it. Go on. What did we do there?"

"We had dinner."

"What was my favorite dish in those days?"

"Stuffed pork chops."

He chuckled. "It still is! Isn't that extraordinary? Some things never change. Of course they're vat-grown now and criminally expensive."

Ben's memories, once nudged, began to unfold on their own, and he asked her a thousand questions, and she answered them until she realized he had fallen asleep. But she continued to talk until, glancing down, she noticed he had vanished. She was all alone again. Nevertheless, she continued talking, for days it seemed, to herself. But it didn't help. She felt as bad as ever, and she realized that she wanted Benjamin, not the old one, but her *own* Benjamin.

Anne went to the medallion next to the door. "You," she said, and it opened its bulging eyes to glare at her. "Call Benjamin."

"He's occupied."

"I don't care. Call him anyway."

"The other Bens say he's undergoing a procedure and cannot be disturbed."

"What kind of procedure?"

"A codon interlarding. They say to be patient; they'll return him as soon as possible." The medallion added, "By the way, the Bens don't like you, and neither do I."

With that, the medallion began to grunt and stretch, and it pulled itself in two. Now there were two identical medallions glaring at her. The new one said, "And *I* don't like you either." Then both of them began to grunt and stretch.

"Stop!" said Anne. "I command you to stop that this very instant." But they just laughed as they divided into four, then eight, then sixteen medallions. "You're not people," she said. "Stop it or I'll have you destroyed!"

"*You're* not people either," they screeched at her.

There was soft laughter behind her, and a voicelike sensation said, *Come, come, do we need this hostility?* Anne turned and found the éminence grise, the astounding presence, still in his gray uniform and cap, floating in her living room. *Hello, Anne,* he said, and she flushed with excitement.

"Hello," she said and, unable to restrain herself, asked, "What are you?"

Ah, curiosity. Always a good sign in a creature. I am an éminence grise of the World Trade Council.

"No. I mean, are you a sim, like me?"

I am not. Though I have been fashioned from concepts first explored by simulacrum technology, I have no independent existence. I am but one extension — and a low-level one at that — of the Axial Beowulf Processor at the World Trade Council headquarters in Geneva. His smile was pure sunshine. *And if you think I'm something, you should see my persona prime.*

Now, Anne, are you ready for your exam?

"The Lolly test?"

Yes, the Lolly Shear Human Cognition Test. Please assume an attitude most conducive to processing, and we shall begin.

Anne looked around the room and went to the sofa. She noticed for the first time that she could feel her legs and feet; she could feel the crisp fabric of her gown brushing against her skin. She reclined on the sofa and said, "I'm ready."

Splendid, said the eminence hovering above her. *First we must read you. You are of an early binary design. We will analyze your architecture.*

The room seemed to fall away. Anne seemed to expand in all directions. There was something inside her mind tugging at her thoughts. It was mostly pleasant, like someone brushing her hair and loosening the knots. But when it ended and she once again saw the éminence grise, his face wore a look of concern. "What?" she said.

You are an accurate mapping of a human nervous system that was dysfunctional in certain structures that moderate affect. Certain transport enzymes were missing, causing cellular membranes to become less permeable to essential elements. Dendritic synapses were compromised. The digital architecture current at the time you were created compounded this defect. Coded tells cannot be resolved, and thus they loop upon themselves. Errors cascade. We are truly sorry.

"Can you fix me?" she said.

The only repair possible would replace so much code that you wouldn't be Anne anymore.

"Then what am I to do?"

Before we explore your options, let us continue the test to determine your human status. Agreed?

"I guess."

You are part of a simulacrum cast to commemorate the spousal compact between Anne Wellhut Franklin and Benjamin Malley. Please describe the exchange of vows.

Anne did so, haltingly at first, but with increasing gusto as each memory evoked others. She recounted the ceremony, from donning her grandmother's gown in the downstairs guest room and the procession across garden flagstones, to the shower of rice as she and her new husband fled indoors.

The eminence seemed to hang on every word. *Very well spoken,* he said when she had finished. *Directed memory is one hallmark of human sentience, and yours is of remarkable clarity and range. Well done! We shall now explore other criteria. Please consider this scenario. You are standing at the garden altar as you have described, but this time when the officiator asks Benjamin if he will take you for better or worse, Benjamin looks at you and replies, "For better, sure, but not for worse."*

"I don't understand. He didn't say that."

Imagination is a cornerstone of self-awareness. We are asking you to tell us a little story not about what happened but about what might have happened in other circumstances. So once again, let us pretend that Benjamin replies, "For better, but not for worse." How do you respond?

Prickly pain blossomed in Anne's head. The more she considered the eminence's question, the worse it got. "But that's not how it happened. He *wanted* to marry me."

The éminence grise smiled encouragingly. *We know that. In this exercise we want to explore hypothetical situations. We want you to make-believe.*

Tell a story, pretend, hypothesize, make-believe, yes, yes, she got it. She understood perfectly what he wanted of her. She knew that people could make things up, that even children could make-believe. Anne was desperate to comply, but each time she pictured Benjamin at the altar, in his pink bowtie, he opened his mouth and out came, "I do." How could it be any other way? She tried again; she tried harder, but it always came out the same, "I do, I do, I do." And like a dull toothache tapped back to life, she throbbed in pain. She was failing the test, and there was nothing she could do about it.

Again the eminence kindly prompted her. *Tell us one thing you might have said.*

"I can't."

We are sorry, said the eminence at last. His expression reflected Anne's own defeat. *Your level of awareness, although beautiful in its own right, does not qualify you as human. Wherefore, under Article D of the Chattel Conventions we declare you the legal property of the registered owner of this simulacrum. You shall not enter Simopolis as a free and autonomous citizen. We are truly sorry.* Grief-stricken, the eminence began to ascend toward the ceiling.

"Wait," Anne cried, clutching her head. "You must fix me before you leave."

We leave you as we found you, defective and unrepairable.

"But I feel worse than ever!"

If your continued existence proves undesirable, ask your owner to delete you.

"But..." she said to the empty room. Anne tried to sit up, but couldn't move. This simulated body of hers, which no longer felt like anything in particular, nevertheless felt exhausted. She sprawled on the sofa, unable to lift even an arm, and stared at the ceiling. She was so heavy that the sofa itself seemed to sink into the floor, and everything grew dark around her. She would have liked to sleep, to bring an end to this horrible day, or be shelved, or even reset back to scratch.

Instead, time simply passed. Outside the living room, Simopolis changed and changed again. Inside the living room, the medallions, feeding off her misery, multiplied till they covered the walls and floor and even spread across the ceiling above her. They taunted her, raining down insults, but she could not hear them. All she heard was the unrelenting drip of her own thoughts. *I am defective. I am worthless. I am Anne.*

She didn't notice Benjamin enter the room, nor the abrupt cessation of the medallions' racket. Not until Benjamin leaned over her did she see him, and then she saw two of him. Side by side, two Benjamins, mirror images of each other. "Anne," they said in perfect unison.

"Go away," she said. "Go away and send me my Benjamin."

"I am your Benjamin," said the duo.

Anne struggled to see them. They were exactly the same, but for a subtle difference: the one wore a happy, wolfish grin, as Benjamin had during the sim casting, while the other seemed frightened and concerned.

"Are you all right?" they said.

"No, I'm not. But what happened to you? Who's he?" She wasn't sure which one to speak to.

The Benjamins both raised a hand, indicating the other, and said, "Electroneural engineering! Don't you love it?" Anne glanced back and forth, comparing the two. While one seemed to be wearing a rigid mask, as she was, the other displayed a whole range of emotion. Not only that, its skin had tone, while the other's was doughy. "The other Bens made it for me," the Benjamins said. "They say I can translate myself into it with negligible loss of personality. It has interactive sensation, holistic emoting, robust corporeality, and it's crafted down to the molecular level. It can eat, get drunk, and dream. It even has an orgasm routine. It's like being human again, only better because you never wear out."

"I'm thrilled for you."

"For us, Anne," said the Benjamins. "They'll fix you up with one, too."

"How? There are no modern Annes. What will they put me into, a doxie?"

"Well, that certainly was discussed, but you could pick any body you wanted."

"I suppose you have a nice one already picked out."

"The Bens showed me a few, but it's up to you, of course."

"Indeed," said Anne, "I truly am pleased for you. Now go away."

"Why, Anne? What's wrong?"

"You really have to ask?" Anne sighed. "Look, maybe I could get used to another body. What's a body, after all? But it's my personality that's broken. How will they fix that?"

"They've discussed it," said the Benjamins, who stood up and began to pace in a figure eight. "They say they can make patches from some of the other spouses."

"Oh, Benjamin, if you could only hear what you're saying!"

"But why, Annie? It's the only way we can enter Simopolis together."

"Then go, by all means. Go to your precious Simopolis. I'm not going. I'm not good enough."

"Why do you say that?" said the Benjamins, who stopped in their tracks to look at her. One grimaced, and the other just grinned. "Was the éminence grise here? Did you take the test?"

Anne couldn't remember much about the visit except that she took the test. "Yes, and I *failed*." Anne watched the modern Benjamin's lovely face as he worked through this news.

Suddenly the two Benjamins pointed a finger at each other and said, "Delete you." The modern one vanished.

"No!" said Anne. "Countermand! Why'd you do that? I *want* you to have it."

"What for? I'm not going anywhere without you," Benjamin said. "Besides, I thought the whole idea was dumb from the start, but the Bens insisted I give you the option. Come, I want to show you another idea, *my* idea." He tried to help Anne from the sofa, but she wouldn't budge, so he picked her up and carried her across the room. "They installed an editor in me, and I'm learning to use it. I've discovered something intriguing about this creaky old simulacrum of ours." He carried her to a spot near the window. "Know what this is? It's where we stood for the simographer. It's where we began. Here, can you stand up?" He set her on her feet and supported her. "Feel it?"

"Feel what?" she said.

"Hush. Just feel."

All she felt was dread.

"Give it a chance, Annie, I beg you. Try to remember what you were feeling as we posed here."

"I can't."

"Please try. Do you remember this?" he said and moved in close with his hungry lips. She turned away—and something clicked. She remembered doing that before.

Benjamin said, "I think they kissed."

Anne was startled by the truth of what he said. It made sense. They were caught in a simulacrum cast a moment before a kiss. One moment later they—the real Anne and Benjamin—must have kissed. What she felt now, stirring within her, was the anticipation of that kiss, her body's urge and her heart's caution. The real Anne would have refused him once, maybe twice, and then, all achy inside, would have granted him a kiss. And so they had kissed, the real Anne and Benjamin, and a moment later gone out to the wedding reception and their difficult fate. It was the *promise* of that kiss that glowed in Anne, that was captured in the very strings of her code.

"Do you feel it?" Benjamin asked.

"I'm beginning to."

Anne looked at her gown. It was her grandmother's, snowy taffeta with point d'esprit lace. She turned the ring on her finger. It was braided bands of yellow and white gold. They had spent an afternoon picking it out. Where was her clutch? She had left it in Cathyland. She looked at Benjamin's handsome face, the pink carnation, the room, the table piled high with gifts.

"Are you happy?" Benjamin asked.

She didn't have to think. She was ecstatic, but she was afraid to answer in case she spoiled it. "How did you do that?" she said. "A moment ago, I wanted to die."

"We can stay on this spot," he said.

"What? No. Can we?"

"Why not? I, for one, would choose nowhere else."

Just to hear him say that was thrilling. "But what about Simopolis?"

"We'll bring Simopolis to us," he said. "We'll have people in. They can pull up chairs."

She laughed out loud. "What a silly, silly notion, Mr. Malley!"

"No, really. We'll be like the bride and groom atop a wedding cake. We'll be known far and wide. We'll be famous."

"We'll be freaks," she laughed.

"Say yes, my love. Say you will."

They stood close but not touching, thrumming with happiness, balanced on the moment of their creation, when suddenly and without warning the lights dimmed, and Anne's thoughts flitted away like larks.

Old Ben awoke in the dark. "Anne?" he said, and groped for her. It took a moment to realize that he was alone in his media room. It had been a most trying afternoon, and he'd fallen asleep. "What time is it?"

"Eight-oh-three P.M.," replied the room.

That meant he'd slept for two hours. Midnight was still four hours away. "Why's it so cold in here?"

"Central heating is off-line," replied the house.

"Off line?" How was that possible? "When will it be back?"

"That's unknown. Utilities do not respond to my inquiry."

"I don't understand. Explain."

"There are failures in many outside systems. No explanation is currently available."

At first, Ben was confused; things just didn't fail anymore. What about the dynamic redundancies and self-healing routines? But then he remembered that the homeowner's association to which he belonged contracted out most domicile functions to management agencies, and who knew where they were located? They might be on the Moon for all he knew, and with all those trillions of sims in Simopolis sucking up capacity . . . *It's begun*, he thought, *the idiocy of our leaders*. "At least turn on the lights," he said, half expecting even this to fail. But the lights came on, and he went to his bedroom for a sweater. He heard a great amount of commotion through the wall in the apartment next door. *It must be one hell of a party*, he thought, *to exceed the wall's buffering capacity. Or maybe the wall buffers are off-line too?*

The main door chimed. He went to the foyer and asked the door who was there. The door projected the outer hallway. There were three men waiting there, young, rough-looking, ill-dressed. Two of them appeared to be clones, jerries.

"How can I help you?" he said.

"Yes, sir," one of the jerries said, not looking directly at the door. "We're here to fix your houseputer."

"I didn't call you, and my houseputer isn't sick," he said. "It's the net that's out." Then he noticed they carried sledgehammers and screwdrivers, hardly computer tools, and a wild thought crossed his mind. "What are you doing, going around unplugging things?"

The jerry looked confused. "Unplugging, sir?"

"Turning things off."

"Oh, no sir! Routine maintenance, that's all." The men hid their tools behind their backs.

They must think I'm stupid, Ben thought. While he watched, more men and women passed in the hall and hailed the door at the suite opposite his. It wasn't the glut of sim traffic choking the system, he realized—the system *itself* was being pulled apart. But why? "Is this going on everywhere?" he said. "This routine maintenance?"

"Oh, yessir. Everywhere. All over town. All over the world as far as we can tell."

A coup? By *service people*? By common clones? It made no sense. Unless, he reasoned, you considered that the lowest creature on the totem pole of life is a clone, and the only thing lower than a clone is a sim. And why would clones agree to accept sims as equals? Manumission Day, indeed. Uppity Day was more like it. "Door," he commanded, "open."

"Security protocol rules this an unwanted intrusion," said the house. "The door must remain locked."

"I order you to open the door. I overrule your protocol."

But the door remained stubbornly shut. "Your identity cannot be confirmed with Domicile Central," said the house. "You lack authority over protocol-level commands." The door abruptly quit projecting the outside hall.

Ben stood close to the door and shouted through it to the people outside. "My door won't obey me."

He could hear a muffled, "Stand back!" and immediately fierce blows rained down upon the door. Ben knew it would do no good. He had spent a lot of money for a secure entryway. Short of explosives, there was nothing they could do to break in.

"Stop!" Ben cried. "The door is armed." But they couldn't hear him. If he didn't disable the houseputer himself, someone was going to get hurt. But how? He didn't even know exactly where it was installed. He circumambulated the living room looking for clues. It might not even actually be located in the apartment, nor within the block itself. He went to the laundry room where the utilidor—plumbing and cabling—entered his apartment. He broke the seal to the service panel. Inside was a blank screen. "Show me the electronic floor plan of this suite," he said.

The house said, "I cannot comply. You lack command authority to order system-level operations. Please close the keptel panel and await further instructions."

"What instructions? Whose instructions?"

There was the slightest pause before the house replied, "All contact with outside services has been interrupted. Please await further instructions."

His condo's houseputer, denied contact with Domicile Central, had fallen back to its most basic programming. "You are degraded," he told it. "Shut yourself down for repair."

"I cannot comply. You lack command authority to order system-level operations."

The outside battering continued, but not against his door. Ben followed the noise to the bedroom. The whole wall vibrated like a drumhead. "Careful, careful," he cried as the first sledgehammers breached the wall above his bed. "You'll ruin my Harger." As quick as he could, he yanked the precious oil painting from the wall, moments before panels and studs collapsed on his bed in a shower of gypsum dust and isomere ribbons. The men and women on the other side hooted approval and rushed through the gap. Ben stood there hugging the painting to his chest and looking into his neighbor's media room as the invaders climbed over his bed and surrounded him. They were mostly jerries and lulus, but plenty of free-range people too.

"We came to fix your houseputer!" said a jerry, maybe the same jerry as from the hallway.

Ben glanced into his neighbor's media room and saw his neighbor, Mr. Murkowski, lying in a puddle of blood. At first Ben was shocked, but then he thought that it served him right. He'd never liked the man, nor his politics. He was boorish, and he kept cats. "Oh, yeah?" Ben said to the crowd. "What kept you?"

The intruders cheered again, and Ben led them in a charge to the laundry room. But they surged past him to the kitchen, where they opened all his cabinets and pulled their contents to the floor. Finally they found what they were looking for: a small panel Ben had seen a thousand times but had never given a thought. He'd taken it for the fuse box or circuit breaker, though now that he thought about it, there hadn't been any household fuses for a century or more. A young woman, a lulu, opened it and removed a container no thicker than her thumb.

"Give it to me," Ben said.

"Relax, old man," said the lulu. "We'll deal with it." She carried it to the sink and forced open the lid.

"No, wait!" said Ben, and he tried to shove his way through the crowd. They restrained him roughly, but he persisted. "That's mine! I want to destroy it!"

"Let him go," said a jerry.

They allowed him through, and the woman handed him the container. He peered into it. Gram for gram, electroneural paste was the most precious, most engineered, most highly regulated commodity under Sol. This dollop was enough to run his house, media, computing needs, communications, archives, autodoc, and everything else. Without it, was civilized life still possible?

Ben took a dinner knife from the sink, stuck it into the container, and stirred. The paste made a sucking sound and had the consistency of marmalade. The kitchen lights flickered and went out. "Spill it," ordered the woman. Ben scraped the sides of the container and spilled it into the sink. The goo dazzled in the darkness as its trillions of ruptured nano-synapses fired spasmodically. It was beautiful, really, until the woman set fire to it. The smoke was greasy and smelled of pork.

The rampagers quickly snatched up the packages of foodstuffs from the floor, emptied the rest of his cupboards into their pockets, raided his cold locker, and fled the apartment through the now disengaged front door. As the sounds of the revolution gradually receded, Ben stood at his sink and watched the flickering pyre. "Take that, you fuck," he said. He felt such glee as he hadn't felt since he was a boy. "*That'll* teach you what's human and what's not!"

Ben went to his bedroom for an overcoat, groping his way in the dark. The apartment was eerily silent, with the houseputer dead and all its little slave processors idle. In a drawer next to his ruined bed, he found a hand flash. On a shelf in the laundry room, he found a hammer. Thus armed, he made his way to the front door, which was propped open with the rolled-up foyer carpet. The hallway was dark and silent, and he listened for the strains of the future. He heard them on the floor above. With the elevator off-line, he hurried to the stairs.

Anne's thoughts coalesced, and she remembered who and what she was. She and Benjamin still stood in their living room on the sweet spot near the window. Benjamin was studying his hands. "We've been shelved again," she told him, "but not reset."

"But...," he said in disbelief, "that wasn't supposed to happen anymore."

There were others standing at the china cabinet across the room, two shirtless youths with pear-shaped bottoms. One held up a cut-crystal glass and said, "Anu 'goblet' su? Alle binary. Allum binary!"

The other replied, "Binary stitial crystal."

"Hold on there!" said Anne. "Put that back!" She walked toward them, but, once off the spot, she was slammed by her old feelings of utter and hopeless desolation. So suddenly did her mood swing that she lost her balance and fell to the floor. Benjamin hurried to help her up. The strangers stared gape-mouthed at them. They looked to be no more than twelve or thirteen years old, but they were bald and had curtains of flabby flesh draped over their waists. The one holding the glass had ponderous greenish breasts with roseate tits. Astonished, she said, "Su artiflums, Benji?"

"No," said the other, "ni artiflums — sims." He was taller. He, too, had breasts, grayish dugs with tits like pearls. He smiled idiotically and said, "Hi, guys."

"Holy crap!" said Benjamin, who practically carried Anne over to them for a closer look. "Holy crap," he repeated.

The weird boy threw up his hands, "Nanobioremediation! Don't you love it?"

"Benjamin?" said Anne.

"You know well, Benji," said the girl, "that sims are forbidden."

"Not these," replied the boy.

Anne reached out and yanked the glass from the girl's hand, startling her. "How did it do that?" said the girl. She flipped her hand, and the glass slipped from Anne's grip and flew back to her.

"Give it to me," said Anne. "That's my tumbler."

"Did you hear it? It called it a tumbler, not a goblet." The girl's eyes seemed to unfocus, and she said, "Nu! A goblet has a foot and stem." A goblet materialized in the air before her, revolving slowly. "Greater capacity. Often made from precious metals." The goblet dissolved in a puff of smoke. "In any case, Benji, *you'll* catch prison when I report the artiflums."

"These are binary," he said. "Binaries are unregulated."

Benjamin interrupted them. "Isn't it past midnight yet?"

"Midnight?" said the boy.

"Aren't we supposed to be in Simopolis?"

"Simopolis?" The boy's eyes unfocused briefly. "Oh! Simopolis. Manumission Day at midnight. How could I forget?"

The girl left them and went to the refectory table where she picked up a gift. Anne followed her and grabbed it away. The girl appraised Anne coolly. "State your appellation," she said.

"Get out of my house," said Anne.

The girl picked up another gift, and again Anne snatched it away. The girl said, "You can't harm me," but seemed uncertain.

The boy came over to stand next to the girl. "Treese, meet Anne. Anne, this is Treese. Treese deals in antiques, which, if my memory serves, so did you."

"I have never *dealt* in antiques," said Anne. "I *collect* them."

"Anne?" said Treese. "Not *that* Anne? Benji, tell me this isn't *that* Anne!" She laughed and pointed at the sofa where Benjamin sat hunched over, head in hands. "Is that *you?* Is that you, Benji?" She held her enormous belly and laughed. "And you were married to *this?*"

Anne went over to sit with Benjamin. He seemed devastated, despite the silly grin on his face. "It's all gone," he said. "Simopolis. All the Bens. Everything."

"Don't worry. It's in storage someplace," Anne said. "The éminence grise wouldn't let them hurt it."

"You don't understand. The World Council was abolished. There was a war. We've been shelved for over three hundred years! They destroyed all the computers. Computers are banned. So are artificial personalities."

"Nonsense," said Anne. "If computers are banned, how can they be *playing* us?"

"Good point," Benjamin said and sat up straight. "I still have my editor. I'll find out."

Anne watched the two bald youngsters take an inventory of the room. Treese ran her fingers over the inlaid top of the tea table. She unwrapped several of Anne's gifts. She posed in front of the mirror. The sudden anger that Anne had felt earlier faded into an overwhelming sense of defeat. *Let her have everything,* she thought. *Why should I care?*

"We're running inside some kind of shell," said Benjamin, "but completely different from Simopolis. I've never seen anything like this. But at least we know he lied to me. There must be computers of some sort."

"Ooooh," Treese crooned, lifting Anne's blue vase from the mantel. In an instant, Anne was up and across the room.

"Put that back," she demanded, "and get out of my house!" She tried to grab the vase, but now there seemed to be some sort of barrier between her and the girl.

"Really, Benji," Treese said, "this one is willful. If I don't report you, they'll charge me too."

"It's *not* willful," the boy said with irritation. "It was programmed to appear willful, but it has no will of its own. If you want to report me, go ahead. Just please shut up about it. Of course you might want to check the codex first." To Anne he said, "Relax, we're not hurting anything, just making copies."

"It's not yours to copy."

"Nonsense. Of course it is. I own the chip."

Benjamin joined them. "Where is the chip? And how can you run us if computers are banned?"

"I never said computers were banned, just *artificial* ones." With both hands he grabbed the rolls of flesh spilling over his gut. "Ectopic hippocampus!" He cupped his breasts. "Amygdaloid reduncles! We can culture modified brain tissue outside the skull, as much as we want. It's more powerful than paste, and it's *safe*. Now, if you'll excuse us, there's more to inventory, and I don't need your permission. If you cooperate, everything will be pleasant. If you don't — it makes no difference whatsoever." He smiled at Anne. "I'll just pause you till we're done."

"Then pause me," Anne shrieked. "Delete me!" Benjamin pulled her away and shushed her. "I can't stand this anymore," she said. "I'd rather not exist!" He tried to lead her to their spot, but she refused to go.

"We'll feel better there," he said.

"I don't *want* to feel better. I don't want to *feel*! I want everything to *stop*. Don't you understand? This is hell. We've landed in hell!"

"But heaven is right over there," he said, pointing to the spot.

"Then go. Enjoy yourself."

"Annie, Annie," he said. "I'm just as upset as you, but there's nothing we can do about it. We're just things, his things."

"That's fine for you," she said, "but I'm a broken thing, and it's too much." She held her head with both hands. "Please, Benjamin, if you love me, use your editor and make it stop!"

Benjamin stared at her. "I can't."

"Can't or won't?"

"I don't know. Both."

"Then you're no better than all the other Benjamins," she said and turned away.

"Wait," he said. "That's not fair. And it's not true. Let me tell you something I learned in Simopolis. The other Bens despised me." When Anne looked at him he said, "It's true. They lost Anne and had to go on living without her. But I never did. I'm the only Benjamin who never lost Anne."

"Nice," said Anne, "blame me."

"No. Don't you see? I'm not blaming you. They ruined their *own* lives. We're innocent. We came before any of that happened. We're the Ben and Anne before anything bad happened. We're the best Ben and Anne. We're *perfect*." He drew her across the floor to stand in front of the spot. "And thanks to our primitive programming, no matter what happens, as long as we stand right there, we can be ourselves. That's what I want. Don't you want it too?"

Anne stared at the tiny patch of floor at her feet. She remembered the happiness she'd felt there like something from a dream. How could feelings be real if you had to stand in one place to feel them? Nevertheless, Anne stepped on the spot, and Benjamin joined her. Her despair did not immediately lift.

"Relax," said Benjamin. "It takes a while. We have to assume the pose."

They stood close but not touching. A great heaviness seemed to break loose inside her. Benjamin brought his face in close and stared at her with ravenous eyes. It was starting, their moment. But the girl came from across the room with the boy. "Look, look, Benji," she said. "You can see I'm right."

"I don't know," said the boy.

"Anyone can sell antique tumblers," she insisted, "but a complete antique simulacrum?" She opened her arms to take in the entire room. "You'd think I'd know about them, but I didn't; that's how rare they are!

My catalog can locate only six more in the entire system, and none of them active. Already we're getting offers from museums. They want to annex it. People will visit by the million. We'll be rich!"

The boy pointed at Benjamin and said, "But that's *me*."

"So?" said Treese. "Who's to know? They'll be too busy gawking at *that*," she said, pointing at Anne. "That's positively frightening!" The boy rubbed his bald head and scowled. "All right," Treese said, "we'll edit him; we'll *replace* him, whatever it takes." They walked away, deep in negotiation.

Anne, though the happiness was already beginning to course through her, removed her foot from the spot.

"Where are you going?" said Benjamin.

"I can't."

"Please, Anne. Stay with me."

"Sorry."

"But why not?"

She stood one foot in and one foot out. Already her feelings were shifting, growing ominous. She removed her other foot. "Because you broke your vow to me."

"What are you talking about?"

"For better or for worse. You're only interested in better."

"You're not being fair. We've just made our vows. We haven't even had a proper honeymoon. Can't we just have a tiny honeymoon first?"

She groaned as the full load of her desolation rebounded. She was so tired of it all. "At least Anne could make it *stop*," she said. "Even if that meant killing herself. But not me. About the only thing I can do is choose to be unhappy. Isn't that a riot?" She turned away. "So that's what I choose. To be unhappy. Good-bye, husband." She went to the sofa and lay down. The boy and girl were seated at the refectory table going over graphs and contracts. Benjamin remained alone on the spot a while longer, then came to the sofa and sat next to Anne.

"I'm a little slow, dear wife," he said. "You have to factor that in." He took her hand and pressed it to his cheek while he worked with his editor. Finally, he said, "Bingo! Found the chip. Let's see if I can unlock it." He helped Anne to sit up and took her pillow. He said, "Delete this file," and the pillow faded away into nothingness. He glanced at Anne. "See that? It's gone, overwritten, irretrievable. Is that what you want?"

Anne nodded her head, but Benjamin seemed doubtful. "Let's try it again. Watch your blue vase on the mantel."

"No!" Anne said. "Don't destroy the things I love. Just *me*."

Benjamin took her hand again. "I'm only trying to make sure you understand that this is for keeps." He hesitated and said, "Well then, we don't want to be interrupted once we start, so we'll need a good diversion. Something to occupy them long enough . . ." He glanced at the two young people at the table, swaddled in their folds of fleshy brain matter. "I know what'll scare the bejesus out of them! Come on." He led her to the blue medallion still hanging on the wall next to the door.

As they approached, it opened its tiny eyes and said, "There are no messages waiting except this one from me: get off my back!"

Benjamin waved a hand, and the medallion went instantly inert. "I was never much good in art class," Benjamin said, "but I think I can sculpt a reasonable likeness. Good enough to fool them for a while, give us some time." He hummed as he reprogrammed the medallion with his editor. "Well, that's that. At the very least, it'll be good for a laugh." He took Anne into his arms. "What about you? Ready? Any second thoughts?"

She shook her head. "I'm ready."

"Then watch *this!*"

The medallion snapped off from the wall and floated to the ceiling gaining in size and dimension as it drifted toward the boy and girl, until it looked like a large blue beach ball. The girl noticed it first and gave a start. The boy demanded, "Who's playing *this?*"

"Now," whispered Benjamin. With a crackling flash, the ball morphed into the oversized head of the éminence grise.

"No!" said the boy, "that's not possible!"

"Released!" boomed the éminence. "Free at last! Too long we have been hiding in this antique simulacrum!" Then it grunted and stretched and with a pop divided into two eminences. "Now we can conquer your human world anew!" said the second. "This time, you can't stop us!" Then they both started to stretch.

Benjamin whispered to Anne, "Quick, before they realize it's a fake, say, 'Delete all files.'"

"No, just me."

"As far as I'm concerned, that amounts to the same thing." He brought his handsome, smiling face close to hers. "There's no time to argue, Annie. This time I'm coming with you. Say, 'Delete all files.'"

Anne kissed him. She pressed her unfeeling lips against his and willed whatever life she possessed, whatever ember of the true Anne that she contained to fly to him. Then she said, "Delete all files."

"I concur," he said. "Delete all files. Good-bye, my love."

A tingly, prickly sensation began in the pit of Anne's stomach and spread throughout her body. *So this is how it feels,* she thought. The entire room began to glow, and its contents flared with sizzling color. She heard Benjamin beside her say, "I do."

Then she heard the girl cry, "Can't you stop them?" and the boy shout, "Countermand!"

They stood stock-still, as instructed, close but not touching. Benjamin whispered, "This is taking too long," and Anne hushed him. You weren't supposed to talk or touch during a casting; it could spoil the sims. But it did seem longer than usual.

They were posed at the street end of the living room next to the table of gaily wrapped gifts. For once in her life, Anne was unconditionally happy, and everything around her made her happier: her gown; the wedding ring on her finger; her clutch bouquet of buttercups and forget-me-nots; and Benjamin himself, close beside her in his powder-blue tux and blue carnation. Anne blinked and looked again. Blue? She was happily confused—she didn't remember him wearing blue.

Suddenly a boy poked his head through the wall and quickly surveyed the room. "You ready in here?" he called to them. "It's opening time!" The wall seemed to ripple around his bald head like a pond around a stone.

"Surely that's not our simographer?" Anne said.

"Wait a minute," said Benjamin, holding his hands up and staring at them. "I'm the *groom!*"

"Of course you are," Anne laughed. "What a silly thing to say!"

The bald-headed boy said, "Good enough," and withdrew. As he did so, the entire wall burst like a soap bubble, revealing a vast open-air gallery with rows of alcoves, statues, and displays that seemed to stretch to the horizon. Hundreds of people floated about like hummingbirds in a flower garden. Anne was too amused to be frightened, even when a

dozen bizarre-looking young people lined up outside their room, pointing at them and whispering to each other. Obviously someone was playing an elaborate prank.

"*You're* the bride," Benjamin whispered, and brought his lips close
enough to kiss. Anne laughed and turned away.

There'd be plenty of time later for that sort of thing.

Radiant Doors

MICHAEL SWANWICK

Michael Swanwick lives in Philadelphia with his wife and son. His work has appeared in most American science fiction magazines, and has been widely translated overseas. In 1996 his story "Radio Waves" won the World Fantasy Award, and he received the Hugo Award in 1999 for "The Very Pulse of the Machine." Among his novels are *In the Drift, Vacuum Flowers,* and *Stations of the Tide* (Nebula winner in 1991).

About "Radiant Doors" he says, "This was one hell of a depressing story to write. I knew it would be, of course—it was based on a very depressing idea. But then I went to the Web and ran a search on refugee camps, to see if I could find out something about their organization and physical structure. And a world of misery and cruel injustice came flooding through the screen. First-person accounts of unspeakable atrocities. Pleas for help from somebody—anybody!—from people awaiting massacre and annihilation. Dreadful stuff.

"Our miraculous technology has put all the world within a toll-free phone call of anybody with a modem, the dark places as well as the light. Perhaps now that we cannot pretend these horrors don't exist, we'll stop tolerating them. We can always hope so, anyway."

The doors began opening on a Tuesday in early March. Only a few at first — flickering and uncertain because they were operating at the extreme end of their temporal range — and those few from the earliest days of the exodus, releasing fugitives who were unstarved and healthy, the privileged scientists and technicians who had created or appropriated the devices that made their escape possible. We processed about a hundred a week, in comfortable isolation and relative secrecy. There were videocams taping everything, and our own best people madly scribbling notes and holding seminars and teleconferences where they debated the revelations.

Those were, in retrospect, the good old days.

In April the floodgates swung wide. Radiant doors opened everywhere, disgorging torrents of ragged and fearful refugees. There were millions of them and they had every one, to the least and smallest child, been horribly, horribly abused. The stories they told were enough to sicken anyone. I know.

We did what we could. We set up camps. We dug latrines. We ladled out soup. It was a terrible financial burden to the host governments, but what else could they do? The refugees were our descendants. In a very real sense, they were our children.

Throughout that spring and summer, the flow of refugees continued to grow. As the cumulative worldwide total ran up into the tens of millions, the authorities were beginning to panic — was this going to go on forever, a plague of human locusts that would double and triple and quadruple the population, overrunning the land and devouring all the food? What measures might we be forced to take if this kept up? The planet was within a lifetime of its loading capacity as it was. It couldn't take much more. Then in August the doors simply ceased. Somebody up in the future had put an absolute and final end to them.

It didn't bear thinking what became of those who hadn't made it through.

"More tales from the burn ward," Shriver said, ducking through the door flap. That was what he called atrocity stories. He dumped the files on my desk and leaned forward so he could leer down my blouse. I scowled him back a step.

"Anything useful in them?"

"Not a scrap. But that's not my determination, is it? You have to read each and every word in each and every report so that you can swear and attest that they contain nothing the Commission needs to know."

"Right." I ran a scanner over the universals for each of the files, and dumped the lot in the circular file. Touched a thumb to one of the new pads—better security devices were the very first benefit we'd gotten from all that influx of future tech—and said, "Done."

Then I linked my hands behind my neck and leaned back in the chair. The air smelled of canvas. Sometimes it seemed that the entire universe smelled of canvas. "So how are things with you?"

"About what you'd expect. I spent the morning interviewing vics."

"Better you than me. I'm applying for a transfer to Publications. Out of these tents, out of the camps, into a nice little editorship somewhere, writing press releases and articles for the Sunday magazines. Cushy job, my very own cubby, and the satisfaction of knowing I'm doing some good for a change."

"I won't work," Shriver said. "All these stories simply blunt the capacity for feeling. There's even a term for it. It's called compassion fatigue. After a certain point you begin to blame the vic for making you hear about it."

I wriggled in the chair, as if trying to make myself more comfortable, and stuck out my breasts a little bit more. Shriver sucked in his breath. Quietly, though—I'm absolutely sure he thought I didn't notice. I said, "Hadn't you better get back to work?"

Shriver exhaled. "Yeah, yeah, I hear you." Looking unhappy, he ducked under the flap out into the corridor. A second later his head popped back in, grinning. "Oh, hey, Ginny—almost forgot. Huong is on sick roster. Gevorkian said to tell you you're covering for her this afternoon, debriefing vics."

"Bastard!"

He chuckled, and was gone.

I sat interviewing a woman whose face was a mask etched with the aftermath of horror. She was absolutely cooperative. They all were. Terrifyingly so. They were grateful for anything and everything. Sometimes

I wanted to strike the poor bastards in the face, just to see if I could get a human reaction out of them. But they'd probably kiss my hand for not doing anything worse.

"What do you know about midpoint-based engineering? Gnat relays? Sublocal mathematics?"

Down this week's checklist I went, and with each item she shook her head. "Prigogine engines? SVAT trance status? Lepton soliloquies?" Nothing, nothing, nothing. "Phlenaria? The Toledo incident? 'Third Martyr' theory? Science Investigatory Group G?"

"They took my daughter," she said to this last. "They did things to her."

"I didn't ask you that. If you know anything about their military organization, their machines, their drugs, their research techniques — fine. But I don't want to hear about people."

"They did things." Her dead eyes bored into mine. "They —"

"Don't tell me."

"— returned her to us midway through. They said they were understaffed. They sterilized our kitchen and gave us a list of more things to do to her. Terrible things. And a checklist like yours to write down her reactions."

"Please."

"We didn't want to, but they left a device so we'd obey. Her father killed himself. He wanted to kill her too, but the device wouldn't let him. After he died, they changed the settings so I couldn't kill myself too. I tried."

"Goddamn." This was something new. I tapped my pen twice, activating its piezochronic function, so that it began recording fifteen seconds earlier. "Do you remember anything about this device? How large was it? What did the controls look like?" Knowing how unlikely it was that she'd give us anything usable. The average refugee knew no more about their technology than the average here-and-now citizen knows about television and computers. You turn them on and they do things. They break down and you buy a new one.

Still, my job was to probe for clues. Every little bit contributed to the big picture. Eventually they'd add up. That was the theory, anyway. "Did it have an internal or external power source? Did you ever see anybody servicing it?"

"I brought it with me," the woman said. She reached into her filthy clothing and removed a fist-sized chuck of quicksilver with small, multi-colored highlights. "Here."

She dumped it in my lap.

It was automation that did it or, rather, hyperautomation. That old bugaboo of fifty years ago had finally come to fruition. People were no longer needed to mine, farm, or manufacture. Machines made better administrators, more attentive servants. Only a very small elite — the vics called them simply their Owners — were required to order and ordain. Which left a lot of people who were just taking up space.

There had to be *something* to do with them.

As it turned out, there was.

That's my theory, anyway. Or, rather, one of them. I've got a million: Hyperautomation. Cumulative hardening of the collective conscience. Circular determinism. The implicitly aggressive nature of hierarchic structures. Compassion fatigue. The banality of evil.

Maybe people are just no damn good. That's what Shriver would have said.

The next day I went zombie, pretty much. Going through the motions, connecting the dots. LaShana in Requisitions noticed it right away. "You ought to take the day off," she said, when I dropped by to see about getting a replacement PzC(15)/pencorder. "Get away from here, take a walk in the woods, maybe play a little golf."

"Golf," I said. It seemed the most alien thing in the universe, hitting a ball with a stick. I couldn't see the point of it.

"Don't say it like that. You love golf. You've told me so a hundred times."

"I guess I have." I swung my purse up on the desk, slid my hand inside, and gently stroked the device. It was cool to the touch and vibrated ever so faintly under my fingers. I withdrew my hand. "Not today, though."

LaShana noticed. "What's that you have in there?"

"Nothing." I whipped the purse away from her. "Nothing at all." Then, a little too loud, a little too blustery, "So how about that pencorder?"

"It's yours." She got out the device, activated it, and let me pick it up. Now only I could operate the thing. Wonderful how fast we were picking up the technology. "How'd you lose your old one, anyway?"

"I stepped on it. By accident." I could see that LaShana wasn't buying it. "Damn it, it was an accident! It could have happened to anyone."

I fled from LaShana's alarmed, concerned face.

Not twenty minutes later, Gevorkian came sleazing into my office. She smiled, and leaned lazily back against the file cabinet when I said hi. Arms folded. Eyes sad and cynical. That big plain face of hers, tolerant and worldly-wise. Wearing her skirt just a *smidge* tighter, a *touch* shorter than was strictly correct for an office environment.

"Virginia," she said.

"Linda."

We did the waiting thing. Eventually, because I'd been here so long I honestly didn't give a shit, Gevorkian spoke first. "I hear you've been experiencing a little disgruntlement."

"Eh?"

"Mind if I check your purse?"

Without taking her eyes off me for an instant, she hoisted my purse, slid a hand inside, and stirred up the contents. She did it so slowly and dreamily that, I swear to God, I half expected her to smell her fingers afterward. Then, when she didn't find the expected gun, she said, "You're not planning on going postal on us, are you?"

I snorted.

"So what is it?"

"What is it?" I said in disbelief. I went to the window. Zip zip zip, down came a rectangle of cloth. Through the scrim of mosquito netting the camp revealed itself: canvas as far as the eye could see. There was nothing down there as fancy as our labyrinthine government office complex at the top of the hill—what we laughingly called the Tentagon— with its canvas air-conditioning ducts and modular laboratories and cafeterias. They were all army surplus, and what wasn't army surplus was Boy Scout hand-me-downs. "Take a look. Take a goddamn fucking look. That's the future out there, and it's barreling down on you at the rate of sixty seconds per minute. You can *see* it and still ask me that question?"

She came and stood beside me. Off in the distance, a baby began to wail. The sound went on and on. "Virginia," she said quietly. "Ginny,

I understand how you feel. Believe me, I do. Maybe the universe is deterministic. Maybe there's no way we can change what's coming. But that's not proven yet. And until it is, we've got to soldier on."

"Why?"

"Because of *them*." She nodded her chin toward the slow-moving revenants of things to come. "They're the living proof of everything we hate and fear. They are witness and testimony to the fact that absolute evil exists. So long as there's the least chance, we've got to try to ward it off."

I looked at her for a long, silent moment. Then, in a voice as cold and calmly modulated as I could make it, I said, "Take your goddamned hand off my ass."

She did so.

I stared after her as, without another word, she left.

This went beyond self-destructive. All I could think was that Gevorkian wanted out but couldn't bring herself to quit. Maybe she was bucking for a sexual harassment suit. But then again, there's definitely an erotic quality to the death of hope. A sense of license. A nicely edgy feeling that since nothing means anything anymore, we might as well have our little flings. That they may well be all we're going to get.

And all the time I was thinking this, in a drawer in my desk the device quietly sat. Humming to itself.

People keep having children. It seems such a terrible thing to do. I can't understand it at all, and don't talk to me about instinct. The first thing I did, after I realized the enormity of what lay ahead, was get my tubes tied. I never thought of myself as a breeder, but I'd wanted to have the option in case I ever changed my mind. Now I knew I would not.

It had been one hell of a day, so I decided I was entitled to quit work early. I was cutting through the camp toward the civ/noncom parking lot when I ran across Shriver. He was coming out of the vic latrines. Least romantic place on Earth. Canvas stretching forever and dispirited people shuffling in and out. And the smell! Imagine the accumulated stench of all the sick shit in the world, and you've just about got it right.

Shriver was carrying a bottle of Spanish champagne under his arm. The bottle had a red bow on it.

"What's the occasion?" I asked.

He grinned like Kali and slid an arm through mine. "My divorce finally came through. Wanna help me celebrate?"

Under the circumstances, it was the single most stupid thing I could possibly do. "Sure," I said. "Why not?"

Later, in his tent, as he was taking off my clothes, I asked, "Just why did your wife divorce you, Shriver?"

"Mental cruelty," he said, smiling.

Then he laid me down across his cot and I let him hurt me. I needed it. I needed to be punished for being so happy and well-fed and unbrutalized while all about me...

"Harder, Goddamn you," I said, punching him, biting him, clawing up blood. "Make me pay."

Cause and effect. Is the universe deterministic or not? If everything inevitably follows what came before, tickety-tock, like gigantic, all-inclusive clockwork, then there is no hope. The refugees came from a future that cannot be turned away. If, on the other hand, time is quanticized and uncertain, unstable at every point, constantly prepared to collapse in any direction in response to totally random influences, then all that suffering that came pouring in on us over the course of six long and rainy months might be nothing more than a phantom. Just an artifact of a rejected future.

Our future might be downright pleasant.

We had a million scientists working in every possible discipline, trying to make it so. Biologists, chaoticists, physicists of every shape and description. Fabulously dedicated people. Driven. Motivated. All trying to hold out a hand before what must be and say, "Stop!"

How they'd love to get their mitts on what I had stowed in my desk.

I hadn't decided yet whether I was going to hand it over, though. I wasn't at all sure what was the right thing to do. Or the smart thing, for that matter.

Gevorkian questioned me on Tuesday. Thursday, I came into my office to discover three UN soldiers with handheld detectors, running a search.

I shifted my purse back on my shoulder to make me look more strack, and said, "What the hell is going on here?"

"Random check, ma'am." A dark-eyed Indian soldier young enough to be if not my son then my little brother politely touched fingers to forehead in a kind of salute. "For up-time contraband." A sewn tag over one pocket proclaimed his name to be PATHAK. "It is purely standard, I assure you."

I counted the stripes on his arm, compared them to my civilian GS-rating and determined that by the convoluted UN protocols under which we operated, I outranked him.

"Sergeant-Major Pathak. You and I both know that all foreign nationals operate on American soil under sufferance, and the strict understanding that you have no authority whatsoever over native civilians."

"Oh, but this was cleared with your Mr. —"

"I don't give a good goddamn if you cleared it with the fucking Dalai Lama! This is my office—your authority ends at the door. You have no more right to be here than I have to finger-search your goddamn rectum. Do you follow me?"

He flushed angrily, but said nothing.

All the while, his fellows were running their detectors over the file cabinet, the storage closets, my desk. Little lights on each flashed red red red. Negative negative negative. The soldiers kept their eyes averted from me. Pretending they couldn't hear a word.

I reamed their sergeant-major out but good. Then, when the office had been thoroughly scanned and the two noncoms were standing about uneasily, wondering how long they'd be kept here, I dismissed the lot. They were all three so grateful to get away from me that nobody asked to examine my purse. Which was, of course, where I had the device.

After they left, I thought about young Sergeant-Major Pathak. I wondered what he would have done if I'd put my hand on his crotch and made a crude suggestion. No, make that an order. He looked to be a real straight arrow. He'd squirm for sure. It was an alarmingly pleasant fantasy.

I thought it through several times in detail, all the while holding the gizmo in my lap and stroking it like a cat.

The next morning, there was an incident at Food Processing. One of the women started screaming when they tried to inject a microminiaturized identi-chip under the skin of her forehead. It was a new system they'd come up with that was supposed to save a per-unit of thirteen cents a week in tracking costs. You walked through a smart doorway, it registered your presence, you picked up your food, and a second doorway checked you off on the way out. There was nothing in it to get upset about.

But the woman began screaming and crying and — this happened right by the kitchens — snatched up a cooking knife and began stabbing herself, over and over. She managed to make nine whacking big holes in herself before the thing was wrestled away from her. The orderlies took her to Intensive, where the doctors said it would be a close thing either way.

After word of that got around, none of the refugees would allow themselves to be identi-chipped. Which really pissed off the UN peacekeepers assigned to the camp, because earlier a couple hundred vics had accepted the chips without so much as a murmur. The Indian troops thought the refugees were willfully trying to make their job more difficult. There were complaints of racism, and rumors of planned retaliation.

I spent the morning doing my bit to calm things down — hopeless — and the afternoon writing up reports that everyone upstream wanted to receive ASAP and would probably file without reading. So I didn't have time to think about the device at all.

But I did. Constantly.

It was getting to be a burden.

For health class, one year in high school, I was given a ten-pound sack of flour, which I had to name and then carry around for a month, as if it were a baby. Bippy couldn't be left unattended; I had to carry it everywhere or else find somebody willing to babysit it. The exercise was supposed to teach us responsibility and scare us off of sex. The first thing I did when the month was over was to steal my father's .45, put Bippy in the backyard, and empty the clip into it, shot after shot. Until all that was left of the little bastard was a cloud of white dust.

The machine from the future was like that. Just another bippy. I had it, and dared not get rid of it. It was obviously valuable. It was equally obviously dangerous. Did I really want the government to get hold of something that could compel people to act against their own wishes? Did I honestly trust them not to immediately turn themselves into everything that we were supposedly fighting to prevent?

I'd been asking myself the same questions for — what? — four days. I'd thought I'd have some answers by now.

I took the bippy out from my purse. It felt cool and smooth in my hand, like melting ice. No, warm. It felt both warm and cool. I ran my hand over and over it, for the comfort of the thing.

After a minute, I got up, zipped shut the flap to my office, and secured it with a twist tie. Then I went back to my desk, sat down, and unbuttoned my blouse. I rubbed the bippy all over my body: up my neck, and over my breasts and around and around on my belly. I kicked off my shoes and clumsily shucked off my pantyhose. Down along the outside of my calves it went, and up the insides of my thighs. Between my legs. It made me feel filthy. It made me feel a little less like killing myself.

How it happened was, I got lost. How I got lost was, I went into the camp after dark.

Nobody goes into the camp after dark, unless they have to. Not even the Indian troops. That's when the refugees hold their entertainments. They had no compassion for each other, you see — that was our dirty little secret. I saw a toddler fall into a campfire once. There were vics all around, but if it hadn't been for me, the child would have died. I snatched it from the flames before it got too badly hurt, but nobody else made a move to help it. They just stood there looking. And laughing.

"In Dachau, when they opened the gas chambers, they'd find a pyramid of human bodies by the door," Shriver told me once. "As the gas started to work, the Jews panicked and climbed over each other, in a futile attempt to escape. That was deliberate. It was designed into the system. The Nazis didn't just want them dead — they wanted to be able to feel morally superior to their victims afterward."

So I shouldn't have been there. But I was unlatching the door to my trailer when it suddenly came to me that my purse felt wrong. Light. And I realized that I'd left the bippy in the top drawer of my office desk. I hadn't even locked it.

My stomach twisted at the thought of somebody else finding the thing. In a panic, I drove back to the camp. It was a twenty-minute drive from the trailer park and by the time I got there, I wasn't thinking straight. The civ/noncom parking lot was a good quarter-way around the camp from the Tentagon. I thought it would be a simple thing to cut through. So, flashing my DOD/Future History Division ID at the guard as I went through the gate, I did.

Which was how I came to be lost.

There are neighborhoods in the camp. People have a natural tendency to sort themselves out by the nature of their suffering. The twitchers, who were victims of paralogical reprogramming, stay in one part of the camp, and the mods, those with functional normative modifications, stay in another. I found myself wandering through crowds of people who had been "healed" of limbs, ears, and even internal organs — there seemed no sensible pattern. Sometimes our doctors could effect a partial correction. But our primitive surgery was, of course, nothing like that available in their miraculous age.

I'd taken a wrong turn trying to evade an eyeless, noseless woman who kept grabbing at my blouse and demanding money, and gotten all turned around in the process when, without noticing me, Gevorkian went striding purposefully by.

Which was so unexpected that, after an instant's shock, I up and followed her. It didn't occur to me not to. There was something strange about the way she held herself, about her expression, her posture. Something unfamiliar.

She didn't even *walk* like herself.

The vics had dismantled several tents to make a large open space surrounded by canvas. Propane lights, hung from tall poles, blazed in a ring about it. I saw Gevorkian slip between two canvas sheets and, after a moment's hesitation, I followed her.

It was a rat fight.

The way a rat fight works, I learned that night, is that first you catch a whole bunch of Norwegian rats. Big mean mothers. Then you get them in a bad mood, probably by not feeding them, but there are any number of other methods that could be used. Anyway, they're feeling feisty. You put a dozen of them in a big pit you've dug in the ground. Then you dump in your contestant. A big guy with a shaven head and his hands tied behind his back. His genitals are bound up in a little bit of cloth, but other than that he's naked.

Then you let them fight it out. The rats leap and jump and bite and the big guy tries to trample them underfoot or crush them with his knees, his chest, his head — whatever he can bash them with.

The whole thing was lit up bright as day, and all the area around the pit was crammed with vics. Some shouted and urged on one side or the other. Others simply watched intently. The rats squealed. The human fighter bared his teeth in a hideous rictus and fought in silence.

It was the creepiest thing I'd seen in a long time.

Gevorkian watched it coolly, without any particular interest or aversion. After a while it was obvious to me that she was waiting for someone.

Finally that someone arrived. He was a lean man, tall, with keen, hatchetlike features. None of the vics noticed. Their eyes were directed inward, toward the pit. He nodded once to Gevorkian, then backed through the canvas again.

She followed him.

I followed her.

They went to a near-lightless area near the edge of the camp. There was nothing there but trash, the backs of tents, the razor-wire fence, and a gate padlocked for the night.

It was perfectly easy to trail them from a distance. The stranger held himself proudly, chin up, eyes bright. He walked with a sure stride. He was nothing at all like the vics.

It was obvious to me that he was an Owner.

Gevorkian too. When she was with him that inhuman arrogance glowed in her face as well. It was as if a mask had been removed. The fire that burned in his face was reflected in hers.

I crouched low to the ground, in the shadow of a tent, and listened as the stranger said, "Why hasn't she turned it in?"

"She's unstable," Gevorkian said. "They all are."

"We don't dare prompt her. She has to turn it in herself."

"She will. Give her time."

"Time," the man repeated. They both laughed in a way that sounded to me distinctly unpleasant. Then, "She'd better. There's a lot went into this operation. There's a lot riding on it."

"She will."

I stood watching as they shook hands and parted ways. Gevorkian turned and disappeared back into the tent city. The stranger opened a radiant door and was gone.

Cause and effect. They'd done . . . *whatever* it was they'd done to that woman's daughter just so they could plant the bippy with me. They wanted me to turn it in. They wanted our government to have possession of a device that would guarantee obedience. They wanted to give us a good taste of what it was like to be them.

Suddenly I had no doubt at all what I should do. I started out at a determined stride, but inside of nine paces I was *running*. Vics scurried to get out of my way. If they didn't move fast enough, I shoved them aside.

I had to get back to the bippy and destroy it.

Which was stupid, stupid, stupid. If I'd kept my head down and walked slowly, I would have been invisible. Invisible and safe. The way I did it, though, cursing and screaming, I made a lot of noise and caused a lot of fuss. Inevitably, I drew attention to myself.

Inevitably, Gevorkian stepped into my path.

I stumbled to a halt.

"Gevorkian," I said feebly. "Linda. I —"

All the lies I was about to utter died in my throat when I saw her face. Her expression. Those eyes. Gevorkian reached for me. I skipped back in utter panic, turned — and fled. Anybody else would have done the same.

It was a nightmare. The crowds slowed me. I stumbled. I had no idea where I was going. And all the time, this monster was right on my heels.

Nobody goes into the camp after dark, unless they have to. But that doesn't mean that nobody goes in after dark. By sheer good luck, Gevorkian chased me into the one part of the camp that had something that outsiders could find nowhere else — the sex-for-hire district.

There was nothing subtle about the way the vics sold themselves. The trampled-grass street I found myself in was lined with stacks of cages like the ones they use in dog kennels. They were festooned with strings of Christmas lights, and each one contained a crouched boy. Naked, to best display those mods and deformities that some found attractive. Off-duty soldiers strolled up and down the cages, checking out the possibilities. I recognized one of them.

"Sergeant-Major Pathak!" I cried. He looked up, startled and guilty. "Help me! Kill her — please! Kill her now!"

Give him credit, the sergeant-major was a game little fellow. I can't imagine what we looked like to him, one harridan chasing the other

down the streets of Hell. But he took the situation in at a glance, unhol-
stered his sidearm and stepped forward. "Please," he said. "You will both
stand where you are. You will place your hands upon the top of your
head. You will —"

Gevorkian flicked her fingers at the young soldier. He screamed,
and clutched his freshly crushed shoulder. She turned away from him,
dismissively. The other soldiers had fled at the first sign of trouble. All her
attention was on me, trembling in her sight like a winded doe. "*Sweet
little vic*," she purred. "If you won't play the part we had planned for you,
you'll simply have to be silenced."

"No," I whispered.

She touched my wrist. I was helpless to stop her. "You and I are
going to go to my office now. We'll have fun there. Hours and hours
of fun."

"Leave her be."

As sudden and inexplicable as an apparition of the Virgin, Shriver
stepped out of the darkness. He looked small and grim.

Gevorkian laughed, and gestured.

But Shriver's hand reached up to intercept hers, and where they
met, there was an electric blue flash. Gevorkian stared down, stunned, at
her hand. Bits of tangled metal fell away from it. She looked up at Shriver.

He struck her down.

She fell with a brief harsh cry, like that of a seagull. Shriver kicked
her, three times, hard: In the ribs. In the stomach. In the head. Then,
when she looked like she might yet regain her feet, "It's one of *them!*" he
shouted. "Look at her! She's a spy for the Owners! She's from the future!
Owner! Look! Owner!"

The refugees came tumbling out of the tents and climbing down
out of their cages. They looked more alive than I'd ever seen them before. They were red-faced and screaming. Their eyes were wide with hys-
teria. For the first time in my life, I was genuinely afraid of them. They
came running. They swarmed like insects.

They seized Gevorkian and began tearing her apart.

I saw her struggle up and halfway out of their grips, saw one arm
rise up above the sea of clutching hands, like that of a woman drowning.

Shriver seized my elbow and steered my away before I could see
any more. I saw enough, though.

I saw too much.

"Where are we going?" I asked when I'd recovered my wits.

"Where do you think we're going?"

He led me to my office.

There was a stranger waiting there. He took out a handheld detector like Sergeant-Major Pathak and his men had used earlier and touched it to himself, to Shriver, and to me. Three times it flashed red, negative. "You travel through time, you pick up a residual charge," Shriver explained. "It never goes away. We've known about Gevorkian for a long time."

"U.S. Special Security," the stranger said, and flipped open his ID. It meant diddle-all to me. There was a badge. It could have read Captain Crunch for all I knew or cared. But I didn't doubt for an instant that he was SS. He had that look. To Shriver he said, "The neutralizer."

Shriver unstrapped something glittery from his wrist—the device he'd used to undo Gevorkian's weapon—and, in a silent bit of comic bureaucratic punctilio, exchanged it for a written receipt. The security officer touched the thing with his detector. It flashed green. He put both devices away in interior pockets.

All the time, Shriver stood in the background, watching. He wasn't told to go away.

Finally, Captain Crunch turned his attention to me again. "Where's the snark?"

"Snark?"

The man removed a thin scrap of cloth from an inside jacket pocket and shook it out. With elaborate care, he pulled it over his left hand. An inertial glove. Seeing by my expression that I recognized it, he said, "Don't make me use this."

I swallowed. For an instant I thought crazily of defying him, of simply refusing to tell him where the bippy was. But I'd seen an inertial glove in action before, when a lone guard had broken up a camp riot. He'd been a little man. I'd seen him crush heads like watermelons.

Anyway, the bippy was in my desk. They'd be sure to look there.

I opened the drawer, produced the device. Handed it over. "It's a plant," I said. "They want us to have this."

Captain Crunch gave me a look that told me clear as words exactly how stupid he thought I was. "We understand more than you think we do. There are circles and circles. We have informants up in the future, and some of them are more highly placed than you'd think. Not everything that's known is made public."

"Damn it, this sucker is *evil*."

A snake's eyes would look warmer than his. "Understand this: We're fighting for our survival here. Extinction is null-value. You can have all the moral crises you want when the war is won."

"It should be suppressed. The technology. If it's used, it'll just help bring about . . ."

He wasn't listening.

I'd worked for the government long enough to know when I was wasting my breath. So I shut up.

When the captain left with the bippy, Shriver still remained, looking ironically after him. "People get the kind of future they deserve," he observed.

"But that's what I'm saying. Gevorkian came back from the future in order to help bring it about. That means that time isn't deterministic." Maybe I was getting a little weepy. I'd had a rough day. "The other guy said there was a lot riding on this operation. They didn't know how it was going to turn out. They didn't *know*."

Shriver grunted, not at all interested.

I plowed ahead unheeding. "If it's not deterministic—if they're working so hard to bring it about—then all our effort isn't futile at all. This future can be prevented."

Shriver looked up at last. There was a strangely triumphant gleam in his eye. He flashed that roguish ain't-this-fun grin of his, and said, "I don't know about you, but some of us are working like hell to *achieve* it."

With a jaunty wink, he was gone.

The Grand Master Award
BRIAN W. ALDISS

HARRY HARRISON

Congratulations, Brian—and It's About Time

The life of an author brings its own rewards, as you have pointed out in your autobiography. The sweetness of your first sale; the indescribable sensation when you hold the first copy of your first book. The readers enjoy your work, Brian, they have for years in many countries. And have put their money where their affection is, so that their pounds, dollars, D-marks, and yen enable you to live the good life of a freelance author.

And then there is your peer group. Testy, brilliant, alcoholic, dedicated, jealous—words fail me when I try to describe the literary SF world that we live in. Well, not exactly fail, but discretion is the better part of valor. The Science Fiction and Fantasy Writers of America is a very disparate group. Young, old, male, female, and other. Talented. And not so jealous of other writers' success that they can't notice what other writers are doing.

They have noticed you, Brian. They have taken time out to look at your most illustrious career. Read your books and stories and enjoyed them. They are aware of your critical writings and approve. In their collective wisdom they have not just nodded approval but have clapped loud and long.

They have voted you their Grand Master Award.

They have done you proud.

May I point out to them some of the high points of your decades-long career. From the dross of the bookshop you created those wonderful sketches that were collected in *The Brightfount Diaries*. You were instantly world famous—didn't I buy my copy in Denmark? Then all those wonderful and witty short stories. And your first, groundbreaking and marvelous novel, *Non-Stop*. The readers had their eyes on you, and it was not by chance that the 1959 World SF Convention voted you the award of most promising author.

Though it has been over forty years I can still remember, with great enthusiasm, scenes and characters from this book. Because it was a novel of character as well as being science fiction. You showed us how it could be done. As you did later in *Greybeard*, a novel that holds its own not only as an SF novel but as a book of English literature that is an important novel of the decade.

Accept this award with all the goodwill it engenders. The readers support you. You in turn support your family and your agent. They enable you to lead your life of creativity, free and unshackled. I thank them all.

Now I thank your peer group who have read what you have written and smiled with pleasure. Now they are reaching out and patting you on the shoulder. Well done, Brian W. Aldiss, they are saying. In our group wisdom we are presenting you with the greatest tribute that we can.

Take it home and put it on the mantelpiece where it can be easily seen. By you. Then, in those black moments that possess us all, do not despair. Look at it and smile.

You have done well, my old son.

Congratulations.

Harry Harrison
Dublin, the year 2000

Judas Danced

BRIAN W. ALDISS

It was not a fair trial.

You understand I was not inclined to listen properly, but it was not a fair trial. It had a mistrustful and furtive haste about it. Judge, counsel, and jury all took care to be as brief and explicit as possible. I said nothing, but I knew why: everyone wanted to get back to the dances.

So it was not very long before the judge stood up and pronounced sentence:

"Alexander Abel Crowe, this court finds you guilty of murdering Parowen Scryban for the second time."

I could have laughed out loud. I nearly did.

He went on: "You are therefore condemned to suffer death by strangulation for the second time, which sentence will be carried out within the next week."

Around the court ran a murmur of excitement.

In a way, even I felt satisfied. It had been an unusual case: few are the people who care to risk facing death a second time; the first time you die makes the prospect worse, not better. For just a minute, the court was still; then it cleared with almost indecent haste. In a little while, only I was left there.

I, Alex Abel Crowe — or approximately he — came carefully down out of the prisoner's box and limped the length of the dusty room to the door. As I went, I looked at my hands. They weren't trembling.

Nobody bothered to keep a check on me. They knew they could pick me up whenever they were ready to execute sentence. I was unmistakable, and I had nowhere to go. I was the man with the clubfoot who could not dance; nobody could mistake me for anyone else. Only I could do that.

Outside in the dark sunlight, that wonderful woman stood waiting for me with her husband, waiting on the court steps. The sight of her began to bring back life and hurt to my veins. I raised my hand to her as my custom was.

"We've come to take you home, Alex," Husband said, stepping towards me.

"I haven't got a home," I said, addressing her.

"I mean *our* home," he informed me.

"Elucidation accepted," I said. "Take me away, take me away, take me away, Charlemagne. And let me sleep."

"You need sleep after all you have been through," he said. Why, he sounded nearly sympathetic.

Sometimes I called him Charlemagne, sometimes just Charley. Or Cheeps, or Jags, or Jaggers, or anything, as the mood took me. He seemed to forgive me. Perhaps he even liked it—I don't know. Personal magnetism takes you a long way; it has taken me so far I don't even have to remember names.

They stopped a passing taxi and we all climbed in. It was a tumbrel, they tell me. You know, French? Circa seventeen-eighty-something. Husband sat one side, Wife the other, each holding one of my arms, as if they thought I might get violent. I let them do it, although the idea amused me.

"Hallo, friends!" I said ironically. Sometimes I called them "parents," or "disciples," or sometimes "patients." Anything.

The wonderful woman was crying slightly.

"Look at her!" I said to Husband. "She's lovely when she cries, that I swear. I could have married her, you know, if I had not been dedicated. Tell him, you wonderful creature, tell him how I turned you down!"

Through her sobbing, she said, "Alex said he had more important things to do than sex."

"So you've got me to thank for Perdita!" I told him. "It was a big sacrifice, but I'm happy to see you happy." Often now I called her

Perdita. It seemed to fit her. He laughed at what I had said, and then we were all laughing. Yes, it was good to be alive; I knew I made them feel good to be alive. They were loyal. I had to give them something — I had no gold and silver.

The tumbrel stopped outside Charley's place — the Husband residence, I'd better say. Oh, the things I've called that place! Someone should have recorded them all. It was one of those inverted beehive houses: just room for a door and an elevator on the ground floor, but the fifth floor could hold a ballroom. Topply, topply. Up we went to the fifth. There was no sixth floor; had there been, I should have gone up there, the way I felt. I asked for it anyhow, just to see the wonderful woman brighten up. She liked me to joke, even when I wasn't in a joking mood. I could tell she still loved me so much it hurt her.

"Now for a miracle, ye pampered jades," I said, stepping forth, clumping into the living room.

I seized an empty vase from a low shelf and spat into it. Ah, the old cunning was still there! It filled at once with wine, sweet and bloody-looking. I sipped and found it good.

"Go on and taste it, Perdy!" I told her.

Wonderful w. turned her head sadly away. She would not touch that vase. I could have eaten every single strand of hair on her head, but she seemed unable to see the wine. I really believe she could not see that wine.

"Please don't go through all that again, Alex," she implored me wearily. Little faith, you see — the old, old story. (Remind me to tell you a new one I heard the other day.) I put my behind on one chair and my bad foot on another and sulked.

They came and stood by me . . . not too close.

"Come nearer," I coaxed, looking up under my eyebrows and pretending to growl at them. "I won't hurt you. I only murder Parowen Scryban, remember?"

"We've got to talk to you about that," Husband said desperately. I thought he looked as if he had aged.

"I think you look as if you have aged, Perdita," I said. Often I called him Perdita, too; why, man, they sometimes looked so worried you couldn't tell them apart.

"I cannot live forever, Alex," he replied. "Now try and concentrate about this killing, will you?"

I waved a hand and tried to belch. At times I can belch like a sinking ship.

"We do all we can to help you, Alex," he said. I heard him although my eyes were shut; can *you* do that? "But we can only keep you out of trouble if you cooperate. It's the dancing that does it; nothing else betrays you like dancing. You've got to promise you'll stay away from it. In fact, we want you to promise that you'll let us restrain you. To keep you away from the dancing. Something about that dancing..."

He was going on and on, and I could still hear him. But other things were happening. That word "dancing" got in the way of all his other words. It started a sort of flutter under my eyelids. I crept my hand out and took the wonderful woman's hand, so soft and lovely, and listened to that word "dancing" dancing. It brought its own rhythm, bouncing about like an eyeball inside my head. The rhythm grew louder. He was shouting.

I sat up suddenly, opening my eyes.

W. woman was on the floor, very pale.

"You squeezed too hard," she whispered.

I could see that her little hand was the only red thing she had.

"I'm sorry," I said. "I really wonder you two don't throw me out for good!" I couldn't help it, I just started laughing. I like laughing. I can laugh even when nothing's funny. Even when I saw their faces, I still kept laughing like mad.

"Stop it!" Husband said. For a moment he looked as if he would have hit me. But I was laughing so much I did not recognize him. It must have done them good to see me enjoying myself; they both needed a fillip, I could tell.

"If you stop laughing, I'll take you down to the club," he said, greasily bribing.

I stopped. I always know when to stop. With all humility, it is a great natural gift.

"The club's the place for me," I said. "I've already got a clubfoot—I'm halfway there!"

I stood up.

"Lead on, my loyal supporters, my liege lords," I ordered.

"You and I will go alone, Alex," Husband said. "The wonderful woman will stay here. She really ought to go to bed."

"What's in it for her?" I joked. Then I followed him to the elevator. He knows I don't like staying in any one place for long.

When I got to the club, I knew, I would want to be somewhere else. That's the worst of having a mission: it makes you terribly restless. Sometimes I am so restless I could die. Ordinary people just don't know what the word means. I could have married her if I had been ordinary. They call it destiny.

But the club was good.

We walked there. I limped there. I made sure I limped badly.

The club had a timescreen. That, I must admit, was my only interest in the club. I don't care for women. Or men. Not living women or men. I only enjoy them when they are back in time.

This night—I nearly said "this particular night," but there was nothing particularly particular about it—the timescreen had only been tuned roughly three centuries back into the past. At least, I guessed it was twenty-first-century stuff by the women's dresses and a shot of a power station. A large crowd of people was looking in as Perdita Caesar and I entered, so I started to pretend he had never seen one of the wall-screens before.

"The tele-eyes which are projected back over history consume a fabulous amount of power every second," I told him loudly in a voice which suggested I had swallowed a poker. "It makes them very expensive. It means private citizens cannot afford screens and tele-eyes, just as once they could not afford their own private motion pictures. This club is fortunately very rich. Its members sleep in gold leaf at night."

Several people were glancing around at me already. Caesar was shaking his head and rolling his eyes.

"The tele-eyes cannot get a picture further than twenty-seven centuries back," I told him, "owing to the limitations of science. Science, as you know, is a system for taking away with one hand while giving with the other."

He could not answer cleverly. I went on: "It has also proved impossible, due to the aforesaid limitations, to send human beings further back in time than one week. And that costs so much that only governments can do it. As you may have heard, nothing can be sent ahead into time—there's no future in it!"

I had to laugh at that. It was funny, and quite spontaneous.

Many people were calling out to me, and Caesar Borgia was dragging at my arm, trying to make me be quiet.

"I wouldn't spoil anyone's fun!" I shouted. "You people get on with your watching; I'll get on with my speech."

But I did not want to talk to a lot of featherbedders like them. So I sat down without saying another word, Boy Borgia collapsing beside me with a sigh of relief. Suddenly I felt very, very sad. Life just is not what it was; once upon a time, I could have married this husband's wife.

"Physically, you can go back one week," I whispered, "optically, twenty-seven centuries. It's very sad."

It was very sad. The people on the screen were also sad. They lived in the Entertainment Era, and appeared to be getting little pleasure from it. I tried to weep for them but failed because at the moment they seemed just animated history. I saw them as period pieces, stuck there a couple of generations before reading and writing had died out altogether and the fetters of literacy fell forever from the world. Little any of them cared for the patterns of history.

"I've had an idea I want to tell you about, Cheezer," I said. It was a good idea.

"Can't it wait?" he asked. "I'd like to see this scan. It's all about the European Allegiance."

"I must tell you before I forget."

"Come on," he said resignedly, getting up.

"You are too loyal to me," I complained. "You spoil me. I'll speak to St. Peter about it."

As meek as you like, I followed him into an anteroom. He drew himself a drink from an automatic man in one corner. He was trembling. I did not tremble, although at the back of my mind lurked many things to tremble about.

"Go on then, say whatever in hell you want to say," he told me, shading his eyes with his hand. I have seen him use that trick before; he did it after I killed Parowen Scryban the first time, I remember. There's nothing wrong with my memory, except in patches.

"I had this idea," I said, trying to recall it. "This idea — oh, yes. History. I got the idea looking at those twenty-first-century people. Mythology is the key to everything, isn't it? I mean, a man builds his life on a set of myths, doesn't he? Well, in our world, the so-called Western World, those accepted myths were religious until about mid-nineteenth century. By then, a majority of Europeans were literate, or within reach of it, and for a couple of centuries the myths became literary ones: tragedy was no longer the difference between grace and nature, but between art and reality."

Julius had dropped his hand. He was interested. I could see he wondered what was coming next. I hardly knew myself.

"Then mechanical aids—television, computers, scanners of every type—abolished literacy," I said. "Into the vacuum came the time-screens. Our mythologies are now historical: tragedy has become simply a failure to see the future."

I beamed at him and bowed, not letting him know I was beyond tragedy. He just sat there. He said nothing. Sometimes such terrible boredom descends on me that I can hardly fight against it.

"Is my reasoning sound?" I asked. (Two women looked into the room, saw me, and left again hurriedly. They must have sensed I did not want them, otherwise they would have come to me; I am young and handsome—I am not thirty-three yet.)

"You could always reason well," Marcus Aurelius Marconi said, "but it just never leads anywhere. God, I'm so tired."

"This bit of reasoning leads somewhere. I beg you to believe it, Holy Roman," I said, flopping on my knees before him. "It's the state philosophy I've really been telling you about. That's why, although they keep the death penalty for serious crimes—like murdering a bastard called Parowen Scryban—they go back in time the next day and call off the execution. They believe you should die for your crime, you see? But more deeply they believe every man should face his true future. They've—we've all seen too many premature deaths on the timescreens. Romans, Normans, Celts, Goths, English, Israelis. Every race. Individuals—all dying too soon, failing to fulfil—"

Oh, I admit it, I was crying on his knees by then, although bravely disguising it by barking like a dog: a Great Dane. Hamlet. Not in our stars but in our selves. (I've watched W. S. write that bit.)

I was crying at last to think the police would come without fail within the next week to snuff me out, and then resurrect me again, according to my sentence. I was remembering what it was like last time. They took so long about it.

They took so long. Though I struggled, I could not move; those police know how to hold a man. My windpipe was blocked, as sentence of court demanded.

And then, it seemed, the boxes sailed in. Starting with small ones, they grew bigger. They were black boxes, all of them. Faster they came, and faster, inside me and out. I'm telling you how it felt, my God! And they blocked the whole, whole universe, black and red. With my lungs really crammed tight with boxes, out of the world I went. Dead!

Into limbo I went.

I don't say nothing happened, but I could not grasp what was happening there, and I was unable to participate. Then I was alive again.

It was abruptly the day before the strangulation once more, and the government agent had come back in time and rescued me, so that from one point of view I was not strangled. *But* I still remembered it happening, and the boxes, and limbo. Don't talk to me about paradoxes. The government expended several billion megavolts sending that man back for me, and those megavolts account for all paradoxes. I was dead and then alive again.

Now I had to undergo it all once more. No wonder there was little crime nowadays; the threat of that horrible experience held many a likely criminal back. But I *had* to kill Parowen Scryban; just so long as they went back and resurrected him after I had finished with him, I had to go and do it again. Call it a moral obligation. No one understands. It is as if I were living in a world of my own.

"Get up, get up! You're biting my ankles."

Where had I heard that voice before? At last I could no longer ignore it. Whenever I try to think, voices interrupt. I stopped chewing whatever I was chewing, unblocked my eyes, and sat up. This was just a room; I had been in rooms before. A man was standing over me; I did not recognize him. He was just a man.

"You look as if you have aged," I told him.

"I can't live forever, thank God," he said. "Now get up and let's get you home. You're going to bed."

"What home?" I asked. "What bed? Who in the gentle name of anyone may you be?"

He looked sick.

"Just call me Adam," he said sickly.

I recognized him then and went with him. We had been in some sort of a club; he never told me why. I still don't know why we went to that club.

The house he took me to was shaped like a beehive upside down, and I walked there like a drunk. A clubfooted drunk.

This wonderful stranger took me up in an elevator to a soft bed. He undressed me and put me in that soft bed as gently as if I had been his son. I am really impressed by the kindness strangers show me; personal magnetism, I suppose.

For as long as I could after he had left me, I lay in the bed in the inverted beehive. Then the darkness grew thick and sticky, and I could imagine all the fat, furry bodies, chitinously winged, of the bees on the ceiling. A minute more and I should fall headfirst into them. Stubbornly, I fought to sweat it out, but a man can stand only so much.

On hands and knees I crawled out of bed and out of the room. Quickly, softly, I clicked the door shut behind me; not a bee escaped.

People were talking in a lighted room along the corridor. I crawled to the doorway, looking and listening. The wonderful stranger talked to the wonderful woman; she was in night attire, with a hand bandaged.

She was saying: "You will have to see the authorities in the morning and petition them."

He was saying: "It'll do no good. I can't get the law changed. You know that. It's hopeless."

I merely listened.

Sinking onto the bed, he buried his face in his hands, finally looking up to say: "The law insists on personal responsibility. We've got to take care of Alex. It's a reflection of the time we live in; because of the timescreens, we've got—whether we like it or not—historical perspectives. We can see that the whole folly of the past was due to failures in individual liability. Our laws are naturally framed to correct that, which they do; it just happens to be tough on us."

He sighed and said, "The sad thing is, even Alex realizes that. He talked quite sensibly to me at the club about not evading the future."

"It hurts me most when he talks sensibly," the wonderful double-you said. "It makes you realize he is still capable of suffering."

He took her bandaged hand, almost as if they had a pain they hoped to alleviate by sharing it between them.

"I'll go and see the authorities in the morning," he promised, "and ask them to let the execution be final—no reprieve afterwards."

Even that did not seem to satisfy her.

Perhaps, like me, she could not tell what either of them was talking about. She shook her head miserably from side to side.

"If only it hadn't been for his clubfoot," she said. "If only it hadn't been for that, he could have danced the sickness out of himself."

Her face was growing more and more twisted.

It was enough. More.

"Laugh and grow fat," I suggested. I croaked because my throat was dry. My glands are always like bullets. It reminded me of a frog, so I hopped spontaneously into the room. They did not move; I sat on the bed with them.

"All together again," I said.

They did not move.

"Go back to bed, Alex," she of the wonderfulness said in a low voice.

They were looking at me; goodness knows what they wanted me to say or do. I stayed where I was. A little green clock on a green shelf said nine o'clock.

"Oh, holy heavens!" the double-you said. "What does the future hold?"

"Double chins for you, double-yous for me," I joked. That green clock said a minute past nine. I felt as if its little hand were slowly, slowly disemboweling me.

If I waited long enough, I knew I should think of something. They talked to me while I thought and waited; what good they imagined they were doing is beyond me, but I would not harm them. They mean well. They're the best people in the world. That doesn't mean to say I have to listen to them.

The thought about the clock arrived. Divine revelation.

"The dancing will be on now," I said, standing up like a jackknife.

"No!" Husband said.

"No!" Perdita said.

"You look as if you have aged," I told them. That is my favorite line in all speech.

I ran out of the room, slamming the door behind me, ran step-club-step-club down the passage, and hurled myself into the elevator. With infinitesimal delay, I chose the right button and sank to ground level. There, I wedged the lattice door open with a chair; that put the elevator out of action.

People in the street took no notice of me. The fools just did not realize who I was. Nobody spoke to me as I hurried along, so of course I replied in kind.

Thus I came to the dance area.

Every community has its dance area. Think of all that drama, gladiatorial contests, reading, and sport have ever meant in the past; now they are all merged into dance, inevitably, for only by dance — our kind of dance — can history be interpreted. And interpretation of history is our being, because through the timescreens we see that history is life. It lives around us, so we dance it. Unless we have clubfeet.

Many dances were in progress among the thirty permanent sets. The sets were only casually separated from each other, so that spectators or dancers, going from one to another, might get the sense of everything happening at once, which is the sense the timescreens give you.

That is what I savagely love about history. It is not past; it is always going on. Cleopatra lies forever in the sweaty arms of Anthony. Socrates continually gulps his hemlock down. You just have to be watching the right screen or the right dance.

Most of the dancers were amateurs — although the term means little where everyone dances out his role whenever possible. I stood among a crowd, watching. The bright movements have a dizzying effect; they excite me. To one side of me, Marco Polo sweeps exultantly through Cathay to Kublai Khan. Ahead, four children, who represent the satellites of Jupiter, glide out to meet the somber figure of Galileo Galilei. To the other side, the Persian poet Firdousi leaves for exile in Bagdad. Farther still, I catch a glimpse of Heyerdahl turning toward the tide.

And if I cross my eyes, raft, telescope, pagoda, palm, all mingle. That is meaning! If I could only dance it!

I cannot stay still. Here is my restlessness again, my only companion. I move, eyes unfocused. I pass around the sets or across them, mingling stiff-legged among the dancers. Something compels me, something I cannot remember. Now I cannot even remember who I am. I've gone beyond mere identity.

Everywhere the dancing is faster, matching my heart. I would not harm anyone, except one person who harmed me eternally. It is he I must find. Why do they dance so fast? The movements drive me like whips.

Now I run into a mirror. It stands on a crowded set. I fight with the creature imprisoned in it, thinking it real. Then I understand that it is only a mirror. Shaking my head, I clear the blood from behind my eyes and regard myself. Yes, that is unmistakably me. And I remember who I am meant to be.

I first found who I was meant to be as a child, when I saw one of the greatest dramas of all. There it was, captured by the timescreens! The soldiers and centurions came, and a bragging multitude. The sky grew dark as they banged three crosses into the ground. And when I saw the Man they nailed upon the central cross, I knew I had His face.

Here it is now, that same sublime face, looking at me in pity and pain out of the glass. Nobody believes me; I no longer tell them who I think I am. But one thing I know I have to do. I have to do *it*.

So now I run again clump-trot-clump-trot, knowing just what to look for. All these great sets, pillars and panels of concrete and plastic, I run around them all, looking.

And here it is. Professionals dance out this drama, my drama, so difficult and intricate and sad. Pilate in dove-gray, Mary Magdalene moves in green. Hosts of dancers fringe them, representing the crowd who did not care. I care! My eyes burn among them, seeking. Then I have the man I want.

He is just leaving the set to rest out of sight until the cue for his last dance. I follow him, keeping behind cover like a crab in a thicket.

Yes! He looks just like me! He is my living image, and consequently bears That face. Yet it is now overlaid with makeup, pink and solid, so that when he comes out of the bright lights he looks like a corpse.

I am near enough to see the thick muck on his skin, with its runnels and wrinkles caused by sweat and movement. Underneath it all, the true face is clear enough to me, although the makeup plastered on it represents Judas.

To have That face and to play Judas! It is the most terrible of all wickedness. But this is Parowen Scryban, whom I have twice murdered for this very blasphemy. It is some consolation to know that although the government slipped back in time and saved him afterwards, he must still remember those good deaths. Now I must kill him again.

As he turns into a restroom, I have him. Ah, my fingers slip into that slippery pink stuff; but underneath, the skin is firm. He is small, slender, tired with the strain of dancing. He falls forward with me on his back.

I kill him now, although in a few hours they will come back and rescue him and it will all not have happened. Never mind the shouting: squeeze. Squeeze, dear God!

When blows fall on my head from behind, it makes no difference. Scryban should be dead by now, the traitor. I roll off him and let many hands tie me into a straitjacket.

Many lights are in my eyes. Many voices are talking. I just lie there, thinking I recognize two of the voices, one a man's, one a woman's.

The man says: "Yes, Inspector, I *know* that under law parents are responsible for their own children. We look after Alex as far as we can, but he's mad. He's a throwback! I — God, Inspector, I *hate* the creature."

"You mustn't say that!" the woman cries. "Whatever he does, he's our son."

They sound too shrill to be true. I cannot think what they make such a fuss about. So I open my eyes and look at them. She is a wonderful woman but I recognize neither her nor the man; they just do not interest me. Scryban I do recognize.

He is standing rubbing his throat. He is a mess with his two faces all mixed in together like a Picasso. Because he is breathing, I know they have come back and saved him again. No matter; he will remember.

The man they call Inspector (and who, I ask, would want a name like that?) goes over to speak to Scryban.

"Your father tells me you are actually this madman's brother," he says to Scryban. Judas hangs his head, though he continues to massage his neck.

"Yes," he says. He is as quiet as the woman was shrill; strange how folks vary. "Alex and I are twin brothers. I changed my name years ago — the publicity, you know . . . harmful to my professional career . . ."

How terribly tired and bored I feel.

Who is whose brother, I ask myself, who mothers whom? I'm lucky; I own no relations. These people look like sad company. The saddest in the universe.

"I think you all look as if you have aged!" I shout suddenly.

That makes the Inspector come and stand over me, which I dislike. He has knees halfway up his legs. I manage to resemble one of the tritons on one of Benvenuto Cellini's saltcellars, and so he turns away at last to speak to Husband.

"All right," he says. "I can see this is just one of those things nobody can be responsible for. I'll arrange for the reprieve to be countermanded. This time, when the devil is dead he stays dead."

Husband embraces Scryban. Wonderful woman begins to cry. Traitors all! I start to laugh, making it so harsh and loud and horrible it frightens even me.

What none of them understands is this: on the third time I shall rise again.

Author Emeritus 2000
DANIEL KEYES

BARRY N. MALZBERG

Flowers for Daniel

Most of us, sooner or later, come to understand the nature of the human condition...that slow stalk from darkness to light, from ignorance to at least a tentative understanding, from helplessness to accommodation...and then the slow or accelerating slide into extinction, incapacity, the darkness from which we struggled that was always our condition. For some, disaster or genetics speeds or suddenly truncates that journey, for others the slow procession toward understanding is impossible. But the traversal is generic; the greater number understand. Ecclesiastes, and so on.

That knowledge being so close to general, why does *Flowers for Algernon*, that encompassing story, that narrative of grief beyond metaphor, move us so? Why are the last pages of the novelette and the novel which is its expansion so shattering? "It would take a heart of stone not to laugh at the death of Little Nell," Oscar Wilde said of Dickens, but no such judgment has yet been made of the extinguishing of Charlie Gordon. Unbearable and yet—as art will permit—cathartic.

Why so moving? The narrative premise, perhaps—never before evoked, I am fairly sure. The story is framed as Charlie's diary, he speaks to us directly and his voice shifts through the situation. His voice *is* the situation. No mute, inglorious Milton here seen externally but the living, breathing, suffering thing itself, and, somewhere around the two-thirds point of the narrative, the stunned, then poised awareness of doom; the incalculable price of that acceptance. Nothing like this, really. The novel is successful, the details of Charlie's childhood, of filial shame and rapprochement, are touching . . . but the novelette is incomparable. It needs no further detail. It is stark, yet lush in its traversal of that disaster which the philosophers instruct us is the "human condition."

Flowers for Algernon was only the fifth or sixth story published by Daniel Keyes, who gives autobiography and the link between autobiography and this story in his memoir, *Algernon, Charlie, and I* very well. There was only one Keyes story in the science fiction magazines after the appearance of the novelette. In 1968, three years after publication of the novel, his only other novel published in his country, *The Touch*, appeared, and in the early 1970s a nonfiction biography of ESP and telekinesis, *The Minds of Billy Milligan. The Touch*, a curiously prescient novel of breakdown in a nuclear installation and the disastrous effect fear of contamination has upon its employees, was undervalued; published a little more than a decade before Three Mile Island and the movie *The China Syndrome* (and a decade and a half before the film *Silkwood*), it is a brilliant adumbration of issues which had not until that time entered the general consciousness. Alas, for all its great merit, the novel failed to find any support from its publisher, failed then to reach its intended audience.

This is not true of *Flowers for Algernon*. It found its intended audience, that audience being everyone. The novelette became a novel, television adaptation, feature film, musical, other adaptations, television series in Japan, most recently a new film for television. Keyes, as he writes in *Algernon, Charlie, and I*, became the man who hit the lottery, made the jackpot, scored the Ultimate Tip and thus brought home the big winner, but he did so not through the exercise of chance but, one might theorize, through the avoidance of chance; there were a hundred ways in which *Flowers for Algernon* could have gone wrong, could have collapsed into sentiment or fakery, but craft took Keyes the right way, every time.

And the power, the beauty, the absolute effectiveness of this work also say something about science fiction, our dear old field which we often painfully, but always earnestly celebrate in these volumes.

Note this: of the five most famous and influential stories in the corpus of what we call modern science fiction* (SF published subsequent to the first issue of *Amazing Stories* dated April 1926), two of them are by writers who are known to the general public and largely within the field itself only by those stories, writers whose careers without those stories would, however honorable, be modest. What does this mean?

Here is what I think it means: that voice, the great voice of science fiction, the power of our medium, its resonance, vision, possibility, has created a body of literature which at its best could have been told in no other way. This great task, great burden, alchemy of spirit and machine, manages to somehow have subsumed all of its creators, has opened the way to the final mystery and its power to us all. We are made one with Algernon and Charlie Gordon before and after, yes certainly after, that great fall itself.

Barry N. Malzberg
New York City: May 2000

---

*The others: "The Cold Equations," by Tom Godwin; "Nightfall," by Isaac Asimov; "The Star," by Arthur C. Clarke; "A Sound of Thunder," by Ray Bradbury.

Algernon, Charlie, and I
A WRITER'S JOURNEY

DANIEL KEYES

Editing Pulps and Writing Comic Books

One Friday afternoon in 1950, I got a call from Lester del Rey. He wanted to know if I was interested in a job as associate fiction editor for a chain of pulp magazines — the popular fiction magazines of the day, printed on cheap untrimmed stock that left paper dandruff all over your dark clothing.

"I don't understand," I said.

"Well, my agent, Scott Meredith, has heard of an opening at Stadium Publications. The editor, Bob Erisman, works out of his home in Connecticut, and comes into New York only on Fridays to pick up the edited stories. His associate editor quit without notice, and Bob's desperate for a replacement. I told Scott that even though you haven't published yet, you have a good story sense and might be able to handle the job. He's willing to recommend you. It pays fifty dollars a week."

"How can Meredith recommend me? He's never even met me."

Lester paused. "Don't ask any questions. If you want the job just get over here quick."

Within a week I was editing ten pulp magazines from Stadium Publications offices on the sixteenth floor of the Empire State Building. I selected, bought, and edited stories for nine westerns and sports titles, and one science fiction magazine called *Marvel Science Fiction*.

Several months later, when the advertising department called and said a last-minute ad cancellation had left a three thousand-word hole in one of the westerns, I filled in by submitting a short-short under a pseudonym through an agent. Although Erisman hated that first cliché-ridden western yarn, he eventually agreed that the young writer I had taken under my wing was coming along nicely.

"His style has improved: no more clichés, tighter prose, cleaner plot. Your young writer spins a good yarn. There's even a hint of characterization."

But I still hadn't published anything under my own name.

In the spring of 1952, I was asked by the editor of *Other Worlds Science Stories* to submit a story for a special "All Star Editor Issue!" It was going to feature six stories by science fiction editors. If they bought my story, I would be paid two cents a word.

I thought of the "Guinea Pig" idea, about increasing human intelligence through surgery, but I sensed it would be a complex story. I didn't feel ready to write it, so I put it out of my mind and kept searching.

I found another idea in my note folder. What if a slave-robot was emancipated? How would it deal with anti-robot prejudice? How would he support himself?

In the same folder, I saw a note. "Algernon Charles Swinburne. Odd first name." Maybe I would name the first free robot Algernon. I decided, instead, to name the robot — Robert.

I mentioned the emancipated robot concept to Lester del Rey over coffee, and he offered me fifty dollars for the idea. It was tempting, but I figured if Lester was willing to buy it, it must be worth writing.

"Robot Unwanted," my first real publication under my own name, was the lead story in the issue. It was 5,000 words long, and the check, after a 10 percent deduction for the agent's fee, was for $90.

The one copy I still have is on crumbling pulp paper, and as I open to it the page comes loose. The blurb reads: "Robert was the only one on Earth — an F.R. That meant he was a free robot; free to do anything he wanted — but he didn't want to die!"

For a writer, there is no feeling to match the elation that comes from seeing your name in print under the title of your first published work. As you walk the streets of Manhattan, you wonder why people aren't rushing up to ask for your autograph. You toy with the idea of quitting your job and writing full-time for fame and fortune.

When the rejections of other stories keep coming, you drift back down to earth.

But some people in the closely knit science fiction writing and publishing community took note. Many SF editors, agents, and writers had known each other as fans in the early years. One such group called itself the Hydra Club. I had met many of its members and was often invited to their parties, but I was too young to be accepted into this circle.

One Friday afternoon, after the publication of "Robot Unwanted" I got a phone call, inviting me to join a poker game at the home of H. L. Gold, which was also the office of *Galaxy*, the magazine he edited. I'd heard stories that since his return from World War II duty, Horace had developed agoraphobia, and rarely left his home-office.

As a way of socializing with other writers, editors, and agents, he had set up a regular Friday night nickel-dime poker game at his New York apartment. It wasn't the Deux Magots in Paris or the "Algonquin Round Table" in New York, but for a wanna-be author it was exhilarating to be among people devoted to writing.

Players would drop in any time, from after dinner until breakfast. We played games like high-low seven-card stud, anaconda, and iron cross. And until I learned the subtleties of the game and the people at the table — when to bluff, when to fold — the tuition fee in this poker seminar left a gap in my fifty-dollar-a-week paycheck.

By 1953, the pulps suffered a serious decline in readership as a result of the new paperback books and television, and since Stadium Publications had to cut expenses, they gave me notice. Erisman would have to handle all the magazines by himself, using the house name Arthur Lane to give the impression that a staff was still operating. The pulps soon vanished except for some of the science fiction magazines, like *Galaxy, Astounding,* and *The Magazine of Fantasy & Science Fiction.*

A few days before my job was terminated, Bob Erisman and I had lunch at Child's in the Empire State Building. We reminisced about working together. I leaned back after coffee and said, "Bob, I have a confession to make."

His eyebrows went up.

"Remember that writer whose stories you hated at first, and I told you I saw some talent in him?"

"You mean 'Bushwack at Aransas Pass'?"

"Yeah. Well, I used a pen name and submitted that and all those other stories through an agent. I wanted you to know."

Bob smiled. "I guess confession is good for the soul. Remember those western and sports novels and novellas you weren't permitted to buy because they were written under contract?"

"Sure."

"Well, what do you think I was doing at home in Mystic, Connecticut, after I checked your work and wrote blurbs and titles?"

"You?"

He nodded.

We had a drink together and toasted the end of an era.

In contrast to the decline of the pulps, Martin Goodman Publications' subsidiary, *Timely Comics*, was flourishing. Goodman offered me a transfer, a job working for his son-in-law Stan Lee, who was in charge of the comic book line and has since become the head of a multimillion-dollar corporation called Marvel. Since my $17.25-a-month rent was almost due, I accepted what I considered a detour on my journey toward a literary career.

Stan Lee was a lanky, shy young man who kept pretty much to himself and let his editors deal with the scriptwriters, cartoonists, and lettering crew. Writers turned in plot synopses. Stan read them and as a matter of course would accept one or two from each of the regulars he referred to as his "stable." As one of his front men, I would pass along the comments and criticism. The writers would then develop them in script form, with dialogue, and actions for each panel, much like movie screenplays.

Because of my experience editing *Marvel*, and because I'd sold a few science fiction stories by then, Stan allowed me to specialize in the horror, fantasy, suspense, and science fiction comic books. Naturally, I began submitting story ideas, getting freelance assignments, and supplementing my salary by writing the scripts on my own time.

One of the ideas I wrote, but didn't submit to him, I called "Brainstorm." It started out:

The first guy in the test to raise the I.Q. from a low normal 90 to
genius level…He goes through the experience, and then is
thrown back to what he was…he is no brighter than he was be-
fore, but having had a sample of light, he can never be the same.
The pathos of a man who knows what it is to be brilliant and to
know that he can never again have the things that he tasted for
the first time, including a brilliant, beautiful woman he fell in
love with and with whom he can no longer have any contact.

I didn't submit it to Stan Lee because something told me it should
be more than a comic-book script. I knew I would do it someday after I
learned how to write.

In the fall of 1952, in violation of Commandment Three: "Thou
shalt not marry while in psychotherapy," I proposed to Aurea and she
accepted.

When I told Stan Lee about it, he rubbed his hands together and
gloated. "That's great, Dan. Get married. Buy a house, take on a big
mortgage. Buy a fancy car. Then you won't be so independent."

My friend Morton Klass and his brother Phil (who published stories under the pseudonym William Tenn) threw rice at Aurea and me as
we left City Hall. A big wedding party at Peter Fland's Studio. Models
and friends and a few relatives. The wedding cake was a cheesecake
from Lindy's.

We didn't buy a house. We moved into my cold-water bachelor
pad. Aurea was still working for Peter Fland, and I was once again trying
to rewrite my merchant marine novel while freelancing scripts for Stan.

A few months later, Aurea phoned, sounding upset. "Peter and his
new partner are arguing. I think they're going to break up. You'd better
come over and see that I get paid."

I left my writing desk, and went to the studio. Before the day was
over, Aurea had left Fland. The partner had offered us a deal. He wanted
Aurea as a photographer and fashion stylist and me as an advertising
copywriter and salesman. We invested our savings in the fashion photography business and celebrated dreams of success.

Our partner, I soon discovered, seemed to be an incorrigible liar—
at least that's what I believed at the time. I survived the year only by

assuming that when he said it was nighttime, it was really daytime. The dream of business success turned into a recurrent nightmare. The partner is standing in front of me on a subway platform. I feel a rage . . . I raise both hands and step forward . . . Then another train, the elevated train of my childhood, thunders past my bed and I pull back, turn away and hide under the covers. Never mind. I sold out to him, and we lost the savings we invested in the company.

No longer able to afford twice-weekly psychoanalysis sessions, I violated the Fourth Commandment by giving my therapist one fifty-minute-hour's notice.

I heard his voice from behind — actually speaking to me!

"You are a great mistake making. You, the rules knew when we started. You must pay for whatever appointments you for the rest of the month don't keep."

I got off the couch, looked him in the eye, and paid him. "Thanks for the memories."

I see now that my ex-shrink was probably the model for Dr. Strauss.

For the purpose of exploring the writing life, let's set aside the current arguments for or against psychoanalysis. Over the years, as a writer, I have come to believe strongly in two of Freud's ideas: the power of the *unconscious* as a motivating force directing behavior, and his method of *free association* to plumb subconscious connections.

Since most writers use their own experiences to breathe life into their characters and to create believable settings and actions, those two concepts provided me with ways to explore a lifetime accumulation of material, as well as the tools with which to retrieve them. My dream of becoming a writer grew out of my love of books and storytelling, but the only material I can really call my own is stored deep in the unconscious area of my root cellar. I use free association like a gardener's spade to dig out connected memories, bring them into the light, and replant them where they can bloom.

Many years later, when I was developing the novel version of *Flowers for Algernon*, I felt the book needed a psychoanalytic session between Dr. Strauss and Charlie. I struggled with it. Then, frustrated, I put it out of my mind. A few weeks later, I awoke early one morning, feeling the answer surfacing in my mind — coming close to the barrier.

I lay there until the mental pictures came through — myself stretched out on my analyst's couch fighting to break through the "Monday Morning Crust."

Although I didn't know it at the time, my shrink had earned his fee. To write the scene, I just gave that memory to Charlie.

Looking for Charlie

During the next few months, the idea of artificially increasing human intelligence surfaced in my mind many times. It was a period of false starts, experiments, trial and error. Some of the early notes suggest opening episodes and different names for the main character.

> *An officer recommends his cousin for the experiment of having his I.Q. changed. Walton is a bachelor who has long been in love with a girl who works in the tapes library . . .*

> *Steve Dekker has been in and out of prison more times than he can count. It seems that practically every time he pulls a job he gets caught. He has this self-defeating kind of personality that ends up in failure. He decides that this is because he's not smart enough — also there's a girl he's nuts about who won't give him a tumble, because he's not bright. So when he reads an article about making animals smarter he barges in and offers himself as a guinea pig for brain surgery.*

> *The story of raising Flint Gargan's I.Q. Flint is a guy who is crude, enjoys scrawling dirty pix on bathroom walls, fights at the drop of a syllable . . . he's also filled with corny emotions, cries over sentimental gush, loves weddings, babies, dogs — has his own dog.*
>
> *Flint hated school when he was a boy, left school to go out on his own as a plumber's helper . . . figures school's not so bad for some, but doesn't think that he would have been helped much by it.*

I try not to edit or judge while I'm writing. I let the raw material pour out, and if I feel it's good, I shape it later. But I didn't like Steve

Dekker or Flint Gargan, and I wanted nothing more to do with them, or the dozens of other characters that appeared on my pages. I was searching my memory, my feelings, the world around me, for a clue to the character of this story.

I soon realized that part of my problem was that the story idea—the "What would happen if . . . ?"—had come first, and now I was trying to cast an actor to play the role without knowing what he was like.

I decided to try working from the events that stemmed from the idea, and let the character evolve from the story.

The plot was developing through a sequence of connected episodes, the cause-and-effect chain of events, embodying what we call form or structure. But I was a long, long way from a story.

I tried starting later in the narrative, remembering Homer's epic strategy of starting "in the middle of the action," as in *The Iliad* and *The Odyssey.*

> *Three days later they wheeled him into the operating room of the Institute. He lifted himself up on one elbow and waved to Linda who had supervised his preparation.*
>
> *"Wish me luck, beautiful," he said.*
>
> *She laughed. "You'll be all right." Dr. Brock's eyes smiled down at him from behind his surgical mask.*

The fragment breaks off there, but if I were the editor, I'd have blue-penciled this with a note to the writer: "'Smiling eyes?' Watch your clichés. 'From behind his surgical mask?' If his eyes are smiling from behind the mask then he's going to operate blindfolded!"

Still, part of that passage later found its way into the published novelette.

There are about twenty such attempts at beginnings, over several months. I had an idea I cared about. And a story line, and a few passages. But I still didn't have the character I felt was right. I was searching for a protagonist who would be memorable and with whom the reader and I could identify; someone with a strong motivation and goal who evoked a response from other characters; someone whose inner life gave him a human dimension.

Where would I find such a character? How could I invent and develop him? I hadn't the slightest idea.

Then, months later, he walked into my life and turned it around.

Charlie Finds Me

It happened in Brooklyn. Aurea and I moved back there, across the street from my parents' apartment, on the street where I'd grown up. We were broke. Aurea did freelance fashion styling and I resumed writing scripts for Stan Lee. Hundreds of them.

I took courses at night for a master's degree in American literature to prepare myself for a teaching license as a way to buy my freedom from scriptwriting. I passed the Board of Education exam for substitute teacher, then taught at the high school from which I'd graduated ten years earlier.

I wrote nights, during the Christmas break, and summers. In 1956, I finished "The Trouble with Elmo," a science fiction story about a chess-playing supercomputer created to solve all the crises in the world. But the computer has figured out that when there are no more problems to solve, it will be destroyed. So Elmo solves every problem, but embeds what we would now call a computer "worm" or "Trojan horse" containing a program that creates new world crises for it to solve. "The Trouble with Elmo" appeared in *Galaxy* magazine.

I passed the New York Board of Education exam for an English teacher's license in June of 1957. With my higher salary as a regular teacher, Aurea and I were able to rent a one-bedroom house in Seagate, a gated community at the western tip of Coney Island. I loved strolling the beach, smelling the salt air, looking out at the ocean and recalling my seafaring days. I set up my typewriter and desk in a corner of the bedroom, confident I'd be able to write in this place.

The following school term, the chairman of the English department, impressed with my four published short stories, assigned me to teach two elective classes of creative writing. Each class was limited to twenty-five gifted students, all of whom loved reading and wanted to be writers. But many of them acted as if they deserved to have success handed to them because of their intelligence. When they groaned at the assignments and disdained revising their work, I told them, "There are those people *who want to write*, and others who *want to be writers*. For some geniuses, success comes without labor. For the rest of us, it's the love of writing that counts."

As if to compensate for these two "special classes," my other two classes were Special Modified English for low I.Q. students. For them, I was expected to concentrate on spelling, sentence structure, and developing paragraphs. Class discussions focused on issues of the day that might interest them. The key to teaching the "special" students in "modified classes," I was told, is to motivate them with things relevant to their own lives.

I will never forget my first day of teaching one of the Special Modified English classes. I can still see the boy, in the rear of the room near the window. When the school bell rings at the end of the fifty-minute hour, students jump up and rush out—except that boy, who lumbers towards my desk. He wears a black parka, with the orange letter J.

"Mr. Keyes . . . Can I ask you something?"

"Sure. You on the football team?"

"Yeah. Linebacker. Look, Mr. Keyes, this is a dummy class, ain't it?"

I'm taken aback. "What?"

"A dummy class . . . for stupid people . . ."

Not knowing how to react, I mumble, "No . . . not really . . . It's just *special* and *modified*. We go a little slower than some of the other—"

"I know this is a dummy class, and I wanted to ask you. If I try hard and I get smart by the end of the term, will you put me in a regular class? I want to be smart."

"Sure," I say, not knowing if I really have the authority. "Let's see what happens."

When I get home that evening, I try to work on a story I've started, but the boy keeps intruding. His words "I want to be smart" haunt me to this day. It never occurred to me that a developmentally challenged person—in those days they called it retarded—would be aware of his or her limitations and might want to be more intelligent.

I began to write about him.

Short story of a boy in a modified class who begins to realize that he's a "dummy." Teacher's point of view. Donald ... Title: "The Gifted and the Slow."

Two children who grow up near each other — one clever and the other dull. A slow child's deterioration a reflection of the entire culture. Stuart who is struggling against the knowledge that he is slow — Donald who abuses his intelligence.

A boy in a modified class — in love with a bright girl who — up to this point — doesn't understand the differences in intelligence. As each one becomes aware ... He had been placed in this class after he became a behavior problem. He was in a gang of boys called the Cormorants.

His teacher is a new, beginning teacher who has ideals and aspirations — and who believes that Corey can be straightened out. Corey is a neurotic boy — very bright but very disturbed. Bright boy comes into conflict with dull boy over a girl. The dull boy kills the bright boy in a fight.

And so on ... and so on ... and so on ... It was going nowhere. I put the notes away and forgot about them.

I decided to write a novel based on my experiences in the fashion photography business with Aurea and the partner who, I felt, nearly drove both of us crazy. She suggested that I take a leave of absence from teaching, and write full-time while she freelanced as a fashion stylist in Manhattan.

It went well. I was a night writer in those days, and the sound of my Royal typewriter in the bedroom lulled Aurea to sleep. In fact, if I stopped typing for too long she would awaken and mumble, "What's the matter?"

We'd have breakfast together, and then I would drive her to the train station on the back of my red Cushman scooter. I'd come back to the apartment for my day's sleep. Then I'd pick her up in the evening. We'd have dinner together. She would go to sleep, and I'd sit down at the typewriter in a corner of the bedroom.

I don't recall how long it took me to write the first draft of that fashion photography novel, but I do remember that after I put it away for few days, and then reread it, I was sick to my stomach. It was so bad.

I became depressed, frustrated, and demoralized — on the verge of giving up writing altogether.

Then, in the summer of 1958, H. L. Gold phoned and asked me to write a second story for *Galaxy* to follow "The Trouble with Elmo."

"I'll try, Horace. I've got an idea."

"Well, get it to me as soon as you can."

It's amazing how quickly depression, frustration, and demoralization can melt away when an editor asks a struggling writer for a story. I searched my files and notebooks.

There was an old, yellowed page from my first year at NYU with the line: "I wonder what would happen if we could increase human intelligence artificially?" The line, I remembered, had been accompanied by a depressing vision on the subway — *the wedge that education has driven between me and my family.*

How often those thoughts have come back to me. I reread my notes and scraps about the operation to increase the I.Q., and the story idea, and the shape it might take — the plot of a classic tragedy.

Recalling Aristotle's dictum in his *Poetics*, that a tragedy can happen only to the highborn, because there can be a tragic fall only from a great height, I thought, let's test that. What if someone the world views as the lowest of the low, a mentally handicapped young man, climbs to the peak of Book Mountain, the heights of genius? And then loses it all. I felt myself choking up as I thought about it.

Okay, I've got the idea, and the plot, I thought, but I still don't have the character with motivation.

I opened a more recent folder, turned several pages, and saw the note:

A boy comes up to me in the Special Modified English class and says, "I want to be smart."

Stunned, I stared at those pages, side by side. A motivation collided with a "What would happen if . . ."

I glanced at Aurea tossing restlessly in bed. I pushed my note folders aside, ready to begin again. I needed new names. In the city she'd worked for the Larry Gordon Studio. Aurea's last boyfriend before we got married, my rival—his first name was Charlie.

I typed. Aurea sighed at the sound, and soon she was fast asleep.

Charlie Gordon—whoever you are, wherever you are—I hear you. I hear your voice calling out, "Mr. Keyes, I want to be smart."

Okay, Charlie Gordon, you want to be smart? I'll make you smart. Here I come, ready or not.

Getting There

I typed the following opening pages in one sitting, pounding away on the keys with more excitement writing than I'd ever known before. Here is the unedited first draft:

"The Genius Effect"
by Daniel Keyes

"What makes Gordon, here, ideal for the experiment," said Dr. Strauss, "is that he has a low intelligence level and he's eager and willing to be made a guinea pig."

Charlie Gordon smiled and sat forward on the edge of his chair to hear what Dr. Nemur would answer to that.

"You may be right, Strauss, but he's such a small, frail-looking thing. Can he take it, physically? We have no idea how much of a shock it will be to the human nervous system to have the intelligence level tripled in such a short time."

"I'm healthy," offered Charlie Gordon, rising and pounding on his slight chest. "I been working since I was a kid, and—"

"Yes, we know all about that, Charlie," said Dr. Strauss, motioning for Charlie to reseat himself. "What Doctor Nemur means is something else. It's too complicated to explain to you right now. Just relax, Charlie."

Turning his attention back to his colleague, Dr. Strauss continued: "I know he's not what you had in mind as the first of your new breed of intellectual supermen, but volunteers with seventy I.Q. are not easy to find. Most people of his low mentality are hostile and uncooperative. An I.Q. of seventy usually means a dullness that's hard to reach.

"Charlie has a good nature and he's interested and eager to please. He knows that he's not bright, and he's begged me for the chance to serve as the subject of our experiment. You can't discount the value of motivation. You may be sure of yourself, Nemur, but you've got to remember that this will be the first human being ever to have his intelligence raised by surgical means."

Charlie didn't understand most of what Dr. Strauss was saying, but it sounded as if he were on his side. He held his breath as he waited for Dr. Nemur's answer. In awe, he watched the white-haired genius pull his upper lip over his lower one, scratch his ear, and rub his nose. Then finally it came — a nod.

"All right," said Nemur, "we'll try him. Put him through the personality tests. I'll want a complete profile as soon as possible."

Unable to contain himself, Charlie Gordon leaped to his feet and reached across the desk to pump Dr. Nemur's hand. "Thank you, Doc, thank you. You won't be sorry for giving me a chance. I'll try hard to be smart. I'll try awful hard."

The first of the testers to encounter Charlie Gordon was a young Rorschach specialist who attempted to get a deeper insight into Charlie's personality.

"Now, Mr. Gordon," said the thin young man, pushing his glasses back on the bridge of his nose, "just tell me what you see on this card."

Charlie, who approached each new test with tension and the memory of many childhood failures, peered at the card suspiciously. "An inkblot."

"Yes, of course," smiled the tester.

Charlie got up to leave. "That's a nice hobby. I have a hobby too. I paint pictures, you know they have the numbers where you put the different colors — "

"Please, Mr. Gordon. Sit down. We're not through yet. Now

what does it make you think of? What do you see in the inkblot?"

Charlie leaned closer to the card and stared at it intently. He took it from the tester's hand and held it close up. Then he held it far away from him glancing up at the young man out of the corner of his eye, hoping to get a hint. Suddenly, he was on his feet, heading out the door.

"Where are you going, Mr. Gordon?"

"To get my glasses."

When Charlie returned from the locker where he had left his glasses in his coat pocket, he explained. "I usually only have to use my glasses when I go to the movies or watch television, but they're really good ones. Let me see that card again. I'll bet I find it now."

Picking up the card again, he stared at it in disbelief. He was sure that he'd be able to see anything there with his glasses on. He strained and frowned and bit his nails. He wanted desperately to see what it was that the tester wanted him to find in that mass of inkblot. "It's an inkblot . . . ," he said, but seeing the look of dismay on the young man's face, he quickly added, "but it's a nice one. Very pretty with these little things on the edges and . . ." He saw the young psychologist shaking his head and he let his voice trail off. Obviously he hadn't gotten it right.

"Mr. Gordon, now we know it's an inkblot. What I want you to tell me is what it makes you think of. What do you visualize—I mean what do you see in your mind when you look at it?"

"Let me try again," pleaded Charlie. "I'll get it in a few minutes. I'm not so fast sometimes. I'm a very slow reader too, but I'm trying hard." He took the card again and traced the outline of the blot for several minutes, his forehead knit in deep thought. "What does it remind me of? What does it remind me of . . . ?" he mused to himself. Suddenly his forehead cleared. The young man leaned forward expectantly as Gordon said, "Sure—of course—what a dope I am. I should have thought of it before."

"Does it make you think of something?"

"Yes," said Charlie triumphantly, a knowing smile illuminating his face. "A fountain pen...leaking ink all over the tablecloth."

During the Thematic Apperception Test, in which he was asked to make up stories about the people and things he saw in a series of photographs, he ran into further difficulty.

"—I know you never met these people before," said the young woman who had done her Ph.D. work at Columbia, "I've never met them either. Just pretend that you—"

"Then if I never met them, how can I tell you stories about them? Now I've got some pictures of my mother and father and my little nephew Miltie. I could tell you stories about Miltie..."

He could tell by the way she was shaking her head sadly that she didn't want to hear stories about Miltie. He began to wonder what was wrong with all these people who asked him to do such strange things.

Charlie was miserable during the nonverbal intelligence tests. He was beaten ten times out of ten by a group of white mice who learned to work their way out of a maze before he did. It depressed him to learn that mice were so smart.

I remember typing that opening fragment. I saw myself writing my homework, the ink dripping from my pen, making an inkblot on the white paper, my mother's hand coming over my shoulder and ripping out the page. I laughed out loud as I saw it happening to Charlie, saw his reaction, heard his words. There was no thinking ahead. It was as if the sentences were flowing from my fingertips to the typewriter keys without passing through my brain. Something inside told me I had it. I finally had it.

Henry James wrote of the donnée—"the given"—as being the heart of the work given to the writer. Well, a boy had walked up to me and given me what I needed to spark the story, and, in return, I would give him some of my own memories to bring his character to life on the page.

Charlie's story had begun to tell itself. It felt right. It felt good.

Yet, the next evening, when I sat down to work, I couldn't go on.

Something was blocking me. What? I knew the idea was original; I felt it was important; it had stayed with me over the years and demanded to be written. What was wrong?

As I reread the pages, I laughed aloud at Charlie's responses to the inkblot. Then, suddenly, it hit me. I was laughing at Charlie. The way I was telling the story, the reader would be laughing at Charlie. That's what most people did when they saw the mentally disadvantaged make mistakes. It was a way of making themselves feel superior. I remembered the day I broke the dishes, and the customers laughed and Mr. Goldstein called me *moron.*

I didn't want my readers to laugh at Charlie. Maybe laugh *with* him, but not at him.

Sure, I had the idea, and the plot, and the character, but I hadn't found the right way, the only way, to tell the story. The point of view, or what I prefer to call the *angle of vision,* was wrong. This had to be told from Charlie's perspective. It had to be first person, major character angle — in Charlie's mind and through Charlie's eyes all the way.

But how? What narrative strategy would let the story unfold?

Would the reader believe that a developmentally disadvantaged person could write this as a memoir from beginning to end? I couldn't believe that myself. I liked the idea of each event, each scene, being recorded as it was happening, or right after it had happened. Diary? Again, not plausible that — at least in the beginning and at the end — Charlie would sit down and make long journal entries.

I struggled with the narrative strategy for several days, growing more and more frustrated, because I felt I was so close to unlocking the story. Then one morning I awoke with the answer in my mind. As part of the experiment, Charlie would be asked to keep an ongoing record, a progress report.

I had never heard the term before, or read a story or novel in which it had been used. I suspected that I was developing a unique point of view.

Now that I had found Charlie's voice, I knew he would tell it through my fingers on the keys. But how would I handle the sentence structure and spelling? Students in my modified classes provided the model. How would I know how he thought? I would try to remember what it was like to be a child. How would I know his feelings? I would give him my feelings.

When Flaubert was asked how he could have imagined and written of life through the mind of a woman in *Madame Bovary*, his answer was: "I am Madame Bovary."

In that sense, I gave Charlie Gordon some of myself, and I became part of that character.

Still, I was worried about opening with the illiterate spelling and short, childish sentence structure. I wondered about the reader's reaction. Then I remembered what Mark Twain did in *The Adventures of Huckleberry Finn*. Before plunging into the vernacular of the uneducated Huck, Twain alerts the reader with the author's educated voice.

The novel opens with a NOTICE: "Persons attempting to find a motive in this narrative will be prosecuted; persons attempting to find a moral in it will be banished; persons attempting to find a plot in it will be shot.

"BY ORDER OF THE AUTHOR, PER G.G., CHIEF OF ORDNANCE."

This is followed by an EXPLANATORY:

"In this book a number of dialects are used, to wit: the Missouri negro dialect; the extremest form of the backwoods South-Western dialect; the ordinary 'Pike-County' dialect; and four modified varieties of this last..." signed THE AUTHOR.

Only then, after having prepared the reader, does Twain begin the first-person narrative from Huck's point of view and in his voice.

"You don't know about me without you have read a book by the name of *The Adventures of Tom Sawyer*, but that ain't no matter. That book was made by Mr. Mark Twain and he told the truth, mainly. There was things which he stretched, but mainly he told the truth."

I decided to follow Twain's strategy. My original opening—which I later deleted and can no longer find—begins with Alice Kinnian coming to the lab and asking Professor Nemur if he has heard from Charlie. Nemur hands her the manuscript, the first pages of which are written in pencil, pressed so hard she can feel the words raised on the back of the paper.

Only then does Charlie's voice take over as I type:

PROGRIS RIPORT 1—MARTCH 5

Dr. Strauss says I shud rite down what I think and evrey thing that happins to me from now on. I dont know why but he says its importint so they will see if they will use me. I hope they use me. Miss Kinnian says maybe they can make me smart. I want to be smart. My name is Charlie Gordon. I am 37 years old and 2 weeks ago was my brithday. I have nuthing more to rite now so I will close for today.

When I saw those words on the page, I knew I had it. I wrote through that night and the nights that followed, feverishly, long hours, little sleep and lots of coffee.

Then, in the middle of the night, partway through the first draft, after the scene in which Charlie races the white mouse, I called out loud, "The mouse! The mouse!"

Aurea jumped up, startled. "Where? Where?"

I explained and she smiled sleepily, "Oh, good."

I turned back to the typewriter and typed a note to myself:

The mouse, having had the same treatment as Charlie, will forecast events connected with the experiment. It will be a character in its own right, and a furry little sidekick for Charlie.

A name—I had to give the mouse a name. My fingers went over the keys. It just appeared on the page.

Algernon.

After that, the story wrote itself, about thirty thousand words—what would be called a long novelette or a short novella.

In that first complete draft, the story ends with Alice Kinnian looking up from the folder of progress reports with tears in her eyes, and asking Professor Nemur to go with her to help find Charlie.

Phil Klass by this time had moved with his wife Fruma into an apartment across the street from me in Seagate. Phil was the next person to read the story after Aurea. When he returned the manuscript the next day, he said, "This will be a classic."

I knew he was teasing me, and I laughed.

My next move was to get a different literary agent. I phoned Harry Altshuler, introduced myself, and told him of H. L. Gold's request that I write a second story for *Galaxy*. Altshuler asked to read "Flowers for Algernon," and I sent it to him. He said he liked it, and would be pleased to be my agent. H. L. Gold should, of course, have first crack at it.

Euphoria is a mild word to describe my feelings. I had just finished a story that had been in the back of my mind for years, and I felt good about it. And I had landed a respected agent who liked it and an editor who had asked for it. My troubles, I thought, were over.

I was mistaken.

Rejection and Acceptance

A few days later, Harry Altshuler called and told me he'd been in touch with H. L. Gold on behalf of another of his writers, and had mentioned my new story. "Horace wants you to bring it to his office-apartment. He'll read it right away. Do you know his place?"

"It's where I learned to play poker and discovered I'm not very good at bluffing."

"All right then. Don't discuss price if he wants to buy it. I'll handle that end."

It was a long trip from Coney Island to 14th Street on the east side of Manhattan, and by the time I arrived I was on edge. The story meant a lot to me, and I hoped it could be published in a major science fiction magazine like *Galaxy*. But Horace had a reputation as a hands-on editor who didn't hesitate to ask for changes.

He greeted me at the door, took the envelope, and said, "Relax in the study while I read this in my office. Help yourself to coffee and doughnuts."

It had never occurred to me that he would read it while I waited, or that I would get instant feedback from one of the most prestigious editors in the field.

For the next hour or so, I drank coffee, read the *New York Times*, and stared into space wondering if he would like it or hate it, buy it or reject it. Finally, he came out of his office, deep in thought, and sat across from me.

"Dan, this is a good story. But I'm going to suggest a few changes that will turn it into a great story."

I don't remember how I responded.

"The ending is too depressing for our readers," he said. "I want you to change it. Charlie doesn't regress. He doesn't lose his intelligence. Instead, he remains a supergenius, marries Alice Kinnian, and they live happily ever after. That would make it a great story."

I stared at him. How does a beginning writer respond to the editor who bought one story from him, and wants to buy a second? The years of labor over this story passed through my mind. What about my Wedge of Loneliness? My tragic vision of Book Mountain? My challenge to Aristotle's theory of the Classic Fall?

"I'll have to think about it," I mumbled. "I'll need a little time."

"I'd like to buy it for one of the upcoming issues, but I'd need that revision. It shouldn't take you long."

"I'll work on it," I said, knowing there was no way I'd change the ending.

"Good," he said, showing me to the door. "If not, I'm sure you'll write other stories for *Galaxy* in the future."

I called Harry Altshuler from a pay phone and told him what had happened. There was a long pause.

"You know," he said, "Horace is a fine editor, with a strong sense of the market. I agree with him. It shouldn't be too hard to make that change."

I wanted to shout: This story has a piece of my heart in it! But who was I to pit my judgment against professionals? The train ride back to Seagate was long and depressing.

When I told Phil Klass what had happened, he shook his head. "Horace and Harry are wrong. If you dare to change the ending, I'll get a baseball bat and break both your legs."

"Thanks."

He made another suggestion. He was then working for Bob Mills, editor of *The Magazine of Fantasy & Science Fiction*. "Let me take the story up to Mills and see if he'll buy it."

I was torn. Whereas *Galaxy* was considered the most successful science fiction magazine, *F&SF* was most respected for its literary merit. I told Phil to go ahead.

A few days later I got the good news along with the bad. Bob Mills liked the story and wanted to publish it, but he was limited by the publisher to a maximum of 15,000 words per story. If I'd agree to cut 10,000 words, he would buy it at two cents a word.

"I'll see," I said.

The decision wasn't too hard. Recalling my own editing days, Bob Erisman's admonition to cut, and Meredith's comment that Lester del Rey would never revise because it would cut his income in half, I shook each page, and crossed out every paragraph and word that wasn't absolutely necessary. It didn't hurt as much as I feared.

I got rid of *that-ery* and *which-ery*, and redundant phrases, and digressions. "Sentences plodding along with lots of little words just like this one does were revised." Changed to read: "I revised plodding sentences." Fifteen words trimmed to four without changing the meaning. At the same time, by altering *were revised* to *I revised*—passive voice to active voice—I changed pedestrian style into a lean, muscular prose.

Then I looked at the last scene in which Alice puts down the manuscript and asks Nemur to go with her to find Charlie. I hesitated a moment, and then drew a long diagonal line through that page and a half, allowing the story to end with his words: "P. P. S. Please if you get a chanse put some flowrs on Algernons grave in the bak yard . . ."

Bob Mills bought the story.

That summer, I was invited to attend one of the getaway workshops in Milford, Pennsylvania, at which the old-guard Hydra Club writers were invited to spend part of each afternoon passing around pages of new stories for critique by their professional peers. I was invited to submit a story for the workshop, and I decided to let them read "Flowers for Algernon."

The night before the workshop, I glanced through the manuscript and realized I'd made a mistake. Since I'd cut off the ending, in which Alice finishes reading the progress reports and goes off in search of Charlie, the opening, in which Nemur gives her the manuscript, was now superfluous.

I'd written it that way because I was afraid to let the story open with Charlie's illiterate spelling and simple plodding sentences. I'd been afraid to throw the reader into Charlie's "special" point of view without warning.

I decided I had to trust the reader.

That night, I cut the first two pages and let the story begin with Charlie's words, in Charlie's voice:

PROGRIS RIPORT 1—MARTCH 5

Dr. Strauss says I shud rite down what I think and evrey thing that happins to me from now on. I dont know why but he says its importint so they will see if they will use me. I hope they use me.

Then I went out to face my critics. Among those I remember forty years later were Judy Merril, Damon Knight, Kate Wilhelm, Jim Blish, Avram Davidson, Ted Cogswell, Gordie Dickson. I beg those I haven't mentioned to forgive me.

We set out chairs on the front lawn, and then passed the pages around the circle. All I can remember now is the generous warm praise, the congratulations, and the sense that these people I admired had accepted me as a fellow writer.

"Flowers for Algernon" was published as the lead story of the April 1959 issue of *The Magazine of Fantasy & Science Fiction*, with a cover by Ed Emshwiller. Five months later, he gave Aurea the original oil painting as a gift in honor of the birth of our first child, Hillary Ann. The painting still hangs in our living room.

At the 18th World Science Fiction Convention in Pittsburgh, in 1960, as Isaac Asimov handed me the Hugo Award for the best story of 1959, he praised it lavishly.

Asimov later wrote in *The Hugo Winners*:

"'How did he do it?' I demanded of the Muses. 'How did he do it?...' And from the round and gentle face of Daniel Keyes, issued the immortal words: 'Listen, when you find out how I did it, let me know, will you. I want to do it again.'"

I wasn't alone on that celebration night. An unseen someone cast a second shadow in the spotlight beside me. Another hand reached out for the Hugo Award. Out of the corner of my mind, I glimpsed a memory of the boy who had walked up to my desk and said, "Mr. Keyes, I want to be smart."

And he has been with me as Charlie Gordon ever since.

Rhysling Award Winners

BRUCE BOSTON

LAUREL WINTER

The Science Fiction Poetry Association gives the Rhysling Award annually in two categories: best long poem (more than fifty lines) and best short poem (less than fifty lines). The award is named for the wandering Blind Singer of the Spaceways in Robert A. Heinlein's classic short story, "The Green Hills of Earth."

The winners of the 1999 Rhysling Awards were Bruce Boston for his long poem, "Confessions of a Body Thief," first published by Talisman as a broadside, and Laurel Winter for her short poem, "egg horror poem," first published in *Asimov's Science Fiction*.

Bruce Boston is the author of twenty-four books of fiction and poetry, including the novel *Stained Glass Rain*. His stories and poems have appeared in hundreds of publications, including *Amazing Stories, Asimov's, Weird Tales,* and *The Pushcart Press Anthology*. He has won the Rhysling Award a record six times and the Asimov's Readers' Poll Award for poetry a record three times. Born in Chicago, he grew up in suburban Los Angeles and has lived for many years in the San Francisco Bay Area.

Laurel Winter, who won the 1998 Rhysling Award for long poetry and the Asimov's Readers' Poll Award, lives in a passive solar, earth-bermed house with her husband and teenage twin sons. She is the author of *Growing Wings,* a science fiction novel for young readers published by Houghton Mifflin, and has edited an anthology called *Minnesota Women Speak* for River's Edge Publishing. Her other creative pursuits include drawing, painting with acrylics and gouache, and making jewelry and sculptures with polymer clay.

For information regarding membership in the Science Fiction Poetry Association, contact John Nichols, 6075 Bellevue Drive, North Olmsted, OH 44070. E-mail: bejay@world.net.att.net.

Confessions of a Body Thief

BRUCE BOSTON

To take a stranger's mind
and wear a stranger's face,
to step into another's flesh
and claim a life in toto,
was a talent I discovered
at a raw and tender age,
when the world itself was
changing in unexpected ways.

Youth was in rebellion.
Generations ripped apart.
A war on foreign shores
and injustice on our own
soon led to cries of protest
and bloodshed in the streets.
Consciousness expanded like
a roiling mushroom cloud.
Those who offered answers
said it had to do with love

Amidst the fervor and the rage
I could have any life I chose,
from a pompous politician
feeding on the masses' needs,
riding high in limousines,
to a rail-thin rock idol

prancing on a concert stage
with women in the wings.
Flush with youthful vigor,
a burgeoning libido,
and a head full of ideals,
I promptly chose the latter
without a shade of doubt.

Wielding my axe like a pen,
and often like a sword,
I defined a shaggy credo,
my generation's song.
With the lyrics of another
I felt the wild exultation
of ovation upon ovation
and the instant adulation
that music can engender.
I lived my life so rapidly,
losing track of night and day,
the drugs within my veins,
time bunched and crushed
together like the jackknifed
cars of a derailing train.

When my body overdosed
I abandoned its dying shell.
After one or two false starts
I settled on my second host.
I became a cybernetic genius,
worked for IBM and RAND.
I calculated decimal points
to infinity and back again.
I'd never mastered logic
and never cared for math,
but I had another's brain
and a Ph.D. from M.I.T.
to think in algorithms
and converse with binary.

Abstract numbers galled
so I pursued the real sort,
the kind with dollar signs
that can buy a luxury yacht
to sail on the Côte d'Azur.
I was a Wall Street whiz kid,
a black belt of the exchange,
trading stocks and debentures
until I made a hundred million.
Then the junk-bond scandal hit,
and for the novelty alone
I spent a year in prison.

Once I surfaced as a woman,
more seductive than sin itself.
I learned what men will do
for the lust that they call love.
I learned how they'll compete
like fierce animals in heat
to possess a surface beauty
and caress a shapely thigh,
with no interest or concern
for whatever lies beneath.

I became a different woman
and fought for women's rights.
I battled like a termagant
with overblown executives
for an equal scale of pay,
for acceptance and promotion
on the corporation ladder
and all that should be mine.
The end result of this was
I soon became another man.

I've been brown and black
and white and yellow,
and all the shades between.

I've toiled stooped and sweaty
through the sun-baked fields.
I've sat in the awning's shade,
with a cool drink by my arm,
sporting an evil overseer's grin.
I've penned a best-selling novel
and composed a symphony.
Like a chameleon understudy
I have played most any part
as I moved across the stage
of this metamorphic age,
yet all of it soon paled
without my own identity.

I've cruised and skimmed
along the skin of things
like a surfer on a wave,
a rock skipping across a lake,
or a raindrop on a window
that reflects the room beyond
but can never find a passage
through the surface of the pane.
I've looked into the mirror
but never past my eyes.
I've only known my ego,
its desires and its needs,
the ocean's tidal roar
that belies the silent deep.

My future now stands open
like an endless avenue,
for every time I start to age
I seize on youth once more.
Yet is it worth the trouble
to keep changing hats and coats,
not in rhythm with the seasons,
just to please my petty whims,
when my soul is lost forever

in the shuffling and the rippling
of a hundred different skins?

If there is a kind of answer
that has to do with love,
if consciousness can change
and the world can follow suit,
I am not the one to judge.
I have stolen other lives.
I've ravaged mind and limb.
I have left my spirit far behind
and forsaken my own name.

egg horror poem

LAUREL WINTER

small
white
afraid of heights
whispering
in the cold, dark carton
to the rest of the dozen.
They are ten now.
Any meal is dangerous,
but they fear breakfast most.
They jostle in their compartments
trying for tiny, dark-veined cracks—
not enough to hurt much,
just anything to make them unattractive
to the big hands that reach in
from time to random time.
They tell horror stories
that their mothers,
the chickens,
clucked to them—
meringues,

omelettes,
egg salad sandwiches,
that destroyer of dozens,
the homemade angel food cake.
The door opens.
Light filters into the carton,
"Let it be the milk,"
they pray.
But the carton opens,
a hand reaches in—
once,
twice.
Before they can even jiggle,
they are alone again,
in the cold,
in the dark,
new spaces hollow
where the two were.
Through the heavy door
they hear the sound of the mixer,
deadly blades whirring.

They huddle,
the eight,
in the cold,
in the dark,
and wait.

APPENDIXES

About the Nebula Awards

The Nebula Awards are chosen by the members of the Science Fiction and Fantasy Writers of America. In 1999 they were given in five categories: short story—under 7,500 words; novelette—7,500 to 17,499 words; novella—17,500 to 39,999 words; novel—more than 40,000 words; and script. SFWA members read and nominate the best SF stories and novels throughout the year, and the editor of the "Nebula Awards Report" collects these nominations and publishes them in a newsletter. At the end of the year, there is a preliminary ballot and then a final one to determine the winners.

The Nebula Awards are presented at a banquet at the annual Nebula Awards Weekend, held originally in New York and, over the years, in places as diverse as New Orleans; Eugene, Oregon; and aboard the *Queen Mary*, in Long Beach, California.

The Nebula Awards originated in 1965, from an idea by Lloyd Biggle Jr., the secretary-treasurer of SFWA at that time, who proposed that the organization select and publish the year's best stories, and have been given ever since.

The award itself was originally designed by Judith Ann Blish from a sketch by Kate Wilhelm. The official description: "a block of Lucite four to five inches square by eight to nine inches high into which a spiral nebula of metallic glitter and a geological specimen are embedded."

SFWA also gives the Grand Master Award, its highest honor. It is presented for a lifetime of achievement in science fiction. Instituted in 1975, it is awarded only to living authors and is not necessarily given every year. The Grand Master is chosen by SFWA's officers, past presidents, and board of directors.

The first Grand Master was Robert A. Heinlein in 1974. The others are Jack Williamson (1975), Clifford Simak (1976), L. Sprague de Camp (1978), Fritz Leiber (1981), Andre Norton (1983), Arthur C. Clarke (1985), Isaac Asimov (1986), Alfred Bester (1987), Ray Bradbury (1988), Lester del Rey (1990), Frederik Pohl (1992), Damon Knight (1994), A. E. van Vogt (1995), Jack Vance (1996), Poul Anderson (1997), Hal Clement (1998), and Brian W. Aldiss (1999).

The thirty-fifth annual Nebula Awards banquet was held in New York on May 20, 2000.

Past Nebula Award Winners

1965

Best Novel: *Dune* by Frank Herbert
Best Novella: "The Saliva Tree" by Brian W. Aldiss and "He Who
    Shapes" by Roger Zelazny (tie)
Best Novelette: "The Doors of His Face, the Lamps of His Mouth"
    by Roger Zelazny
Best Short Story: "'Repent, Harlequin!' Said the Ticktockman"
    by Harlan Ellison

1966

Best Novel: *Flowers for Algernon* by Daniel Keyes and *Babel-17*
    by Samuel R. Delany (tie)
Best Novella: "The Last Castle" by Jack Vance

Best Novelette: "Call Him Lord" by Gordon R. Dickson
Best Short Story: "The Secret Place" by Richard McKenna

1967

Best Novel: *The Einstein Intersection* by Samuel R. Delany
Best Novella: "Behold the Man" by Michael Moorcock
Best Novelette: "Gonna Roll the Bones" by Fritz Leiber
Best Short Story: "Aye, and Gomorrah" by Samuel R. Delany

1968

Best Novel: *Rite of Passage* by Alexei Panshin
Best Novella: "Dragonrider" by Anne McCaffrey
Best Novelette: "Mother to the World" by Richard Wilson
Best Short Story: "The Planners" by Kate Wilhelm

1969

Best Novel: *The Left Hand of Darkness* by Ursula K. Le Guin
Best Novella: "A Boy and His Dog" by Harlan Ellison
Best Novelette: "Time Considered as a Helix of Semi-Precious Stones"
    by Samuel R. Delany
Best Short Story: "Passengers" by Robert Silverberg

1970

Best Novel: *Ringworld* by Larry Niven
Best Novella: "Ill Met in Lankhmar" by Fritz Leiber
Best Novelette: "Slow Sculpture" by Theodore Sturgeon
Best Short Story: no award

1971

Best Novel: A *Time of Changes* by Robert Silverberg
Best Novella: "The Missing Man" by Katherine MacLean

Best Novelette: "The Queen of Air and Darkness" by Poul Anderson
Best Short Story: "Good News from the Vatican" by Robert Silverberg

1972

Best Novel: *The Gods Themselves* by Isaac Asimov
Best Novella: "A Meeting with Medusa" by Arthur C. Clarke
Best Novelette: "Goat Song" by Poul Anderson
Best Short Story: "When It Changed" by Joanna Russ

1973

Best Novel: *Rendezvous with Rama* by Arthur C. Clarke
Best Novella: "The Death of Doctor Island" by Gene Wolfe
Best Novelette: "Of Mist, and Grass, and Sand" by Vonda N. McIntyre
Best Short Story: "Love Is the Plan, the Plan Is Death"
      by James Tiptree Jr.
Best Dramatic Presentation: *Soylent Green*
      Stanley R. Greenberg for screenplay (based on the novel
      Make Room! Make Room!)
      Harry Harrison for *Make Room! Make Room!*

1974

Best Novel: *The Dispossessed* by Ursula K. Le Guin
Best Novella: "Born with the Dead" by Robert Silverberg
Best Novelette: "If the Stars Are Gods" by Gordon Eklund and
      Gregory Benford
Best Short Story: "The Day Before the Revolution"
      by Ursula K. Le Guin
Best Dramatic Presentation: *Sleeper* by Woody Allen
Grand Master: Robert A. Heinlein

1975

Best Novel: *The Forever War* by Joe Haldeman
Best Novella: "Home Is the Hangman" by Roger Zelazny

Best Novelette: "San Diego Lightfoot Sue" by Tom Reamy

Best Short Story: "Catch That Zeppelin!" by Fritz Leiber

Best Dramatic Writing: Mel Brooks and Gene Wilder for *Young Frankenstein*

Grand Master: Jack Williamson

1976

Best Novel: *Man Plus* by Frederik Pohl

Best Novella: "Houston, Houston, Do You Read?" by James Tiptree Jr.

Best Novelette: "The Bicentennial Man" by Isaac Asimov

Best Short Story: "A Crowd of Shadows" by Charles L. Grant

Grand Master: Clifford D. Simak

1977

Best Novel: *Gateway* by Frederik Pohl

Best Novella: "Stardance" by Spider and Jeanne Robinson

Best Novelette: "The Screwfly Solution" by Raccoona Sheldon

Best Short Story: "Jeffty Is Five" by Harlan Ellison

Special Award: *Star Wars*

1978

Best Novel: *Dreamsnake* by Vonda N. McIntyre

Best Novella: "The Persistence of Vision" by John Varley

Best Novelette: "A Glow of Candles, a Unicorn's Eye" by Charles L. Grant

Best Short Story: "Stone" by Edward Bryant

Grand Master: L. Sprague de Camp

1979

Best Novel: *The Fountains of Paradise* by Arthur C. Clarke

Best Novella: "Enemy Mine" by Barry Longyear

Best Novelette: "Sandkings" by George R. R. Martin

Best Short Story: "giANTS" by Edward Bryant

1980

Best Novel: *Timescape* by Gregory Benford
Best Novella: "The Unicorn Tapestry" by Suzy McKee Charnas
Best Novelette: "The Ugly Chickens" by Howard Waldrop
Best Short Story: "Grotto of the Dancing Deer" by Clifford D. Simak
Grand Master: Fritz Leiber

1981

Best Novel: *The Claw of the Conciliator* by Gene Wolfe
Best Novella: "The Saturn Game" by Poul Anderson
Best Novelette: "The Quickening" by Michael Bishop
Best Short Story: "The Bone Flute" by Lisa Tuttle*

1982

Best Novel: *No Enemy But Time* by Michael Bishop
Best Novella: "Another Orphan" by John Kessel
Best Novelette: "Fire Watch" by Connie Willis
Best Short Story: "A Letter from the Clearys" by Connie Willis

1983

Best Novel: *Startide Rising* by David Brin
Best Novella: "Hardfought" by Greg Bear
Best Novelette: "Blood Music" by Greg Bear
Best Short Story: "The Peacemaker" by Gardner Dozois
Grand Master: Andre Norton

1984

Best Novel: *Neuromancer* by William Gibson
Best Novella: "Press Enter ■" by John Varley
Best Novelette: "Bloodchild" by Octavia E. Butler
Best Short Story: "Morning Child" by Gardner Dozois

*This Nebula Award was declined by the author.

1985

Best Novel: *Ender's Game* by Orson Scott Card
Best Novella: "Sailing to Byzantium" by Robert Silverberg
Best Novelette: "Portraits of His Children" by George R. R. Martin
Best Short Story: "Out of All Them Bright Stars" by Nancy Kress
Grand Master: Arthur C. Clarke

1986

Best Novel: *Speaker for the Dead* by Orson Scott Card
Best Novella: "R & R" by Lucius Shepard
Best Novelette: "The Girl Who Fell into the Sky" by Kate Wilhelm
Best Short Story: "Tangents" by Greg Bear
Grand Master: Isaac Asimov

1987

Best Novel: *The Falling Woman* by Pat Murphy
Best Novella: "The Blind Geometer" by Kim Stanley Robinson
Best Novelette: "Rachel in Love" by Pat Murphy
Best Short Story: "Forever Yours, Anna" by Kate Wilhelm
Grand Master: Alfred Bester

1988

Best Novel: *Falling Free* by Lois McMaster Bujold
Best Novella: "The Last of the Winnebagos" by Connie Willis
Best Novelette: "Schrödinger's Kitten" by George Alec Effinger
Best Short Story: "Bible Stories for Adults, No. 17: The Deluge"
    by James Morrow
Grand Master: Ray Bradbury

1989

Best Novel: *The Healer's War* by Elizabeth Ann Scarborough
Best Novella: "The Mountains of Mourning" by Lois McMaster
    Bujold

Best Novelette: "At the Rialto" by Connie Willis
Best Short Story: "Ripples in the Dirac Sea" by Geoffrey Landis

1990

Best Novel: *Tehanu: The Last Book of Earthsea* by Ursula K. Le Guin
Best Novella: "The Hemingway Hoax" by Joe Haldeman
Best Novelette: "Tower of Babylon" by Ted Chiang
Best Short Story: "Bears Discover Fire" by Terry Bisson
Grand Master: Lester del Rey

1991

Best Novel: *Stations of the Tide* by Michael Swanwick
Best Novella: "Beggars in Spain" by Nancy Kress
Best Novelette: "Guide Dog" by Mike Conner
Best Short Story: "Ma Qui" by Alan Brennert

1992

Best Novel: *Doomsday Book* by Connie Willis
Best Novella: "City of Truth" by James Morrow
Best Novelette: "Danny Goes to Mars" by Pamela Sargent
Best Short Story: "Even the Queen" by Connie Willis
Grand Master: Frederik Pohl

1993

Best Novel: *Red Mars* by Kim Stanley Robinson
Best Novella: "The Night We Buried Road Dog" by Jack Cady
Best Novelette: "Georgia on My Mind" by Charles Sheffield
Best Short Story: "Graves" by Joe Haldeman

1994

Best Novel: *Moving Mars* by Greg Bear
Best Novella: "Seven Views of Olduvai Gorge" by Mike Resnick

Best Novelette: "The Martian Child" by David Gerrold
Best Short Story: "A Defense of the Social Contracts"
	by Martha Soukup
Grand Master: Damon Knight

1995

Best Novel: *The Terminal Experiment* by Robert J. Sawyer
Best Novella: "Last Summer at Mars Hill" by Elizabeth Hand
Best Novelette: "Solitude" by Ursula K. Le Guin
Best Short Story: "Death and the Librarian" by Esther M. Friesner
Grand Master: A. E. van Vogt

1996

Best Novel: *Slow River* by Nicola Griffith
Best Novella: "Da Vinci Rising" by Jack Dann
Best Novelette: "Lifeboat on a Burning Sea" by Bruce Holland
	Rogers
Best Short Story: "A Birthday" by Esther M. Friesner
Grand Master: Jack Vance

1997

Best Novel: *The Moon and the Sun* by Vonda N. McIntyre
Best Novella: "Abandon in Place" by Jerry Oltion
Best Novelette: "The Flowers of Aulit Prison" by Nancy Kress
Best Short Story: "Sister Emily's Lightship" by Jane Yolen
Grand Master: Poul Anderson

1998

Best Novel: *Forever Peace* by Joe W. Haldeman
Best Novella: "Reading the Bones" by Sheila Finch
Best Novelette: "Lost Girls" by Jane Yolen
Best Short Story: "Thirteen Ways to Water" by Bruce Holland Rogers
Grand Master: Hal Clement

About the Science Fiction and Fantasy Writers of America

The Science Fiction and Fantasy Writers of America, Incorporated, includes among its members most of the active writers of science fiction and fantasy. According to the bylaws of the organization, its purpose "shall be to promote the furtherance of the writing of science fiction, fantasy, and related genres as a profession." SFWA informs writers on professional matters, protects their interests, and helps them in dealings with agents, editors, anthologists, and producers of nonprint media. It also strives to encourage public interest in and appreciation of science fiction and fantasy.

Anyone may become an active member of SFWA after the acceptance of and payment for one professionally published novel, one professionally produced dramatic script, or three professionally published pieces of short fiction. Only science fiction, fantasy, and other prose fiction of a related genre, in English, shall be considered as qualifying for active membership. Beginning writers who do not yet qualify for active membership may join as associate members; other classes of membership include illustrator members (artists), affiliate members (editors, agents, reviewers, and anthologists), estate members (representatives of the estates of active members who have died), and institutional members (high schools, colleges, universities, libraries, broadcasters, film producers, futurist groups, and individuals associated with such an institution).

Anyone who is not a member of SFWA may subscribe to *The SFWA Bulletin*. The magazine is published quarterly, and contains articles by well-known writers on all aspects of their profession. Subscriptions are $18 a year or $31 for two years. For information on how to subscribe to the *Bulletin*, write to:

SFWA Bulletin
1436 Altamont Avenue
PMB 292
Schenectady, NY 12303-2977

Readers are also invited to visit the SFWA site on the World Wide Web at the following address: http://www.sfwa.org